Before the Next Mistake

Cate Perry

Black Rose Writing | Texas

This is a work of fiction. Names, characters, businesses, places, events, and incidents are either the products of the author's imagination or used in a fictitious manner. Any resemblance to actual persons, living or dead, or actual events is purely coincidental.

ISBN: 978-1-68513-581-2
PUBLISHED BY BLACK ROSE WRITING
www.blackrosewriting.com

Printed in the United States of America
Suggested Retail Price (SRP) $23.95

Before the Next Mistake is printed in Minion Pro

*As a planet-friendly publisher, Black Rose Writing does its best to eliminate unnecessary waste to reduce paper usage and energy costs, while never compromising the reading experience. As a result, the final word count vs. page count may not meet common expectations.

Cover art by Bob Paltrow

Praise for
Before the Next Mistake

Cate Perry was a top ten finalist for the 2015 Ink and Insights Writing Contest for her novel-length manuscript *Not Looking* and a Judge's Favorite in the 2018 Ink and Insights Writing Contest for *Before the Next Mistake.*

"Prepare to be captivated by the unlikely friendships formed by three women, each traversing distinct paths in life, yet united in their support for one another through trials of love, career, and family. Within these pages lies not just a compelling narrative, but an intimate glimpse into the inner workings of the book publishing world. With a perfect blend of romance, humor, and an uplifting conclusion, this book will make you laugh, cry, and want to read it all over again. A true gem."
–Andrea Hurst, bestselling Amazon author of *The Guestbook*

"A complicated relationship among three women destined to save or ruin their future—like Solomon's *The Ex-Talk* meets Korelitz's *The Plot!*"
–Cam Torrens, award-winning author of the *Tyler Zahn* suspense mystery series

"Cate Perry's *Before the Next Mistake* is a must-read for lovers of women's fiction... Perry has a knack for creating tremendously dramatic scenes, lacing them with robust humor. I could not help laughing as I watched Carolyn's world clash with her ex-husband's and all her other interactions. I relished the lively conversations accompanied by witty, introspective commentary...Perry is a very gifted author. I loved this book."
–Readers' Favorite

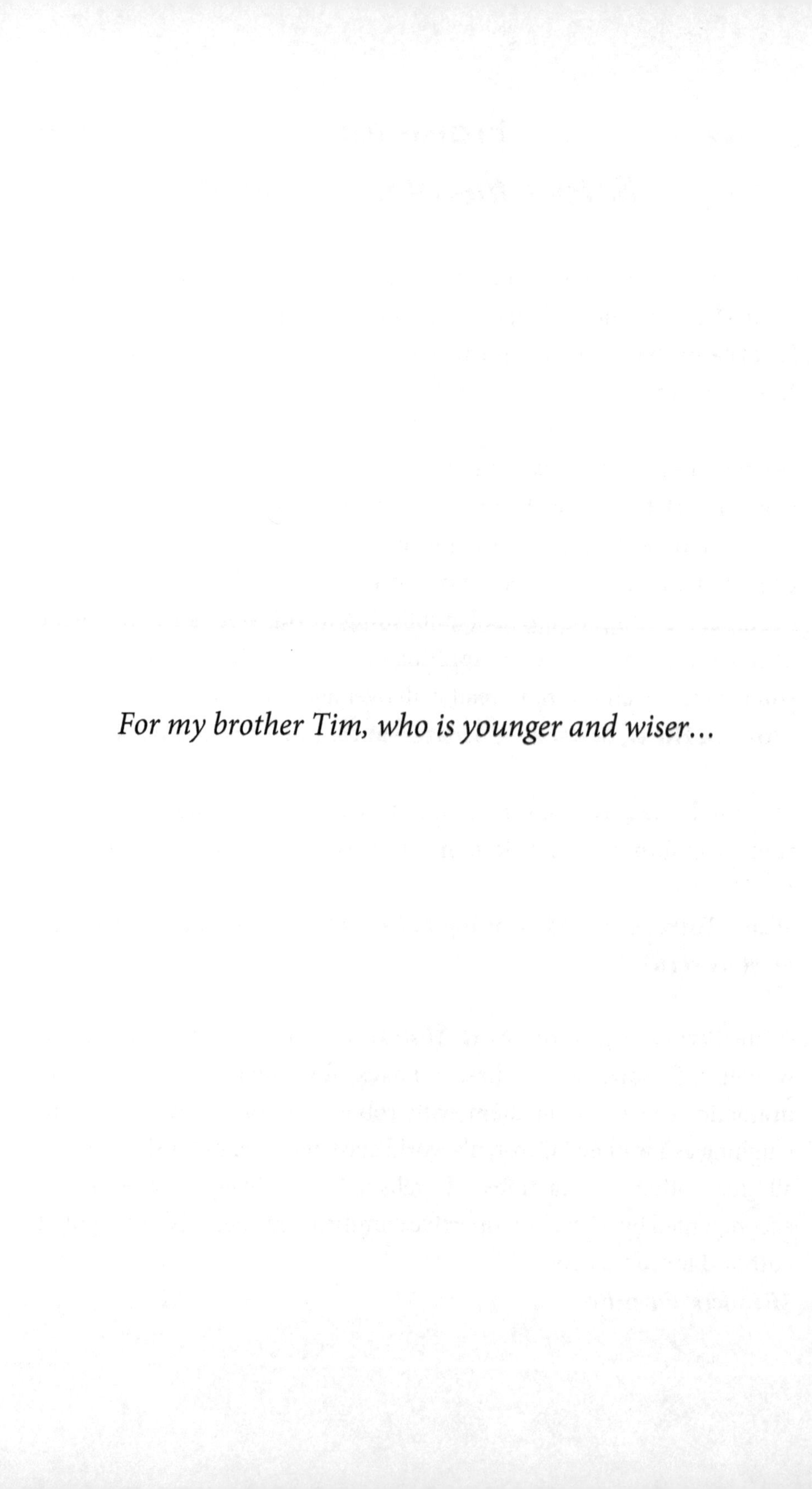

For my brother Tim, who is younger and wiser…

Before the Next Mistake

Under the Bus

Carolyn

By her second glass of wine, Carolyn Ford felt the welcome buzz. Everything in the penthouse martini bar was in order for the New York Bestsellers party, already packed wall-to-wall with booksellers, reporters, and reviewers. Carolyn took note of the heavy hitters to ensure her author didn't miss any opportunities. She lifted her long flute glass of Syrah across the room, toward Ira from *Booklist*. He waved back, a solid connection, sure—but where was Wendy from the *New York Times*?

Carolyn's eyes rested on the belle of the ball, Morgan St. John, the author and survivor. She had been a sophomore at the high school when that horrific shooting took the lives of twelve students and a teacher. Now in her early forties, just a couple years younger than Carolyn, Morgan moved gracefully about the room in her black silk jumpsuit and soft chiffon wrap.

"The Colorado tragedy set the trend for school shootings," stated a reporter in Carolyn's current standing circle. She strained to hear him over the surrounding conversations.

"A *precedent*," Monique Jameson, *Glamour Magazine's* book reviewer, corrected. She looked surprisingly unglamorous for a *Glamour* associate, in crop pants and a loose-knit sweater. Her hair was sleeked back, her bun on-trend in its intended messiness.

"It's not like it was the first school shooting in history," added a junior editor, stepping aside for a caterer carrying a tray of bacon-wrapped prawns.

"Yet it unleashed a whole culture of mass shootings," the first reporter said, then leaned in towards Carolyn. "But what sets her memoir apart from the other victims' stories told over the last twenty-five years?"

Although this was Carolyn's favorite question, she let the reporter wait as she gently twirled the stem of her glass between her thumb and index finger. Her elongated reflection showed her auburn hair much paler in the glass, the bob style longer, and her green eyes appeared almost translucent. "Everyone knows of the trauma and carnage involved in this landmark case," she began. "Morgan's story, however, is draped in miracles. She was a foster child who'd found her place on the wrong side of the tracks; a student stalked by one of the shooters prior to the tragedy; a victim who found safety in a custodial closet; and a young high school graduate who fell in love with, and ultimately married, the very E.M.T. who rescued her from hiding that day."

The words may have been canned, but the message caused Carolyn's heart to swell. After establishing herself as the most successful publisher her age to put out bestselling genre fiction—the kind stocked on market and airport shelves—she'd finally found a narrative, an *experience*, that could change readers' lives. It was almost too good to be true—an editor on her team had even said as much. How many readers were thinking differently about their lives and those around them?

Carolyn watched the reporter scribble notes on his pad, the book reviewer thumb-tap her phone screen, and the junior editor move off to grab a refill at the bar. Morgan and her husband were now standing in a corner, giving yet another interview. Carolyn noticed how Morgan clung to her husband's arm with a white-knuckled grip. He'd saved her once; he would get her through this, too.

As the sun set over Manhattan, caterers lit tea lights at the tables. Smooth jazz played from a speaker in the corner, a little too loudly for

Carolyn's taste. People had to speak over the music, but at least it generated a palpable, eager tension throughout the room. While everyone else talked books, Carolyn's mind ran numbers, profit margins, and percentage distributions.

"Ma'am?"

Carolyn glanced up to find a server carrying a tray of wine glasses. She knew that a third glass of wine was seldom a good idea. It seemed reasonable, though, to have a glass in her hand, to avoid being interrupted by other servers during interviews.

She began to move toward Ira, who'd been waiting patiently for over a half-hour to speak with her, when she noticed how flushed both Morgan and her husband's faces had become. Mr. St. John was standing almost nose-to-nose with the reporter, spitting words she couldn't quite make out.

Carolyn made her way across the room, edging past a caterer here, nodding towards a *Post* reporter there, until she drew close enough to hear Morgan stammering, "The attendance records showed I was at school."

"When school started, yes," the reporter agreed, adjusting his dark-framed glasses. "I'm asking where you were at the time of the shooting."

"And I'm *telling* you to back off," Morgan's husband hissed.

Carolyn's jaws clenched and she felt her nostrils flare. She'd put these questions to rest well over a year ago, but something about this reporter gave her that slow motion feeling before the crash.

"*There* you are, Morgan," Carolyn cut in, as though she'd been searching all over. "*Booklist* is waiting to speak with you at the bar."

"Let's go," Morgan's husband said, his hand on her back to usher her away.

Morgan didn't move, as though she were frozen to the floor. Her husband's hand moved to her shoulder and gave it a squeeze.

"If you insist on evading the question," the reporter said, flipping his tablet cover shut, "I'll go ahead with what I have."

The chatter that surrounded them slowly subsided. Without moving her head, Carolyn looked right and left to see guests raising eyebrows at each other, taking out their pads or setting their phones to record whatever was going on in their corner.

"Mr. —?" Carolyn glanced at the reporter's name tag. "Mr. Wiley, why don't you and I set up an appointment to continue this interview—"

"You're Ford, right? The publisher?" The reporter's black-framed glasses slid down his nose as he reopened his tablet cover to go through his notes. He pushed them back at the bridge and met Carolyn's gaze. "After some investigative reporting, I was able to unearth a video today that reveals a hole in Ms. St. John's story."

Carolyn opened her mouth to tell Mr. Wiley what he could do with his hole when she noticed the color drain from Morgan's face. Heart racing, Carolyn took a sip of her Syrah.

Wiley crossed his arms and tapped an index finger to his chin as though he were thinking something through. He narrowed his eyes at Morgan's husband and said, "Or perhaps Mr. St. John was in on it, too?"

Carolyn stepped between the two men before Morgan's husband could get back in the reporter's face. "We're going out those doors to the terrace, *now*," Carolyn commanded through clenched teeth, steering Wiley by his elbow and glaring at Morgan to follow them out.

Carolyn turned her back on Mr. Wiley and walked the few steps over to the couple. "Mr. St. John," she said, her voice low, "we need you for damage control. Please stay inside and let the reporters know there's nothing important going on out here."

The husky E.M.T. gave a brief nod and stayed in place as Morgan fell in step behind Carolyn and their interrogator. Carolyn knew the surrounding reporters were on high alert now, watching them cross to the French doors, taking notes and frantically searching for whatever video Mr. Wiley was talking about.

The Manhattan winter was bitterly cold—the kind that made Carolyn long for the mild, rainy winters of her childhood on the opposite coast. Stepping onto the balcony, she tightened her Burberry wool sweater at her neck and took another sip of the warm, red wine. Then she turned to face the reporter and said, "Cut to the chase."

"It would seem Ms. St. John cut class at the time of the shooting," he said. "Security footage from the 7-11, down the street from the school, shows her buying a Diet Coke and a pack of gum when it happened."

From the Manhattan street five stories below, tires squealed, followed by honking and cursing. Carolyn raised her voice to be heard over it. "I don't know what footage you're referring to, but anyone can doctor a video—"

"Oh, it's official." He closed his tablet cover and adjusted his glasses once again. "The date and time at the bottom of the screen list the same time as the shooting, down to the second."

"So, in your investigation of Morgan St. John, you just happened to find a 25-year-old surveillance video with some teenage girl at a corner store?" Carolyn held out her glass, swilling it to show she was awaiting his response.

Morgan stepped up and jutted her chin. "It obviously wasn't me. You're trying to create some scandal to boost your own ratings. This is nothing but a hoax."

"Oh, it's a hoax, all right," Mr. Wiley said, then turned to Carolyn. "My investigation of an unsolved robbery did, as a matter of fact, lead me to this tape of your client. They keep all surveillance videos for unsolved cases in an evidence locker at the precinct. This video captured a week's worth of surveillance, and the shooting had happened a few days before the robbery. It's all here, if you'd like to see it."

"I don't need to view some old convenience store video to know it's not me," Morgan said. "I was hiding in a closet, listening to the gunshots that took the lives of twelve—"

"I'll take a look," Carolyn said evenly. She watched as the reporter brought out his tablet again and scrolled. With a final tap of his finger, he held out the tablet.

The recording was grainy. Carolyn watched as the cashier took money from a man in a ball cap. Then the door opened and a girl in a hoodie emerged, her movements jerky from the old tape used to record it. Her hair was black, parted down the middle—much like the pictures they'd included of Morgan in the brief photo section of her book.

"Notice anything familiar?" Mr. Wiley asked. "The nose ring, perhaps?"

Morgan rolled her eyes. "Thousands of girls had nose rings twenty-five years ago. Can we get back to the party now?"

"Nose rings were the trend," Carolyn agreed, trying not to let the doubt register in her voice. Even she herself had sported a little diamond stud at the side of her nose. But few girls had worn the kind of nose ring Morgan had—a hoop at the base of her septum, like some old cartoon bull.

"Keep watching," Mr. Wiley said. "She'll pay the cashier any second now."

"This is ridiculous!" Morgan threw up her hands. "What does that have to do with anything?"

Carolyn silently begged the same question as she watched the girl reach into her backpack and pull out a wallet. Carolyn looked up from the screen and met Morgan's gaze. "You had an ATM card?" she asked.

"We'll be breaking the story online tonight," Mr. Wiley said. "Then in the morning papers—"

"Morgan, say something," Carolyn urged her client. "Tell him it's someone else in that video…" She trailed off, watching Morgan's face for any sign of defiance against this tabloid hack. This was impossible. She had done her homework, checked school records and hospital records.

Carolyn felt her stomach plunge to her feet. It had never occurred to her to check Morgan's bank statements for a debit purchase made at the same time as the shooting. She forced a breath deep into her lungs and worked to regain a firm stance before turning back to face Mr. Wiley. "Can you give us a day or two to confirm this?" Her voice sounded as hollow and distant as the sirens blaring from the street below. "We'll meet with you in exchange—give you an exclusive, in-depth interview."

"You duped your readers," Wiley reminded her. "Why would I—or any of *my* readers—believe a word either of you have to say now?"

"This news comes as a complete surprise to me," Carolyn said. "Be sure to include that in your article."

"It will only make you look negligent." Wiley shrugged. "But I suppose that's a step up from creating a hoax."

Carolyn took Morgan's elbow and guided her toward the patio entrance. The glass rattled when she slammed the French doors shut behind them. Feeling all eyes in the room on her, Carolyn took a gulp of wine and immediately felt her stomach turn sour. She conjured images of tomorrow's headlines in *The Times, The Post,* and every other rag represented at the event. If Wiley's assertion was true, the book would be pulled from store shelves and the hate mail would begin. She envisioned the stacks of thousands of books in the warehouse that would never be shipped. Thousands of hours wasted holding Morgan's hand through the editing process, setting up galleys, editing again, printing, binding. How many trees had been killed to print this woman's lies?

"I can explain," Morgan murmured. "If we could just find a place to meet alone for a few minutes—figure out how to change the pitch lines so that…"

Morgan's voice faded under the rushing sound in Carolyn's ears. Surrounded by reporters, it took every ounce of her being to keep from shrieking questions at the woman. For starters, how exactly did Morgan plan to explain away her lies to all the people who had bought them for so long? Women who had posted and reposted the article about the teenage girl from the wrong side of the tracks. Women who had cried when they read about the young E.M.T. finding her alone and hysterical in the custodial closet—who had checked on her in the hospital and had fallen in love with her after she'd graduated high school. Had Morgan consciously created this mythology, or was she delusional? Had she stalked the E.M.T. after high school, acting as though she were one of the students he had saved? Or was he in on the lie, too?

Carolyn took one more swig from her glass to get her through her imminent Uber ride back to her apartment. She would have to spend all night contacting printers, booksellers, her attorney, and crafting a press release—which would include the publisher seeking legal remedy from the author. This was beyond damage control. She was ruined.

Morgan's husband approached them, wearing a thick wool overcoat. He helped Morgan on with her wrap. While his eyebrows appeared knitted in concern, Carolyn couldn't help but wonder what their ride home would be like. Would they laugh maniacally as they planned an escape to a tropical paradise with all the money they'd scammed? Or would he prod her for answers until he discovered that he'd found someone else in that closet, and that the last twenty-five years of his life had been the biggest hoax of all?

Before they turned to leave, Morgan asked, "Can we meet tomorrow to sort all this out?"

Caroline shook her head in disbelief. The woman truly was deluded.

"Don't keep your husband waiting," she said. Then she took one last look at the fraud standing beside her and said, "Party's over."

Ava

Ava stood before the house, looking from the business card in her hand to the address by the door. She'd expected Howard Mercer Literary and Associates to be in one of Seattle's skyscraping buildings, or at least in a business office of some sort. But this appeared to be the agent's personal home, overlooking what would have been the glossy waters of Lake Union and the Space Needle beyond, had the January sky not been so overcast and threatening snow.

She knocked on the door and stood back. The beat of footsteps sounded on the other side, then a sliding chain lock, and at last the deadbolt before the door finally swung open.

"Ava Perkins?" a young woman asked.

"Yes," Ava said, holding out her hand to shake. "I'm here to interview for the literary agent position."

"Yes, the junior literary agent position." The breeziness in the young woman's voice off-set the correction that had somehow just put Ava in her place.

"Junior," Ava repeated, "of course."

"I'm Dahlia," the young woman said. "Howard's assistant."

Ava nodded her acknowledgment, estimating Dahlia to be only a couple years younger than herself, fresh-faced and fresh out of college. Except that where Ava had dressed in her most formal bohemian wear, this young woman wore a classic beige cardigan, a gold necklace, and kept her shoulder-length blonde hair back with a cream-colored hairband. She was utterly unintimidating, were she not holding Ava's future in her loosely folded, French manicured hands. "If you wouldn't mind coming in and having a seat, Howard and I need to go over a couple of things before he can begin."

"Of course," Ava said, thankful for the chance to decompress before the interview.

As Dahlia walked off down the hallway, Ava scanned the walls. They were littered with framed pictures of Mr. Mercer hanging out with all the local literary legends, from Tom Robbins to Kristin Hannah to Elizabeth George. Somehow, these accomplishments conflicted with the sound of Mr. Mercer's laundry churning down the same hallway. Ava could even hear the man himself going over the day's itinerary with his intern.

Ava knew she should be scanning her notes for the millionth time—not fumbling through her purse for her cell to check in with Gavin. Yet, as she tapped in her passcode, she knew she was doing more checking *up* on her fiancé than checking *in*. She chided herself for picking up an expensive Merlot last night to toast her potential success this morning—expensive for them, anyway. Gavin's glass had inevitably led to an empty bottle by the evening's end. What if he'd slept in for work again?

Her cell glowed to life with the picture of them beaming after Gavin had proposed to her on a sailboat ride last spring. Although, her grin turned into a grimace when she saw the "888" number on the voicemail alert from creditors calling again—one of the many reasons she was desperate for this job. But then she saw Gavin had beaten her to the first text—that he had, indeed, woken up in time. She beamed as she opened the text, squinting to read the words.

I'm sorry. There's just no way—

"Ava?"

Her head shot up. Howard Mercer stood before her, waving his hand weakly as though he'd been saying her name more than once. He wore business casual, which made sense, since he worked from home—khakis, a navy polo shirt, and what appeared to be house sandals. The sandy hair she'd seen in all of his pictures now showed specks of gray at the temples and thinned slightly at the crown. He was handsome, in a mid-forties way—a man who, in the summer, probably sported the kind of tan that came from playing golf and tennis.

"Hello, Mr. Mercer." Ava rose, reluctantly placing the cell back into her purse so she could shake his hand. What was it Gavin needed to apologize for? Snoring too loudly? That there was just no way he could get that plastered on a work night again? Or had he been stashing money away for their honeymoon and was sorry he'd kept it from her?

Mr. Mercer's kind blue eyes crinkled behind his wire-frame glasses. "Please, call me Howard," he said as he beckoned her to follow him down the hall. Her heels clicked along the hardwood floor, louder than she would have liked.

Howard extended a hand to an empty chair at a worktable. Dahlia was already seated on a stool in the corner. Before Ava could come up with any other excuses to look at her phone or think of any more possible endings to Gavin's cryptic half-sentence, Howard Mercer took his seat and cleared his throat.

"I'm afraid our senior editor won't be in for about another hour," he said, "so he won't be able to join us for the interview."

"That's fine," Ava said, hoping that one less body at the table would mean a less intimidating interview.

"We're eager to hear about your experience," he said, glancing back and forth between Ava and the piece of paper he was holding, presumably her resume.

"I graduated from the University of Washington magna cum laude, with a Bachelor's in Literature and a certificate in editing. I interned for a year with *Seattle Weekly* before taking a job working in acquisitions at *Klipsun Literary Magazine*."

"Agenting is becoming more and more difficult—even impossible—in the current publishing climate," Howard said. "What is it about agenting that you're hoping to experience?"

Ava crossed one knee over the other and folded her hands on top. She couldn't tell him the exact truth—that she needed to sign a billion-dollar book deal to make enough commission to settle hers and Gavin's debts. This brought her back to Gavin's text, which she struggled to banish into the furthest, most cobwebbed corner of her mind. But then, thoughts of her father crept into the open spaces—a worn flannel shirt stretched over his broad shoulders, sleeves rolled up to the elbows, forever typing sweeping fantasy novels on a perpetually out-of-date computer. No one had ever wanted to publish them, though, so she couldn't very well bring him up, either.

Finally, she leaned forward and said, "I'm an avid reader, of course, but I've always loved being that link between promising authors and publishers—sort of a gate-keeper, right?"

Howard chuckled.

"But to be that person who could make it possible to put an author's name on the map. And, someday, maybe my own name on the map— like my publishing idol, Carolyn Ford."

Howard raised his eyebrows, obviously impressed. "Do you know Ms. Ford?"

Ava shrugged. "We had lunch recently."

She grinned at Howard, hoping he hadn't heard the little squeak in her voice—that he couldn't detect her stretching the truth to its snapping point. But if a white lie of having "had lunch" with Carolyn Ford could land her the job, then she still wasn't as much of a liar as most of the industry. He didn't need to know she'd only seen her seated across a restaurant a few years back, when she was in town for the Association of Writers and Publishers Conference. And she had no doubt but that she'd meet Carolyn Ford, eventually.

"You're obviously experienced," Howard leaned forward, "but we require an agent training period to adjust to the agency. There's a modest salary, of course, and as soon as you start taking queries, you'll make a small percentage of the royalties and work your way up as you continue to take on more responsibilities. And there are writers' conferences in New York, California…"

Ava nodded, clinging first to the word "salary," which she knew few agencies were able to offer, and then five more words repeated themselves in her mind: "As soon as you start…"

She had the job.

The unspoken fact hung palpable in the air. Ava waited for the offer while Dahlia thanked her. She waited for it as Howard cleared his throat and offered his hand to shake—still waited for it as he said, "Thanks for coming in. We have a few more applicants to review, but we'll be in touch."

"Awesome," Ava replied, still clinging to his hand because he hadn't yet officially offered her the position.

Feeling his hand grow limp, Ava loosened one finger at a time until he was free. She tried not to notice him massaging his knuckles as Dahlia put a gentle hand on her back and said, "I'll see you out."

In the hallway, Dahlia chattered on about her experiences working for Mercer Literary. As they approached the front door, she leaned in with a conspiratorial whisper. "You're the most qualified of the applicants, even if you did mention…"

"What?" Ava asked, breathless.

"Carolyn Ford." Dahlia shrugged. "Howard's always avoided her, but after what happened with her author a couple of days ago, you know."

"Oh!" Ava expelled it in a breath as though she'd been punched in the gut. Carolyn Ford had always been her heroine, having single-handedly climbed the ranks of the publishing world until she'd become New York royalty. What could be wrong with her that Howard didn't like her? And what big news had she missed two days before? She cringed to think she'd come off looking uninformed.

Ava gave Dahlia a restrained handshake and opened the front door to the morning wind. The air felt like frosted powder, and when she turned her face to the sky, tiny flakes tickled her nose, cheeks, and eyelashes. Eyes closed, she wondered if her runaway mouth had lost her the job. Why had she brought up Advance Publishing? Why hadn't she stuck to the script—been honest, at least? She wasn't a liar by nature, but over-eagerness had always been a weakness of hers.

Ava opened her eyes and walked down the sidewalk to her car, rifling through her purse for the keys—but when her knuckles brushed against her phone, she grabbed that instead.

Snowflakes fluttered against the screen and melted into drops. She looked up from the phone long enough to see she was approaching an intersection. The red from the pedestrian light glared at her from across the street. Obeying reflexively, she shivered and smeared her password on the snow-spotted screen so she could look up what on earth had happened with Carolyn Ford. But when the screen lit with her text inbox, she remembered Gavin's message from earlier.

The light changed. Ava started across the crosswalk before finally bringing up the text. What she read stopped her legs, her breath—her world.

Her lips mouthed words she could no longer see. Her foggy exhalations came shorter and faster, her head woozy. A high-pitched squeal rang in her ears. From the middle of the crosswalk, she looked out into the street and saw yellow.

And then she saw black.

Jazmine

Jazmine sat in shock. Her breaths came fast and shallow. She felt a pounding in her left elbow, where she'd smacked the window when the bus whirled around. Everything else seemed to be intact. Her heart hammered against her rib cage and her hands and fingers shook in the aftermath of—what? A loss of control? A collision?

She opened the school bus STOP sign and turned on the hazards. Snow flurried against the gigantic windshield. The seats behind her were eerily silent—the calm before the inevitable trauma began. But then, as she checked the mirror above her, Rylan began screaming, followed by Frankie, rocking back and forth. If it weren't for the double-breasted seatbelt restraining him, he would surely bludgeon his forehead against the seat in front of him.

"What happened?" came the voice of Gabby, Jazmine's bus assistant, in the seat to her right, over the wailing of several more special needs students.

"Ice," Jazmine managed, her voice sounding raw and hollow.

"Did we hit anything?" Gabby asked with wide brown eyes.

"I don't think so," Jazmine said, praying that the glow she'd seen from the center of the road had been some kind of trick of the light. All she could recall was rounding the corner up the street when they slid. And when she slammed on the brakes, her small school paratransit had whipped around until it finally stopped against a curb.

"I'll check on the children," Gabby said, rising from her seat and edging her way down the aisle. Jazmine felt a deep appreciation for the reserved calm that this lovely middle-aged Latina woman brought to an otherwise stressful job, not to mention the overall chaos of her life.

Jazmine reached for the radio. After going to the emergency channel with dispatch, she breathed in deeply before speaking. "There's been an accident," she said hoarsely. "We're on…" She glanced around desperately for a street sign. Normally, she knew each road like every other part of her regimented daily routine, but with today's unfamiliar snow route and the collision, she was too shaken. "Shoot, I don't know what road we're on…"

The dispatcher's voice crackled back. "Stay calm, Jazmine. The Ranger has your GPS. Do you know if anyone is injured?"

"We're checking now." Jazmine forced her voice to be heard over the noise of the children and glanced back at Gabby, who shook her head back at her. "Nobody hurt so far."

"Secure your bus and set out your emergency triangles while we call 911," the dispatcher said. "We have a supervisor on his way."

Jazmine set the receiver back down and looked again at the rearview mirror, this time at the cars lining up behind the bus, all of them accumulating snow except for the rainbow shape their wipers left on each windshield. She closed her eyes and shook away the thought of the traffic holdup. With a little special needs boy of her own, it seemed like her whole life inconvenienced the rest of the world.

Rising slowly from her seat, Jazmine tested her shaking legs to make sure they would hold her up enough to join Gabby in checking on the children. She found little Taylor rolling her head and batting at her ears. Only the thumb-less mittens strapped around her hands kept her from pulling at her hair.

"It's okay," Jazmine murmured. "We're safe now."

She looked up at Gabby to see if everyone was still okay. Gabby met her gaze and furrowed her brow, pointing to her arm. "You're bleeding."

Jazmine put her hand to her elbow, feeling around until her fingers came back warm with blood. She looked back at her seat and saw where the impact of her elbow had cracked the side window.

"Oh my God," Gabby whispered fiercely, "Someone was hit!"

Jazmine looked frantically at each of the children, but she couldn't see anything out of the usual.

"No, someone on the street," Gabby said louder.

Jazmine followed her assistant's finger, pointing out the window where, through the snowflakes, Jazmine made out a form—someone bent over a heap on the ground.

"Oh my God," Jazmine said and moved towards the front of the bus, shooting a pleading, this-can't-be-real look back at Gabby.

"I'll take care of the kids," Gabby said, shooing Jazmine off the bus.

Jazmine reached for the first aid kit and the long plastic box behind her driver's seat before opening the double doors, this time without the lift. She stepped carefully off of the bus onto the snow-slick sidewalk, trying to remember the date. February 14. She'd run a person down on Valentine's Day. This was the date that could read on the person's gravestone.

No. Jazmine wouldn't go there. Not now.

People were coming out of the surrounding homes to see what was happening. Jazmine rounded the front of the bus to the street, where a man was kneeling over a woman on the ground. Blood streamed down the side of her head and tears ran across the bridge of her nose and down the opposite cheek.

"Is she okay?" Jazmine asked, realizing immediately how asinine the question was.

"Yes," he said. "She's unresponsive, but she's breathing."

Jazmine's breath caught in her throat. To think she'd come so close to snuffing the life out of a woman like that—who couldn't be older than twenty-five. She wondered when had the tears begun. Had they burst out on impact? Or were they just now seeping out, as the woman lay there unconscious?

"Are you trained in First Aid?" she called.

"Trained in CPR, back when I was a lifeguard," the man answered, removing his steamed-up glasses and setting them in the snow. "Call 911."

"They're on the way," Jazmine said as she approached. She opened the First Aid kit and set it on the ground next to him. "I need to put out triangles, unless you need immediate help."

"No, I've got it," he said.

Jazmine turned back to the bus and flipped open the long plastic box, already covered by a half-inch of fresh snow. She reached in for the reflective triangles and unfolded them into shape. She set one on the traffic side of the bus, then trudged to place one behind the bus.

Jazmine made her way back to the front to place the last triangle. As she crouched to set it in place, she noticed a small rectangle in the snow beside the curb. Her mind flashed back to the jolt she felt after swerving on the ice. Then, her memory shifted into slow motion as the bus slid down the hill—to the glow in the center of the street. A steady glow, right there in the middle of the road. What had the woman been doing, just standing there like that?

She shuffled through more snow toward the light still glowing a couple of feet away from the newly placed triangle. If she could just save the phone. Save the phone and she could save the woman. The growing number of drivers lined up behind the bus were now pulling U-turns to take different routes to work. More residents watched the man work to revive the victim.

Her victim.

Jazmine used the back of her glove to shield her eyes from the brights of the nearest waiting car. She crouched down to dust off the accumulating snow when she noticed a spot of blood. And then two. A gash beside her left eye was still bleeding. The throbbing in her head began anew as she turned her focus back on the phone—the shattered screen and corner seal gaping open to revealing the wiring inside. Jazmine began all but gasping for air at everything that lay broken in this street.

Jazmine heard a bus window slide open, but she couldn't turn around before Gabby's voice poured down on her. "All's good in here, Jazmine. What about outside there?"

As if by reflex, Jazmine pocketed the phone. "I'll fill you in when I get back in there," she said, realizing her pocketed hand still gripped the cell phone. An ambulance finally made it past the traffic, lights whirling, to park two feet next to where she still knelt.

"Are you okay, Ma'am?" came the shouting voice of a medic through an ambulance window three feet directly above her head. Jazmine looked up at the blaring, glaring EMT rig, but couldn't just take out the phone and place it back in the snow where she'd found it.

"No. I'm fine," Jazmine said, but the man was having none of it.

"You're bleeding, Ma'am," he yelled again. "Did this bus hit you?"

"I'm the driver of the bus," she called back. "My arm hit the side window, but the woman over there needs your immediate attention." She pointed with her un-pocketed hand.

Two police cars eased next to the bus in the thickening snow, their sirens and lights also blaring. Jazmine could only imagine how terrified the children on the bus must be—and poor Gabby, taking care of them all alone. As the police officers from one car rushed to the woman in the road, Jazmine made her way back to the bus to meet with the officers from the second car.

Two officers turned around to face her. The man was tall and thin, while the woman was short and squat.

"Do you know anything?" Jazmine asked, feeling the tears rim her eyelids. "Is she at all responsive?"

"I'm sorry, but we won't know that answer until she's examined in the hospital," the female officer said. Her police uniform name indicator read *Robertson*.

Jazmine brushed away the blood now trailing down her cheek.

"I'm getting a medic for that eye," the male officer told Jazmine. "Then I'll check the bus."

"Can you tell us what happened here, Ma'am?" the remaining officer asked.

Jazmine replayed the scene in her mind as she spoke, the bus careening down the hill.

"I can't believe Seattle didn't close their schools this morning," Officer Robertson murmured. "At least give a late start to let the ice melt. I have to ask you to take a mandatory breathalyzer test, though."

"Of course," Jazmine said. As the officer held the apparatus out to her, she opened her mouth and blew as much air as her shortness of breath would allow. She felt horrible enough without being treated as a reckless driver. Ultimately, her quick maneuvering may have saved that woman's life, and certainly the lives of the children on board the bus. They should have been throwing her a parade, not shoving breathalyzers in her face—much less the drug test she expected from the school district before the day was through.

But what if it got much worse? What if that woman didn't make it? Would she be charged with manslaughter? Would the state take her son away? Where would he go? Who would take on a severely autistic three-year-old? Certainly not his father, the loser who had left them both two years prior.

Jazmine looked back to the bus, where she could hear Rylan's continued screaming—high-pitched and endless once he started. The eight-year-old seemed never to come up for air. Through the window, Frankie still rocked back and forth, and Taylor banged at the bald spots by her ears, desperate to remove the hand coverings so she could pull at her remaining tufts of hair.

"Could I ask you to please turn off those lights?" Jazmine asked, pointing at the spinning lights atop the police cars. "And ask the ambulance drivers to turn off the siren. These are special needs children, for God's sake. Do you have any idea how these things are adding to their trauma?"

"I'm afraid we have to keep the strobe lights on," Officer Robertson said, "to alert oncoming traffic. I'll see about getting them to turn the siren off, though." She turned away and spoke into her radio.

"It's about time," Robertson's male partner told the medic when he finally arrived to help Jazmine.

He had Jazmine sit in a fold-out chair while placing a foil blanket around her shoulders. She winced when he applied some antibiotic to the wound before bandaging the cut beside her eye. Jazmine sat dazed, watching as residents peered out their windows, reporters made their way from police officer to medic, and crowd members huddled along the sidewalk.

Finally, the supervisor arrived with the operations manager in a district van. The kids needed to get to an EMT unit and then the hospital for observation. While the operations manager worked with Gabby to transfer the students into the van, Dan Stewart, the supervisor, pulled Jazmine aside for some questions of his own.

"Did anything precede the ice?" he asked, after she'd given him the now-automated run-down of what had happened. "Did one of the kids throw something? Or perhaps another car honked and startled you?"

"I don't recall anything preceding the accident," Jazmine said dully, hoping her statement would be generic enough to walk back later during the inevitable school district investigation. She'd have to explain that she'd been up until three in the morning with her son, screaming from more night terrors. That she'd woken up tired as hell—utterly exhausted from both lack of sleep and from the physical exertion of having to rein her son in—not just a few hours before, but constantly, day after week after month. That she'd run out of both sick and personal leave time and couldn't afford to take an unpaid day off. And that she'd stood in front of her bathroom mirror telling herself that she felt just fine. She'd catch a nap after the morning rounds. All she had to do was make it through a couple of hours. She'd done it before— everybody did at some point.

But for now, she only added, "I need to speak with an attorney."

As vans from local news agencies pulled alongside the police cars, Dan Stewart went over the legalities and all the what-would-happen- now scenarios. He'd be accompanying them to the hospital, where there would be a blood draw and drug test and basic medical observation. The ensuing investigation would entail district and police officials going over the video from the bus camera and interviewing

Gabby, the students, and the woman in the street—who was now on a stretcher in the ambulance. Jazmine shook her head in disbelief. Why hadn't the lady just crossed the street? Why on God's white, snowy pavement had she just stood there?

Snowflakes drifted lazily down, hoping to attach to her silver blanket, only to slide down the foil like a bus on an icy morning road. Jazmine silently thanked the numbness growing inside her for forcing a distance between herself and this nightmare from which she would never wake up.

Broken Connections

Carolyn

Carolyn signaled from the driver's seat of her mother's Buick. Traffic had increased in Seattle in the past twenty-two years, and she'd forgotten how awful Washington drivers were when snow touched the ground. The only remnants she could see from last week's snowstorm had been pushed against the sides of the road, although the dusky clouds above made the ice much harder to detect.

After four days of Hoax Hell that followed the disastrous Manhattan party, not to mention the last six hours on a plane, the car indeed felt like a luxury vehicle—a couple notches too warm and so comfortable that it wouldn't take much for Carolyn to nod off. Her mother had insisted on coming to get her, no matter how many times she'd told her she'd rather call an Uber.

And now her mother sat in the passenger seat, smelling of powder and menthol. In her lap sat Trixie, her miniature white Chihuahua. The dog shook out of fear, or perhaps habit. It couldn't possibly be cold with the heat set to *inferno*. But Carolyn didn't dare turn it down, lest she unleash an unnecessary diatribe about the effects that a couple degrees might have on winter contagion.

Carolyn drove them over the West Seattle Bridge toward her mother's house on a bluff above Alki Beach. Five years prior, she'd bought her mother the rental when she agreed to take care of Carolyn's twelve-year-old daughter for the summer. With 16-hour days spent building up her list enough to get into one of the Big Five publishing houses, Carolyn hadn't been able to give Sophie the time she needed. Not to mention her cheat of an ex-husband was too much of a playboy to trust to take parenting seriously.

The summer stay was only intended to give Sophie a chance to get to know her grandmother better. When she returned to New York, Carolyn would have everything in place to give her daughter a stable upbringing and every opportunity. But then, Sophie never came back. Carolyn told herself that once she landed a job with publishing royalty, it would be worth it. And she really thought it had been once she rose to the top. Now, having been fired without so much as a severance package, she knew with heartbreaking clarity that it had all been for naught.

"Carolyn, listen," her mother said, nodding to the radio. As she turned up the volume knob, Trixie stood on shaky legs, glanced around, then curled up in her lap again.

"*After this, we'll hear from a Colorado school shooting survivor about the Morgan St. John memoir hoax—and the Seattle-born publisher who allowed it to happen.*"

"Have you spoken to the news yet?" her mother asked.

"I already gave my statement to the Associated Press. The only person I have any plans to speak with now that I'm back in Seattle is Quentin Sims," Carolyn said, signaling to her exit onto Harbor Avenue.

"Quentin who?" Vivian asked. "Is he a reporter?"

"Dr. Sims is a child behavior specialist," Carolyn answered, "and one of my best-selling authors. I need to make sure he doesn't find another publisher before I can figure all of this out."

Giving a quick shoulder check before changing lanes, Carolyn's eyes grazed her mother's profile, which seemed somehow more familiar than her face head-on. Her hair had faded and was shorter, thinner. But the arched slope of her forehead into her straight, Roman nose, and the curve of her upper lip down to her much fuller bottom lip would forever be imprinted in her memory.

"So how have things been going with you?" Carolyn asked, desperate to shift the focus from her recent fall from success.

"A little lonely since Sophie moved out," her mother said with a sigh, "but now I've got you to keep me company." She reached over and patted Carolyn's knee. "By the way, I have one more box for Sophie. I thought you could take it to her dorm next week. Give you a chance to wish your daughter a happy birthday."

"Looking forward to it," Carolyn said through clenched teeth. While she appreciated an excuse to drop in on her daughter, she didn't exactly welcome the implication that she wouldn't have remembered her nineteenth birthday if her mother hadn't reminded her.

Driving past the cafés and businesses along Alki Avenue, Carolyn kept her eyes ahead, determined not to glance at one restaurant in particular. The memories that came with it were too much to process right now, and she suddenly felt feverish.

"What are you doing?" her mother asked.

"It's too hot," Carolyn said as she continued to press for the window to roll down, which it wouldn't. Childproof driver control buttons weren't intended for forty-somethings. "I need some fresh air."

Trixie stirred in Vivian's lap, sniffing at the cold breeze coming through the window that Carolyn had finally managed to open. The Puget Sound was almost impossible to discern from the clouds at this point in the evening. Soon it would be dark. When Carolyn turned back to see if the light had turned, she caught another glimpse of her mother's profile. Old family pictures flashed through her mind.

In pictures where her dad had played photographer, her mom smiled delicately at the camera, her face full and clear, tentatively happy and beautiful in her youth. Then came the pictures of them together. Her dad was never thrilled at the prospect of posing for pictures. He sported plaid suits, the collar points reaching the end of each shoulder. Sideburns and big, black-framed eyeglasses, with a hand holding a scotch glass to complete each look. And then there was her mother— from beehives to bobs—always draped around him somehow, looking to him for...what? Guidance? Acceptance?

When the light turned green, Carolyn pressed the accelerator, fully aware of the answer because she had seen the same profile of her own face, in her own family pictures. But instead of looking to Marcus, her smile had shined on her daughter Sophie, so certain that everything she'd given up for her would be worth it. Her move to New York, her marriage to a philanderer and the subsequent divorce had led to her desire to prove herself in the publishing industry and, ultimately, to lose her daughter to someone who could give her the one thing Carolyn couldn't: Time.

"Dear, please close the window," her mother said. "It's freezing out there, and the wind is too loud for me to hear the news."

As the window rose to a close, a voice came clearer from the Buick's stereo system.

"That so-called 'memoir' is nothing more than sacrilege." The interviewee sniffled. *"For someone to take our very real trauma as her own, to make money off our classmates'—our friends'—deaths. The shooters can now share the blood on their hands with Morgan St. John, not to mention the publishers, who were too busy making money to do their research."*

Carolyn gritted her teeth as the reporter chimed in. *"Carolyn Ford, the memoir's publisher, and a Seattle native, declined to comment."*

"This is ridiculous," her mom said, snapping off the radio. "You need to give them your side of this story."

Carolyn shook her head. "I have no interest in making my case in the court of public opinion." After all, she had come home to escape the calls from reporters, booksellers, printers, and Morgan's incessant apologies. She'd already been blasted in countless newspapers and magazines around the world. Her name in the publishing industry was right up there with syphilis. She was done for and had bowed out gracefully, yet the industry and the public wouldn't let it go until she'd suffered for making them believe a story she'd fallen for herself. Carolyn eased her foot on the brakes at a traffic light and looked past her mother to the beach. "I'll let the mob simmer, thanks. In a month, maybe I'll be 'yesterday's' news."

"You're home now. Our reporters aren't like those New York sharks. They'll sympathize with you. Now, if I could just…"

Carolyn noticed the shine of a cell phone screen in her mother's hand as she mumbled to herself about where to find such-and-such number.

"Mom, what are you—"

"Wait, I've got it."

"Got what?"

"Hush now, it's ringing."

Carolyn held her breath, barely noticing that frozen snow had begun to smack the windshield. Her passenger-seat driver of a mother reached to turn on the windshield wipers.

The rhythm of the wipers felt to Carolyn like a ticking clock. She gripped the steering wheel and asked, "What's ringing, Mom?"

"It's not ringing anymore, dear." Carolyn drew in a much-needed breath until her mom added, "I'm on hold. Now close your window, will you? I won't be able to hear them when they answer."

"When *who* answers?"

"Hello, this is Vivian Ford, and we just heard your uneven coverage of the Colorado memoir hoax."

"Mom, hang up the phone." Carolyn grabbed for it, but her mother's sleight of hand in getting it to her other ear was exceptional. Trixie snapped at Carolyn. Her mom practically had to shout to be heard.

"My daughter is the publisher. What's that?"

Carolyn scanned the side of the road for a place to pull over, but the plowed snow piles filled every empty parking spot.

"Yes, she's sitting right here with me now," her mother continued while Trixie snarled from her lap. "She'd love to tell you the *real* story behind the—Carolyn, what are you doing?"

Carolyn had hold of the phone, trying to wrench it out of her mother's grasp, but her mother's fingers were like the talons of a hawk.

"Carolyn, really, let go," her mother insisted.

Carolyn twisted this way and that, steering with her left hand and pulling with every fiber of every muscle in her right arm until her mother suddenly released the phone. Carolyn's hand jerked towards her own chest and wound up flinging the device out the window.

Trixie clambered over the console between them, yipping incessantly at the phone that had disappeared into the flurries.

"Now look what you've done," Vivian huffed. "Would you close that godforsaken window before Trixie jumps out after it?"

Carolyn swerved the car into a loading zone and slammed on the brakes. "I'll go look for it." But, as the window went up, Carolyn could hear the crunch of the phone under the tires of oncoming traffic. Then she saw it out of the corner of her eye, spinning across the road until it shattered against the opposite curb and then dropped into a sewage grate.

Keeping her gaze on the windshield, she could sense her mother looking at her, agape. "I'll get you a new phone," Carolyn said as she shifted the car into drive.

"It wasn't mine, dear," her mother said dryly. "It was yours."

Ava

Numb from painkillers, Ava stared into a distance only she could see. The events floated as tufts of snow. Singular moments knit themselves into a fuzzy blanket of memory. A revolving door of nurses and doctors and orderlies and officers came and went. Some brought food and drink that others later whisked away, untouched. One of those people sat in the visitor's chair now, looking every bit as bleak as Ava felt.

The woman opened her mouth to speak, then closed it. She slumped into the chair, then sat up. Who was she? Ava was too numb to care as she sat among the snowflakes, flashing cryptic clues of what had brought her to this hospital bed.

The last kiss—long and languid—tasting of spicy warm Merlot.
A soft voice welcoming her inside.
The glow of the cell phone screen.
The Puget Sound waters, dark and glassy.
Howard Mercer's arching eyebrows.
Headlights—a bus?
I'm sorry.

Ava's eyes fell once again on the woman sitting in the visitor's chair. Had she just spoken those same words—*I'm sorry*—that had glared at Ava from a cell phone screen?

"I shouldn't be here," the woman murmured.

Ava squinted to make her out. She wore a brown purse slung bandolier-style over one shoulder of her faded purple jacket, jeans, and scuffed, faux suede booties. She didn't look like any of the officers or hospital staff Ava had seen.

"They told me not to say anything that could be used against me," the woman continued. "But it's obviously causing you more harm."

More harm? Ava looked harder at the woman, whose dark hair was as frazzled as her voice. The morning light streamed through the window, blanching her skin.

"My son's in the occupational therapy wing," the woman said. "His appointment is almost over, so I should get going. I just figured it was the right thing to do—to come by and tell you how sorry I am. Even though…" Her wide brown eyes turned glassy. "It was the ice, you know? And something shining from the middle of the crosswalk—you, just stopped there, cold."

"I was…" Ava furrowed her brow, working hard to process the woman's words. She'd said something about the ice, the shining. "What did you say? That I stopped in the road?"

"I'm not asking you to explain—"

"Who are you?"

"—I only wanted to see if I could do anything to help. And I found your phone. Thought you might like it back, although I'm afraid it's in even worse shape than you are."

Ava reached to take it from her, but something pulled against her hand—a clear tube and tape. She looked left to find the tube hooked into an I.V. bag. "How long have I been here?"

"The accident happened two days ago," the woman answered, placing the phone in her palm. Attached to the screen was a sticky note with the name *Jazmine Johnston* scrawled in green ink and a phone number beneath. The numbers blurred and swam.

Two days ago.

Tell you how sorry I am.

More harm…

The woman—Jazmine, apparently—looked from Ava to the phone and back to Ava. "It looks pretty busted. It'll be a miracle if it turns on."

Ava held the power button and waited, gazing numbly at the spiderweb pattern of the shattered screen until it eventually lit up.

"Well, I'll be," Jazmine mused.

Ava couldn't make out the numbers for her passcode, let alone remember them, but somehow recalled the zig-zag pattern they made. Once she was in, she handed the phone back to Jazmine.

"You need me to read something for you?" she asked.

Ava willed her mind to process what she needed, but the flurries kept her from it.

"A text?" Jazmine prodded. "An email?"

"Text!" Ava burst, thrilled to have made some kind of breakthrough. "I need you to read the text."

"Which one?" Jazmine asked.

"I don't know," Ava said. "Start with the first one you see."

As the woman clicked into the phone, Ava watched her hold the cracked screen up to her face.

Ava closed her eyes to better hear the words. "Enabler" and "toxic" and "recovery" seeped through her waiting ears. Without opening her eyelids, she bolted upright—the image of Gavin, the one she'd seen a hundred times stood in the doorway of their modest mother-in-law-type cottage. He'd come home from work or wherever, business suit rumpled, and was trying his best to act sober. She wasn't fooled, but she knew better than to call him on it. Fully lit, Gavin always closed the door behind him a bit too hard or too soft, depending on how the booze was hitting his mood at that moment. Not this time. She turned away to look out the small living room window, too icy to see through, too frozen for Seattle winters, and when she looked back, the door was wide open. Gavin was gone. Ava opened her eyes to see this strange woman again still holding her phone.

"Says he'll be gone a few days to give you a chance to pack and find a place to stay," she continues. "Damn. That's cold. Do you have a place to go?"

Ava stared numbly at the wall and gave her default place to stay. "My dad's."

Jazmine's expression turned puzzled, and she shook the phone. "It died on me."

"Try the button again," Ava said, feeling her stomach tighten.

Jazmine pressed at the side of the phone, but the screen remained dark.

"I don't get it," Ava said.

"It'll take some time to sink in," Jazmine said, her voice no longer frazzled, but low and soothing.

"No, I mean I really don't understand. What is he saying? 'Enabler' and 'toxic' to his 'recovery'?"

"Honey," Jazmine crouched down beside the bed and put a warm hand over Ava's. "His text says that if he's going to have any chance at becoming clean and sober, he can't stay with you. He needs help."

"But *I* can help him," Ava argued weakly.

"From the sound of this text, he thinks you've been helpful in all the wrong ways."

Once again, the woman's words made no sense and Ava's head pounded all over again. She laid her head back on the pillow and closed her eyes.

"He needs professional help, sweetheart," Jazmine said. "Look, is there anything I can do? Anything you need?"

"I need *him*," Ava said, her voice weak in its desperation. She couldn't help but wonder what he might say if he knew his text had put them both in recovery. Her brain was too swollen to send a command to laugh or cry. More likely, the painkillers were dulling her reactions, warping all these strange flurries of memory.

"I'm afraid I'm not anyone who should be giving relationship advice," Jazmine said. "I really am so sorry."

Ava gave a hopeless shrug. Under her closed eyelids, the snowflakes blurred together, coming at her as though she were the windshield of a racing car. The months she'd paid their rent, washed the dishes while Gavin studied for his bar exam, lied to his partners about why he wouldn't be in for work this time, put stacks of bills on her credit card while he put law school tuition on his.

In a surge of anger, Ava opened her eyes wide. The thin, cold fluorescent tubes of light blinded her. She sat up and blurted, "Do you need a place to stay?"

Jazmine cocked her head and froze. "Me? I know my job's in trouble, but I didn't run the bus through my apartment building."

Ava felt herself warm through the drug-induced haze. "I can't pay the rent on my dad's place without you-know-who. I don't even know if I have a job—wait, you're in trouble, too?"

"I'm on leave while they investigate," Jazmine said. "The accident, you know? I can take care of my son, which is a good thing. He's got some issues—speaking of which, his appointment just ended. I need to get going."

An image flashed of snowflakes fluttering against the glowing cell phone screen and, underneath her feet, a white stripe of the crosswalk. She had been standing still in the middle of the street. And now this woman's job was in trouble.

Ava opened her mouth to apologize when a vague realization of the job itself began to dawn. Her head continued to throb and the ache grew sharper as a sense of vertigo set in. She was fraternizing with the very woman who had put her in this bed. This was the driver.

"You okay, there?" Jazmine asked.

Ava's eyes began to roll back.

"Hey, why don't you rest your head." Jazmine's voice was soft and calm. "I'll have a nurse come check on you." There was a distant crinkle of plastic. "For what it's worth, I'll put the phone back on the windowsill."

"I'm…" Ava started, struggling to remember what word she needed to say to apologize to this woman before she left. "I need—"

"A new phone?" Jazmine asked. "I'd be happy to pick one up for you, if you'd like."

Ava laid her head back. Yes, she needed a phone. She murmured her father's address so Jazmine could bring it to her. She had to call Gavin. No, not Gavin. Stupid Gavin. No, that other man—the one who raised his eyebrows while holding up her resume. Yes. Howard Mercer, the literary agent man with the job.

"I would really appreciate that," she said and closed her eyes, letting her head sink deeper into the pillow as she nodded off, buried under flurries of snow.

Jazmine

Jazmine scooted Henry through the door of Emerald City Cellular. The walls were painted different fluorescent colors—orange, blue, yellow. Three sales reps talked eagerly with customers—a middle-aged couple, an upright businesswoman, and a man in faded jeans and a trucker hat, his face drawn, eyes hollow. He glanced up, sensing her gaze, and put his grease-stained fingers to the rim of the cap's visor.

A young saleswoman whose name tag read *Reya* asked, "Can I help you?"

"I'm picking up a phone," Jazmine said, "for a friend. She's in the hospital right now, so she couldn't be here in person."

As Reya narrowed her eyes, Jazmine feared her fresh wave of public notoriety might be dawning on her. "What's the name?" the young woman asked.

Jazmine set her bag on the counter to search for the folded paper with Ava's full name and additional information. She felt overstimulated and claustrophobic all at once—and if she felt it, she could only imagine what Henry was going through. She slid the paper across the counter and reached for Henry at her side until she felt the soft fluff of his hair.

Inevitably, Henry moved away from her touch and reached for some headphones dangling on a rack. Jazmine pulled him back, his Elmo jacket riding up his little pot belly. He responded with a whimper, and she cursed herself for forgetting his fidget spinner at home. After the seventy-five minutes and three bus transfers it took to get here, she couldn't stand the idea of having to do it all over again later if he threw a fit. The plan was simple: Get the phone, get it to Ava, and get her to drop any-and-all charges.

Reya's eyes never left the screen. "And how are you associated with this account?"

The walls officially closed in as Jazmine searched for some kind of answer that would result in a promise kept. Nothing.

"I'm not," she finally admitted, her fingers still gripping Henry's flailing arms.

"Would your child like this?" asked the businesswoman at the adjacent counter. She held out her tablet to show some kind of colorful stacking game. It was perfect.

"No thanks," Jazmine said. "I'm afraid he would break it."

The woman looked like she'd stepped out of Forbes magazine, wearing what had to be a designer trench coat, straight-leg pants, and shoes that probably cost over three months' rent. Even her red hair was polished, cut just to her jawline. Jazmine's hair would forever be too curly to be considered "polished."

The woman put back the tablet and fished around for something else in her large purse. "How about sticky notes?"

Jazmine looked at the stack of four colors—yellow, teal, raspberry, and green. She could only imagine the mess Henry would make and said, "I'm not sure what he'd do with them…" She trailed off when Henry snatched them from the woman's hand and simply thanked her.

And she truly was grateful. Wallpapering the store with perfectly aligned sticky notes beat the alternative. "Can I pay you for them?"

"Ms. Ford?" The businesswoman's customer service rep asked.

The woman—Ms. Ford, apparently—held up a finger that she'd be right there, then turned back to Jazmine and shook her head. "They're all yours."

Jazmine watched Henry create a line of teal sticky notes all along a shelf of blue-tooth speakers and earbuds. An old man in a veteran's cap entered the store and Henry jolted at the loud "zap" of the security tracking system. Jazmine held her breath as Henry stood paralyzed. When he pulled off another sticky note, she exhaled once again.

The elderly gentleman didn't seem fazed by the noise—perhaps his hearing aids were turned low. Leaning shakily on his cane, he took the middle-aged couple's place at the counter on the opposite corner of the store, but Jazmine was already too deep in thought to notice much. How was she going to pull this off—buying a phone for a woman she hardly knew? A woman she'd run down with a bus on an icy road, no less.

"She's in the hospital," Jazmine insisted. "You can call her and she'll give you her permission over the phone."

"We really can't do that," Reya said. She seemed to be watching Henry, who was now sticky-noting a line of burner phones. "Lots of people in this situation buy temporary phones," she offered.

"But how would a burner give her access to her contacts and texts?" As soon as the words left her mouth, Jazmine thought back to that awkward breakup text and wondered if maybe it wouldn't be better that Ava have a blank slate phone—at least for a little while.

"We can take the SIM card out of that phone and put it in the temporary," Reya said.

Jazmine nodded slowly as she processed the situation. For better or worse, that would give Ava access to her information, and she'd promise to pay for the new phone once Ava was able to pick it up herself. "Sounds like a plan," she said.

As Jazmine reached for the sleek, cellophane-wrapped box and set it on the counter, Reya pointed at the sticky notes. "Would you mind taking those off the merchandise?"

Jazmine looked around for her son and found him at the furthest end of the same shelf. He'd begun placing the raspberry sticky notes on the boxes beneath the line of teal. He hadn't yet noticed the veteran, who was taking a box of earbuds from the middle of the display.

"It's the only thing keeping him calm," Jazmine whispered to Reya. "But I promise I'll remove them before we leave."

At the next station, the customer service rep handed Ms. Ford a plastic bag with her merchandise.

"Excuse me, sir?" Jazmine asked, but the man didn't seem to hear. She raised her voice a decibel and a half. "Sir? Could you take one from one of the top shelves?"

"I didn't take nothin'," he said. "I'm only looking."

"No, I understand." Jazmine worked to keep her voice calm. If he were any closer, she could just take the Post-it and put it on the box that was hanging behind the one the old man had taken. "It's just that my son has this, sort of, project going on, and if you take this away from the teal—"

The veteran lifted his cane and pointed it at her. "I'm not stealing!"

"Is there a problem?" Reya asked, hovering one hand over the printer. Jazmine noticed her make eye contact with the manager, who nodded in reply before putting a phone to his ear, surely to call the police.

"This woman accused me of steal—"

"No, he was taking from the row of *teal*, and I was afraid my son might—"

But it was too late. Henry saw the man holding his teal-posted box. From moan to shriek, everyone moved two feet back, like leaves scattering from a tornado.

The man looked at the sticky note on the box. "I'll give it back," he said, finally understanding what Jazmine had been trying to tell him. He talked in a way one might speak to a puppy. "Now everything is okay."

Jazmine knew Henry was beyond hearing the man at this point. Her son took the box and hit it against his own head three times before Jazmine was able to cross the store and pry the box from his hands. She moved back toward her counter. The man in the trucker hat flinched with each scream, but when his sunken eyes met Jazmine's, he shrugged his consolation.

The store manager came out from behind his counter and stated in the same, firm, professional voice she'd heard so many times before in so many public places: "My apologies ma'am, but I need to ask you to remove your son from the store until you can get him calmed down."

"I'm sorry," Jazmine said, juggling Henry's thrashing body from arm to arm. "He's autistic. It's not his fault."

"I understand completely, ma'am. Why don't you take him out to your car—"

"I don't have a car—"

"Then take him outside!" the man in the trucker hat suddenly spouted, his face now beet red.

"It's freezing out there," Ms. Ford broke in, her voice every bit as firm as the manager's. "Why don't you point us to the restroom?"

Reya gave a sad smile. "I'm sorry, ma'am, we don't have a public restroom."

"A storage room?"

"No customers allowed there. It's policy," the manager said, his voice even.

"A breakroom?" Ms. Ford continued, sounding almost bored with each rejection.

Reya gave a faint shake of her head.

"Come with me," Ms. Ford said, walking past the veteran with a confidence Jazmine hadn't felt since Ben had left her and his son to fend for themselves.

"But…" Jazmine stammered, "what about the phone?"

"I'll have everything ready for you when you come back," Reya said.

Ms. Ford opened the door and waited for Jazmine to corral her squirming, angry octopus of a son and follow her out to a gold Buick. "Your son can sit in the back seat," she said, "and you can either join him there, or me up front, whatever works."

Jazmine wished he was the kind of child she could join in the back seat and hold until he relaxed under the solace of her maternal warmth. But Henry never found comfort in his mother's touch, especially when he was throwing a fit.

Jazmine winced when he kicked the car door and held onto the top of the door frame, squealing like a punctured pipe until Jazmine finally had him in the back seat and shut the door. She opened the front passenger door and slid into the car.

"I'm Carolyn, by the way," the woman said as she jammed the key into the ignition and started the engine.

Jazmine stared at the cellular store in front of them. "Even for Henry, this is a whopper of a meltdown," she told the kind woman. She wondered if the patrons and workers could still hear Henry's piercing screams from inside the store. But soon enough, the trucker, the vet, and the sales staff all disappeared from view under the steam creeping up Carolyn's windshield. "I'm Jazmine," she said, almost as an afterthought, and reached out her bare hand to shake the leather-gloved hand Carolyn extended.

From the back of the Buick, Henry threw his head back over and over into his seat, his cheeks streaked with tears. Jazmine forced her focus on the warming air that blew from the car's vents until it dawned on her that she had no idea what to expect now. Would this generous woman drive them home? Would she be willing to sit here for however long it took for Henry to calm down? Didn't matter. No number of *what-ifs* could amount to Jazmine's undying appreciation at the solitude this car provided.

"I once thought my daughter had Sensory Integration Disorder," Carolyn stated calmly, her voice just loud enough to be heard over Henry's wailing. She fished through her purse until she found the tablet she'd offered in the store. Jazmine listened to her voice like a bedtime story, melting into the plush seat. "It turned out, Sophie was just incredibly sensitive," Carolyn continued. "She'd wear one set of clothes that felt comfortable. She had a closet full of the sweetest dresses and outfits that she refused to wear. I had to buy a seatbelt lock because she'd unbelt herself mid-drive, complaining it was too tight."

When the tablet lit up, Carolyn clicked here and scrolled there.

Henry rammed his head into the back of her seat.

"Henry, stop," Jazmine said.

Carolyn stayed Jazmine by placing a hand softly on her arm. She continued her story with the same soothing, tranquil voice. "Her shoes were always tied too tightly. She wouldn't eat tapioca pudding because of the texture. Soda was 'too spicy' because of the fizz. She feared stepping in puddles, wouldn't even finger paint." Eventually, a game lit on the screen, and Carolyn tapped to move blocks this way and that, like Candy Crush or an old game of Tetris. "I know this isn't the same challenge that your son has, but I can certainly relate."

For a moment, the only sounds were those of Henry's heaving breaths from the backseat, and the dings and clangs of the video game still in Carolyn's hands.

"I'm guessing that if your son would like to play this, you could run into the store to collect your things."

"What do you say, kiddo?" Jazmine asked tentatively. Henry leaned forward for the tablet.

Jazmine nodded at Carolyn, opened the car door, and said, "I'll be right back."

Commiseration

Carolyn

Carolyn stepped carefully down the Seattle sidewalk, adjusting the cake box in her arms as she rounded the corner to the almost completely glassed entrance of Lander Hall. The building was every bit as impressive as it had looked in the pictures on the dorm's website. The only thing the building lacked was a big red bow, since it was Carolyn's most expensive present yet to her daughter. It had been a safety issue, more than anything—a mother's desire to get her daughter out of driving through the horrid Seattle traffic. And she could certainly afford it—*could* being the operative word. What would Sophie think now, when she found out that Carolyn's latest "success" would actually bankrupt her? Would she believe her mother was an incompetent publisher of a bogus memoir, or that she'd been in on the lie?

But Carolyn couldn't think about that now because there was Sophie, sitting on the arm of a brightly colored lounge chair, glancing up from her phone. A smile lit on her face as her eyes went from Carolyn to the cake box and back to Carolyn, and she came rushing to open the door for her.

"Thanks, sweetheart," Carolyn said, then stopped and blinked as she realized this girl was not, in fact, her daughter. She looked so much like Sophie had appeared on her visit to New York last summer—strawberry blonde hair pulled up into a messy bun, jeans with tears all the way down the front. But on closer inspection, Carolyn noticed her eyes were brown, not Sophie's piercing ocean blue, and her smile lacked Sophie's dimples and freckle-spattered nose.

Carolyn straightened up. No harm done. Anyone could have made that mistake through tinted windows, and she'd called plenty of interns "sweetheart." Best to own it and get to the point. "I'm here for Sophie Wheeler."

"I'm Sophie's roommate," the girl said, "Jenna. Some people came by the room just before you got here, so she asked if I could bring you up."

Carolyn shifted the box to the crook of one arm as she came through the door. "Sophie speaks highly of you. She even sent me a photo of you two," she fibbed, feeling a slow sinking feeling in her chest that Sophie had chosen to spend time with friends she probably saw daily, rather than come down to greet her mother herself.

"Actually, that's perfect," Carolyn said with one last definitive nod. "Gives me a chance to bring this cake out of its box and make a real entrance."

"Ooh, cake," Jenna said, "that's so nice. Let's get you signed in and I'll help you with it."

Jenna guided Carolyn to the check-in desk inside the tall glass door, then over to an end table in the lounge. Students lazed about, some playing pool, others chatting, but most of them sat hunched over their phones. Carolyn and her daughter's roommate undid the box at the corners and folded the sides underneath so that the cake sat open on what was now a cardboard platter.

"Oh, we can't have candles here," Jenna said with an apologetic shrug.

Carolyn continued setting the 1 and the 9 candles into the cake. "How about if I leave them unlit?"

"Oh yeah," Jenna said, nodding some kind of impressed approval. "That should work."

"Lovely," Carolyn said. "Now, let's go wish my daughter a happy birthday."

Jenna led Carolyn to an open elevator and pushed the button for the fourth floor.

"How do you and Sophie get along?" Carolyn asked, realizing only after the words were out what a silly question it was—as though this virtual stranger would impart any kind of disdain for her roommate to the roommate's own mother. But then, Carolyn couldn't help feeling awkward, because if they got along, then surely Jenna had received an earful of Sophie's complicated relationship with both of her parents. And as sweet as this undergraduate was, Carolyn couldn't help wondering if her politeness were a mere cover-up for the dark secrets she really knew about Sophie's MIA excuse for a mother.

Ding!

The elevator's ring almost stopped Carolyn's heart completely. She shifted the cake yet again to get a stronger grip.

"We get along great," Jenna answered as she stepped off the elevator. "Sophie's way more fun and interesting than my last roommate. We're just down the hall, here." She led Carolyn right and then past several open-and-closed doors. "We have a great view of Mount Rainier, but with all the clouds lately, it hasn't been out."

It took Carolyn a moment to process Jenna's statement. She hadn't heard that Washington idiom—that the mountain was or wasn't "out" based on whether the clouds allowed it to be visible—in years. As they stepped closer to the room, she felt a familiar flutter in her chest from the nerves that usually accompanied seeing Sophie. She could never figure out why that was. Sophie had always been good-natured. But then, five years ago, she'd chosen to stay with Vivian. Carolyn couldn't blame her for wanting stability and attention, but it had been a massive rejection, just the same.

Jenna stopped abruptly and gestured to their room. Carolyn turned through the open doorway and exclaimed, "Happy birthday, honey!" She stopped short when she caught sight of Sophie and almost sent the cake flying.

Her beautiful daughter, whom she had mistaken for Jenna's twin just moments before, looked nothing like the wide-eyed, sparkling young academic who had led her here.

"Something wrong, Mom?" Sophie asked, tilting a hip to the side as she stood by her bed.

"What did you do to your hair?" Carolyn tried to look past the half-shaven head, the strawberry blonde hair now dyed the color of seaweed—tried to see through the black makeup spackled across Sophie's eyes. She wanted to find the sweet-faced girl she'd worked so hard to give a good life, even if she hadn't been able to be there to mother her through it.

"I didn't do it," Sophie quipped. "Isadore did."

"Isadore?" Carolyn turned to Jenna. "Is that a foreign exchange student on this floor?"

Jenna shook her head and opened the door wider to reveal a woman who appeared to be Natalie Wood, if Natalie Wood had lived into her fifties. Brunette, side-swept hair, dark eyes, smooth skin. The woman carried an easy sophistication. Carolyn's eyes traveled down her arm to her bracelet-clad wrist and noticed a rock the size of Manhattan on the ring finger of a hand resting gently against someone else's arm. Carolyn's gaze drifted upwards until her eyes froze on the face of her ex-husband.

"Can you believe she's nineteen already?" Marcus asked, regarding Carolyn with amusement. He held up a small glass of what appeared to be water. "We've got ourselves a bona fide college girl!"

"Oh my God, Mom!" Sophie exclaimed. "What the hell?"

Carolyn looked down to see the cardboard platter hanging limply from her hands, the cake slipping face-first to the carpeted floor.

"Not to worry," Isadore said in some kind of European accent every bit as silky as the scarves around her neck, flowing behind her as she flitted over to Carolyn.

Numb, Carolyn gave her the cardboard cake box and allowed the woman to scoop the cake back onto it. As Isadore asked Jenna to "dispose" of it in a hallway "receptacle bin" and then find a custodian who could give the carpet a quick steam-clean, Carolyn and Sophie shared an entire conversation with their eyes.

Widened: Why didn't you tell me your dad would be here?

Eyebrow raised: Like that's really what's bothering you.

Narrowed: Well, you could have told me he got married.

Crinkling at the corners: And ruin this fun surprise reunion? Not likely.

Carolyn finally broke away from the staring contest, glancing around the sparse dorm room. The beds were up high, like top bunks, underneath which were their desks, Sophie's was littered with her computer, papers, and books, while Jenna's sat neat and tidy as the dormitory's brochure picture. Her gaze had just landed on Marcus's latest literary masterpiece, *Indemnity*, on Sophie's shelf when he stepped in to break the silence.

"Carolyn, this is Isadore," Marcus said. "Isadore, this is Sophie's mother."

Underneath Carolyn's grin, her teeth were gritted to keep her jaws from grinding. *Sophie's mother*, he'd said, as though she'd been some temporary baby mama and not his wife of eleven excruciating years. In fact, she wondered how many other baby mamas there had been during their marriage and through all the years after the divorce. Just how many half-siblings did Sophie have? And at what point did Marcus decide to send away for this mail-order bride and experiment with fidelity again? And why the hell had Carolyn's mother said nothing about this development in Sophie's father's life in the week since she'd been back home?

"That is a lovely color on you," Isadore said.

Carolyn glanced up to see she'd been addressing her, then looked back down at her belted overcoat. It was dark turquoise, the same shade as her eyes, and a color her New York stylist had told her would set off the red highlights in her auburn hair.

"Thanks," Carolyn said. "Your scarf is very..." she trailed off, wondering why she was at a loss for words, "...stylish." Her eyes rested on Marcus's glass and suddenly her throat felt parched. She turned to

Sophie. "Honey, do you have something to drink? A bottle of water or—"

"Isadore brought some țuică." Sophie grabbed a mug from a shelf and poured something from a nondescript glass bottle. "Try some. They don't even sell it in America."

Carolyn took the mug from her daughter and swished the drink inside. "What is it?"

"A traditional Romanian drink," Sophie said, gesturing eagerly for Carolyn to take a sip. "You can really taste the plums in this one."

Romanian, Carolyn thought, working to keep her gaze from shifting to that damn wedding ring. The sparkling stone was so much larger than the antique ring Marcus had bought Carolyn two decades ago. And why was she so irritated by the fact that Marcus had traded Carolyn in for this older Romanian model? Somehow, it proved a humiliation far more depressing than the typical younger woman cliché.

Carolyn brought the glass to her lips and barely wet her lips. It was all but flavorless.

"Would you like to sit down?" Isadore offered.

"No thank you," Carolyn said, feeling the tiny room close in on her. As the president of her own publishing company, she knew a little something about power moves, and she wasn't about to sit below eye level of this woman. "So, are you an author, too?"

"No, Mom, she works here," Sophie said.

"She's a professor," Marcus said, the smoothness of his voice massaging the salt ever deeper into Carolyn's wounds. "Romanian History, specializing in art and architecture."

"Wait, didn't you publish a textbook, Isadore?" Sophie asked.

"One or two," Isadore said with a sly smile towards Marcus, as though Sophie was adorable in her naive assumption that Isadore had limited herself to writing *only* one or two books.

Normally, this was where Carolyn would pull the Advance Publishing card to show them both just who outranked whom. But she wasn't about to let the nosedive she'd taken from her publishing pedestal land her in a perfect belly flop—especially not in front of her now bestselling ex-husband and his brand-new professor wife. Instead, she took another sip of the plum juice and listened as Sophie's stepmother stole her spotlight.

"I was just telling Sophie that she *must* attend next week's Graffiti Jam," Isadore said, as though she knew she was doing Carolyn a favor by changing the subject. "At the Jam, musicians play their instruments while artists cover each other in paint. It is a night of unity and passion."

Sophie gave a wry grin. "And I was telling Isadore that it sounds more like a geeky finger-painting orgy."

"A passion for life, silly girl," Isadore explained.

Carolyn watched how Isadore interacted with her daughter, wondering just how long this woman had been in the picture to establish this kind of rapport—not to mention the similarities she noticed between Marcus and Sophie, such as the way they both now cocked their head just a little to the side as they laughed. She wished she could take pleasure in the way Marcus' hair had faded the past few years, into a gray that was gradually turning more salt than pepper, but it only made him look more distinguished.

Throughout their divorce, Carolyn had called on karma to do its cosmic job by striking Marcus with impotence, or at the very least, male-patterned balding. When it came to the size of his ego, so little would have gone so far. But karma didn't work on demand. Perhaps it was karma's response to her audacity that had bestowed on Marcus a full head of hair, handsome laugh lines, and a stunning new wife who was an authority on Romanian art and architecture.

And then it hit her. The core grievance she was feeling at this point was that, for *this* woman, Marcus seemed to have chosen to be a faithful man—the man he'd never been for her.

She took another, longer drink and felt her stomach warm. What bothered her most was that while Sophie had chosen to live with her Grandma Vivian—which had been hard enough—spending more time with Marcus after he'd returned to Seattle some four or five years ago had not been part of the deal. As much as she appreciated all of Vivian's help with Sophie, where the hell had her mother been in all of this? Had she shared Sophie with Marcus without so much as a word? Had she just allowed this Romanian woman to give her this ridiculous seaweed haircut? But then, God knows she herself had raised hell twenty years prior, sporting a nose ring and dreadlocks.

As Sophie launched into a story about her college orientation a few weeks back, Carolyn's eyes blurred her daughter's face back through time, to a montage of firsts. The first time Carolyn had seen her infant face and breathed her in. The first tooth cut, and the first tooth lost. The way Sophie's face had glowed when she took her first step morphed into the face shining from her first-grade picture. The tear-stained cheeks when she broke her arm falling off a horse shifted into more defined cheekbones stained by the blush she'd sneaked from Carolyn's makeup bag. Carolyn had been there for it all—until the divorce, the building of her publishing firm, and ultimately, Sophie's decision to stay in Seattle.

Carolyn tried to push the montage into the future, to picture her daughter's hair with more salt than pepper but she couldn't—the same way she never could have pictured Sophie's first day of college years ago at her fifth birthday party. How could she imagine her daughter at age forty-four when Carolyn couldn't believe she'd reached that age herself? It all seemed so impossible. And yet…

Carolyn's eyes refocused and her ears re-engaged in the current conversation, in which Isadore was now reciting possible part-time positions Sophie might want to apply for.

"As it so happens," Carolyn interjected, "I know someone who works at the university who might have a job for you. One of my best-selling authors is a professor in the very department you'd like to major in."

"Psychology?" Sophie asked.

"Exactly." Carolyn nodded and folded her hands in front of her. "I've already got a meeting with Dr. Sims next week to discuss his next book, and I'm hoping to get his help for a friend. I'll ask if he's got a position open for you."

"Dr. Quentin Sims?" Sophie asked. "That would actually be pretty cool."

"That sounds perfect, actually," Isadore added, as though she had any real idea of what was perfect for Carolyn's child. She didn't seem nonplussed, which grated on Carolyn all the more.

Carolyn raised her empty mug for Sophie to refill.

"Try not to drink too fast," Isadore warned.

Carolyn shrugged at Sophie, wondering why this woman would tell her how to pace her special Romanian plum water.

"I thought for sure you'd want to keep your focus in the sciences," Marcus said.

"Psychology *is* science, Dad," Sophie said, rolling her eyes as she handed Carolyn her replenished mug.

"Your father is just so proud of that award you won last spring," Isadore said.

"Award?" Carolyn asked, looking between the three of them.

Sophie shifted her weight, clearly uncomfortable from the sudden spotlight. "It was just a science fair project for my forensics class."

"They teach forensics in high school, now?" Carolyn asked, wondering why she was just now hearing about this. "Like *CSI*? What did you do, solve a murder?"

Marcus nudged Sophie's arm. "Come on, sweetheart, don't be modest. Tell your mom about the DNA project you did."

Sophie shrugged. "I don't know how to explain it. Why don't we talk about the real news going on here?"

Carolyn felt her stomach plummet down to her Jimmy Choos. "I don't see why we need to change the subject to—"

"I agree with your mother," Marcus said. "We can discuss that later."

The last thing Carolyn needed was Marcus's patronization. The three others stood there silently, blinking at her. "I say we discuss it now," she said.

"You just said you didn't want to change the subject," Sophie argued.

"No, let's lay it on the table, right here and now."

Isadore leaned into her new husband and whispered, "What is she talking about?"

"Why, the news, of course," Carolyn said. "About the whole reason I'm taking cover in Seattle."

"Taking cover?" Isadore asked.

"Mom, I was going to say..." Sophie trailed off as she leaned forward.

Carolyn felt her eyes grow wide. This had nothing to do with her job. She had to recover—and fast. "Your father has remarried," Carolyn said, holding up her mug of țuică. "Cheers to a lifetime of fidelity." She drained the mug and held it out to Sophie for more.

"Carolyn, stop," Marcus said, with the exact inflection he'd used for those same two words throughout their marriage. She could hardly imagine he condescended to Isadore this way. In fact, Carolyn opened her mouth to ask that very question when Marcus continued. "Sophie is talking about the news that I won the Seattle Literacy Society Book Critics Award for Literary Fiction."

Carolyn set down her glass and mouthed the words he'd just said. *Award for Literary Fiction.* Of course. *Of course.* Marcus had won one of the Pacific Northwest's most coveted awards, just as Carolyn's own publishing ship was listing and about to keel over. What she'd mischaracterized as patronization had been so much *worse*—it was *pity*, for God's sake!

"Wait, why are you taking cover in Seattle, Mom?" Sophie asked.

"Taking cover?" Carolyn asked, her wheels turning back to what she'd said earlier. "No, not 'taking cover'—I said I'm taking *over* Seattle. I got a job."

The faces around the dorm room stared at her, wide-eyed and agape. She held her face straight, resolved that it was not so much a lie as it was an impending truth.

"Is grandma okay?" Sophie asked. "I just talked to her yesterday, and—"

"She's fine," Carolyn assured her. "She's looking forward to making you an official birthday dinner this weekend."

"But what about your position at the firm?" Marcus asked. "Your place?"

"New York may continue to be the publication capital of the world, rooted in tradition, but I'm tired of history," Carolyn said to the man who had whisked her off to New York in the first place. At least he didn't seem privy to the fact that she'd been fired. "The townhouse is up for sale, and I'm looking forward to moving back to the Pacific Northwest, where the streets are less crowded and the air is fresh and pure. Seattle is the future of publishing." She reached over to put an arm around Sophie's shoulders. "And I'm especially eager to spend more time with my daughter."

The last thing Carolyn had expected was for Sophie to react by putting her head on her shoulder and she felt the flutter again, that her sweet daughter reciprocated the infinite love she held so dearly for her. But then, Sophie whispered into her ear, "No more țuică for you."

"You're cutting me off?" Carolyn stage-whispered back.

"Mom, you're acting a little tipsy."

Carolyn raised her head from where it had rested against Sophie's. "Why on earth would I be tipsy?"

Isadore tilted her head and knitted her eyebrows. "I said that țuică is a traditional Romanian drink."

"Lemonade is a *drink*," Carolyn said. "Ginger ale is a *drink*. I didn't taste any alcohol in this watered-down concoction."

"That's because you *can't* taste the alcohol in this drink," Sophie said. "Why do you think Isadore told you to slow down?"

"And why on earth is she bringing alcohol for our *nineteen*-year-old's birthday?" Carolyn's voice rose.

"Carolyn, calm down," Marcus insisted. "In Isadore's culture, everyone drinks. It's no big deal."

"From what I've heard," Sophie said, "you were hardly a stranger to alcohol at my age."

Carolyn gaped at Marcus, wondering just how much of her past he'd cared to share with their daughter. The room began to feel hot and small and a little off-kilter. She turned her gaze to Sophie for any of signs of the sensory disorder she'd once exhibited as a child in a crowded room such as this one. Nothing. Her grin showed perfect contentment.

"This is my fault," Isadore said. "Let us drive you home, please. I insist."

Carolyn shook her head but stopped when she felt a hand on her shoulder.

"Mom, please," Sophie said. "I only had a couple of sips. Please let Dad and Isadore drive you home so I know you're safe."

Carolyn broke her gaze from her daughter. It was Sophie's birthday, and somehow Carolyn had managed to make a scene. In the end, she knew she would endure any indignity for those pleading, sea blue eyes. Riding home in the back seat of Marcus and Isadore's car would be a case in point. She collected her purse and keys and worked not to stumble toward the door.

"Wait, let's get a quick picture before we go," Marcus said, pulling a phone from his pocket.

Carolyn opened her mouth to object. As much as she would have loved a picture with her daughter, she just wouldn't feel right posing alongside her ex-husband and his current wife.

But then, Marcus handed her his phone, the camera at the ready. "Do you mind?" he asked as he put his arms around Isadore and Sophie.

Carolyn lifted the phone, moving it this way and that. "I can't get you all to fit in the screen."

"Let's give some more space," Isadore offered. It only took each of them a step back to hit the wall on the opposite side of the tiny room.

Carolyn squinted at the phone. "Still not working."

She moved back a step, then back again, until she was out the door, standing in the hallway when the three smiling faces of the happy family finally filled the screen.

Ava

Ava's hand shook as she slid the key into the lock. She hadn't been to her father's bungalow in the last two months for exactly the reason she didn't want to enter now. The gaping void he left when he passed had been almost unbearable. But the emptiness of the home without his booming laugh or the constant rhythm of his fingers tapping the word processor keys made it all too tangible and real. Yet somehow, she noticed as she stepped through the doorway, the scent of him still lingered. For the first time in all the years he'd lived here, there was no fog of smoke wafting through from the steady drags of his pipe. She stood still, closed her eyes, and breathed him in—pungent aroma of marijuana and all—squeezing her eyelids shut all the while to keep any tears from falling.

Finally, Ava shut the door gently and moved further into the house. She shuddered from the cold, exhaling clouds. She crossed the living room for the thermostat, hoping services hadn't been cut. She passed the recliner, the sofa, the desk, sensing the guilt wisp around her like so many ghosts. She should have come here sooner. Shouldn't have seen the home simply as an easy way to pay down their—albeit mostly Gavin's—debts. She ran her fingertips along his desk as she walked by, picking up the thin layer of dust that had accumulated since her father had gone to the hospital those months ago. He'd never been keen on Gavin. But he'd loved Ava and was willing to go along—to bequeath his home to his only child. And now, the bungalow that wouldn't be paying down her debts would at least be providing a refuge for as long as she could afford the mortgage and taxes. Ava bit her lip and closed her eyes, sending a silent plea to the universe for the agenting job. At least she'd been lucid enough at the hospital to arrange for Jazmine to bring her new phone to her father's house today. She sent a silent plea to the universe that the phone would come complete with a voicemail from Howard Mercer's Agency with an official job offer.

Ava's gaze fell on the remote control on the coffee table. She took another deep breath and reached for it, aimed it at the TV, already grateful for the impending noise and distraction. The TV screen came alive with the local news, flashing the yearbook picture of a high school girl, then cut to footage from what appeared to be a convenience store. The bottom of the screen read, "The 1999 Colorado Shooting Victim Hoax."

"The Colorado shooting?" Ava said under her breath. She'd been in diapers when that happened. She turned up the volume.

"The debit exchange matches the date and time of the shooting," the reporter said, "and a handwriting analysis shows that was, indeed, Morgan St. John's signature on the receipt."

Ava toyed with the remote, ready to change the channel.

"While a major printing house is gearing up to sue the publisher, the publishing house insists that extensive research had been done into the life of Morgan St. John. CEO Frank Meyers says that a shakedown has occurred in accordance with the company's guidelines and ethics."

Ava shook her head, wondering what hell that author's agent must be going through. She lifted the remote to turn off the television when she thought she heard Gavin's voice speaking directly to her from the TV. She glanced back to find his face filling the screen.

"If you've been involved in a collision, don't let the insurance companies take what's yours."

Ava's shoulders slumped. She remembered how nervous Gavin had been the night before recording this ad for his law practice, pounding down shots of whiskey, one after the other. And now, she noticed the hint of bloodshot around those piercing baby browns.

The camera changed to show a woman a little younger than Ava. "The insurance companies only allotted me five thousand dollars for my accident. Thanks to Douglass and Burns, it turns out my case was worth one million dollars!"

Gavin's face filled the screen once again. Perhaps only Ava could see beneath the makeup to how drawn and weary he was—how false his brightness and confidence were as he pointed straight into the camera and said, "Call Douglass and Burns…"

"Shut up," Ava murmured.

"…to get a free consultation and don't settle for less…"

"Shut *up!*"

"…than your pain and suffering are worth."

"Shut up, shut up, *shut up!*" Ava shouted and threw the remote against the wall, where it broke into at least three parts before it fell to her father's work desk and scattered into even more pieces. "Dammit," she muttered, trudging over to pick them up.

She reached for the biggest part first, then the top piece, when she noticed a stack of papers arranged back and forth, towering on his desk like a Jenga puzzle. Manuscripts. Good God, so many of them. The top title read: *The Cosmic Circus of Serendipitous Absurdities.* Her lips curled slightly into a rueful grin. Yet another ludicrous title of a farcical book that would never find an agent, let alone a publisher. She lifted the title page to the dedication: *For my Ava—may you ever be your own.*

While Ava's eyes burned with tears at her father's gesture, she couldn't help but wonder what the hell it was supposed to mean. Since when was she not her own? It's not like she was someone else. And having a "circus" of "absurdities" dedicated to her didn't seem entirely complimentary. She lifted the manuscript with one hand while her other hand lifted the next title page—*The Electric Kettle Drummer's Guide to Jazz in the Multiverse*—to reveal another dedication to her. *For my Ava—may you ever be your own.* She set down the first manuscript on the office chair, and then the second to read the third manuscript's dedication. *For my Ava—may you ever be your own.*

By now, she was openly weeping, playing reverse manuscript-Jenga on the office chair as she went down the pile of manuscript dedications. The news reports coming from the television were all just vapid noise until a few of the words registered. She turned to see a reporter on the screen, bundled up for the cold, standing outside the enormous automatic glass doors of the hospital she'd just left. "I'm here at Harborview, where the victim was released earlier this afternoon."

When stock footage filled the television screen with a school bus, she realized the "victim" the reporter had spoken of was *her*. And the bus on screen had been the one that hit her. She was surprised to find it was one of those short buses. It hadn't *felt* short.

"Still no word on what ultimately caused the accident," the reporter continued, "but a school district representative released a statement agreeing with the police report icy conditions were responsible for this horrific scene. Many parents, however, are calling for an investigation before the driver returns to work."

Ava wondered what the investigation might turn up. Had it been more than just ice? From what little she could recall of Jazmine's visit, she couldn't imagine she'd been intoxicated or that she would text while driving a bus load of kids. Not that Ava was innocent in that particular regard, but there was no law against texting and walking, was there?

She shuddered again in her father's barely warming living room, wondering why on earth she'd given the very bus driver who had run her down *permission* to get into her cellular account. She could blame the bus driver for the accident, but she had only herself to blame if the woman used her personal information to stalk her or hack into her bank account or steal her identity. Ava imagined Jazmine taking off with all her money, boarding a plane to the Bahamas, never to be heard from or tracked down. Then it occurred to her that even if Jazmine hacked into every account Ava had, she'd find only enough money to buy a latte at the corner Starbucks.

But ultimately, it was Ava herself who had been standing in the middle of the road. She remembered it vividly, now that a solid night's sleep and a much smaller dose of painkiller had cleared her brain. She'd read Gavin's text and stopped right there in the street in a state of shock. If anyone was to blame for that accident, it was—

"Just me," a voice came from the doorway.

The manuscript in her hands slithered to the floor and Ava turned abruptly to find Jazmine standing there with a child on one arm, a diaper bag on her opposite shoulder, and a white plastic bag in her free hand. The little boy squinted at Ava, then closed his eyes and laid his head against Jazmine's shoulder.

"Sorry," Ava said. "You startled me."

"You left the door open," Jazmine said. "It's freezing in here. You doing okay? Still woozy from those pain killers?"

Even with her little boy on her arm, Jazmine appeared more put together than she had the last time she'd visited Ava in the hospital room. Her hair seemed to be styled with some kind of pomade that gave it curl and texture. Eyeliner brought out her eyes—which weren't lifeless like they were before, but hazel and truly stunning. Ava scanned the same purple jacket and the darker, newer jeans.

"Who is this little guy?" Ava asked in a hushed voice.

"This is my son, Henry," Jazmine murmured back. "I mentioned him last time we spoke. I'm afraid I don't have anyone to watch him this time."

"Look at that sweet face," Ava said, admiring the little O-shape of his mouth as he breathed deeply, in and out.

"Yeah, he's sweet when he's asleep," Jazmine said wearily.

Henry's head slipped off Jazmine's shoulder and he blinked awake, babbling a couple of nonsensical words. Ava watched as Jazmine went tense until his eyelids drifted shut again, his head resting back where it was before. Jazmine closed her eyes too and exhaled softly.

Ava glanced at the bag that Jazmine had brought, ready to get her hands on her new phone. She needed to know about the job and get back to them before they moved on to their second pick. Plus, there was a small chance that Gavin had reached out to her—maybe he'd heard about the accident and changed his mind.

"I was hoping we could talk," Jazmine said, leaning closer to Ava with a new urgency. She gripped the Emerald City Cellular bag tightly in her hand. "About the accident."

Ava gestured to her father's sofa, where they sat on opposite ends. "I'm not supposed to talk about it," she said, repeating Gavin's party line. He was forever telling his clients not to talk with the defendant or the prosecution, depending on which side they were on, and he often came home fuming when they did, which inevitably blew his case out of the water.

But Gavin wasn't here. In fact, Jazmine had been the only person who'd cared enough to visit Ava's hospital room.

"I interviewed for a job just before, you know, the accident. And with all the hospital bills accruing, I need to check my messages to see if they gave me the offer."

"Of course," Jazmine said, handing her the bag.

Ava reached in and brought out a box for a temporary phone.

"They wouldn't let anyone but you get a new phone on your account," Jazmine explained. "But I had them put in your SIM card, so this should work for now. And I brought some cash to pay for your new phone when you're able to get out there to get one. I would take you there myself, but I don't have a car."

Normally, Ava would have quipped about the irony of a bus driver not owning a car, but she was too busy opening the box for the phone, eager to get it going.

"I really am so sorry," Jazmine continued. "If I had any money at all, I wouldn't hesitate to help with the bills. Now that the school district has put me on leave, I'm struggling to take care of Henry. He's autistic."

Ava felt her heart implode. Jazmine had been driving a school bus in order to support her autistic child, and by stopping in the street for that text, Ava may have caused this woman to lose her job. She opened her mouth to come clean, but Gavin's voice came at her again, along with mental images of credit card debt and hospital bills that she would never be able to pay on her own. Ava closed her mouth and directed all of her focus on the phone, growing increasingly desperate when the box refused to give way from all the plastic packaging.

"Can I help?" Jazmine asked.

Ava handed it back and watched as Jazmine worked a key into the side of the box, cutting through the shrink wrap until Henry began to slide down her arm.

"Would it help if I took him?" Ava offered.

"If you don't think he'll be too much?"

"I'm sure I'm fine to hold him as long as I'm sitting down," Ava said, reaching out both hands to take him.

"Whew, that's a weight off," Jazmine said, shaking out the arm that had held him all this time.

She was right about the weight. Henry seemed to weigh twice what he looked in size, probably because he was asleep. Ava rested his head into the crook of her arm and looked down on his angelic face, the hairline damp from sleep.

"What happened was tragic," Jazmine said, gently shaking the box this way and that while she spoke. "That ice ruined my life, too. If you go after the school district, they have money in reserve for situations like this—natural disaster-type events, you know?" The box finally gave way to reveal the glossy new phone. "Would you like me to plug it in?"

Ava nodded, protecting the sleeping, heavy boy who looked to be about three years old. The burden of Henry's weight alone would be enough to bear, but her new knowledge of his autism only added to her remorse over the accident. It would be so easy for Ava to alleviate that guilt with one simple apology. In fact, Ava *could* go after the school district. She could let Jazmine off the hook right here and now. But then, saying too soon that it wasn't the driver's fault might make it appear that Ava was admitting fault, and she'd lose any chance of paying for the inevitably exorbitant price of her hospital stay. Not yet.

"Looks like it's ready to go," Jazmine said when the screen finally lit up.

Ava handed Henry back, his head rolling to the right as he went back to his mother's shoulder. Then she took the phone from Jazmine and went straight to her voicemail. Only one had been left from a number she didn't recognize. That ruled out Gavin. It wasn't the typical "888" number the creditors used, and she didn't recall the Howard Mercer Literary Agency having an out-of-state area code.

"I'll leave you in peace now." Jazmine said, her voice resigned.

Ava reached for the sticky note that Jazmine had placed on her old phone during their last visit. "I have your number," she said, and put the phone to her ear. "I'll think about what you said, okay?"

Jazmine nodded slowly, then rose from her chair and left the house, closing the front door quietly behind her.

The voice in the phone was low and smooth as velvet. "This is Carolyn Ford."

Ava's mind raced. Carolyn Ford. *The* Carolyn Ford?

"…I wanted to see how you're faring since yesterday."

Faring? Since yesterday? Had the news made it all the way to Carolyn Ford in New York? Perhaps that agent she'd interviewed with had identified Ava as an up-and-coming literary agent.

Then it hit her. The assistant had said that Howard didn't work with Carolyn Ford.

The phone beeped and returned Ava to the blank home screen. She straightened her posture, inhaled deeply, and considered calling back.

But then, the screen lit up with a call from the same number. Ava tapped the green *Accept Call* button and managed a breathless, "Hello?"

"So glad you're there! This is Carolyn Ford. Did you get my message?"

Ava forced the stale, frigid air of her father's home into her lungs. "I did, thank you."

"How are you holding up?"

"Feeling much better, thanks."

"Wonderful. And Henry?"

Henry? Ava looked out her window to see the outline of Jazmine's back as she walked down the sidewalk. "He's fine? Great, actually. Never been better."

"That's good," Carolyn replied hesitantly, as though she wasn't sure she believed it.

Ava sat back in her chair. Carolyn Ford was calling for Jazmine? But why? What did that bus driver have to do with the publishing universe?

"I'm back at Emerald City Cellular so I could call you. They dialed for me, so there's no breach of security."

This had to be a different Carolyn Ford. Yes, a different woman altogether.

"I can't talk long," Carolyn continued. "I have an… appointment… to get to. But I need to get my tablet back. I thought you could come by later in the week. We could take a walk on Alki Beach, Henry could arrange all the rocks in a straight line—"

"I'll go!" Ava blurted. "If you can give me your address, I'll be there. I mean, *we'll* be there." Scrambling to get to her father's desk for a pencil, she committed the West Seattle address to her concussed memory. "Thank you, Ms. Ford," Ava gushed.

"Didn't I tell you to call me Carolyn?" she asked. "Please do, and anyway, don't forget that tablet. All my contacts are in it."

Contacts, Ava thought. All the biggest, most powerful names in the literary world—and Jazmine was holding them all in that diaper bag of hers.

Ava thanked Ms.—*Carolyn*—and ended the call, scrambling for Jazmine's phone number. She dialed and Jazmine answered on the second ring.

"Jazmine, it's Ava. You were right. I think we should talk."

Jazmine

Jazmine and Ava stood side by side on Carolyn's porch. The windows on the double front doors reflected Alki Beach behind them. Jazmine shifted the diaper bag slung over her shoulder in order to lean in and guide Henry's finger to push the doorbell. They listened to the pleasant chimes, followed by a series of yips from within. Jazmine's spine went rigid, her jaws clenched. Breathless, she watched Henry. The barking seemed to be too muted to have agitated him—yet.

"Don't forget," Ava said, her voice low. "We met recently and I'm your ride."

Jazmine shrugged. "It's the truth."

On the porch filled with overcast daylight, Ava appeared a whole new woman since her discharge earlier that day. Jazmine wondered if she always wore that much makeup, or if she'd overdone it in an effort to appear more put together. She had to be younger than Jazmine by at least five years, so it's not like she needed makeup to hide any aging. Her hair, which had been matted when Jazmine saw her in the hospital, had since been combed through, now hanging around her shoulders in light brown waves. Foundation had dried and cracked around the scabs along her left temple. Jazmine winced at the evidence of what she—no, the *ice*—had caused.

Three days ago, when Ava had shocked Jazmine by calling to take responsibility for her part in the accident—she'd even *apologized*— Jazmine figured that Ava's offer to drive her to Carolyn Ford's house had been an olive branch, much like Jazmine's olive branch of getting her a new phone. But then, Ava couldn't drive with her concussion, so they'd taken an Uber instead, which was either extra-thoughtful or kind of strange. It was the way Ava had prattled on the entire ride about Ms. Ford—her icon, apparently—that finally gave Jazmine pause. Plus, Ava had offered a *ride*—not to walk Jazmine to the door and possibly inside this woman's house. But what could Jazmine do now? At this point, she was sinking in legal quicksand and regardless of what olive branch Ava was offering, she was holding out a *branch*. And why not give the concussed young woman this opportunity to meet her icon? It was really the least she could do.

Rain pattered against the eave above them, loud enough that Henry covered his ears. Once again, Jazmine froze. Not today, not today…

"It's so modest," Ava said, gazing around the two-story, cabinesque home, dwarfed by mansions and condominium complexes on all sides. She jolted when one of the double-doors whooshed open, grabbing the porch railing to keep her balance.

"You okay?" Jazmine reached out and took her gently by the arm, but wide-eyed Ava didn't seem to notice.

Jazmine followed her gaze to Ms. Ford—who'd insisted she call her Carolyn—standing shoeless at the open door. She wore a belted sweater dress and held a wine glass in one hand. The perfect edges of her dark red hair brushed against the teal crewneck collar. Jazmine's memory reeled back to the cellular store and those damn teal post-it notes that had that poor old man convinced he'd been accused of being a common thief.

Jazmine shook off the recollection just in time to see Henry toddle toward the woman standing in the doorway. The yipping was less muffled now, yet it seemed to come from somewhere deep in the house.

"Welcome, young sir," Carolyn said. "Make yourself at home. And do we have an extra guest?"

Jazmine shifted her focus to the young woman with stars in her eyes beside her. "This is—"

"Ava." The young woman reached out a gloved hand to Carolyn. "I'm Jazmine's…" Her eyes flickered panic and darted to Jazmine.

"Ride," Jazmine finished for her.

"A-vah…" Carolyn drew out the last syllable in thought, swirling the red wine in her glass this way and that. "You remind me of someone."

Jazmine held her breath, watching Henry disappear into the house between Carolyn's leg and the door jamb.

"I'm…" Ava faltered.

"My daughter," Carolyn said.

Jazmine glanced back and forth between them, watching Ava's face register utter confusion.

"But Sophie's younger than you," Carolyn continued, "by a handful of years."

Jazmine dug into the diaper bag for the iPad when Carolyn stepped aside to allow them in. As she walked them down the hallway, Jazmine inhaled the scents of fresh pine, campfire, and what smelled like medicine. "This is my mother's home," Carolyn began.

"That explains it," Ava breathed.

"Excuse me?" Carolyn asked.

Ava froze. "Um, the classic mid-century woodwork. It's like stepping back in time."

"Exactly," Carolyn replied, one eyebrow raised. "It's also temporary, since I've just moved back to Seattle."

"Really?" Ava asked. "From where?"

"New York," Carolyn said curtly.

The hallway opened into a living room and kitchen, separated only by a counter. The side facing the Puget Sound was made entirely of windows, and a sliding glass door led out to a large cedar deck with a tarped picnic table and barbecue grill. Jazmine tried to imagine the view on a warm, sunny day.

Henry found a spot in the living room where he walked in a tight circle so fast, it was a wonder he didn't fall over. Jazmine considered reaching out, but knew Henry needed his circle time as a way to explore his new environment. The fact that he was smiling showed he was feeling excited—maybe even happy.

To her right, Ava rested her forehead against the cool sliding door window and whispered to Jazmine, "I can't believe I'm actually here." She immediately jerked back and wiped away the smudge with her sleeve.

"Hey, how about a drink?" Carolyn offered. "God knows I could use another one."

Before either could answer, she was off to the kitchen.

"I'm not feeling so hot," Ava confided into Jazmine's ear.

"You shouldn't be drinking," Jazmine said, "especially with a concussion."

"I don't want to be rude." Ava's whisper was shrill. "This is the chance of a lifetime."

"Relax, Ava. You'll do fine," Jazmine said before calling toward the kitchen. "Could you pour my designated driver an ice water?" She watched Ava twisting her hands. The last thing anyone that high-strung needed was alcohol.

"How about coffee, Eva?" Carolyn's voice answered. "I can get the Keurig going."

"It's Ava," Jazmine called to the kitchen, then flinched when Ava elbowed her arm.

"I can't believe you corrected her," she hissed, followed by a loud and sweet-toned, "Yes, coffee would be wonderful."

"It's your name, isn't it?" Jazmine rubbed her arm. "What's the deal?"

"I can't think of anything to say," Ava continued in a hush.

"Talk about printing books, or whatever reason you said you had to meet her."

"Publishing," Ava corrected. "But it has to come up organically, in conversation, like figuring out a crossword puzzle."

Jazmine couldn't see how a crossword would give her an in with Carolyn Ford, but none of that mattered when she looked to the living room, where Henry had discovered a new way to turn in circles—the piano round stool, which swiveled one way to rise and the other to lower.

Carolyn poked her head out of the kitchen and said, "I'm having mulled wine. Warm with a spicy kick. That work for you?"

"Perfect," Jazmine answered, making a move to get Henry off the piano stool.

"He's fine," Carolyn insisted. "Why don't you two have a seat at the table?" She disappeared back into the kitchen.

Jazmine followed Ava to a tall-back dining room chair. Carolyn soon entered the room with a tray of two wine glasses and a steaming mug. "Would you like cream or sugar for your coffee?"

"Black is fine, thanks," Ava said.

Jazmine grabbed the tablet from the diaper bag and set it on the table before taking her seat across from Ava, where she could have a view of her son in the living room. Henry pressed his little tummy over the seat and ran his feet around the base of the stool until it raised as high as it could go, then switched directions, all the while throwing down beatboxing rhythms.

Carolyn took the chair beside Jazmine.

"Are you sure Henry's okay to do that?" Jazmine asked, gesturing towards the piano stool.

"I think it's great!" Carolyn said. "Let's keep the little guy happy." When she lifted her glass, Jazmine followed suit.

Jazmine watched Ava lift her mug, which looked every bit as out of place clinking the wine glasses as the young woman sitting there herself. Jazmine let her own mulled wine warm her tongue as she savored hints of cinnamon and cloves.

Carolyn set down her glass. "I'll be meeting with a client of mine in a couple of weeks. He's a local autism specialist who has multiple degrees and several books under his belt. I hope this wasn't too presumptuous, and you're certainly not obligated, but I made an appointment to have Henry evaluated. Dr. Sims may be too booked to take him on personally, but he can refer you to other specialists who can. Are you available to meet him on Friday afternoon?"

"Sure am." Jazmine felt her throat tighten and her eyes burn. She'd been up and down so many avenues trying to find Henry the best treatment she could afford, which was most often government run or young interns with little to no experience. Now, here she was, the closest she'd ever been to finally getting Henry the best of the best treatment, and she had no job. "But I'm afraid I wouldn't be able to afford it."

"Dr. Sims' services are gratis," Carolyn said. "He'll make things happen from there. I have the utmost confidence in him. You'll see what I mean on Friday."

Jazmine bit her lower lip. It was still too soon to get her hopes up, yet she felt her chest lifting with the kind of deep breath she hadn't been able to take in months. "I can't thank you enough."

"Did you hear about that school shooting memoir hoax?" Ava broke in, holding up the newspaper with the crossword puzzle.

Jazmine cocked her head, wondering whether concussions caused some kind of conversational Tourette's, where one blurts out non sequiturs. And what it was with that newspaper?

Carolyn narrowed her eyes at Ava, as if she were still trying to place her face. She set down her wine glass. "Is that why you're here?"

If Ava could have gone any paler, she would have been translucent. She looked down and faltered. "It's right here in the paper. I thought you'd be interested, being a publisher and all."

Jazmine glanced from Ava to Carolyn. For a woman able to show such uncommon patience with her son, why would some memoir strike such a raw nerve? "Is something wrong, Carolyn?"

The laser beams streaming from Carolyn's eyes remained fixed on Ava. "How did you know I'm a publisher?"

"You just talked about that autism specialist and his books."

"I never said I published them." Carolyn swallowed hard and glared Ava down. "You're a reporter, aren't you?"

"Of course not," Ava said.

"I knew I'd seen you on the news." She turned to Jazmine. "You brought a reporter into my home? I was good to you, and you brought a—"

Jazmine shook her head vehemently. "I have no idea what's happening here."

Carolyn's mouth dropped open and she looked away. "It was my mom. She called you, didn't she? So, you could get *my* side of the story?"

Ava's face took on an ashen sheen, and her stricken expression reminded Jazmine of the look she'd had when the bus ran her down just days before.

Carolyn didn't wait for Ava's answer as she stomped over to the staircase. "*Mother! Get up here!*"

Jazmine breathed deeply, squared her shoulders, and set her jaw. "You're right."

Carolyn whirled around.

"I need to lie down," Ava murmured.

"You did see Ava on the news," Jazmine powered on. "You probably heard my name, too. We were in an accident. I was driving a school bus and it slid on an icy patch and hit Ava."

"It gave me a concussion," Ava said, "and I'm starting to feel—"

Ava leaned over and vomited all over Carolyn's mother's floor. She dropped her mug in the process, sending coffee pouring onto the hardwood as well, until the mug stopped in front of Jazmine's feet.

Jazmine winced and turned away. Henry went silent. It was Carolyn's turn to blanch. Jazmine could only imagine what was going through that kind woman's mind. Ms. Ford would have nothing to do with her or her son again.

"I've got this," Jazmine offered, pointing to the floor. "Just find a place where Ava can lie down while I clean up, and we'll be out of here as soon as I'm done."

Carolyn seemed at a loss. Jazmine thought of the wine glass in her hand when she'd first opened the front door. This publisher woman was good and buzzed.

"Good God!" Carolyn's mother stood at the top of the stairs. "Care Bear, don't just stand there—get that poor woman to the sofa."

Carolyn side-stepped the mess on the floor and took Ava gently by the elbow. Downstairs, the dog started yipping again, agitated by

Carolyn's mother's sudden absence, or perhaps having heard her distress.

"It's the concussion," Ava cried. "They said I might feel nauseous. They said bed rest for the remainder of the week. But then you called and…and…I couldn't miss my chance to meet you."

"And why is that?" Carolyn asked Ava. Her tone had no sudden kindness, but she was no longer interrogating Ava with veiled anger either. She spread a blanket over the sofa before helping Ava onto it.

"Because…because you're my hero," Ava managed before breaking down.

Henry toddled up to Jazmine. She held up her palm and said, "Stand back, little man. This is yucky."

For once, Henry followed her directive, his eyes wide. He began to coo his little owl sound, each "Hoo" growing in volume until Jazmine tried to shush him. She wished someone would shush that stupid dog before Henry lost it completely.

"He's fine," Carolyn's mother whispered as she worked a plastic bag over the mess on the floor the way she probably picked up after the dog. "He's dealing with the tension, I know. I'm Vivian, by the way."

"Thanks," Jazmine replied, taking the antibacterial spray and wet jet mop that Vivian offered with the hand that wasn't holding the plastic bag. As Vivian carried the bag out the front door, presumably to the outside garbage bin, Jazmine sprayed the floor and went over it with the mop. She wished she could be done here, free to take Henry back to the safety of their home.

"Do you think your little boy would like to meet my dog?" Vivian asked when she came back into the house.

Henry stopped "hoo-ing" and looked up at Vivian in awe. Jazmine pressed her lips together and shook her head as inconspicuously as possible.

"Oh, darn, I almost forgot." Vivian crouched down to Henry's level. "Trixie needs a nap before she can meet you. How about taking this container out to the living room with me?"

Jazmine watched Vivian hand Henry a disposable plastic container, presumably for Ava, should she need to spill her guts all over again. Jazmine glanced over to see Carolyn tucking Ava in on the couch. She couldn't help but feel abandoned by her accomplice, knowing that as soon as Ava drifted off, Jazmine would be left to explain the accident and the plan that had gotten her off the hook. But so much of what was being said about 'hoaxes' and 'reporters' flat out confused her.

Once she'd finished, Carolyn came back and took her place back at the dining room table. Vivian sat in what had been Ava's chair. Jazmine took her seat, as well. She glanced into the living room. "Where did Henry go?"

"He's lying down on the love seat," Vivian said. "Seems he saw the young woman close her eyes for a nap, and he followed suit."

Carolyn stared straight into Jazmine's eyes. "Why did you bring this woman to my home?"

"Calm down, dear," Vivian said.

Jazmine felt her throat close and averted her gaze. "It was Ava's idea. I knew it was—"

"Betraying me?" Carolyn asked. "I'd like to hear you say it."

"It was a stupid deal Ava came up with. I thought that if it worked—"

"No, not a deal," Carolyn said. "You sold me out. And here I'd set up a meeting for you with Dr. Sims, the most prestigious autism specialist on the West Coast."

"Oh, enough with the guilt trip." Vivian waved away Carolyn's words.

"Why don't you go back down to Wheel of Fortune, Mother?"

"You called me up here, Carolyn Grace." Vivian turned to Jazmine. "Thank you for taking care of the floor, honey."

"Of course," Jazmine said, feeling her heart sink to her toes.

Jazmine managed to meet Carolyn's eyes again to find them ablaze. She saw something behind the anger, though. The alcohol had lit up the green in her eyes to the color of limes. And it had slurred her speech, so that "Wheel of Fortune" had come out "Wheel of Forshin."

"Carolyn is right," Jazmine said. "I sold her out. I didn't want to lose everything."

Carolyn broke her gaze, as though she'd lost. Vivian patted her daughter's hand and said, "We've all been there, dear. Even Carolyn."

"Are you serious?" Carolyn glared at her mother. "Are *you* actually throwing the hoax in my face now?"

"I was actually referring to the time you left Marcus," Vivian said. "I seem to remember you doing whatever it took, as well."

Jazmine watched Carolyn's muscles slump, almost one by one, as the tension left her.

Vivian smiled at Jazmine. "Well, I'll let you two talk, now. Wheel of Fortune is over, but Jeopardy awaits." She pushed back her chair, rose, and made her way back down the stairs.

"You deserved so much better from me," Jazmine said. "I really am so—"

"Don't say it. As my mother said, I've been betrayed before. By countless people in publishing, although this last one…I should have seen it coming. By my ex-slut of a husband." Carolyn shook her head.

"I feel terrible," Jazmine said, "If I could drive Ava to her house right now and walk Henry to ours, I would. Since the accident, my license was temporarily revoked and—"

"Why is it he can be faithful to *her*?"

"Who?" Jazmine glanced around, knowing the only "he" in the room was her son.

"All his adult life, he's been a cheat. But once this *Isadorrrre* came into the picture, he straightened up. Eight years after the divorce, and *this* feels like the ultimate betrayal." Carolyn's chair legs scraped against the hardwood as she pushed back from the table and rose, making her way to the kitchen.

"It pisses me off that my ex-husband traded Henry in for a 'normal' child," Jazmine said.

"What's that?" Carolyn's voice echoed from the kitchen.

"Ben left us because he couldn't handle Henry's…" She glanced into the living room to see if he was listening and found him fast asleep beside the piano stool. "His outbursts. Ben's one of those ultra-orderly guys, you know? Needs life to proceed in the order of his daily agenda. It always had before Henry came along."

Carolyn took her seat again and set down her wine glass with one hand, holding the wine bottle in the other to top off Jazmine's glass.

Jazmine took out her phone and tapped into Facebook. "Henry relies on structure, too, of course. But we didn't know yet that he was autistic." Jazmine scrolled through pictures on the phone. "If Ben had known there were strategies and all those lists to study and follow, maybe he wouldn't have left. Now, he's happily married, with a bouncing baby girl."

Jazmine held out her phone. Carolyn reached for her reading glasses off the table and squinted at the screen. "Oh," she said. "Wow. So that's where Henry got those intense brown eyes."

"I tell myself to stop the self-torture of looking them up, cyberstalking the life that should be mine—mine and Henry's."

"My fiancé left me for Alcoholics Anonymous," came a raspy voice from the living room.

The two women turned to see Ava propped up on three or so throw pillows, apparently listening in. Jazmine chuckled. It had to be the concussion talking.

"I didn't even drink before I met him. Before I knew it, I became his drinking buddy, trying to keep up. Then he broke off the wedding because he said I was an…" Ava trailed off again, making more noises that sounded like crying, "an enabler."

Jazmine shared a look with Carolyn, both rising to move into the living room to console this poor, broken girl. But then, the noises bubbled out as chuckles.

"He's an alcoholic. Missed work all the time. If it weren't for all the excuses I've made for him, he'd be unemployed."

She was shaking with laughter now, the kind that turns breathless and silent, then resumes all over again. Carolyn walked to the love seat and Jazmine sat down on the recliner.

"But now *I'm* the toxic one, and after he goes through his twelve steps, some woman will get herself a great catch while I'm paying the debts I accrued to enable him!" This time, her laughter came out tired and sad. "Why wasn't *I* worth getting clean for?"

"Don't do that to yourself," Jazmine said, her voice low and fierce. "It was a case of bad timing."

"You haven't sat around wondering why you and Henry weren't worth staying for?" Carolyn asked.

Jazmine looked at Carolyn, unsure whether to feel offended or chalk her tactlessness up to having one too many. "If that's your logic, then do you believe you weren't worth being faithful to?"

Carolyn pursed her lips. "It's not so much that as the feeling that Isado*rrrr*e has something I never did—something that *is* worth it for him. What galls me is that I can't for the life of me put my finger on what she has that I don't."

The three women gazed into the fireplace. It was rare that Jazmine allowed herself to turn over the lost hopes, question the injustice of it all. She seldom had time, for one thing, and dwelling on anything frivolous was a diversion she couldn't afford. But here, she belonged—not just with these two women, but with a legion of women out there in the world who'd had men leave them to become the men they'd wished they'd been for them. "We're the ones who need a support group," Jazmine said absently.

"For enablers?" Ava asked.

"No," Carolyn said, her eyes shining, "to keep us from falling into the same trap again. To help us find the addiction-free, non-controlling, faithful men."

Jazmine narrowed her eyes. "And how do you suppose we'll figure out how to navigate this better?"

"For one thing," Ava said, sitting up straighter, "now that we know what the red flags are, once we see them in a guy, we rule them right out." Her eyes rolled a bit, and she laid her head back down.

Carolyn reached over to help Ava get comfortable. "And by pooling our red flags, we keep from making the bigger mistakes."

"Where do we find this red flag support group?" Jazmine asked.

"Seems to me, we already have," Carolyn said.

The women nodded their newfound allegiance to each other, until Henry toddled up to Jazmine and said, "Dod."

"What's that, little man?" Jazmine asked.

"Dod, dod, dod," he repeated, walking in a little circle as he did so.

"I think he's saying 'dog'?" Carolyn asked. "Probably because of my mother's chihuahua. It was all I could do to ensure they were both out of the room when you came."

Jazmine felt Carolyn's words wash over her as a feeling swelled from within. It had been so long, she had to search for the word—much less recall the last time she'd felt it. A memory emerged from her mind's fog, of the moment she dared look at the stick and saw the plus sign. Despite the sinkhole opening in the left side of her brain, swallowing all of her aspirations of college and career in one swift gulp, she was swept away by an overwhelming sense of elation—that was the word. Elation. Jazmine's heart sang, and she felt her love for her son fill her eyes.

"We could go somewhere else," Carolyn said, "if it's a prob—"

"No." Jazmine had to push the word through her throat as she shook her head. Her words came out as a rough, breathless whisper. "It's his first word. Dog. His first real word."

Carolyn's own eyes grew glassy. "Here, Henry's saying his first word, and I'm at a loss for words! Come here."

Jazmine allowed Carolyn to envelop her in a hug. Realizing she got to share this moment—albeit it with a woman who was little more than a stranger—made her doubly elated.

"Dod, dod, dod."

Jazmine, Carolyn, and even Ava laughed at the gleeful sound of his first word, and the laughter sent a tear down Jazmine's cheek.

"I'm so excited for you," Ava said. "And I'm sorry to you both."

Jazmine and Carolyn shared a look.

"I'm sorry I imposed on this visit," Ava continued. "Carolyn, you've been a role model to me for a long time now, and when I saw a chance to meet you, I couldn't pass it up. And Jazmine, I never intended to manipulate you. I would have dropped the charges against you whether or not you'd brought me here with you tonight."

"I believe you," Jazmine said.

"I'm afraid I'm not much of a role model these days," Carolyn added, "but it helps to hear that I made a difference. I appreciate your candor."

"What better difference can you make than bringing the most poignant and powerful literature to the masses?" Ava asked.

"Dod," Henry chimed, as though in agreement.

"I couldn't have said it better myself." Carolyn chuckled.

Jazmine raised her glass. "To first words!"

"And to role models," Ava said as she lifted her mug.

A *ding* from Ava's cell phone interrupted the toast. She clicked on it and scrolled until her face broke out in a smile. She hugged the phone to her chest and said, "The agency gave me the job."

"With an agency," Carolyn murmured, her eyes narrowing as though she were connecting the dots. For the first time since their arrival, her shoulders appeared to relax. "So, you're really not a reporter?"

On the House

Carolyn

Carolyn stood alone in the waiting room of the University of Washington's Psychology Department, glancing around the empty receptionist's desk until she spotted a sticky note with her name on it and pulled it from the counter.

Carolyn—We're between receptionists right now. I'm down the hall in Office 204, third door on your right. Q

Carolyn straightened her navy pin-striped pencil skirt and started down the hallway.

In the seven years that Advance Imprint had been working with Dr. Quentin Sims, Carolyn had yet to actually meet him. It seemed any time she'd flown into Seattle to spend her holidays with family, Quentin had flown out to spend them with his. Carolyn admired how Quentin had pulled off a kind of kid-friendly sophistication throughout the gray-blue hallway leading towards his office. The hall was lamp-lit, rather than fluorescent, and decorated with framed pictures of crayon drawings by whom she presumed were his patients.

When Carolyn found the open door of Office 204, Quentin waved her in just as he finished a phone call. She took in the spacious room, painted sage; the potted plants, arranged on various shelves; and, through his picture window, the incredible view of the city skyline and the water beyond. There was a bubbling sound coming from the corner table, where Carolyn found an opaque vase glowing yellow and emitting a vapor mist into the air. She breathed in the fragrance of eucalyptus and lavender oils.

Quentin hung up the phone and came around his desk with that familiar baritone voice she'd heard on many of their own phone calls. "Well if it isn't Carolyn Ford, in the flesh." He extended a large hand, which enclosed hers in a handshake, then gestured to an ergonomic leather chair on the other side of his glossy walnut desk. "To what do I owe this honor, other than finally meeting, and checking to ensure your friend and her son will be in good hands?" He clasped his hands in front of him, which were a little darker than the walnut desk. Carolyn noticed he'd had his hair cut in a different style since the author headshot they'd used for his last book. Shaved, actually—close to the scalp all the way around.

"I'd love to know how things went with Jazmine and little Henry last week," she said.

"You know I'm not at liberty to discuss my clients," he said, then gave a wry smile, "but I'll let it slip that they were a pleasure to work with, and that I was able to refer Henry to an especially gifted specialist who uses a sliding scale."

"That's wonderful to hear," she said.

"I'm glad you made the connection." Quentin leaned back in his chair and steepled his long fingers, tapping his thumbs together.

Carolyn fidgeted with the sticky note in her hand. "You mentioned you're between receptionists. I have a potential applicant to fill the position. My daughter is a freshman at the University of Washington this year, and she could use a job. You know, a work-study type thing."

Quentin nodded as she spoke and reached for a pad of paper on the desk. He scribbled something with a felt-tip pen, then peeled off the top note and handed it to her.

"Have her go to this Web address and fill out the online application," he said. "We'd love to fill the position as soon as possible, and I'm sure your daughter, assuming she inherited your work ethic, would be an asset to the department."

Carolyn smoothed the note over the first one she'd picked up at the receptionist's desk until it adhered. "This is very much appreciated. It's secondary to the actual reason I'm here, which is, of course, business. I wanted to tell you in person that I'm about to take the reins of a local imprint."

"That's wonderful, Carolyn," Quentin said. "I'm so happy you're going to be able to persevere through all of that…" he trailed off.

"Yes. All of that," Carolyn finished for him, eager to skirt the details of the disastrous hoax. "More to the point, this imprint will be perfect to launch *Opposite Ends of the Spectrum*."

Quentin regarded her, his eyes the color of melting chocolate. Carolyn held her breath. Like with most effective sales pitches, when her offer was on the table, she forced herself to stay quiet until he responded. When Quentin finally leaned in, she held her breath. His voice came out deep and gentle. "Random House wants it."

Carolyn's insides wilted, starting with her lungs, then her heart, then her stomach. The corner vaporizer gave the room a humid feel, the eucalyptus suddenly overwhelming her senses. "You gave it to Random House without discussing it with me first?"

"I tried, on several occasions," Quentin replied, maintaining his even baritone. "My agent and I both left messages on your voicemail, email, instant messaging. But for almost a month, you've been M.I.A."

"I was working on my next direction," Carolyn insisted. "I needed time. Did you sign with them, or can you still change your mind?"

Quentin shook his head. "My preference was to sign again with you."

"You could rescind?"

"Have you had authors who rescinded on their contracts?"

"Seldom," Carolyn relented. She avoided the earnest sincerity glistening in his eyes by watching a sparrow fluttering in the window, landing on a brick, and pecking at whatever seeds the winds may have driven to the outside sill.

"Keep in mind the opportunity my agent presented to me," Quentin said. "We're talking about Random House."

"No," Carolyn said curtly, forcing her disappointment deep into her deflated gut. She was still Carolyn Ford, after all, and she would walk out of this office with her head held high. "All right, then. Thank you for your time." The constant bubbling sound from the corner had become so obnoxious, she knew she'd better collect her things before she took it and tossed it at Quentin's skyline view. She imagined the sparrow darting away as the vaporizer hit the glass.

Quentin stopped her before she picked up her handbag. "Have you considered launching your imprint with an emerging author?"

"I have more bestsellers waiting in the wings," she said breezily, rising from her seat.

Quentin picked up what appeared to be a small newspaper from his desk. He held it up so she could read the headline.

University students by day, single mothers by night
By Jazmine Johnston

"I referred Jazmine to you for help with her son," Carolyn said. "Since when is she reporting for the university newspaper?"

"She attended the University of Washington five years ago," Quentin said, handing the paper to her.

Carolyn skimmed the first paragraph, then the second, the third, the fourth. She began to feel overcome with the sad irony that Jazmine had written this piece before Henry had been conceived. Probably even before her ex-husband—what was his name? Oh yes, Ben—had come into her life. While the topic itself was difficult, Jazmine's voice rang through, painfully naive in its message of maternal empowerment.

"If I'm not mistaken," Quentin said, "the woman can *write*—"

"It's fine," she quipped, then leveled a hard stare at Quentin. She found it interesting that Quentin had so much background on Jazmine's academic status—was so willing to go above and beyond for this particular patient. The corner of her mouth tugged up slyly. "What's really going on here?"

Quentin leaned forward again with his elbows on the glossy, walnut desk. "I can't help wondering if maybe you're projecting some kind of defensiveness onto—"

Carolyn shook her head. "I'm talking about Jazmine."

"So am I."

"Exactly," Carolyn shot back. "You're interested in her."

Quentin's eyebrows raised over wide eyes.

"You're looking her up on the university computer, reading her past newspaper articles, and pitching her to me as a potential author. You've taken her under your wing. I'm simply wondering why."

"You took her under your wing first," he said.

"Now who's defensive?"

Quentin nodded, pressed his lips together in thought. "You need a writer and Jazmine knows how to write." He pushed back from his desk. "Did it occur to you that maybe I was trying to help *both* of you?"

As Quentin stood, Carolyn worked to contain the humiliation she felt—at losing Quentin to Random and at the prospect of launching a new imprint with nothing more than a writing novice.

Quentin held the office door open for her and held out his hand once again. "I'll be in touch about job openings for your daughter," he said.

Carolyn gave his hand a firm shake before making her way down the gray-blue hallway. What stung her most was the fact that Quentin was right. Jazmine's writing showed promise, to the extent that she wanted to encourage her to get back into the game. If Carolyn was having to start over in publishing, she just might do well with someone who was starting over, too.

Ava

Two weeks after her interview, Ava knocked once again on Howard Mercer's front door as his new junior literary agent. She ran her fingers through her hair, straightened her jacket, and shifted her laptop bag, hoping her makeup was enough to cover the fading bruises. And, once again, Dahlia swung open the door, looking every bit as put-together as she had at Ava's job interview. Her blonde hair was pulled into a sleek ponytail at the base of her neck, and it complemented her crisp, belted trench coat and black pumps. She smiled at Ava, then cringed at seeing her face.

Ava immediately lowered her head, pulling locks of hair into her face to hide the abrasions.

"No, please don't," Dahlia said. "I'm so sorry about the accident. I saw it covered on KING-5 News that night. I just wasn't thinking—I mean, of course you have a few bruises. You look fine, though, really. Please, come in."

Ava began to smile at Dahlia's babbling apology until the pain from the welt on her cheekbone caused her to wince. It hurt to smile ever since the accident although, aside from her time with Jazmine and Carolyn last week and her news at getting the job, she'd had little reason to so much as grin.

"How are you feeling?" Dahlia asked.

"Better every day," Ava said, but the mounting pressure in her temples kept her from proving it with a full-on smile.

"Howard is still in his office getting his files together for our meeting this morning," Dahlia explained as she led Ava through the entry and the hallway. Ava scanned the pictures of Howard with the Pacific Northwest's finest authors as they went, imagining similar pictures lining her own walls someday. "He's impressed that you're ready to get to work, although we really should have come to your house for this meeting."

"Believe me, I'd much rather be here," Ava said as Dahlia opened the French doors and gestured her into the same meeting room she'd interviewed in two weeks prior.

"Howard usually takes that seat," Dahlia said, "but you can sit wherever else you'd like. I'm headed out to grab some coffee for everyone. Anything you'd like, in particular?"

Ava's shoulders relaxed at the idea of a caffeine hit. She'd been in too big a rush to grab coffee that morning. "A non-fat, tall Chai latte would be sublime," she said, reaching into her laptop bag for her wallet. "I can give you some money—"

"Oh, God no!" Dahlia waved her away. "Howard always pays. I'll be back in a few!"

Left alone in the meeting room, Ava gazed out the window at the perfect view of the Space Needle, which had been too cloud-covered for her to see during her interview. She focused on the space-aged disc at the top, flashing back to the time her father had taken her to the famous landmark—insisted she ride up the glass-plated elevator, no matter how she clung to the safety rail in fear. He'd been right though. As she recalled the view at the top and the protective feeling of her father's arm around her, she felt the tension melt from her shoulders.

A feeling of contentment fell over her, happy to meet at Howard's place rather than her father's bungalow. She wasn't much of a housekeeper—even less so since the accident. Howard's insistence that she take time to recuperate before getting started with the agency had left Ava shuffling aimlessly through her tiny new home, feeling her loneliness reverberate through every room until she remembered how last week's "Red Flag Society" had helped her realize that maybe she'd gotten off easy when the drunken, neophyte lawyer had bolted. Sure, she'd supported him throughout law school—paying most of the rent, editing his briefs and reviews, quizzing him before exams—only to have him abandon ship. But what if she'd married him and wasted more years of her life, only to have him leave her to raise the kids on her own while he chased another, "better" life?

Ava shook her head. No way. She extracted her laptop from the bag and set it on the table in order to appear busy when she noticed an envelope on the table—the squarish Hallmark kind with her name written in the middle of it. She reached for it, unsure whether to open it now or when all were present. Since it hadn't been sealed, she figured it couldn't hurt to take a quick peek. It was a pretty, floral *Get Well* card, signed in beautiful cursive by Dahlia, in a scrawled signature by Howard, and in block letters by Max.

Ava sat back. *Max?*

She closed the card and inserted it back into the envelope when the French doors opened and a man juggling a steaming mug and a gigantic bouquet stepped through. A couple of days ago, plied with pain killers, she might have actually thought it was a body that had sprouted a head of flowers.

"Sorry I'm late," he announced, setting down a steaming mug with one hand and holding out the flowers with the other. Now that there were no flowers to obstruct his view, he seemed to realize that no one but Ava was there. She recognized him immediately—his cool, urban hipster vibe, handsome, angular face, bedhead hair, and dark, thick-framed glasses.

"Oh, hey. I'm Max. You must be our new junior agent?"

"I've seen you before," Ava said, studying his face. "Are you a doctor?"

Max chuckled. "No, I'm Howard's senior agent. But I checked on you in the hospital to make sure you were okay. I hope that's all right. Freaky coincidence, but I was the first person on the scene, so you gave me a hell of a scare. All of us, actually."

"You saved me?" Ava asked with an air of wonder.

Max laughed again. "All I really did was keep you going till the EMT got there."

"Thank you," Ava breathed.

Max adjusted his black-rimmed glasses and scratched his unshaven jaw. "Yeah, Howard asked me to pick them up for you. He felt terrible about your accident."

Ava had been thanking him for saving her life, not for the flowers, but she let it go at that.

Ava sat in awe that her new colleagues would work so hard to make her feel welcome. She couldn't remember being treated so well before, personally or professionally. "Well, it certainly wasn't his fault," Ava said, eager to make a positive impression with her new colleague. Maybe she'd even click with him in a way that they could become a formidable agenting duo, signing the most prolific authors in the land!

The late-morning sun lit up the flowers—yellow roses, lilies, and baby's breath. "These are beautiful," she said, then nodded at his drink. "That looks good."

"Just green tea," he said as he set it back down on the table. The fog on his lenses shrank into ever-smaller circles until his dark, almond-shaped eyes appeared in clear focus.

"Yum," Ava said, although her insides gave a little shiver at the thought of such a flavorless drink.

"Takes the chill off," Max said. "Kind of funny how much time I spend in coffee houses when I don't even drink caffeine."

"Ah," Ava nodded. "Is it a religious thing?"

Max chuckled. "More of a lifestyle choice. I don't want to depend on any substance—caffeine, sugar, alcohol, or any other chemical."

Ava beheld Max's still smiling face, which suddenly radiated golden rays of sunshine. The man was a non-addict—an anti-Gavin, if ever there was one. She wondered if maybe she should cut out chemicals too and turn into one of those my-body-is-my-temple types. She could meditate, do yoga, and, well, that's all she could think of.

"There's more tea steeping in the kitchen," he said. "Would you like me to make you a cup?"

"That would be lovely," Ava said, although she wasn't so sure. The only green drink she enjoyed was a cold Midori sour, and the only tea that didn't taste like weakly flavored water was a nice, syrupy Chai. She considered letting him know that Dahlia would be bringing her a Chai tea soon enough, but somehow it seemed only polite to join him in a cup before she came back. It was the least she could do since he'd brought her such pretty flowers, even if they'd ultimately been Howard's idea.

As Max left to pour her tea, Ava found herself running him through the completely infallible red flag protocol that she, Carolyn, and Jazmine had discussed last week. She had little to go on at this point, though. His mussed hair and charcoal V-neck sweater that had seen better days only showed her that he probably wasn't a control freak like Jazmine's ex-husband. And he didn't appear to be hiding a flask like Gavin, Esq. had always done to stiffen his resolve during his own business meetings.

"Here you go," Max said, making his way back into the room.

"Thanks so much," Ava said. She took a sip, then worked to keep her expression neutral as she swallowed. "Oof, that's hot. I'll wait a couple of minutes for it to cool down."

"Suit yourself," Max said, taking his seat across from her again.

"How long have you worked at Howard Mercer?" Ava asked.

"About five years now," he said before taking a sip from his cooling tea.

"I bet it's been amazing," Ava said wistfully. She had so much she could hardly wait to learn.

"It's been a good run," he said, somewhat noncommittally. When his phone dinged with a text, he pulled it from his jeans pocket, clicked it on, skimmed it, then set it face-down on the table.

"Ah! My senior and junior agents are already hard at work, I see," Howard said from the doorway with his assistant, each of them holding steaming cups of coffee. He stood aside to allow Dahlia through. She placed Ava's Chai in front of her and set down a small stack of file folders next to it.

Howard came into the room and offered a hand to shake. Ava noticed his outfit was similar to the one he'd worn for her interview, except that today's polo was burgundy and his REI-style cargo pants were gray. His salt-and-pepper hair appeared darker than last time, perhaps still damp from his morning shower. Ava's hand almost melted in the surprising warmth of his—especially since he was the one who had just come out of the cold—and once again, she held onto his hand a beat too long.

"Welcome to Howard Mercer Literary," he said, his voice and smile every bit as warm as his hand. "We're looking forward to having you on our team."

"I can't wait to begin this new chapter with your agency," Ava replied, feeling her headache subside as she breathed in the cinnamon spice steaming from the little hole in the takeout cup in front of her.

"Pun intended, right?" Dahlia asked playfully as she set down the folders.

Ava shrugged weakly, ready for a groan from at least one of the men for a play on words they'd probably heard a thousand times. Instead, Max lifted his mug as though to clink it with Ava's and said, "Here! Here!"

Ava tipped her cup to his before allowing herself a grateful sip of the sweet ambrosia.

Howard took a seat in the corner and shuffled through the stack of files. "Dahlia, did you grab the contract?"

The assistant, now seated in the corner, scrolled through her phone. "Bottom folder," she replied without so much as looking up.

"Ah, yes. Here we go." Howard handed over a stapled packet with the agency's insignia at the top. "You can look this over and get it back to us within the week."

Ava nodded and took the packet. Normally, she would have Gavin look it over. Hell, normally, he'd be representing her in the whole bus accident debacle. But nothing had been normal since Valentine's Day and her near-demise. As Ava tried to peruse the pages, scanning for dollar signs, followed by numbers, she thought about the envelopes piling up on her coffee table marked *CREDIT PAYMENT PAST DUE* and *FINAL NOTICE*. All she needed once she signed on with Howard was a bestselling author, and she could settle all the debts Gavin had left her with.

"We also brought a list of agency related websites you can browse," Howard continued, his sky-blue eyes peering into hers as if to ensure she was tracking his directions.

Dahlia opened another file. "Here's the password for our email," she said. "I'll mark the queries you might be interested in, so you can see if there's anything you'd consider representing. Then you'll meet with Howard to discuss which choices best fit the agency."

Ava scanned the paperwork. She felt downright giddy. Skimming query letters sure beat waiting up on too many weeknights for Gavin to return from AA meetings so he might have a twenty-third second-chance at sobriety.

"You can look up Publisher's Marketplace," Howard continued. "Get a sense of what's selling. Literary magazines, blogs, you name it. Take your time with it. Agenting is like sifting for gold. Most of it's crap, but once you turn up an author like J.K. Rowling or Lianne Moriarty, it's more than worth it."

Ava typed in the address for Publisher's Marketplace, which opened with the headline: "Advance Imprint's Humiliating Hoax."

Ava shook her head. "The media are really raking her over the coals, aren't they? It's not like she's the first publisher to be duped."

"Which is exactly why she should have done a better job of vetting the whole story," Howard answered. He pressed his lips together and peered into the laptop screen.

"I actually saw her last week," Ava said.

"Carolyn?" Howard looked up from the screen.

Ava nodded. "She's in Seattle—getting away from it all, I guess." She bit her lip, considering how much to share, and could only come up with, "I sort of feel sorry for her."

"She deserved better." Howard nodded. "But Carolyn's always been a powerhouse. She'll get through this."

Ava sat in silent consideration of Howard's insights. She stole glances at him out of the corner of her eye and, for some reason, resorted to the 'red flag' game again. Not for herself, of course—just for practice in general. His career seemed solid, so no neediness there. It would take some time before she could determine whether he had any addiction issues, although she couldn't imagine how he could run his own agency—which he'd been doing at least twenty years—if he did. He was confident, but not arrogant. He was polite and authentic, which ruled out charm or any hint of smarminess—traits Ava could only assume ran rampant in the world of publishing. She made a mental note to bring him up when she met up with Jazmine and Carolyn again at the "Red Flag Society's" first official support and accountability meeting.

Ava changed the subject by clicking on different books coming on the market. "Hey, look!" she said, pointing at the laptop screen. "There's Wes McBride."

Howard squinted to read the screen, then nodded. "You a fan of Western fiction?"

"Not really." Ava shook her head. "I edited a couple of his stories for *Klipsun.*"

"You've worked with Wesley McBride?" Max asked, taken aback. "*The* Wesley McBride?"

"Sure," Ava said. "I didn't realize it was that big of a deal. I've known him since I was a kid. He and my dad played poker all the time."

Howard squinted to read the rest of the information under Wesley's name. "Says here, he recently fired his agent of fifteen years over a licensing dispute."

"Really?" Ava asked, leaning in to read it for herself.

"What do you think the chances are that you could talk him into signing with us?" Max leaned forward. "You can hit him up at the upcoming writers conference."

Ava's chest swelled at the thought. He'd always been impeccably polite to her—that easy swagger and old Southern charm—whether during a poker game or on a more professional level, when she'd edited a couple of his short stories for *The Klipsun*. She'd known he'd published a couple of books, but she hadn't realized until now that he was rather renowned. She could actually sign an author that would make her enough money to at least stop the threatening credit letters. And she could do it all without stupid Gavin's help.

Then she thought of her father's manuscripts collecting dust inside his musty bungalow. Sure, most of the manuscript pile had been the ramblings of a pot-head eccentric, but that one at the top—*The Cosmic Circus of Serendipitous Absurdities*—had been his magnum opus. The ramblings of a genius.

"You know, my father was a writer," Ava offered.

"Oh, yeah?" Howard asked, his voice far milder than it had been over Wes McBride. "Published?"

"Well, no," Ava stammered, "but do you think I'd be able to get any of his work published? Posthumously?"

Max winced—no, actually, he gave a full-on cringe—which caused Ava to wince in turn.

"It would be a conflict of interest for our agency to sign the work of an agent's relative," Howard explained.

"Nepotism," Max said with a shrug.

Of course. Nepotism. Conflict of interest. Why hadn't Ava thought of that. She needed to get the subject back on track, STAT! "I'd be happy to introduce Wes to either of you at the conference," she offered.

"I'd love an introduction," Max said with an earnest smile. "And, if Ava's going to join us at the conference, we'd better train her to take pitches in person."

"I've never taken a pitch before," Ava said, thankful to shrug off her faux pas and go back to what had become her normal disposition as the nervous and awestruck newbie.

"Oh, they're easy, once you know what you're looking for," Howard said. "It's more about putting the author at ease than anything. Want to try one?"

"Sure," Ava said, feeling far less than sure. In fact, after the excitement of getting her contract, she was ready for a nap. Still, she nodded and brought herself closer to the edge of her seat, squaring her posture.

"Max, how about you play the part of the aspiring writer?"

"So, um," Max started, adjusting his glasses and wringing his hands like a nervous first-time conference-goer. "I've written a fictional novel about a man grieving his deceased wife, all the while trying to put his life back together with his kids and step kids."

"Sounds interesting," Ava said, at a loss for how to follow up.

"Ask about genre," Howard coached softly.

Ava nodded. "Would you classify this novel as literary fiction?"

"I'm not sure what that means." Max ran a hand over his hair. "I've been told by friends that it's funny, though. The story's taken from my own experiences."

"You mean, it's a memoir?" she asked.

"I don't really do labels, but if that's what you want to call it." Max shrugged. "Anyway, in the end, he becomes a better person."

Ava felt her eyes go wide and her mouth drop open. "You mean, like the kind of person his wife had wanted him to be all along?"

"Exactly."

Ava leaned forward. "Why do men do that?"

Howard chuckled. "Well, an answer to that question would definitely put the pitch session over the time limit."

"I know," Ava said with a half-hearted grin. "It's completely irrelevant to what we're doing here. It's just something that's been weighing on my mind."

"I'm not sure what you're talking about." Max cocked his head, his eyes shining with amused intrigue.

"I'm wondering why men seem to become better people after the fact?" Ava clarified.

Howard sat back in his chair and crossed an ankle over his knee. "Well, before I could answer that question, I'd have to make two arguments."

Ava raised an eyebrow for him to proceed.

"First, guys don't *always* become better people, and second, it's not always the *guys* who become better people."

"Why, did someone do this to *you*?" Ava's eyes brightened.

Dahlia looked up from her phone, as though this was a completely unexpected response from the big boss—or perhaps hoping that Howard might share something that even she didn't already know about him.

"I was about your age. She was dating a total asshole."

Ava saw Dahlia's eyes widen even more than her own. Apparently, Howard wasn't one to swear.

"Anyway, I fell for her, hard. And I thought she felt the same way— that she was going to leave him. Next thing I know, she moves across the country."

"So, she became a better person for the asshole?" Max asked.

Howard stopped mid-nod. "Actually, no. She became a better person once she found out he was an asshole and divorced him."

"So, she became a better person in *spite* of him," Ava said thoughtfully.

Howard raised an eyebrow back at her, as though she were testing his patience.

"Okay, then." Ava gave a pursed-lip grin. "I'm glad to know women aren't the only ones to go through it."

"I haven't gone through it," Dahlia said with a shrug, going back to her phone.

"Huh," Max mused, flipping through the Seattle Writers Conference paperwork. "I didn't see Roxi Fischer on the roster they put out last week."

"They just added her," Dahlia murmured.

Ava scanned the conference page, her eyes resting on a woman with straight black hair and severe makeup. "What's wrong with Roxi Fischer?" she asked, trying to sound casual.

"She's the worst kind of agent." Howard shook his head. "She's known for making writers cry during pitch sessions. She's also known in the industry to be a duplicitous backstabber."

Max raised his eyebrows, as though this were news to him. "Well, I've gotta head out," he said, rising from his seat. "I'm meeting with Jocelyn about her sequel to *Into the Sun*."

"Have you been following the numbers for *Sun*?" Howard asked.

Ava looked from Max, to Howard, and back again, watching as Max's expression turned wooden. His voice was even as he said, "I always follow the numbers, Howard."

"Just remember that the sales for a sequel can be about fifty percent—"

"—of the sales for the first book," Max finished for him. "Yes, I'm well-aware of that. But a sequel also has the potential to boost the numbers of the first book, so…"

Howard held the senior agent's gaze until Max finally snatched up his phone from the table and said, "Nice to meet you, Eva," and walked out, taking all the oxygen in the room with him. His mug still sat there, steaming lazily.

"My apologies," Howard said with a weak smile. "I'll be sure to remind Max of your actual name when I talk to him later."

"No worries. People make that mistake all the time." Ava sat there at a loss, trying to process the exchange she'd just witnessed. It was the first time that anything at Howard's agency had felt less than perfect.

Jazmine

Snow and ice continued to line the Seattle streets; sun rays pierced the windows of the northbound commuter rail. The train's heat, coupled with the warmth emanating from Henry's sleeping body, overwhelmed Jazmine with lethargy. Her head bobbed to the unsteady rattle and bounce of the train, snapped up at random intervals. Then she sank back into slumber again.

Through the fog of sleep and memory, Jazmine walked up the front step and reached for an envelope on her townhouse door. She let go of Henry's hand to open it and pull out the letter—a notice.

Eviction.

The walls of the townhouse began to crumble, the concrete steps beneath her cracked, and when she reached for Henry's hand, he was gone.

Her head snapped up.

A dream.

No.

While Henry still slept heavily against her, the actual eviction notice lay somewhere in her purse, folded as many times as she could bend the paper.

The train slowed to a stop at the Edmonds Depot. A few people in business attire and a teenager in a hoodie ambled towards the door and out into the frosty air. A slick young man in a suit and tie entered the train and made his way to the seat across from Jazmine, followed by a haggard woman whose skin appeared gray under a layer of filth. She took a seat a couple of rows in front of Jazmine, yet her stench knew no bounds. Jazmine breathed out of her mouth and prayed the woman wouldn't start pacing or ranting, or both. But who was she to judge, being one conversation away from homelessness herself?

Jazmine shifted Henry in her lap, gazing out at the Puget Sound where a ferry made its way past a barge five times its size. Eventually the train slowed, and she glanced out the windows across the aisle to see the Edmonds Station whir slowly past before the train stopped completely. From the corner of her eye, Jazmine saw the slick young man gather his things and rise to leave. Henry yawned, rubbing his eyes with the back of his hand.

"Ready to see Pops and Nonny?" Jazmine asked him.

Henry squirmed to get out of her arms, but judgment or not, she pressed him against her as they made their way past the homeless woman.

Stepping onto the platform, Jazmine set Henry down and took his hand while she scanned the scattered crowds for her stepmother. She found Lucinda standing beside a trash can and waved. Her stepmother's eyes lit with recognition and she opened her arms wide for Henry. He ran towards her and then backed in for his hug. "How you doing, Henry?"

Then, she greeted Jazmine in a tone that rang both routine and false, followed by a one-armed, half-hearted squeeze. "You must being very busy," she said in her clipped, Filipino accent as they turned to walk to the car. "Your father been calling five times, at least."

Jazmine gave a faint nod and directed Henry to Lucinda's car.

Henry started singing, "Nonny, Nonny, Nonny!"

"He talking now?" Lucinda asked, clearly stunned.

"That makes three words," Jazmine told her, thankful he'd at least had the decency to add "Ma" to his vocabulary before adding Lucinda.

When they were belted in, Jazmine spent the ride giving Lucinda the run-down of the bus accident.

Lucinda's voice was wistful as she said, "That poor girl." She shook her head and clucked her tongue. "And the students on your bus?"

"No injuries," Jazmine said. Behind her, Henry made beatboxing noises that sounded uncannily like songs they'd listened to on the radio—complex beats and off-beats. "I was told there were some sore backs the next day, but that's it. And the woman I hit dropped the charges against me."

"So you have your job back?"

Jazmine pursed her lips and took a breath to calm herself. "The district is still running the investigation."

"Of course," Lucinda said. Her ambiguity had always put the "passive" in passive aggressive, which mystified Jazmine to no end. In every other aspect of her life, Lucinda was a caring and outgoing person—a loving wife to Jazmine's father, a devoted friend, and she adored Henry as though he were her own grandchild. In her spare time, she volunteered for community outreach, like Meals on Wheels and the Edmonds Food Bank. Jazmine had nothing but respect for Lucinda and wondered why she never seemed to reciprocate the sentiment. Was Jazmine a perpetual reminder of her father's first wife? Had she put so much time and energy into fulfilling her daughterly duties to her mother that she'd failed to come through for the father who hadn't come through for her?

As Lucinda turned the car into the driveway, Jazmine unbuckled her seatbelt. By the time she had Henry out of his car seat, her stepmother had disappeared into the house, leaving the front door wide open.

A scent of warm ginger greeted them inside. Jazmine sat on the bench in the foyer to pull off her shoes and set them beside her father's gargantuan work boots and Lucinda's flats, which weren't much bigger than Henry's shoes. On the hallway wall, younger versions of her father and Lucinda watched her from their wedding picture. Her father looked sharp and fit in his Navy uniform. He'd never be able to fit in that uniform now, after years of being plied with Lucinda's amazing lumpia. Lucinda herself had somehow maintained the same figure that was clad in a traditional Filipino two-piece wedding dress with butterfly sleeves.

Her father had met and married Lucinda while stationed in the Philippines. Jazmine hadn't been at the wedding. She'd been too busy taking care of her dying mother to make the trip.

Jazmine took a deep breath and made her way into the kitchen. In addition to the usual toys Lucinda had set up for Henry to play with—stacked in order of color and/or size—her stepmom had cooling racks lining the kitchen island. All were stacked high with gingerbread men. Lucinda had obviously put so much time and thought into this fun activity that it pained Jazmine to envision the argument about to ensue—when, inevitably, Lucinda would try to get Henry to see the face and buttons on each cookie, only to have Henry line up one unbroken chain of raisins from top to bottom.

Jazmine's vision went dark as her father placed his hands over her eyes. "Guess who?" he asked, his deep voice raspier than usual.

Under normal circumstances, Jazmine would say a snide, "Hi, Dad," before turning to give him a hug. Today, she couldn't manage it through her tightening throat. She turned around to bury her head in his shoulder before he could see her cry. It made no sense, really. Despite almost two decades of resenting his abandonment, she'd spent all morning yearning for the comfort of his booming bass voice and the smell of his Aqua Velva aftershave. Yet now, those very things reduced her to tears. As he pulled her in, she could hear the eviction notice crinkle inside her purse.

"So, you get pay leave, or you finding new job?" Lucinda asked from behind the kitchen counter.

Jazmine resisted pulling away from her father. "Can we talk in the other room?" she murmured into his ear.

"Wha's that?" Lucinda asked. "Your father ears going bad, you know."

Jazmine's father chuckled. "I always hate to admit when she's right. You'll need to speak up, champ."

"I need to talk to you. Can we sit down—in the living room, maybe?"

"Of course!" he said, putting a hand on her back. "Luci, you mind watching Henry for a few minutes?"

"No problem," Lucinda replied in a way that may have come off cool and easy to Jazmine's father, but the way her eyes bore into Jazmine's signaled that there most certainly was a problem.

Jazmine sat on the end of the sofa, nearest to her father's recliner. He swiveled the chair to face her head-on and leaned forward to listen. She'd last seen him at Christmas, yet his head seemed balder, and his once deep brown eyes were faded and watery.

"You know about the accident," Jazmine started. When her father put a hand to his ear, she repeated, "The accident," in a loud, clear voice.

"Oh, yes." He nodded. "Luci and I were talking about that this morning."

"Well, the district put me on leave, but it isn't paid. And the superintendent of the townhouse we've been staying in told me we're…" She couldn't say it. "It isn't set up for a child with Henry's…"

Lucinda whisked into the room with glasses of ice water in each hand. "Then where will you go?"

"I thought maybe I could run the family motel for a while."

"We offered you that position years ago," her father said, "before you married—"

"Yes, but—"

"We can't fire Vince because you deciding to take the position," Lucinda interjected.

"Of course not, I just thought—"

"Working the motel doesn't fit with Henry's school schedule," her father said, his voice firm, but gentle. "That's why you said you needed to drive a school bus."

This wasn't going the way Jazmine had planned. Living in the manager's station would have allowed her independence from…from *this*. "Bus driving is no longer an option for me, Dad."

"You could live here," her father offered.

"Of course," Lucinda agreed airily, taking a seat on the arm of the recliner. Jazmine wanted to ask her what had happened to watching

Henry in the kitchen, but then Lucinda continued. "Our house not so good for Henry. Things will be very different for him."

"Different, how?" Jazmine asked.

"We have rules—"

"As do I." Jazmine pushed the words through clenched teeth.

"Discipline, too."

"As do I." Jazmine tensed to rise.

Lucinda shot Jazmine's father a shocked look, but he nodded in a way that let her know he'd have it handled. She pushed herself up from the arm of his chair and padded back into the kitchen.

Jazmine's father regarded her, waiting until she met his eyes—an older, male version of her own irises. "Honey, what do you want?"

Jazmine glanced away. Her father was never this direct. "I want to do right by Henry."

"That's obvious. But you'll never be able to do right for him if you're not doing right by yourself."

Jazmine scoffed. Was this what her father had thought when he'd moved to the other side of the world and left her to take care of her ailing mother? He was taking care of himself out of love for Jazmine? Not likely.

"You're talking like I have a choice in the matter. I don't think you understand. Ben left us with nothing. You should see him now, Dad—his new wife, and their perfectly beautiful, non-disabled daughter."

"So, what's new? Ben never had your strength, and I never once saw him do right by you. But don't be a victim, now. Do *you*—"

"Victim?" Jazmine screeched. Did it ever occur to him that maybe she wound up with a jerk like Ben because of his non-existence in her life? "How about giving me some credit here! You should be *commending* me on how I—"

"Want to finish school?" her father prodded gently.

Jazmine's head swam. She felt attacked—ambushed—and all in the name of being selfish?

"Travel?" he pushed.

Jazmine squinted at him in utter disbelief. Did this man understand her situation at all? No, her father lived in an entirely different reality—always had. Not everyone could whisk away and recreate their lives, like her father and son of a bitch ex-husband. Some people were just made to be the ones left behind to do the dirty work, and Jazmine had long since learned that she was one of those people. Her father was more of a wildcard, which was why she even chose, reluctantly, to see if he might help her with a job at the motel. College and travel were abstract luxuries in Jazmine's world, which ran on a steady diet of *need to* and *have to*. "Want" was a frivolity that had long left her vocabulary.

"Sweetheart, this accident has given you the gift of time. Use it. Search your heart, search your *soul*. Dig deep into all that muck, past everyone else, past every obstacle. The world didn't shut down on you when Ben walked out, so don't you go shutting yourself down to it."

"But—"

"Providing opportunities for your child is honorable, but it's a waste if it's at the expense of your *soul*. I'm going to provide an opportunity for *my* child."

Jazmine sat there stunned, to the extent that she could practically hear the cartoonish thud of her chin hitting the floor. Her father had never put her first before, but now that he was, her head swam from the overwhelming idea of going back to finish her degree. Okay, so the last thing she needed in her life was to feel beholden to her suddenly attentive father and passive-aggressive stepmother—who would surely hold it over her head forever. But the only thing she wanted now—no, *needed*—was a full night's sleep, followed by an afternoon nap the next day. She could figure out the rest later.

Lifting her gaze to meet her father's pale, watery eyes, she asked, "Where would we sleep?"

"We converted our downstairs into a mini-apartment so we could get in on that Airbnb action."

Even though she felt the walls closing in on her, for the first time since Jazmine and Henry had walked through her father's front door, she could feel her ribs expand enough to take a full breath. She hadn't been supported like this since Henry was born—since *ever*, really. And then, as she heard Lucinda's soothing voice in the kitchen guiding Henry with his gingerbread raisin line-making, she thought maybe this arrangement could be just as positive for Henry as for herself. But only if Lucinda's brand of care-taking didn't devolve into raising her iron fist in the name of disciplining him into "normal." No matter. If it came to that, Jazmine could pick right back up and leave.

"I'll pay rent, of course," she finally said.

"I'll only accept it if you promise not to leave here the same person you are in this room with me now. Find yourself—decide what *you…*"

"…want…"

"…and this temporary home is on the house."

Jazmine nodded her appreciation and watched her father grow blurry through her own watery eyes.

The Better Man

Carolyn

Carolyn crammed a coffee pod into the Keurig with one hand and worked a diamond stud into her earlobe with the other. The earring dropped to the floor, bouncing twice before rolling under the counter. She didn't have time for this. She fished her phone from the pocket of her blazer. On her hands and knees now, she shined the flashlight, hoping it might pick up the sparkle. She felt hot breath on her neck and heard Trixie sniffing her perfume.

"Look," she whispered, pulling at the lobe that had the other earring in it. "Can you find this for me? Somewhere under the counter?" Trixie licked the earring and watched her expectantly.

The doorbell rang. Carolyn bonked the underside of the counter when the dog yipped in her ear. She rubbed the crown of her head while Trixie scrambled off to the front door.

"I'll get it," Vivian called in a sing-song voice from the living room.

Under her breath Carolyn sang back, "And I'll let you." She crawled from one end of the counter to the other, again rubbing her head as she scanned the floor. No shiny object. Screw it. She'd find another pair or go without. She froze at shouts coming from down the hall—a voice calling desperately, "Mom? Mom!"

Carolyn jolted upward, hitting her head against the counter again. Dizzy, she felt for a welt as she shuffled on her knees to the kitchen door. "Sophie?"

"Mom, I need you!" Sophie called breathlessly, her footsteps racing toward the kitchen until she rounded the corner and ran her knee right into Carolyn's shoulder, tripping heels overhead.

"Ow!" Carolyn cried. "Sweetie, are you okay?" She crawled to where her daughter lay splayed on the bisque-colored rug. Trixie dashed over and licked all over Sophie's face from chin to forehead.

"What the hell, Mom?" Sophie shifted herself onto an elbow and rubbed the shaved side of her head. Carolyn was pleasantly surprised to see that the hair on top hanging over the other side had gone from seaweed-green to streaks of various fluorescent colors. Her cheeks were still ruddy from the brisk late-March air. "What are you doing—"

"I'm getting ready for a meeting."

"On the floor?"

"Honey, what's going on?" Carolyn rose stiffly to her feet, brushing off any of Trixie's hair still clinging to her pants. Her skull seemed unbruised, but even after testing her arm, she couldn't yet tell about the shoulder. "You came into the house sounding like you'd been mugged."

Sophie searched her mother's eyes. "I need you..."

Carolyn held out her hand to help Sophie back up. Her heart pounded. Sophie hadn't *needed* Carolyn in almost a decade—ever since she'd chosen to stay with Grandma Vivian. "Anything," she said.

"...to tell me who you dated before Dad," Sophie stated bluntly.

Carolyn stood frozen, her heart pulsing from her throat, where it had jumped when Sophie asked this bizarre question.

"I doubt your mother kept track of *all* the boys she dated," Vivian said as she shuffled into the kitchen in her robe and house slippers. Her strawberry blonde hair appeared dull and dented in the back from sleeping. Trixie pranced on her heels. It was a wonder the dog never got trampled—a thought Carolyn didn't find all that unappealing. "Coffee?" Vivian asked, holding out an empty mug towards Sophie.

"Definitely," Sophie said, then turned back to Carolyn. "Jesus, Mom. How many guys were there?"

Carolyn dug through her purse for her keys. "This is the last thing I need to get into," she said, noticing that her daughter seemed to take inordinate pleasure in frustrating her at this most inopportune time. "I've got to get to my meeting."

"Which isn't for another two hours," Vivian interjected as she handed Carolyn her coffee mug, steaming with the aroma of fully loaded dark roast. "Why don't you put your Type-A personality aside and spend an hour with your daughter?"

"I love your hair," Carolyn offered. "I think it's about time you broke free from the mold."

"Of course, your mother likes it," Vivian said. "She always was my rebellion hellion."

"Oh please," Sophie argued. "Mom's as strait-laced as they come."

Vivian walked into the living room, all the way to the bookcase. She used her index finger to scan the books there and pulled out a photo album and what appeared to be Carolyn's high school annual.

Carolyn's shoulders sank. "Mom, I'm sure Sophie has better things to do than—"

"I've got all morning," Sophie said, gazing out her grandmother's floor-to-ceiling windows at the low sun shining over Alki Beach.

Carolyn's mind raced, mentally flipping through the pages Vivian was about to share with her daughter. She knew full well Sophie wasn't as interested in seeing Carolyn's rebellious stages as she was in seeing the guys posing with Carolyn for various occasions.

Vivian took a seat beside her granddaughter and opened the photo album. "Oh look, your mother's prom picture."

"Where?" Sophie scanned the page, as though there were any other pictures to see. "Wait, that's *you*?"

Carolyn hadn't seen that picture in decades. On the opposite side of the table from them, she could only view it upside-down, and even from that direction she was impressed by the volume of her hair.

Carolyn suddenly welcomed the photo album as a way of avoiding Sophie's barrage of questions. Her daughter had never shown interest in her past life before.

"You were so vampy," Sophie said, tracing Carolyn's teenage face with her finger. "Black hair, black lips. Your date's wearing more makeup than you! And that hair…"

Vivian laughed. "I still hold those two solely responsible for the hole in the ozone layer."

"Where's your prom date now?" Sophie asked.

"Works at Boeing," Carolyn said, "at least he did at our twenty-fifth high school reunion. At the time he was about to get divorced—"

Sophie's eyes lit up.

"—and remarried that same year, I heard. Three kids, total."

Sophie's face fell.

"And what would you have me do if he was available now?" Carolyn asked, moving towards the dining room chair where she'd placed her briefcase. "Call him up? Ask him out for a drink?"

"Well, *yeah*," Sophie said. "That's the whole point."

"The point?" Carolyn worked to keep her tone breezy as she clicked open the briefcase and shuffled through the same paperwork she'd already double and triple-checked the night prior.

"You're my subject," Sophie said with a shrug, as though Carolyn should have known this all along. "It's research for Soc 103."

"Your sociology professor assigned you to research my former love life?" Carolyn's voice was flat.

"Yes!" Sophie reached across the counter for her book bag. "We have to do a study—"

"—for which you waited until the last minute, no doubt."

Sophie rolled her eyes. "We're supposed to choose a certain demographic…"

Carolyn studied her daughter, seeing Marcus in her demeanor—the way she set her chin in determination, the way she furrowed her brows in thought. She even saw Isadore in the way her hand floated a gesture to embellish everything she said. The tone, however, reminded her of her own mother's tone—the one that contained a warning that there would be a catch of some sort.

"I chose the middle age demographic," Sophie said, "and their interactions through technology."

"Then why are we wasting time going through your mother's pictures?" Vivian asked, then beamed. "I'd love to be a subject in your study."

"Maybe…" Sophie stammered. "I mean, you're a Baby Boomer. I was talking about middle age. You know, Generation X'ers, like Mom."

Carolyn raised her eyebrows at her daughter. "Middle-aged?"

"You're forty-two."

"I'm begging you to get to the point," Carolyn said.

"There are all these divorced people getting in contact with their high school sweethearts over the internet," Sophie started. "And a bunch of them are getting back together again, after all these years."

Vivian chimed in. "I have a friend at the pool who found her high school prom date on Facebook," she said, handing Sophie a cup of coffee, fresh from the Keurig. "They just got married—at eighty years old!"

Sophie gave an impressed nod. "Do you have any old sweethearts, Grandma?"

"Your granddad was my first date, my first kiss, my first…" She paused, then giggled.

"Mom, please!" Carolyn said, then turned to her daughter. "See, Sophie? This is how you're supposed to react to your mother's relationship stories. You're supposed to be grossed out by them—not *engrossed*."

This conversation was rapidly feeling irrelevant. Carolyn yearned to beat the traffic downtown and find a quiet corner to review her notes, her sales pitches and, well, demographics.

Vivian pointed to a picture in Carolyn's yearbook—the one where Carolyn had pulled back her then-purple hair and combed a thick, straight row of bangs over her forehead. She stood in a black lace dress, bright orange tights, and a pair of clunky Doc Martens next to the president of both the Associated Student Body and the Future Business Leadership Association.

"Carolyn Ford: Most likely to Take Over the World," Sophie read.

Carolyn took a sip of coffee and gave a wry grin. "Still working on that one—and the way things have been going, it might need to be a different planet in a different solar system."

Vivian reached around Sophie's shoulder and gave her a squeeze as they laughed together. Carolyn leaned forward and turned the page for them. Senior pictures. Graduation.

"You had *dreadlocks*?" Sophie asked.

"New wave turned to grunge turned to ska." Carolyn gave a shrug as though to say, *What was a poor girl to do?*

Carolyn reflected on her '90s wardrobe, which had consisted only of flannel shirts and cut-off jeans over tights, along with a nose and belly button ring. Then came the tattoos. There was always some sort of inner maverick in Carolyn's quest to express herself.

Sophie continued flipping pages. Pictures of Carolyn with her college friends, girls' nights out, various dates. "What about him?" Sophie asked. "And him?"

"Married," Carolyn replied. "And married."

"Well now, some turned gay," Vivian added. "I'm not saying your mother is to blame—it just worked out that way, you know."

"Mom, please," Carolyn said, then clicked her briefcase closed with an air of finality. "I'm off. Looks like you'll need to call your dad to help you out." In her head, she added that he'd had plenty more 'sweethearts' than Carolyn ever had, herself.

"Dad's taken," Sophie whined. "Isn't there someone?"

"There was that one young man," Vivian said, searching Carolyn's face. "But that was after college, wasn't it?" She turned to Sophie. "Does it count for your study if it's an after-college sweetheart?"

"That was just Marcus," Carolyn lied.

"No, before Marcus," Vivian argued. "At the place you worked down on First."

"That's where Mom met Dad," Sophie said, her tone turning to one of glum resignation.

Carolyn tried to hide the gleam in her eyes. She really didn't want to get into this—especially not in this particular company. But for once in her life, Sophie was coming to *her* for help.

"Don't you remember?" Vivian kept on. "Your father invited him in once, when he'd driven you home one evening. Your father must have asked him a million questions…" Vivian trailed off. "I remember he had such a nice smile. And his eyes—so blue that I could have dived right in."

"It was a tech guy at work," Carolyn blurted, then bit her lips together.

Sophie gasped. "Before Dad?"

Carolyn forced breath into her lungs, both horrified and relieved that her mother had finally cajoled her into un-padlocking Pandora's can of worms. She nodded to the first question and figured she'd let the nod speak to the second—a half-truth that seemed more productive than telling Sophie that this had all happened during her dating relationship with Marcus.

"So?" Sophie asked.

"We worked together." Carolyn shrugged. "He was in a band. Gave me CDs to listen to. All the angst-ridden post-punk stuff coming out of Seattle." As Carolyn reminisced, his image came to life in her mind.

"What?" Sophie asked coyly. "Why are you smiling like that?"

"I just…" Carolyn stammered and gave a soft smile, biting softly on the bottom corner of her lip. "I liked his dimples when he smiled."

"Do you remember his name?" Sophie asked.

Carolyn shook her head—another unspoken half-truth, as she'd recognized it immediately when she heard it a few weeks ago—but that was one detail she wasn't about to share in present company. When Carolyn saw her daughter's shoulders slump, she added, "Let me see what I can do."

"With technology, right?" Sophie's face brightened. "Facebook? Snapchat? Instagram?"

"I'll start with the Google and let you know how it goes."

"Mom, it's not *the* Google."

Carolyn took one last swig of coffee. "I'm out of here."

"I should get going, too," Sophie said. "Don't want to be late for work."

Carolyn narrowed her eyes and put a hand on her hip. "I thought you said you had all afternoon?"

Sophie shrugged. "I lied."

"How is work going, anyway? Your new boss isn't going easy on you because of me, is he?"

"It's been really fun working for Quentin, actually." Sophie rose from her stool to join Carolyn on her walk to the front door, where they shared a goodbye hug. "I hope it works out, Mom. The meeting, that is. I don't feel like I've ever really seen you happy before, you know?"

"Agreed," Vivian said, standing in the hall behind them while Trixie barked. "Go get 'em, honey."

"I appreciate that." Briefcase in hand, Carolyn stood tall. "How do I look?"

Sophie smiled a genuine smile. "Ready to take over the world."

Ava

An unemployed publisher, a school bus driver on investigation, and a novice/fledgling literary agent walk into a bar, Ava thought to herself as she strolled through the underground Cider House. She scanned the room for Carolyn and Jazmine, eager to see them again after a full month. The dim lighting didn't help, coming only from single cord lamps hanging from the ceiling, as well as tea lights flickering at each table. Her nerves calmed at the sound of an acoustic guitar coming from a corner stage, played by a man who sang in a soft, whispery voice.

The women weren't sitting at any of the vacant wooden tables in the middle of the bar. She noticed one woman sitting at a table against the antiquated brick wall, but she was neither Jazmine nor Carolyn.

Meeting in a bar meant an official "Girls' Night Out"—something Ava hadn't enjoyed since she'd starting dating Gavin, which meant she hadn't enjoyed one since college. In preparation, Ava had spent the past two hours trying on outfits that would make her look as though she'd just thrown on a pair of skinny jeans and fitted top and happened to look amazing in them. The same went for her long, chestnut tresses, meticulously curled, then mussed and scrunched into beach-tousled waves.

With so many breweries around, the hard cider establishment tended to be more of a women-slash-couples place. Mead also topped the menu. Ava was sure that the few men seated at the bar sipping the ancient Viking brew spent their weekends donning costumes for both

Comic-Con and Renaissance Faires, which weren't exactly the sort of single men that topped her wish list. But then, at this point, Ava was looking for an anti-Gavin, and it was sure to be challenging to find a perfectly sober man in a bar. If nothing else, perhaps she would happen upon a talented writer who would make them both millions. She scanned the people at the bar, wishing writers wore some kind of uniform to distinguish them—or that there were T-shirts for "FUTURE BESTSELLERS."

Ava finally spotted her new friends at a tall table in the farthest corner, both dressed as casual as she, although Carolyn's idea of casual still had her looking like she was ready to lead an editorial board meeting. They broke the conversation as Ava sat in one of the iron-backed stools at the high table.

"Good to see you again, Ava." Jazmine's voice was warm. "You look great—I mean, you know, the bruises have healed nicely."

Ava's gaze landed on Jazmine's hazel eyes. The irises glowed with sincerity through what appeared to be new, burgundy-framed glasses. Ava struggled briefly to figure out what else made Jazmine look different tonight. Up until now, Ava hadn't seen Jazmine's hair pulled back into a high ponytail, bursting with tightly coiled curls. Despite her reservations, Ava admired how Jazmine's ribbed sweater hugged her every curve without looking slutty, as well as the way her olive-toned skin glowed from within the warm fuchsia sweater—a color that Ava would never be able to pull off with her alabaster complexion. Before now, Ava had viewed Jazmine as a disheveled, overworked single mom, and here she was at their table looking every bit as sleek and put together as Howard's intern, Dahlia.

"Physically, the doctors say my shoulder is healing right on track," Ava replied, after hesitating a bit too long. "I wish I wasn't mixing up days and times, though, showing up for work at noon on Monday, thinking it's nine in the morning on Thursday. Thankfully, my new boss has been super patient with me. I guess he had a concussion once, too."

Carolyn leaned over for a side hug. Ava looked down at the floor, hiding her dropped jaw. *I'm on hugging terms with Carolyn Ford?* she thought, although that kind of greeting was probably commonplace in the New York metropolis. Jazmine beckoned the rail-thin server to their corner table.

"My mother wanted to give you her attorney's card," Carolyn said, handing Ava an ordinary beige business card with dark brown block lettering. "She swears by this woman and says she's willing to take on contingency cases."

Ava pursed her lips. "But why wouldn't she give this to Jazmine? She's going to have legal trouble, too."

"I have a lawyer through my union," Jazmine said. "Plus, the district has already decided that it was the ice at fault."

"That's exactly what Mom assumed, on both counts," Carolyn said. "So, since you'll be going after the district, and not our new friend here," she reached over and placed a hand on Jazmine's wrist, "she wants you to have solid representation—not those smarmy ambulance chasers you see on daytime television commercials."

"What, like Douglass and Burns?" Ava chuckled ruefully. "Anyone but guys like that."

"Now, tell me about this new job offer you got," Carolyn said. "You'd said something about an agency—I thought maybe real estate?"

Ava swelled with pride. "I'm an associate with a literary agency." Her cheeks burned, and she could only imagine how brightly they were blushing when she saw Carolyn's eyes grow wide.

"No kidding?" Carolyn asked. "Which one?"

Ava's wheels spun for a way around it. If Howard didn't work with Carolyn, who was to say what Carolyn thought of him? But Carolyn's eyes bore into her and Ava knew she may as well come clean with it now. "Howard Mercer."

The impressed expression on the New York publisher changed to one of intrigue and confusion.

"Howard Mercer," Carolyn's voice was barely audible. Both Ava and Jazmine leaned in to hear more, but Carolyn pulled back and looked toward the mead-drinkers at the bar.

Ava pulled back too and stared at the musician on stage. What was it Dahlia had said exactly? That Howard didn't do business with Carolyn Ford? No, that wasn't it. More like he hadn't done any business with Carolyn Ford, which simply meant they hadn't done business up to this point. Nevertheless, she decided to veer the subject before things went too sour.

"I have a question for you, actually," Ava started. "I found a manuscript by my dad—a bunch of them, actually. He used to write all the time before he, you know, passed away."

"I'm sorry for your loss," Carolyn said. "Did you read it?"

"I did," Ava said. "And it's good. Fantastic, really. His other books were good, too, but wacky and weird. Agents never seemed to get them. But this one seems to draw upon his life and it's exquisite. It should be read, you know?"

"I do know," Carolyn replied. "It's why I've spent so many years bringing books to the world."

"But Howard says it would be a conflict of interest—nepotism, or whatever—for his agency to sign it, since I work there."

"He isn't wrong," Carolyn said. "And publishers seldom print posthumous books because what's the point of gaining a readership they can't keep growing with more books?"

"You could always self-publish," Jazmine offered.

Ava bristled. "*Anyone* can self-publish. If he'd wanted that, he could have done that with all of his books. But he didn't. He said he'd know he'd made it once he got through all the gate-keepers."

Carolyn placed her hand on Ava's. "I can help you navigate self-publishing. I know it isn't what you're hoping, but you'd be surprised how many independent authors take off. It can actually be quite lucrative."

Ava opened her mouth to thank her when the server arrived, pulling an electronic tablet from his apron pocket and tapping it to life. "What can I get for you this evening?"

Ava paused, taking stock of the drinks already on the table—a white wine for Carolyn and a hard cider for Jazmine. Ava pointed at Carolyn's wine glass and said, "I'll have what she's having."

"Pinot grigio?" the waiter asked.

"Exactly," Ava said, having no idea what he'd just said. She'd never been big on wine and would have preferred Jazmine's bubbly cider or a syrupy-sweet Midori sour, but what better way to emulate her publishing hero than to mirror her wine selection?

"Put it on my tab," Carolyn said, then called out, "And please bring a glass of water."

The server nodded as he dashed away. Ava noticed Carolyn eyeing the guitar player as she adjusted her mauve pashmina wrap before folding her hands on the table. She smelled light and fresh, with hints of lemon and lavender. A month had passed since they'd agreed to join forces in support of one another, and in that time, Carolyn's dark circles had faded and the forehead creases were now hidden under newly cropped bangs. In fact, the woman's face radiated serenity.

"He's cute," Ava said, feeling like a high school gossip. "Handsome, I mean."

"For you, maybe," Carolyn said, raising one eyebrow. "He's a little young for me."

"Oh, please," Jazmine said. "He's at least your age—thirty-seven, maybe?"

"Which makes me older by at least five years," Carolyn said.

"This is the 21st century," Ava reminded her. "Men love older women. You could be a cougar." Ava's smile faded when Carolyn's unamused eyes told her how unfunny her attempt at age consolation had been. "Well, he's too old for me," she tried again, but stopped when Jazmine nudged her foot under the table to let her know she was only making things worse. "What about you, Jazmine? Are you in your thirties?"

"Thirty-four," Jazmine said, taking a drink from her cider. "But the last thing I need in my life right now is a man."

Ava watched as a man in a windbreaker and rain-spotted glasses entered the bar and glanced around before spotting the woman sitting by the brick wall. He gave a slight nod and made his way to her table.

The folksy singer on the corner stage held a last note and ended his song, eliciting sporadic, polite applause from the guys at the bar. Ava clapped wildly and shouted, "Woo-hoo!" The man glanced up at their table, gave a half-smile, and winked.

"Did you see that, Carolyn?" Ava asked. "He totally winked at you!"

"No, he winked at you," Carolyn answered dryly, "the one making all the noise."

"I'm with Ava on this one," Jazmine chimed. "That man winked at one forty-two-year-old publisher."

"If he did, I'd call that a red flag." Carolyn took a sip from her wine while she sized him up. "And I'm guessing he has a few more where that one came from."

"You don't know that," Ava argued. "He's a musician—that shows he's talented."

Carolyn chuckled. "Yes, and male musicians are also known for their high moral standards in fidelity. Just you watch, he'll be winking and blowing a kiss at another middle-aged woman by the end of his next song. How do you think he gets his tips?"

Ava opened her mouth to object that forty-two was hardly middle aged when her gaze was blocked by the server suddenly standing before her with a tray. He first set down her wine glass. Carolyn motioned for him to place the tall glass of water next to it, directly in front of Ava.

Carolyn nudged Ava and said, "Thought you could alternate between the two."

"Please do," Jazmine said. "I didn't come here to spend my night mopping hardwood floors."

"Oh, God." Ava could feel her cheeks burning at the memory of throwing up all over Carolyn's mother's floor. "I'm so sorry you had to clean up after…"

"Naw, I'm just joking with you," Jazmine said.

Ava turned to Carolyn. "And your mother must think I'm—"

"Don't worry, Ava. Mom's very forgiving," Carolyn insisted. "She had to be. You should have known me as a teen!" She smiled mischievously. Ava couldn't imagine Ms. Ford being anything less than school valedictorian.

"Why don't we open our first official meeting of the Red Flag Society with a toast?" Jazmine asked, raising her glass.

"As well as my new lease of a publishing firm," Carolyn said, "and Ava's new position as a literary agent, and Jazmine's newly discovered writing prowess."

The women clinked glasses, holding each other's gaze as they brought their glasses to their lips. Without moving her head, Jazmine looked over to Ava with raised eyebrows, as though asking what Carolyn had meant by her last comment.

Ava shrugged as she sipped her cold white wine and grimaced.

"Is something wrong?" Carolyn asked.

"It's just really," Ava paused, searching for the right wine-type word, "dry."

Jazmine tilted her head and regarded Ava with a sparkle in her eye. "Pinot grigio is always dry. Why did you order it?"

"It just," Ava stammered, "looked good." She turned to Carolyn. "But I'll drink it or pay for it. I didn't mean to criticize it by making that face."

Carolyn gestured the server over again. "Let's try this again so you can get what you want."

"What did you mean when you said you'd leased a publishing firm?" Ava asked.

"And about my writing—how did you put it—'prowess'?" Jazmine added.

Carolyn held her glass by the stem in an easy-breezy, nonchalant way. "I mean that the out-of-business Rainier Press is now the fledgling Ford Publishing."

"That's fantastic," Ava exclaimed, ever impressed by this woman's ability to persevere.

"As for Jazmine..." Carolyn trailed off as she pulled a thin newspaper from her purse and sat it decidedly on the table in front of her.

"Why would you have an old copy of *The Daily*?" The space between Jazmine's eyes furled and her hands pulled back, not wanting, it seemed, to touch the University of Washington's newspaper.

Carolyn smiled. "My daughter is a freshman there. You should be proud of what you wrote. Very proud."

Ava watched Jazmine narrow her eyes at Carolyn, as though she wasn't buying that her daughter had anything to do with giving her the newspaper. But all she finally said was, "It's just an article I wrote a long time ago."

"You went to the 'U'?" Ava asked, then realized she sounded way too incredulous. "I mean, how were you able to do school with Henry?" She looked at the date on the newspaper, realizing it pre-dated Henry—by about nine months, actually. She leaned in and whispered, "Did you drop out?"

Jazmine nodded, gazing at the newspaper. "Only had fifteen credits to go."

"Is there any chance of going back?" Carolyn asked gently. "Fifteen credits is, what? One more quarter?"

"It's money I don't have," Jazmine spoke in a surprisingly off-hand tone.

"I thought you said the district isn't blaming you," Ava said. "So, you've got your job back, right? You could do night classes?"

Jazmine shrugged. "Turns out, they don't want the public outcry from getting me behind the wheel right away, so they're putting me on paid leave for a couple of months—which almost makes things perfect."

"*Almost* perfect?" Carolyn repeated. "What *isn't* perfect about it?"

"It would take me away from Henry, first of all."

"But your job already did that, didn't it?" Ava asked.

"Right, but this is a chance to really connect with him in a way I haven't been able to," Jazmine explained, then held up a hand when Ava tried to argue. "There's more—Henry finally pitched one loud-ass tantrum too many and got us evicted."

Ava stared at Jazmine, dumbfounded, then glanced at Carolyn to see that she was doing the same.

"Jazmine, come live with me," Ava said. "I have the extra room and, to be honest, I could use the help with the mortgage."

Jazmine gave a half-grin. "You haven't spent enough time around my son. You won't be able to get any work done with him around."

"By the time I ever get home, I'm sure Henry will be long asleep."

"Jazmine, think about it," Carolyn said. "Taking Ava up on her offer would afford you the opportunity to finish your degree *for* your son. Based on this promising sample and then arming yourself with a degree in journalism, I can envision you building an online platform."

"Platform?" Jazmine asked.

"It's like," Ava paused, determined to impress Carolyn with her publishing savvy, "the way you build your readership. Your author website, social media, blogs, any connections you have in the writing industry—"

"But I'm not an author," Jazmine argued. "That was the only article I've ever published, and the journalism class was just a credit requirement for my Communications major. I've thought about their broadcast journalism sequence, maybe to be a news anchor or host some kind of community level show. Ask people questions, you know? Reporting, interviews…"

Ava gasped. "You could interview people on the topic of our support group!"

Jazmine seemed to push back from Ava a little, regarding her out of the side of her eye. "I think you're taking our support group thing a little too literally."

When the server approached the table to ask if anyone needed refills, Ava ordered a hard cider.

"Now you're just ordering what I got," Jazmine said. "What do *you* want?"

"A Midori sour," Ava relented.

The server's nostrils flared with what Ava presumed was a hidden sigh—as though she were making an already-long night that much longer. "You're sure, now?"

"Positive," Ava said.

The waiter placed Ava's barely touched glass of Pinot grigio on his tray and whisked back to the bar.

Jazmine gave Ava a curious look. "You're so good at encouraging me to move in and complete my college degree for myself, but it seems like you're too focused on making everyone else happy. I mean, you can't even order a drink to please yourself."

Ava wanted to argue, but the blandness of the green tea she'd drunk for Max's sake still lingered deep in her taste buds—as well as her immediate reflex to swear off caffeine and alcohol forever in the name of being a non-addict like him. Her various misrepresentations of herself had become like a nervous tick in her anxious need to be accepted.

"I was a people-pleaser when I was your age," Carolyn said.

Ava fought from letting her mouth fall open. She couldn't imagine a cut-throat publisher like Carolyn Ford as a "people-pleaser."

"I tried to save men, too," Carolyn continued, "until I decided to save myself, instead."

"I never tried to save Gavin," Ava said—and it was true. She hadn't.

Jazmine took a sip of her cider, studying Ava's face. "And then you became his drinking buddy."

As much as Ava wanted to deny this allegation, a vague recollection of their conversation at Carolyn's mother's house reminded her that she'd already confessed as much.

Jazmine took in a deep breath and pursed her lips. "I've had plenty of friends who have changed for the guys they were with. They're relationship chameleons."

"Are you insinuating that I'm a lizard now?" Ava asked, just as the server reappeared with her Midori sour. The perplexed look in his eyes let her know how odd her question had sounded outside of any context. And in this case Ava was trying to figure out the context of why she needed to defend her life, such as it was. Thankfully, he was too busy running to the next table to question it.

"Only you know whether you have a history of changing your colors," Carolyn said, twirling the wine stem between her thumb and forefinger.

Ava stared at their drinks, embarrassed at the way she'd changed colors—from white wine to fluorescent green, before taking a too-long sip through the tiny black straw. But even the flavor of Jolly Rancher in all its sour melon splendor couldn't distract her from what Jazmine had said.

She thought about Drew, a musician whom she'd "supported" through several bands by essentially becoming his own personal roadie. And Brian, the runner who'd gotten her into half-marathons and Thai food. And, of course, Gavin, who was most fun when he got that tipsy sheen in his eye. When he'd had enough alcohol to loosen him up enough for singing along to Pandora and, at least for their first year together, to throw his arms around her and dance around the room. As she'd done with the others, she went along, convincing herself that this was the true, unadulterated Gavin—that the beer or vodka or gin had stripped him of his inhibitions and allowed him to love her from the very core of his being.

But his unbridled "love" turned out to be as fleeting as that particular inebriated stage. A couple more drinks, and his eyes changed. His words sloshed in his mouth while his behavior became rougher and raunchier. Whenever Ava had the foresight, she'd excuse herself to bed before his eyes turned wild. Now, she realized it had taken being hit by a bus to see how their whole relationship had been an illusion.

"I thought we were here to support each other through bad relationships," Ava finally said, speaking each word with deliberation. "This feels more like an intervention, after the fact."

"Sort of," Carolyn said, raising her wine glass, "except it's an intervention *before* the next mistake."

Ava toyed with her straw and thought about her father's inscriptions. *For my Ava—may you ever be your own.* As the meaning finally sank in, she swallowed back the sadness welling within her. "Well, I'd rather focus on finding ways to skip past any more fixer-uppers to the better, healthier, standup men." She watched as Carolyn and Jazmine shared a look and braced herself for the inevitable. *But that will only work if you're your best and healthiest self.*

Thankfully, the server at the next table cut off their impending response by whirling around, returning to their table, and whispering almost conspiratorially, "Is there a solution for her?" He pointed toward the corner with his elbow and chin. "That woman over there is in desperate need."

"How so?" Ava turned to view the woman sitting against the brick wall. The man's windbreaker had been laid over the back of his chair and he now sat across from her, sipping his drink.

"She comes in all the time," the server said, tucking his tablet into his apron pocket. "We worked out a system where she can escape bad dates and I make a double tip. That guy there? He showed up forty-five minutes late. Said it was traffic, but I told her she still should've left. Few minutes ago, when he finally shows up, she's starving, and he says he isn't hungry. Orders a glass of water. That's it. *Water!*"

Jazmine shook her head ruefully. "That girl needs to tip big and head for the alley. Two red flags are two too many."

The server held out his fist to bump with Jazmine.

"But what if the first one's a fluke?" Ava asked. "What if he really had been stuck in traffic, but had shown up and ordered the most expensive plate on the menu?"

"Forty. Five. Minutes," Jazmine reminded her. "And it doesn't sound like he even let her know till he got here."

"Okay, look. A small flag and he gets one warning," Carolyn decided. "One gridiron sized flag, and he's gone."

Ava nodded, still unsure. If they were going to use sports terminology, they may as well stick with the three strikes before he's out. But then three becomes four and four becomes five. Gavin had shown his share of flags from day one, and Ava had always rationalized them away. She glanced over again and knew the only thing setting her apart from the woman at that table were the two women at *her* table. No matter how desperately she clung to denial, Jazmine's insightful interviewing skills and Carolyn's shared experiences had shone a light on the enabling part of herself that she could never again unsee.

"She's just going to sit there, hungry, because her date doesn't want to eat?" Jazmine asked.

"No, she ordered anyway," the server replied. "I'm guessing they'll be going Dutch."

"So basically, dinner's on her," Carolyn said.

Jazmine giggled, but Ava shook her head in pity as she watched the woman. Her face was as much in shadow as it was aglow from the tea light on their table, so even though her mouth smiled and her eyes shone, the dark circles beneath them made her look gaunt and somber. Ava reached into her purse for her credit card. "No, it's not. Her dinner's on me."

"Good idea," Jazmine said, pulling some cash from her jeans pocket. "I'll chip in, too. Cocktail karma!"

"Carolyn's taken care of us," Ava said brightly. "We'll take care of that woman." Ava beamed as the server took her card and Jazmine's money, although deep down she knew the last thing she should be doing was charging anything nonessential—let alone a stranger's meal. But then, like Jazmine said, perhaps karma would repay this act of kindness in the end.

"I don't know if she'll ever find her pride," the server said as he turned toward the woman's table, presumably to let the woman know that her bill had been paid.

Ava noticed Carolyn's eyes twinkling with amusement at their overture to the woman by the wall. They watched as the server spoke to the woman, and then waved when she looked their way and smiled.

But then, the woman's smile froze as she seemed to look back and forth between Jazmine and Ava. Ava turned to Jazmine to see if she noticed, but the smile on her face was just as frozen.

"Is something wrong?" Ava whispered.

"I hope not," Jazmine whispered back.

"Do you know her?" Carolyn asked.

"Actually, I do," Jazmine said, running her hand over her napkin as though to iron it out. "She is—was—the assistant on my bus."

"Huh," Ava said, hoping the woman didn't feel like a charity case knowing that a former colleague had paid her dinner bill.

"I must say," Carolyn said to Jazmine, "your gentle prodding with that server would have made for a great interview."

"And the perfect topic," Ava added.

"Not to mention," Carolyn continued, "that establishing a listenership would help you land a communications job once you get your degree."

Jazmine threw up her hands. "Since when did I decide to go back to school? And even if I found some kind of platform, just how would you suppose I supply relationship solutions that none of us are even close to having?"

Ava's shoulders slumped. Jazmine was right. From what little she knew about these two women, and what she knew all too well about herself, they were the *relationship impaired* leading the *relationship impaired.*

"We conduct some real-life research," Carolyn said, smiling up at the server as he set Ava's card and receipt on the table.

Ava felt something click inside her. "We can *all* research. Like, we date guys with the purpose of sorting out the do's from the don't's."

"Sure," Carolyn said, sounding anything but. "Or, you could interview men who've become better people, as well as the new women in their lives for whom they changed. If anyone had the answers, it would be them, wouldn't you think?"

"Answers," Ava murmured, deep in thought. "Oh my God," she suddenly gushed, then made her voice so soft the others had to lean in to hear her. "We could interview each other's exes!"

"Oh, hell no." Jazmine pushed back into her chair.

"Absolutely not," Carolyn agreed.

"In fact, if we're going to collaborate," Jazmine said, rifling through her purse until she brought out a pen and reached across the table for a cocktail napkin, "that's our first rule. No… researching… exes."

"Fine," Ava relented. "You're probably wanting something more like the conversation I had with my boss the other day."

Carolyn set down her wine glass abruptly and blinked a couple times too many. "What's that?"

"I told Mr. Mercer about our conversation the other night, about exes becoming the people we wish they could've been for us, and—"

"You *what?*" Carolyn asked, her eyes narrowing. Ava may not have been able to see the forehead wrinkles, but the vertical lines etched between Carolyn's eyebrows were familiar. The tension from their meeting at Carolyn's mother's house was making a comeback.

Ava gave an equally tense shrug. "He gave me some interesting insight."

"And we'll add a confidentiality clause to our collaboration agreement," Jazmine mumbled, jotting it down on the cocktail napkin.

"Agreed," Carolyn said, her tone matter-of-fact, keeping her gaze firmly fixed on Ava. "What did he say?"

"That men don't *always* get better after a relationship," Ava started.

"Just after relationships with the three of *us*, right?" Jazmine asked.

Ava gave her a half-hearted smile. "And he said it's not always the *men* who go on to become better people. Said he was once in love with someone who went off with some awful guy."

"Off where?" Carolyn asked.

"Don't know," Ava said, mixing her drink with the tiny straw that had come in the glass. She liked the clinking sound the ice cubes made. "He didn't get specific."

"And she became a better person for the 'awful guy'?" Jazmine asked.

"Naw, she left him," Ava said. "I guess she became a better person for herself. Too bad she didn't come back for Howard. He seems pretty much flagless to me."

"I'm sure he does after working for him all of two weeks," Carolyn said wryly, then straightened her posture as though she were ready to resume the main point of their meeting. "Well, women will dump men for all kinds of reasons. I'm sure his ex had hers."

Ava took a slow sip from her black straw and gave a mild shrug. "I once dumped a guy because he didn't like cheese."

Carolyn and Jazmine broke into laughter.

"How is 'not eating cheese' a red flag?" Jazmine asked.

"Who doesn't like cheese?" Ava asked, as though the answer was obvious. "He wasn't lactose intolerant or vegan—he just didn't like it. Plus, he always kept his phone turned over, like he didn't want me to see the texts coming in. I was probably being paranoid, but—"

"I doubt it," Carolyn said. "Marcus told me I was paranoid when I accused him of cheating. If I'd gone with my gut, I could have saved myself years of therapy after the truth surfaced when I finally caught on."

"Seems like red flags won't do us any good if we doubt ourselves when we see them," Jazmine said, then added, "Ooh, that's good." She clicked on her pen again and jotted it down.

They were both right, of course, as Ava recalled the cheese-hater turning over his phone. Funny, though. It made her remember Max at work. He'd done the same thing in the first meeting with Howard. Was his turning over the phone a red flag to monitor? Were these same red flags even applicable to working relationships? Ava didn't want this drinking game to cause suspicion or paranoia to reign.

"Dishonesty is a huge red flag for me," Jazmine said. "I dated a guy who said he lived on his family's estate. Turned out he was living in a trailer in his uncle's driveway."

This time, it was Ava's turn to laugh.

Carolyn waved the server over and gestured to her nearly empty wine glass. "I tried online dating back in New York, and one guy looked so good on paper, but he wore a hat and sunglasses in every picture."

"Let me guess," Jazmine said, "he was bald and had a lazy eye?"

"Spot on," Carolyn said, smiling broadly with her eyes wide in surprise. "The thing is, neither of those things would have bothered me if he'd just been honest in the first place. Then we just happened to 'bump into' his brother—who looked nothing like my short pudgy date and everything like Lorenzo Lamas—"

"Lorenzo who?" Ava asked.

Jazmine leaned in and explained. "He was a TV actor from the '90s who had luscious long hair."

"I think he arranged for him to be there to impress me somehow," Carolyn explained, "but he wound up spending the rest of the date talking with *him*. So then, when I got up to leave he said, 'Hey, I know you had a long drive out here—you're welcome to spend the night at my place.'"

"Ick," Jazmine said, looking as though she'd just bitten into a sour lemon. "All right, dishonesty is going on the list, along with euphemisms and shadiness."

Ava sipped from her black straw until the last of it made a slurping sound. "You'll probably think this is as silly as the cheese thing, but Gavin never put our picture on social media."

"Wait now, let me get this straight," Jazmine said. "You guys were living together, but he never made your relationship 'Facebook Official'?"

Ava felt her cheeks burn. "When you put it that way, it seems so obvious. Gavin just said his personal life was no one else's business and that I was being—"

"Too sensitive," Carolyn and Jazmine said in unison, as though they'd heard the same line themselves a million times.

"So typical," Carolyn said. "They gaslight us and say *we're* the ones who have the problem by being paranoid or too sensitive."

"Ben was always gaslighting me like that," Jazmine said. "But his jokes always seemed to come at my expense. And it was my fault that he was so controlling. If I could just do things right for once, he would loosen up."

Carolyn drained the last of her Pinot grigio, then waved her empty glass in small circles as she spoke. "Marcus told me I was being paranoid when I accused him of cheating. The worst thing, though, was when he'd go on and on and on so that I couldn't interrupt him."

"Sounds like a filibuster to me," a voice came from above them. All three of them looked up to see the server placing a full, chilled glass in front of Carolyn. "My ex filibustered me so much that I swear I had out-of-body experiences—making mental lists of what I would get at the grocery store later, or just imagining being in a relationship with someone who would actually listen to me."

Ava glanced over at Jazmine's cocktail napkin. "Be sure to add filibuster to the list."

Jazmine's list was now so long that she had to flip the cocktail napkin over.

"What list?" the server asked as he reached for Ava's empty glass and mouthed, *Refill?*

"Red flags," Ava said, while nodding to his second question.

"I'll give you a red flag," the server said. "When customers treat me rudely, it takes everything in my power to keep from telling their dates to run as fast and as far as they can. Not that they would listen to the waiter."

"Shoot, I didn't even listen to my dad when he warned me about Ben," Jazmine said. "He'd sniffed him out from the start."

"Just like all my mother's Chihuahuas over the years," Carolyn agreed, somewhat wistfully. "Somehow, with their yippy little snarls, they just knew."

"Your mom has only ever had Chihuahuas?" Ava asked.

"Is there any bigger red flag than that?" Carolyn asked.

The women laughed as the server left for Ava's refill.

"All right," Jazmine said, "any more red flags for us?"

"Neediness," Carolyn said.

"Trying to buy you with gifts," Ava added.

"Using dating to distract from the pain of his last breakup," Carolyn said.

"Being the victim," Ava said.

"Still living with his ex-wife," Carolyn said.

Ava and Jazmine trained an incredulous stare on her.

"You dated a guy who still lived with his ex-wife?" Jazmine asked.

"It was just the one date," Carolyn said, "which ended as soon as he said he was still living with her."

"Talk about a bullet dodged," Jazmine said, shaking her head as she wrote it down.

The server reappeared with Ava's second Midori sour, which she sipped as soon as he'd set it down. Though it felt ice cold on her tongue, it warmed her insides. She'd hit that sweet spot in her drinking, where life was filtered through rosé-colored glasses.

"Looks like you're *our* drinking buddy, now," Jazmine said, then started giggling. The more she giggled, the harder she giggled, until Ava wondered if she'd also hit her own sweet spot.

"But am I your roommate?" Ava asked, slyly.

"Ava, really, I don't want to impose," Jazmine started.

"Don't worry about other people," Ava insisted. "What do *you* want?"

Ava watched as Jazmine looked down and inhaled deeply, as though she were reaching into her core for the answer.

"Okay, roomie," Jazmine said. "Let's do this."

"I'll drink to that," Carolyn said, raising her wine glass.

As soon as Jazmine held up her cider, Ava thrust her glass towards theirs with such gusto, it was a miracle they all didn't shatter on impact. Instead, just as the folk singer strummed his last chord, the bar filled with the sound of their ringing glasses.

Jazmine

When spring quarter started, Jazmine sat in the Communications Building room 228, working to type as rapid-fire as the professor's lecture on Qualitative Communication Research Methodology. While coming back had felt like a homecoming of sorts, she knew she stood out among the twenty-year-olds in the classroom—she could almost pass for their den mother. When she glanced around the room, the boredom on their faces was apparent—and she understood it completely. Four years ago, exhausted by course upon course of media history, media formats, and media skills, she was only counting days till graduation—and she'd been dreading this class, in particular.

Now, it took all of ten minutes into this first day back in class to find herself enthralled by the professor's lecture on the differences between qualitative and quantitative research. She felt almost guilty that she didn't miss Henry the way she assumed most mothers would miss their kids. But the time away to study what she loved provided such relief and respite that she threw herself into her note-taking, checking her phone dutifully every so often for word from Lucinda. Only two texts had come in, from Ava and Carolyn, wishing her a good first day back to college, and she loved them—both the texts and the women sending them.

She typed notes from the professor's slide presentation, trying to refocus on his words, and forcing her thoughts back to her friends, and the image of *The Daily* that Carolyn had set on the Cider House table a few weeks prior. Jazmine still struggled to understand how she had unearthed that old article. She just couldn't buy that it had been her daughter, a Social Sciences major. The only thing Jazmine could figure was that Carolyn had done some research on her, and that didn't make any sense at all.

Jazmine came back into the present moment when the professor announced, "We're going to take these last few minutes to go over your final project, due ten weeks from today."

Jazmine's heart fluttered in panic, and she found it hard to breathe.

"You'll be establishing a media platform on a topic of your choice to…"

Media platform? Jazmine tried to wrap her head around the idea of calling a local radio news outlet to ask for a slot. Or she could do that blog-to-book idea that Carolyn had suggested—and which Ava had rejected on the basis of it being antiquated. Her Gen Z classmates would surely balk. She couldn't even begin to stress out over what topic she would choose when the professor continued.

"…you'll be using interviews and focus groups to collect information regarding a topical situation or social phenomenon involving human issues such as emotions, beliefs, relationships, societal roles or inequities."

This was what Jazmine was all about, yet not at all what she'd been expecting. She'd been looking forward to the monotony of homework—each textbook page opening her mind, her world—and every stroke of her highlighter giving her a picture of her future self. But a media platform? A topic of her own choosing?

With only five more minutes of class, she turned to gaze out the window for a quick mental escape. By some trick of the overcast light, she caught her reflection in it instead of the outside view. She studied her face and appreciated the vagueness—the closest she'd come to having her features airbrushed. Now that she was in her early thirties, her wide eyes had lost their naiveté, but the glass window helped omit the beginnings of crow's feet. Since she'd moved back in with Ava, the student loans she'd secured allowed her a couple minor luxuries such as having her hair done. She'd even started wearing makeup again.

And then, beyond her reflection, Jazmine caught sight of a man's head bobbing above the student traffic on the walkways. He had closely shaven hair and black skin that stood out in stark contrast with the white business collar beneath it. Of course, there were hundreds of black men who attended UW, but the suit this man was wearing narrowed the field—it had to be a professor. Still, it was silly to think it could be him—and even if it were, what then?

Then it hit her. The man on the walkway—the autism specialist Carolyn had referred her to—*he* had been the one who found that copy of *The Daily* and showed the article to Carolyn at one of their publishing meetings. As the professor gave his closing comments, Jazmine slipped quietly into her jacket and slipped her laptop into the computer bag, which she strapped across her chest, bandolier-style. Thankfully, one of the exit doors was right behind her desk, so she was able to leave before the hallways filled completely.

The stacked heels of Jazmine's knee-high boots pounded solid footsteps down the stairs, giving her an air of confidence she wished she actually felt. Once outside, she braced herself against the oncoming blustery spring wind. Although he was a full block ahead of her by now, Jazmine kept her eyes on that head, bobbing above the clusters of students, following him all the way down Skagit Lane. Every so often, he would turn and nod to other professors until, finally, she caught enough of a profile to make out the chiseled features that indeed belonged to Dr. Quentin Sims.

Jazmine stayed well back and watched as he made his way around the colossal library, and then the Drumheller Fountain before angling towards Guthrie Hall—home to the Psychology Department. This came as no surprise to Jazmine, of course, as that was where she'd met with him over a month ago with Henry—and where they'd been referred to the specialist working with Henry now.

As they passed by Rainier Vista, Jazmine could see Mount Rainier sitting majestically against a backdrop of *finally* blue sky. As Dr. Sims walked toward the building, Jazmine leaned her weight forward onto her toes to mute the pounding of her boot heels against the brick walkway and reconsidered whether she should continue following his long-legged gait. She could find a bench at the vista and admire the view.

She checked her phone for the time—fifty minutes until her next class. Jazmine flashed back to her conversation with Carolyn, conjuring the memory of the newspaper on the Cider House table. The feelings surged through her, fresh as when she'd first felt them, fortifying her with strength, will, and a perfectly valid reason for walking around the side of the building to use the same entrance she'd used with Henry. This time, she took the stairs, giving each an extra pound of her step to hear it echo up the stairway chamber. She swung open the door to the Psychology Department, ready to walk straight into his office. She'd forgotten about the receptionist's desk.

"Can I help you?" a student secretary asked. Her hair was shaven around the sides of her head with only the bangs left long.

"I'm here to speak with Dr. Sims," Jazmine said. "Is he in?"

"He is," the student-receptionist said with another head swoop to move the bangs, "but he's setting up to record right now."

Jazmine tilted her head.

"His podcast," she clarified. "*Insights and Information.* You're welcome to have a seat, but he may be awhile."

Jazmine gave a short nod and chose a chair along the wall facing the hallway which housed five professors' offices, including Quentin's. She crossed her legs, bouncing the upper one impatiently.

"Wait, are you here for the interview?" the receptionist asked.

"No," Jazmine said, reaching into her pocket for her phone. "Why? Is there a position opening?"

"I meant for the podcast," the receptionist said. "Sorry, I'm still pretty new here. I just thought maybe—"

"I'm here on other business," Jazmine said, the word *podcast* lingering in her mind. She'd never listened to one before, which she could never admit out loud as a Communications major. But it was a media platform, which she could use to give interviews. Then, Jazmine heard the words coming out of her mouth. "I'm hoping Dr. Sims can advise me."

What was she saying? She'd barely conceived the idea of the podcast, much less a topic. Yet, the words kept tumbling out, as though by saying them aloud, Jazmine could audition the idea the way she would a dress costume for a play, twirling around in front of a three-faced dressing room mirror. So, she sat there spouting the topic idea of relationship challenges to the open-faced receptionist. While putting it into words didn't make it a reality, it made it feel tangible, somehow. And the idea that she could actually make this happen—could actually fulfill her final project and don her graduation cap and the UW's purple and gold honor cords over her robe—caused a positively giddy feeling to bubble up inside her.

"I know who your first guest could be!" the receptionist gushed. "She works right here at the university—a professor in the World History Department. She's my stepmom, actually, but my dad definitely improved himself for her. Maybe she could give you some expert answers."

As the young woman scribbled a name, a door squealed open from down the hall and Quentin's baritone voice called, "Sophie, was that new microphone ever delivered?"

Jazmine watched as the receptionist moved toward a corner of the office to rifle through stacks of packages and manila envelopes. Quentin appeared in the hallway, fidgeting with a couple of power cords as though he were trying to distinguish one from the other.

"I think this might be it." The receptionist held out a small box to him.

Quentin took it and turned it over in his hands. "Perfect. What would I do without you, Sophie?"

"You have someone here to see you," his student-receptionist said.

For the first time, Quentin looked up and saw Jazmine. The slight strain in his expression melted into a broad smile as he made his way into the waiting room and extended a hand.

"Dr. Sims," Jazmine said, her words clipped, although she found herself at a strange fork in the road. The first prong had her chiding Dr. Sims for sharing her article, while the second had her genuinely needing his help for a podcast. In fact, she had him to thank for the very idea of the podcast, as inadvertent as his help in that had been.

"Ms. Johnston," Quentin replied graciously, clasping her hand in both of his.

Jazmine felt as though she'd slipped her hand into a glove her mother had warmed for her on the radiator. She knew she would take the second prong in the road when she lost herself in a sudden image of slipping her fingers through his.

"So good to see you again," he said, drawing Jazmine back from her reverie. "Although I recall we established a first-name basis at our last meeting."

Jazmine broke from his gaze, studying the pattern in the beige carpet. "I was hoping I could have a moment to talk with you."

"I've got my podcast guests coming any time now," Quentin said, glancing hesitantly at the office door. "I may only have a moment right now." He turned from the door until he had her eye. "But for you, I'm all ears."

Jazmine walked beside Quentin down the blue-painted hallway, breathing in his soft, spiced cologne. She glanced at the framed crayon drawings by past patients, hung between office doors. All the while, she wondered what he'd just meant. *But for you…*

"How's the little man?" Quentin asked. "And his new specialist?"

Jazmine quickened her step to keep beside Quentin's long strides, processing his questions. *Little man.* Had he heard her use that term with Henry during their one evaluation session—and cared enough to remember? Or did he use that term for all his male patients whose names he couldn't remember?

"I'm already seeing improvement," she finally said. "Turns out there are ways I can approach him that help preempt or de-escalate his tantrums. I can't tell you how much I appreciate each and every avoided meltdown, especially with so many more school demands on my time."

He held his office door open for her. "Funny how we always think of changing *their* behavior when the key is often changing our own."

"Exactly." Jazmine nodded and looked around his office. She noticed the aroma steamer wasn't on today, like it was when she'd been there a few weeks before to have Henry evaluated. Perhaps he hadn't had a chance to turn it on yet, or maybe he didn't want to record the gurgling sound during his podcast. Finally, Jazmine looked down, pursed her lips, and got back to her purpose for being there.

"To be honest, I'm not here to talk about Henry."

Quentin raised an eyebrow. "That so?"

"Look, with all due respect and appreciation for your help, I'd like to know why you were talking to Carolyn Ford about me."

"When she referred you to me?" he asked.

"No, when you showed her that old article from *The Daily.*"

"Oh, that. It was a good article." He shrugged, as if that were that.

"But how did you even know I wrote for the university paper?" Jazmine asked. "And what about doctor-patient confidentiality?"

"Jazmine, with all due respect—and appreciation for your candor—you didn't write that article during Henry's evaluation. In fact, *The Daily* is a public medium."

Jazmine nodded, tracing the desk's wood grain with her finger in order to avoid his gaze. Had she really resorted to such convoluted rationalization just to talk to Quentin again? The table was so shiny, she was pretty sure his reflection was staring back at her.

"Truth be known," he said, "when I saw Carolyn, I probably focused on your article to create a bit of interference for myself."

"What do you mean, 'interference'? Like I'm an offensive tackle or something?"

She didn't expect Quentin to laugh so robustly. "In a way, but a more delicate bit of distraction, I'd say. I had to let Carolyn know I was going with a different publisher for my new book. I used your article to change the subject. If this made things difficult with you or broke a trust with us, I am sincerely sorry."

"So, Carolyn isn't currying favor with you by encouraging my writing?" she asked.

Quentin folded his hands on the desk. "Ms. Ford's type of overture is extended only to a minute number of talented writers."

Jazmine felt her posture straighten. "Well, sure, if I want to take time away from Henry. Seems like the goal these days is to get the writing to go viral, which shouldn't be more important than the content of what I write."

Quentin nodded, then shook his head and spoke softly. "An industry-savvy trainer wants to help get you ready for the ring. I'm still not getting how that's a bad thing?"

"It's time I don't have and work I don't have the energy to do. I mean, I'm fine to write an editorial for a university paper or coming up with a podcast for my Communications class, but building a platform? I feel like I went from zero to a hundred in the two months I've known this woman."

Quentin gave a hearty laugh. "That sounds like Carolyn. You're in good hands, though. And what *if* your writing went viral? Wouldn't it be worth the work?"

"Not if I'm losing time with my son."

Quentin rubbed his chin with his knuckles. "Why not work from home? You might even get more time with your son that way. But you know," Quentin paused and raised an eyebrow, his deep brown eyes glistening, "she can provide all the guidance you allow her to, but—to quote my nine-year-old niece—she's not the boss of you."

Jazmine felt the corner of her mouth tug into a grin. The thought of this man spending time with his little niece endeared him to her.

"You could tell her 'no' anytime. Tell her to go back where she came from."

Jazmine giggled. "The phone store?"

"Carolyn Ford came from a phone store?" Quentin asked, his face broadening into that smile he'd shone when he first saw Jazmine in the waiting room.

Jazmine couldn't contain her own smile. "No, that's where I met her. She was great with Henry, and we became friends soon after."

Quentin nodded and reached across the desk, as though to put his hand on Jazmine's—but seemed to think better of it when he pulled back. "Look, all I'm saying is that you could take a chance. Accept the fact that for once the universe is conspiring in your favor. Build that platform. Record that podcast."

Jazmine felt her eyes grow wide.

"It's easy," Quentin said. "And fun, even for a technological amateur like me. You could even record your first interview here, when you're ready. I can run the equipment while you do your thing, whatever that may be."

As exciting as the prospect was of spending more time with Quentin Sims, it was even more mortifying to think of him in such close proximity to her fledgling topic of choice. How shallow would it seem that she was exploring pop relationship psychology next to the depth of his research in autism? Jazmine shook her head. There she went again finding reasons not to stretch her own wings. After all, he didn't seem disingenuous about liking her article about single mothers as university students. In fact, he seemed legitimately impressed.

Jazmine jumped in her seat when someone knocked at the professor's door. Sophie poked her head through. "The Hendricksons are here to see you."

An older couple entered the room. Both husband and wife had hair they'd allowed to gray naturally. Their open smiles radiated genuine kindness.

Quentin rose and leaned across his desk to shake each of their hands. "So glad you could come share your experience. Our podcast listeners have a great deal to gain. Actually, I have one of those people here, now—who would gain from hearing about your experience. No idea whether she's a listener."

Jazmine sat there, wondering whether to stand or remain seated. Despite the fact that she'd known full well Quentin had this appointment when he agreed to talk to her, part of Jazmine craved for this couple to leave—to have him back to herself. *But he's a professor,* she reminded herself. *And even if he wasn't, a guy like this couldn't possibly be available.* She shook off her musings of the impossible and rose to greet the couple.

"Nice to meet you," the woman said, and then offered her hand until Jazmine rose to shake it. "Camille Hendrickson." The early-spring coldness of her palm was a bit of a shock after Quentin's warm bear paws. Her husband stood behind her, unzipping his parka.

"Camille heads the Neuropsychology Department here at the U," Quentin said. "And Russell retired from that same department a few years ago. They have an adult daughter with autism who's been able to live on her own in a nearby apartment and is very successful as an information technologist."

"Now we foster autistic kids," Russell said. "Retirement gives me time to take care of the kiddos and have dinner ready for Camille when she gets home."

"That's...amazing," Jazmine said.

"Jazmine has an autistic son," Quentin said. "I evaluated him a few weeks ago. I don't know how Jazmine's been doing it on her own up till now."

Mr. Hendrickson turned and faced Jazmine. "We know the challenges, dear, so I've no doubt you're quite amazing yourself."

"She most definitely is," Quentin said.

Jazmine's cheeks burned at the same time as her jaws clenched. To hear compliments on her parenting—from autism experts, no less—meant the world to her. Still, she couldn't help herself. "You're doing it again."

"Doing what?" Quentin asked. When Jazmine widened her eyes in warning, he nodded. "Ah, yes. My apologies. Jazmine's just okay. Your run-of-the-mill person. No big deal, really."

Jazmine's pursed lips found their way into a wry half-grin and she elbowed him gently, enjoying the feeling of familiarity. Quentin chuckled.

"It's always good to laugh," Russell said. "We never could have survived this wild ride if we hadn't learned to let loose now and then. Right, honey?"

Camille nodded. That explained their expressions entirely. Their wrinkles didn't age them because they were mixed with laugh lines. Jazmine felt a sudden urge to storm them with questions. Would she ever learn to laugh with Henry? Or to laugh through a tantrum? Or was it only in hindsight that the laughter came?

"Let me give you my card," Camille said, her sky-blue eyes earnest and kind as she fumbled through her purse. "Please call on us if you need to talk."

"Or want some help with your son," Russell added. "You probably already have a network, but we'd be happy to be a part of it."

Camille handed Jazmine her business card. "Well, Dr. Sims, shall we take a seat?"

"Please do," Quentin said. "I'll be right back once I see Jazmine off."

He held the door open for her and walked her back down the hall. The fragrance of his cologne warmed her once more. The hallway was narrow enough that they walked closely together—close enough that she could feel the warmth emanating from him, that she had to fight the urge to lean into him.

"Sophie," Quentin said as they rounded the corner to the receptionist's desk. "Would you have a few minutes to walk Jazmine through the process of recording a podcast?"

"Of course," Sophie chirped.

Jazmine glanced at the clock. "I have fifteen minutes for a lightning tour. Thank you," she told Sophie. Then she turned to Quentin. "And you."

This time, when Quentin held Jazmine's gaze, she didn't look away.

Past, Meet Present

Ava

Ava folded her hands on the table, listening to her thirtieth pitch of the day. It was at least her fifteenth pitch of retirees who had finally gotten themselves going on that book they had always wanted to write. In this case, the woman was sweet-faced, wearing a paisley scarf around her head, tied at the nape of her neck. Ava envied her light, flowing maxi-dress, as she herself had dressed far too warmly for late April, which had switched overnight from non-stop rain to 60-degree sunshine. It was all Ava could do not to fan herself with the woman's query letter.

"I wrote a children's story," the woman started, "for my grandchildren. I can already tell you they love it, so I have no doubt it could become very popular."

Ava tried to keep her face placid as she made the first mental check. She was surprised by how many people were willing to spend hundreds of dollars to attend a writers conference without reading what agents were seeking and what they weren't—which, in the case of Howard Mercer Literary, was *not* children's books.

At the table to her right, Howard sat taking his pitches, looking especially professional in a dark gray blazer and a crew neck of the same color. She noticed he'd grown ruddy in his forehead and cheeks.

She could hear the man pitching implore him. "But it's been revised."

Howard leaned in. "It doesn't fit with our list, sir."

The man stood and slammed his palms on the table, spittle flying as he shouted, "You're turning down a bestseller!"

As the writer stomped away, Ava heard Howard mumble, "How many times have I heard that before?"

Ava felt for Howard. In her own interactions, she'd had only positive experiences at the conference—at least, so far. She quietly knocked on the underneath of the pressed wood table, lest she jinx it.

"Oh my," said the elderly woman in front of Ava. There'd been such a long pitch list over the last two hours that she'd already forgotten the woman's name. She glanced at the writer's conference badge. Beverly.

"Anyway, as I was saying, it's about a little girl who finds a fairy and captures her in a glass bottle," Beverly continued. "She leaves her there overnight and finds her dead in the morning."

Before she could stop herself, Ava gasped in horror. "The little girl suffocates the fairy to death?"

"Yes, so then she…"

As Beverly continued to prattle on, Ava wondered about her own father pitching novel after novel, to no avail. Had the agents felt as taken about by his crazy ideas as she did by this woman's fairy killing book? Were they as cruel to him as Roxi Fischer, taking pitches at the table to her left, whose writer was now tearing up and sniffling? Damn. Howard had told Ava how Ms. Fischer prided herself on making authors cry right there at her pitch table. The cutthroat agent appeared almost exactly as Howard had described her, wearing stiletto heels and enough eyeliner to give her an appearance as sinister as her reputation. He'd also mentioned that the woman was determined to sign Wesley McBride.

At any rate, as Beverly got to the end of her pitch, Ava renewed her vow never to make a writer cry. Yet, how on earth could she let this project down gently? Even if there was a moral to the story, which, as Ava listened, there didn't seem to be, there was no way a book that gave children nightmares would ever sell. She glanced surreptitiously at the clock on the far wall. Only two more minutes until the pitch sessions were over. Then, she'd have twenty minutes to find the main conference room for the *Who's New in Publishing* panel.

"I'm glad your grandchildren will treasure your story," Ava said, "but I'm afraid Howard Mercer Literary doesn't represent children's books. Let me highlight the names of a few agents here who do. May I?"

Beverly nodded and handed Ava her conference program, which she flipped through and put a star by three agents' names, itching to get out that door before the big rush. It was imperative that she catch up with Wesley before Roxi did.

"But I didn't sign up for those agents." Beverly's pale green eyes grew watery.

"Tell you what," Ava said. "I'll see if they have any open spots and try getting you in. Do you have a business card?"

"No." The woman sounded defeated. "Should I?"

"How about if I take a quick picture of your name badge?" Ava offered, pulling out her phone.

"I suppose that would be fine," Beverly said, holding it out for Ava to zoom in on. "I appreciate this very much."

"Of course," Ava said. "There's also a presentation on self-publishing coming up soon. That might be a promising option for you, as well."

"Why?" Beverly asked in alarm. "You don't think anyone will publish my book?"

Ava glanced at the open door just as Wesley McBride walked past on the way to his next presentation. Roxi seemed to have noticed him too. They locked eyes. Ava narrowed her eyelids. Roxi raised an eyebrow. It was on.

"I'm sorry," Ava said. "Our time's up and I really need to be going. I wish you all the best and hope you'll keep writing."

Ava shot straight to the door, casting one last glance back at Roxi, who was still finishing her last pitch. She had at least a couple of minutes on her.

Volunteers for the Seattle Writers Conference scurried past Ava in the Westin Hotel hallway. Ava found Wesley turning a corner far down the hall and stepped eagerly behind him, trying to catch up, but her heels against the hotel's carpet were working against her.

"Mr. McBride," she called when she knew she was in earshot.

The tall, stocky man stopped and turned. His weathered face and kind brown eyes gave him a semblance of a man on his way to play poker in some southwest saloon, rather than a best-selling author who regularly signed six-figure deals with any and all of the "Big Five" New York publishers. He shot Ava a broad smile.

"Heya, kid. You here with *Klipsun*? How are things since…?"

Ava lowered her head. She'd gotten used to speaking of her father in the past tense since he'd passed, but talking about him with an old friend carried too much sting for a public setting such as this. And to tell him she was self-publishing his magnum opus—albeit under the guidance of Carolyn Ford—seemed strange to say just before pitching him to sign with her agency. So, she placed her focus on his first question.

"I've gone in a different direction, actually," Ava said as she sidled up beside him. Various writers passed by them, sneaking glances at their conference faculty name badges. Ava reached into her pocket for one of her freshly printed business cards. "For two months now, I've been agenting for Howard Mercer Literary."

"Well, good for you," he said, taking the proffered business card. "Hope Howard knows how lucky he is to have you."

Ava raised an eyebrow. "He will as soon as I land my first major author."

Wesley gave a wry smile. "I guess you've heard, huh?"

"That you're between agents?" Ava asked. "I have—and I'm wondering if we'd be able to discuss Howard's Agency and what we can offer that exceeds our competitors."

Wesley shifted his weight and put his thumbs through his belt loops. "Well, I got weary from all the excuses my last agent couldn't come through for me. Now, I'm in the market for an agent who's available to represent me without a hundred other things going on in their private life to keep them from business as usual."

Ava wanted to scream, *I'm available!* But she knew she had to play this one just right. "It sounds like you need a young agent with no other commitments outside of her job—someone hungry to start building her list." She gestured at herself. "Take me. I have no life."

Wesley's head fell back as he roared with laughter. Passersby slowed down to see what the noise was about.

Ava felt her cheeks burn. "I mean, I have no family obligations, nothing that would stand in the way of selling your books."

Wesley pursed his lips and narrowed his eyes at Ava as though he might be seriously considering her offer. "You make a good point. If you were a little more established—"

"But that's the beauty of going with Howard Mercer Literary," Ava said. "Who's more established in Seattle—on the whole West Coast, really—than Howard? You'd be getting a package deal. With our agency, you'll get sales, not excuses."

Ava gave a jolt when she looked over to find Roxi standing right beside her.

"I overheard Howard asking where you were," Roxi told her. "We've only got ten minutes before the *Who's New in Publishing* panel."

Wesley nodded. "I also need to set up for my presentation on author branding," he said.

"Of course," Ava said, probably too quickly.

Wesley held up her card with one hand and extended his other to shake. "I'll give you a call, kiddo."

"Thank you so much," Ava said, careful not to squeeze the life out of his oversized hand. She released her grip, turned, and hurried back to help Howard set up their own presentation, wanting more than anything to skip down the hallway. She could hardly wait to tell Howard. She didn't even care that Roxi was hitting Wesley up right this minute. She would be nothing more than an annoyance holding him back from his presentation. Ava had gotten to him first and had made a perfect impression. Close enough, anyway. Even when her cell rang in with yet another bill collector's auto-call, she didn't feel the usual stress over the impending repossession of her car. Let them take it! As soon as she sold just one of Wesley McBride's books, she'd treat herself to a nice, silver Porsche.

Once inside the main conference room, Ava made her way along the side wall to the front stage, where Howard was speaking with Ted Cavanaugh, a bigwig with the Seattle Library System and the emcee of their upcoming panel. On the stage, Max was helping the volunteers push two long tables together for the three agencies on the panel. From the conference room floor, Dahlia handed up his coffee cup, probably full of green tea.

Ava gazed out at rows upon rows of aspiring writers, her gait light as she moved toward the stage. She had no words of actual experience for these hopefuls, much less any advice from years invested in the industry. Yet, while she did have memory after memory of her father typing away at each doomed manuscript, it was her moment with Wesley that seemed to have injected her with a hit of confidence. She had the potential to sign any writer out there—the potential to put any one of those open, eager faces on the map. She couldn't wait to have Howard Mercer introduce her as his newest agent on their *Who's New in Publishing* panel. Her kimono-style wrap flowed behind her as she ascended the stairs to the stage, making her feel like Superwoman.

"Shoot," Howard mumbled as he took his seat. "Looks like they've only got two microphones for both tables." He fiddled with the microphone cord and sighed.

"That means we'll have to pass the thing back and forth between you, me, and whoever's sitting here." Ava gestured at the empty spot on the other side of her, then glanced at the nameplate on the table. "TBD," she read aloud. "That's kind of generic." Her own nameplate gave her first and last name and agency, as did every other nameplate at the table.

"To Be Determined," Howard said. "Probably weren't able to get the guy's name in time to print his nameplate."

"All right, boss, one black coffee for you," Dahlia chirped, suddenly standing before them with two steaming cups in her hands and a manila folder pinched precariously between her elbow and ribs. She handed the first cup to Howard, then turned to Ava. "And one white coffee for you."

Ava thanked her, took the warm cup, and stirred it absently with the two little red straws that the assistant had included.

"Everything is in here," Dahlia said. "Conference itinerary, pitch list, presentation notes." She took the empty seat on the other side of Ava, set the folder on the table, and sorted through it with her glossy nails. It appeared she'd taken a curling iron to her hair this morning, and her figure looked especially petite in a fitted, cream-colored cashmere sweater and gold-trimmed brocade miniskirt.

"Much appreciated," Howard said, as she closed the folder and handed it to him. He took it and absently set it aside.

"I was able to get in a good word with Wesley in the hall just now," Ava mentioned, working to sound nonchalant and professional and not at all as giddy as she felt.

Howard paged through the materials in the folder, then looked up into space. Finally, he turned to her. "McBride?" he asked.

"The one and only," Ava said, feeling her giddiness spill over.

"Excellent work," Howard said with an impressed nod.

"How were the pitches?" Dahlia asked them.

"Rough," Howard said. "I can't believe I have to do this all over again in New York next month. I wish I could send you or Max instead."

Ava yearned to go to the Big Apple in Howard's stead, but she knew she was much too green to take on an exponentially longer pitch list than she'd just endured at their little Seattle conference. Plus, she didn't want to miss the Seattle Literary Society Awards Ceremony, now that she'd finally scored an invite. She couldn't wait to represent Howard's agency there, and she knew she'd get her chance to go to New York soon enough.

"Is this your first conference panel?" Dahlia asked Ava. "You must be so excited!"

"And nervous," Ava said. "It's not like this is new to me—I used to have the final say on every work to be published in *Klipsun Literary*—but I hardly ever saw the authors' faces, let alone three hundred of them at once." Ava didn't add that *Klipsun* was a little literary journal, with maybe 2,000 readers. As an agent, her authors had the potential to be read the world over.

"You've got this," Dahlia said. "The agent-editor after-party is the best. Wish I could be there, but I've got a date."

"That's awesome," Ava said, wondering why she insisted on using that insipid word "awesome" in front of Howard Mercer. What was this, 1985? At the same time, her internal organs clenched at the fact that Dahlia had another potential dalliance. But then, Ava reminded herself that she had too much to do in building her career to have any time left over for dating.

"Where did Max go?" Ava asked.

"He's over there talking to Roxi Fischer," Dahlia said, nodding to the opposite side of the room.

Ava glanced over and found Roxi laughing at something Max had said. She felt the butterflies in her stomach suffocate like in that writer's fairy death-jar. It actually looked like that shark was flirting with an agent two-thirds her age. That was all she could surmise until she was distracted by a familiar fragrance of lemon and lavender coming from behind her.

Howard looked up slowly from his folder and turned to ask Dahlia a question.

"Excuse me. I believe this is my seat," someone said to Dahlia.

Ava didn't turn when she saw Howard watching Dahlia's baby blue eyes grow ever wider. Ava couldn't quite place the familiarity at first, but she instantly recognized the voice and spun around to see Carolyn Ford standing over them in all her professional poise and attire.

Without a word, Dahlia vacated the chair designated for "TBD" and slipped into an empty seat along the wall beside the stage. Ava watched her pull out her phone and smile at whatever text or email glowed from the screen.

Carolyn waved to Roxi and Max and, in one motion, eased into her chair with a sophistication matched only by her silk tunic and palazzo pants. Ava wondered whether it was the plum color of her outfit or the crystal chandeliers above them that seemed to turn Carolyn's hair redder and her eyes a brilliant emerald color.

"So good to see you," she whispered to Ava and pulled her over for a side hug. "How are things going with your new roomies?"

"They're great," Ava said, and they were. She wished she could tell Carolyn all about the move-in, but she could feel Howard's eyes on them. The familiar affection Carolyn had shown Ava at the Cider House now felt awkward. As Carolyn released her, Ava could feel herself grow hot, suddenly closed in by the two publishing powerhouses on either side of her.

"What are you doing here?" Ava whispered back. "I thought Advance Publishing had—"

"I want to start by thanking everyone for being here," the panel moderator began, "from our aspiring authors to those published, to our agents and editors on the panel. I'm Ted Cavanaugh, head of Seattle Public Libraries for what? Thirty-seven years now? I was going to start us off with a true Seattle institution and my old friend, Howard Mercer, but it seems to make more sense if we start from one end of the table and go in order."

Ava listened as Mr. Cavanaugh continued. He was a local institution himself—middle-aged with mussed gray hair and forever wearing tweed blazers and brightly colored bow ties. Any other city might have written him off as eccentric, but Seattle had embraced his quirks along with his love for all things literary.

"So, let's start with Seattle native and an old friend to many of us, recently returned to our Apple State from the Big Apple itself: Carolyn Ford."

Howard kept aiming his gaze forward as he took the microphone and passed it across Ava to Carolyn. "Good morning, everyone," she began. "Most of you know me from Advance Publishing, based in New York. But I actually grew up here in Seattle."

Ava listened as the crowd murmured approvingly, although she noted a few people shifting uncomfortably in their seats.

"I even got my start in a little company run by four people in a boxy white building down on First Ave," Carolyn said before glancing Howard's way.

Ava looked at her boss as well and found him scribbling something on his notepad. She pictured Howard and Carolyn in the boxy white building in early '90s Seattle—him with long, grungy hair and a Kurt Cobain-style cardigan, and her in draw-string flared pants, a long, silk blazer, and chunky, stacked loafers. As hard as she tried, she couldn't imagine Carolyn being less professional than she was now.

Carolyn continued, "Today, you might call it a 'start-up,' but for us, it was an experiment—to see if we could launch the first internet bookstore. I'm guessing you've bought from it once or twice since it opened."

The audience chuckled. This time, it was Howard who shifted in his seat.

"Too bad I didn't buy stock in it then," she added, followed by more polite laughter.

"Howard and I always worked well together," Carolyn continued. "Now that we're in closer proximity, perhaps we'll come full circle."

Ava saw through the glowing smile Carolyn shined at the audience to the timid way she raised her eyebrows at Howard. The audience probably saw Howard grinning, but only Ava was close enough to see the jaws grinding behind a forced smile.

Ava listened as Carolyn outlined what Ava already knew about her, although she was more candid than what Ava remembered reading about her in *Publishers Marketplace*. "After my move to New York," she continued, "I used what I'd learned to start a small press."

As Carolyn explained how her small press had been bought as an imprint and absorbed into one of New York's most distinguished publishing houses, Ava noticed Max, seated on the other side of Howard, gazing at the clock on the far wall.

Carolyn was winding down her pitch for her new Ford Publishing when she emphasized her current acquisition list in nonfiction for women's psychology, health, and well-being. Ava couldn't help feeling discouraged that her father's book didn't fit into Carolyn's list, although with her luck, their friendship could well be a conflict of interest.

Carolyn finished her introduction with the words, "No memoir, please." She paused and smiled back at the audience when her last statement earned a rueful chuckle from those in the know. Ava sipped her coffee, admiring how Carolyn had slipped in an acknowledgment of the elephant she owned. Her acknowledgement and disarming smile had probably diffused any attention on the scandal.

Carolyn handed the mic over to Ava when a whispered voice came over the sound system. "…Like it's a joke," a woman rasped, "…promoting a hoax just to scam millions of readers is hardly laughable…"

The audience went silent, everyone looking at the eyes bulging from Roxi Fischer's makeup-spackled sockets.

"Howard," Mr. Cavanaugh started, as though he'd been oblivious to what Roxi had inadvertently blurted to the room, "why don't you introduce yourself—"

Ava began handing the mic to Howard when Carolyn snatched it out of her hands. Screeching feedback pierced the air.

"Excuse me." Carolyn winced at the static as she spoke into the microphone.

Ava expected a cat fight to follow, but then noticed her friend relax. When Carolyn spoke soothingly, it was almost as though everyone in the room had become her confidant.

"I've obviously made my share of mistakes," Carolyn said. "But in this case, I researched everything that was available at the time. Unfortunately, the damning evidence didn't come out until the book was published. If it had come out before, I would have dropped the book immediately."

Hands went up in the audience.

"We'll take questions as soon as introductions are done," Mr. Cavanaugh said, tapping his mic to get order in his court. "Howard, are you ready to introduce your agency and your new agent?"

Once again, Carolyn passed the mic to Ava, who passed it further left to Howard. He unbuttoned his blazer, as though he needed room to breathe.

"I'm Howard Mercer. I opened Howard Mercer Literary in 1997 and have signed and placed hundreds of books with publishers, from sports biographies to YA fantasy to cookbooks. I'm here today with our new literary agent, Ava Perkins, who will tell you a little about herself and what she's looking to sign."

When Howard handed off the cold metal microphone to Ava, she felt tanks of nerves collide in her stomach. She was on.

"Indeed, indeed," Cavanaugh said. "We need to hear from Seattle's newest literary agent, a former editor from Klipsun Press. A warm welcome to the front lines, Ava Perkins."

Carolyn reached under the table to give Ava an encouraging pat on the wrist. Ava glanced at Howard, who appeared too shell-shocked by Carolyn's peace offering to shift his attention to his new associate agent.

"Thank you, Mr. Cavanaugh, and hello to all the hopeful authors out there," Ava said with a wave to the audience. "I know you wouldn't be here if you weren't dedicated to the important craft of writing." She sipped from the water bottle, worrying that her voice was shaking too much and that her wave was too cutesy. "I'm looking forward to helping bring your work together with a world of readers always primed for a compelling read." Ava paused, gulping her water this time. Was she being too over-the-top?

"I'm the new junior agent for Howard Mercer. Since I'm just starting out, I thought I'd tell you a little about the difference I see in being an agent and working as an editor." She continued on with her experience in acquiring short stories and essays for *Klipsun* and described an agent as an intermediary between the author and the editing department of a publishing house. Ava concluded her introduction, hoping she hadn't rambled on, but was comforted when

Howard shot her a steadying wink. She took a deep breath and, with a sweep of her hand, told the audience members that she was now formally open to queries for mainstream, historical, and women's fiction.

"I'm just building my list, but to the writers in my stable, I'm expecting productive relationships." Ava swallowed hard. Had she really said that? Her face reddened. She couldn't even enjoy a successful romantic relationship—how bold a promise to make when she had yet to sign a client?

Howard murmured, "Nice job, kiddo," as Mr. Cavanaugh moved on to Max.

"I started working for Howard Mercer five years ago as a lowly intern." Max paused for the brief audience chuckle. "I've since worked my way up to senior agent. In fiction, I'm looking to sign literary, sci-fi, fantasy, and some Young Adult. In non-fiction, I'm looking for quirky pop-culture and current events."

As Max passed the mic to Roxi, Ava feared that she'd spoken far too long.

Ms. Fischer started in on her beginnings working in a recording company, of all places. She dropped names of musicians and bands from the 1980s, all of which would have been fascinating to Ava if she weren't still annoyed with Roxi for talking behind Carolyn's back over the entire sound system. Ava glanced quickly at Howard, and then Carolyn. Both seemed to stare over the tops of the heads of the assembled writers in the crowd, as disengaged from what Roxi was saying as Ava was, until she finally finished her introduction.

"All right, we're ready for audience participation," Mr. Cavanaugh said. "Who has a question for our agents?" Several hands went up again, and he chose the one nearest to him.

The woman stood up and asked, "Can you tell us more about the author-agent relationship?"

"I'm sure it'll come as no surprise that I believe the cornerstone of any editor-author relationship is honesty," Carolyn said. A few audience members nodded knowingly or whispered to one another, no doubt about the scandal. "Lies can cost both money and careers. I think everyone up here would agree that we'd rather deal with the truth than be blindsided. Are you falling behind in your edits? Do you need more guidance in your revision? We need to hear from you to make sure everyone is—pun intended, here—on the same page."

More audience chuckles. Ava marveled at Carolyn's presence on this stage and how she seemed to loosen the audience up more and more with each comment she made.

Howard reached across Ava for the microphone. "While I agree with Ms. Ford, I would argue that honesty and communication go hand in hand. You don't want to become a nuisance, but your agent—or editor," he acknowledged Carolyn with a polite gesture of his hand, "need to know what's going on. A person might think he—or *she*—is being honest by simply omitting the truth. If the cards aren't all there, laid out face-up on the table, then the relationship itself is doomed."

Ava had to keep herself from glancing back and forth at the conversational volley happening at either side of her. What had started as a discussion on publishing seemed to have morphed into a different topic entirely.

On the other end of the panel, Roxi Fischer answered the question with the authority that comes from years of rejecting writers. "So many people have read so many books that they seem to think they can all write one. But how many of them take the time to learn the craft?"

"Good writing isn't just about the product—it's about the process," Carolyn argued. "There are many ways we all strive to better ourselves." She paused, then regarded the audience, as though she'd forgotten they were there. "You can take classes or hire high-quality editors."

Howard reached for the microphone from the agent on the other side of him. "This is all true, but ultimately, it *is* about the final product." He stopped and looked Carolyn square in the eye. "There are no second chances."

It dawned on Ava that when they'd met at the Cider House, Carolyn hadn't been dismayed by the fact that Ava had shared their conversation with Howard. She'd been appalled because she *was* the woman who had moved across the country for Marcus—or as Howard had referred to him, "the asshole."

A montage of phrases of the past months echoed through Ava's mind.

...She was dating a total asshole...

...my ex-slut of a husband...

...Next thing I know, she moves across the country and starts her own business...

...She became a better person once she found out he was an asshole and divorced him...

...So, she became a better person in spite of him...

The microphone picked up Ava's gasp so that it echoed throughout the conference hall.

"Sorry," Ava said into the mic. She scooted her chair a foot away from the table, and while Max steered the discussion to a more neutral topic, Howard and Carolyn shot a quick look at one another, and then glared in unison at her. She avoided both by looking past Howard at Max, who smiled back at her, completely oblivious to the connection she'd just made.

Carolyn

Carolyn's heels pounded down the sidewalk as she wove through the people in her way. It was a wonder she didn't slip on the rain-slick concrete, yet nothing could slow her down now that humiliation was driving her once more. She'd thought she could outrun it when she left New York. Now that Howard had just humiliated her at that stupid panel, where was she supposed to go?

Each click of her heels brought on the word *STU-pid, STU-pid, STU-pid* like an indignant mantra. She never should have given in to Sophie's request to get in touch with him. She could just as well have lied about reaching out and being rejected, and Sophie would never have known.

STU-pid pictures.

STU-pid memories.

STU-pid her.

At the corner of First Street, she didn't so much as glance at the white, boxy building where they'd worked together. She continued on, down the hill to Alaskan Way, until she found herself in front of the OK Hotel. Her skin and hair grew wet under the misty drizzle as she read the new sign: OK HOTEL APARTMENTS AND ARTIST SUITES.

And then, all she saw was a younger, lankier Howard, leaning against the brick wall in a faded band T-shirt and ripped up jeans. It was the Howard she'd worked with, entering data incessantly into the old Mac Plus computers. The Howard who had driven her home from work, stopping off at Christo's on Alki Avenue for pizza and beer and a midnight stroll on the beach. His hair had been golden brown, hanging to his shoulders on one side and tucked behind his ear on the other. Even now she melted just a little at the memory of his face breaking into a smile. She wanted to put a hand to his cheek and gently stroke that dimple beneath his eye.

Carolyn recalled that night at the OK Hotel—how Howard had breathed the word "wow" into the night air, and how she'd grinned and bit down gently at the side of her bottom lip. Yet as they'd stood in the presence of leering show-goers and homeless men alike, Carolyn had wished she'd put a jacket on over her black lace top that showed through to her black lace bra. She'd pulled her dreads into a bun on top of her head and made up her face with charcoal eyes and lips so crimson dark, they bordered on purple.

The two of them pushed through the crowd, drawn toward the pulsing rhythm, the stage lit up like a warehouse rave. Everywhere Carolyn looked there was a member of one band or another, free to talk amongst themselves.

The singer on stage had Cleopatra eyes and an elaborate headdress. Carolyn had swayed, her arms up in the air, hands moving like those of a Hindu folk dancer, completely lost in the music. The lights rang with vibrancy and the music became tangible in the air; the air breathed with her—it *was* her, and she was it—hot and musty and languid. She made love to the beat of the song, moving her hips slowly, like a belly dancer writhing in ecstasy.

"Carrie, you okay?" he'd asked.

Her head rolled around on her neck, searching for the body that belonged to that voice. Oh, yes, there he was. "I don't think I've ever been so okay in all my life!"

He'd cocked his head and said, "You're dancing with the wall."

Carolyn turned to see the flat surface she'd been rubbing up against, flashing colors from the stage lights, like undulating waves of cotton candy. She turned back to face him and ran a strand of his wavy, shoulder-length liquid caramel through her fingers. "Anyone ever tell you that your hair is delicious?"

He tilted her chin and she was sure he could see straight to her core. Her pulse quickened, her chest swelled, feeling him uncover the secrets within her. The music throbbed in his eyes, his velvet hand on her chin and jawline, and she leaned forward, yearning to drink him in. She bit her bottom lip.

"Carrie," his voice came again, a hand gently shaking her shoulder. "Are you okay?"

Carolyn broke from her daydream and looked up to see Howard's face—his "middle-aged" face, as Sophie would call it. Had he followed her here from the conference? Under the streetlights outside the former music venue, his eyes appeared shadowed and weary, and his mouth was set in a grim line. A ferry horn bellowed across the way as it left the dock, interrupting the pulsing music of her memory. Carolyn wondered if he'd known where to find her because that long-ago night had meant as much to him as it did to her—if they still had that electric connection where he just *got* her. Or, more likely, had he just followed her down the street from the conference?

"I'm fine," Carolyn whispered, even though the opposite was clear in the tears dribbling down her cheeks.

Howard put both of his hands through his clean-cut, graying hair. "Carrie, what are you doing?"

"Look, you made your point, okay? That's the second time in just a few months that I've been humiliated in front of a room full of people. I had to get out of there."

Howard put his hands deep in his pockets. "You always were good at running," he said gently.

"I get it, Howard. You're still angry with me after all these years."

"No, not angry."

"Then what?"

"Where do I start? How about with the out of the blue, blast-from-the-quarter-century-past note—which you sent to my professional email, no less—from someone who's suddenly single, suddenly back in town."

Carolyn's mind froze. How was she supposed to respond? Tell him her daughter made her reach out to him for her school project?

"What's wrong with letting you know that I'm back in town?" Carolyn asked. "I thought it only fair to give you a heads up that we'd be running into each other from time to time—at industry events, like this one. And I'm not *suddenly* single."

Howard seemed to study her face, then he shook his head. "Bullshit."

"It's been over ten years since I divorced Marcus!"

"That's not what I mean, Carrie, and you know it."

Carolyn clenched her jaw. There he stood, seeing through her once again. "Thanks to this lovely inquisition, I am now well-aware that it was a mistake."

"Damn right it was."

Now Carolyn stood, rooted into the concrete. She knew what "it" she was talking about, but what was his? The email? The way she'd left? Their whole relationship in the first place? "And I guess I thought enough time had passed that maybe—"

"I'd be over it?" Howard asked coolly. "Well, I am, thank you very much. It took me a few years, but I got over it just fine. So as much as I appreciate your emailed 'check-in,' I think we're safe to go our separate ways again."

He turned around and took a few steps when Carolyn called, "If you're *so* cock-sure mature, then why part ways?"

Howard whirled around. "Why?" he shouted. "Why? Because I don't trust you!"

Carolyn felt the wind knocked out of her. "I was young and stupid," she shouted back, then gulped more air to add, "and then I got pregnant!"

Howard looked up to the sky. "That's right," he said. "I heard you had a daughter."

"I had to stay with him. It was the right thing to do."

Carolyn searched Howard's eyes for some sign of relent.

"By whose standards?" he asked.

"Are you being serious right now? Are you actually implying I should've moved back so you could help raise someone else's child with me?"

"There was nothing I wouldn't have done for you."

"You were in no position to support a child," Carolyn said.

"I got my 'act together' for you, remember?" he asked, using finger-quotes. "I quit the band, I quit using, I saved every penny to get us to New York. And then I lost everything while you married that asshole author—what's his name? Matthew?"

"Marcus," she muttered.

"Whatever. The band sold out arenas. I'm sure you heard them on your New York radio stations."

Carolyn opened her mouth to remind him that they'd been one of the '90s many one-hit-wonder alternative bands but thought better of imposing on his what-if revisionist whine-fest.

"That was supposed to be *me*," Howard said. "I gave up the band to be with you and in the end, I lost everything."

"But then you built your own literary agency," Carolyn insisted. "Just like I built my imprint after Marcus cheated on me for the gazillionth time."

"What are you trying to say, Carrie? That we're both better off?"

"I'm saying I learned from my mistakes."

"Then it sounds like you're the one who isn't over it," Howard said. "You're ripping at some ancient scar tissue here, Carrie."

Howard turned and walked into the mist and fog. He vanished from her sight like a lost dream. Carolyn stood stock-still until she felt her breath come back. That wasn't the Howard she'd known. Had she caused him to become that guarded—that jaded?

No. Carolyn shook her head and gathered herself together. It was a relief to know where she stood.

When she turned on her heel to leave, a movement caught the corner of her eye. She squinted into the darkness as Howard's shape emerged from the mist again.

Once he approached her, he put his arms around her and she sobbed into his chest. She hadn't cried when she'd discovered Marcus cheating—not the first time or the last. She hadn't even cried when Morgan St. John ignited her publishing reputation and sent it crashing down in flaming shards. She relaxed into Howard and the solace he provided. At the very least, he cared for her as a person and for now, their age-old connection was enough.

But then, a text chimed. Howard reached into his blazer pocket and pulled out his phone.

"It's my fiancée," he said. "I'll get back to her in a few, after I escort you safely back to the conference. Downtown hasn't gotten any less dangerous in the last twenty years—especially at night."

Carolyn appreciated not having to walk back alone. But this time, with every click of her heels, she heard the word, "Fi-AN-cee, Fi-AN-cee, Fi-AN-cee."

Jazmine

Jazmine sat in a chair behind Henry as he played with his railroad set, connecting one wooden track to another. His blue-and-white striped conductor hat lay delicately in her hands—the hat he refused to wear. She'd tried to explain this to her stepmother when she'd brought it back with her after class in a lame attempt to cover up the haircut fiasco. Lucinda had meant well, of course—thought she'd been doing Jazmine a favor. She'd started with her "goo-goo, gah-gah" voice, thinking she could sweet talk Henry into a sense of security, until she put the electric razor to his head and he'd shrieked as though she'd been coming at him with a butcher knife. If nothing else, it gave Jazmine an opportunity to put her new de-escalating skills to the test.

But now, with just ten minutes before Ava would be coming home and Carolyn was set to arrive, Jazmine didn't dare even breathe as she leaned forward to set the hat as weightlessly on his head as she could. When the chair creaked and Henry went still, Jazmine froze right along with him. She stared at his wilderness of hair and the stubbly little trail of scalp that went straight through it. Her muscles remained tense as she waited motionless for him to move again, determined not to detonate her little time bomb just as her friends were due to come walking through that front door.

Finally, Henry crouched down for a piece of the wooden track. Jazmine slowly, painstakingly reached out her hand with the hat. It sat there atop his curls—what was left of them, anyway—limp and lifeless as roadkill. Jazmine stood back up and felt her chest swell with pride. It was her first win of the night.

She tensed when she heard Ava's key in the lock, hoping Henry would stay the course. Sure enough, Ava opened the door and let Carolyn through first. It was funny the way Ava pandered to that woman—kind as she was.

"Oof!" Carolyn waved a hand in front of her nose. "Someone hit the ganja hard in this place."

"I've been trying to air the place out," Ava said, apologetically. "My dad was a big fan of the B.C. bud."

"Ah, yes." Carolyn's voice was wistful. "I remember getting pot from Canada dealers. This fragrance brings me right back to my college apartment, passing around the pipe with my roommates."

Jazmine smiled, trying to picture the sophisticated Carolyn smoking weed in college. She noticed Henry look up and, at the first sight of Carolyn, he chirped, "Dod!" Then, as he leaned over his train set to get up, his precariously placed hat fell to the floor.

Ava tilted her head, then furrowed her eyebrows. "What happened to his hair?"

Jazmine shook her head at her son's unfortunate new hairstyle and took a seat in the faded living room recliner chair to explain. "After I dropped him off before morning classes, Lucinda decided—without asking me, mind you—that his hair needed a shave. She brought out the electric razor and got in one good swipe down the middle of his head before he freaked out."

Jazmine wasn't sure how to take Ava's sudden burst of giggles. Then, Carolyn joined in.

Jazmine followed their gazes back to her son, who had thankfully gone back to his train—so focused that he was oblivious to the laughter happening at his expense—and felt like she was seeing his little reverse mohawk for the first time. Over the past couple of days, she'd been so mired in his meltdown and her ensuing resentment towards her stepmother that she hadn't seen it for what it was—and it *was* hilarious.

Wiping her eyes, Carolyn held up a gift bag. "I brought him a few things, but only in case of an emergency or—Choo! Choo!—if he gets bored with what he's rolling with so far!" She giggled anew.

"Emergency?" Ava repeated. "Like a pair of runaway clippers?"

Jazmine doubled over, waving for them to stop before she laughed herself to death.

"Well, she is a godsend to take care of Henry while you finish that degree," Carolyn finally managed.

"That's true," Jazmine said. "Unfortunately, we have a difference in our parenting philosophies. She believes 'tough love' will cure Henry. I believe that understanding the way he perceives the world will help us both. But she loves him, and that's what counts, right?"

"Hey, what's with the plutonium?" Carolyn asked, pointing to the fluorescent green drinks on the coffee table.

"Oh my God," Ava gushed. "Did you make us Midori sours?"

Jazmine took a couple deeper breaths to ensure she could speak coherently. "That's what you ordered at our meeting last month, right? I figured I'd raid Ava's late father's fully stocked bar and whip these up to see what all the rage is about."

Carolyn took a sip and pulled back, coughing. "You sure that's not plutonium?"

"It's Midori, vodka, lemon and lime juice—"

Ava took a sip, then nodded her approval. "This is even better than the Cider House!"

"But what *is* Midori?" Carolyn asked.

Jazmine shrugged. She'd just grabbed the bottle that said Midori and measured one ounce for each glass.

Ava, still holding her drink, used her other hand to scroll through her phone. "It's a 'melon liqueur,'" she said, with an added tone of sophistication on *liqueur*.

"It's liquid candy," Carolyn said with a grimace. "Like a gateway drink to the harder stuff. Speaking of which, I don't mean to sound unappreciative, but would Ava's father's bar possibly include a bottle of Pinot gris?"

"Will this do?" Jazmine asked, taking a bottle from the end table and holding it up for Carolyn to see the label from an esteemed Napa Valley vintner. The cool glass bottle was covered in tiny beads of sweat, still cold from the fridge.

Carolyn raised an eyebrow. "Very observant. You'll make a top journalist, yet."

"It's the least I can do."

"You've got a nice place, here, Ava," Carolyn said, glancing around to take it all in.

Jazmine followed her gaze and shrugged. Basic, eggshell paint bordered by deep brown maple trim.

"Mid-century minimalist," Ava said.

Jazmine reached for her Midori sour and took a long, thoughtful sip. It wasn't as bad as Carolyn had made it out to be. "So, I have something to share with you both."

"I have something to share with you, too," Ava burst.

Jazmine shot Carolyn an uncertain glance.

"I've been in talks with McBride," Ava started.

"That name sounds familiar," Jazmine said.

"He's an author," Carolyn explained. "He writes those old Westerns for the over-fifty male demographic."

"I know, right?" Ava squealed. "He fired his agent and wants to sign with me!"

Carolyn narrowed her eyes. "Why wouldn't your boss want to sign McBride himself?"

"Well, *I'm* the one who knows Wes personally, for one thing," Ava said, sounding stung. "He and my dad were friends, and I edited a couple of his short stories for *Klipsun Literary*. But that's the kind of guy Howard is. He wants to give me a chance to start strong in building my list. And thank God for that. I can finally pay off—"

"—those hospital bills," Jazmine finished for her. "I wish I could help with those. I know the district is taking forever to get that compensation package together."

But then, Carolyn raised her glass. "I'd say congratulations are in order. If the school district doesn't pay out—which it probably will—your commission on any given McBride book should be enough to cover everything. How's the job going, anyway?"

"I love it," Ava gushed. "I really, really love it. Howard is so kind and patient and gracious, and the senior agent, Max—well, he saved my life."

Something in Ava's statement pulled Jazmine from her stressful court case reverie. "Saved your life? How's that?"

"When I was unconscious—you know, after the bus accident," Ava paused for a moment. "Now that I think about it, you must have seen him, Jazmine. He said he was the first on the scene to come to my aid."

Jazmine thought back to the man crouched over Ava on the snowy street, who said he'd been a lifeguard at some point. "Does he wear glasses?" she asked, remembering when he'd had to remove them because they kept steaming up.

"Yes," Ava said. "That's him!"

Jazmine nodded. "I was very thankful he was there. He was great and made sure you had a pulse and were breathing. But I never saw him perform CPR or First Aid."

Ava shrugged. "He said he was the first to arrive on the scene, and that he kept me going until the EMT got there."

Carolyn and Jazmine shared a look.

"I don't know," Carolyn said. "I got an odd feeling about him at the conference. Did you see him talking with Roxi Fischer? I must have seen them chatting it up on at least three occasions. That's two flags against the man already."

"There was never a first flag," Ava raised her voice defensively. "He didn't lie about the accident. And just because Roxi is a viper doesn't mean Max is, too. He was probably doing some reconnaissance that he could bring back to Howard."

Jazmine felt for Ava, sitting there squirming in her seat. Then she turned her gaze toward Henry, who was now doing his little antsy dance around his train track.

"And the flags don't matter, anyway," Ava continued, "because it's not like I'm trying to have a relationship with him. We just work really well together. He even asked if I could meet him at a coffee shop on Monday morning before work to go over a few things. That sounds like dedication to me."

Jazmine looked to Carolyn, who seemed to be choosing her words.

"Does it seem strange to you that he would schedule a meeting at a coffee house?" Carolyn finally asked. "I mean, why wouldn't he just have the meeting during work hours at the agency?"

"Almost every coffee shop table has people in a meeting," Ava said, clearly frustrated. "This isn't even about Max, is it? Maybe you two don't think I'm talented enough to warrant the attention of a superior. I may be naive sometimes, but I'm good at what I do."

"Hoo-hoo!" Henry chirped from his corner, rolling the wooden train through an intersection. Jazmine held her breath. His "hoo-hoo" noise often predicated a meltdown, but he seemed to be doing fine.

"I have an idea," Jazmine said, getting up from the recliner to find the cocktail napkin in her purse that she'd used at the Cider House. "I want you to look at our list again. If you can't find one red flag, we'll let it drop."

Jazmine handed the napkin to Ava, whose eyes moved back and forth over the list they'd created at the Cider House. She set it down. "There's only one there," she said, "and she shouldn't have even written it because it's barely a flag."

"Which one is that?" Carolyn asked.

"When we first met and he told me he'd been first on the scene and I recognized him from his hospital visit—you know, because he's an upstanding, caring guy who wanted to check in and make sure I was okay—he turned his phone over on the table before he left the room to get me some tea."

Ready to let the subject drop, Jazmine glanced over to Carolyn, afraid she might have more gasoline to throw on the open flame crackling between them.

"Listen, Ava," Carolyn started, "I'm just looking out for you, okay? And Max wasn't the only one to raise red flags at that conference."

Jazmine glanced back and forth between the two women, feeling out of some kind of loop they both now shared.

"Who else?" Ava asked, her face shining intrigue as she leaned in and almost whispered, "Was it Howard?"

Jazmine watched Carolyn's eyes go wide, as though surprised that Ava would suggest her boss as the flag-raiser. "He raised flags for me once," Carolyn said. "A long time ago. But apparently, I was the one to wielding red this time around."

"You know Ava's boss?" Jazmine asked Carolyn.

"We worked together a long time ago," Carolyn said. "He was sort of the one I let get away."

"Oh," Jazmine breathed, finally feeling caught up in the conversation.

"He was so much fun," Carolyn continued, her eyes staring off into some past reverie. "But he was sort of a man-child. Garage band drummer and everything the Seattle music scene entailed."

"Sex, drugs, and rock 'n roll?" Jazmine ventured a guess, wondering which of those Howard had embodied—cheating or addiction? From what she knew of the Seattle music scene, heroin had been rampant among musicians.

Carolyn shrugged and sighed. "Anyhow, when Marcus came along, he seemed to have it more together—a promising writing career, a place of his own. It seemed like the responsible decision to make at the time."

"Wow," Ava breathed. "And now Howard is the better man."

"Underneath a few issues, he really always was," Carolyn said dismally. "I've spent years wondering how my life could have been different with him. When I came back to Seattle, there was this little splinter of hope that maybe he was available. And then, Sophie had this silly project, for which she asked me to get in touch with an old flame—to see if technology could help us rekindle any sparks we once had. It made me think it might actually be possible."

"But he's engaged," Ava said, her voice as downtrodden as Carolyn's expression. And then, she murmured something softly enough for only Jazmine to hear. "There are no second chances."

"Enough about me," Carolyn said, reaching for the bottle on the coffee table to refill her empty wine glass. "Jazmine, would you remind me why we're meeting here?"

"We're here so I can show you the platform you encouraged me to build," Jazmine began, "using the full, surround-sound experience of Ava's father's stereo system."

"What do you mean?" Ava asked.

Jazmine clasped her hands in front of her. "Well, I went back to see Quentin—"

"Quentin?" Carolyn asked. "Sims?"

Jazmine stopped mid-breath. She couldn't tell her how she'd gone to his office to chastise him for talking to Carolyn behind her back. "I asked if he'd show me how to record a podcast."

"Interesting," Carolyn said, drawing out the first syllable.

"Who is Quentin Sims?" Ava asked. Now it was her turn to be out of the loop.

"He's a good man," Carolyn said.

Ava gasped. "Is he single? Handsome? Do you like him?"

"Yeah, right," Jazmine laughed. "An esteemed PhD falls for a school bus driver? I don't think so."

"*Former* school bus driver," Ava reminded her.

"Yeah, thanks for that," Jazmine said, raising an eyebrow. Then she rose and stepped over Henry's railroad tracks to get to her laptop, hooked up to the speakers on Ava's dad's entertainment system. "Anyhow, his receptionist gave me the phone number of my first interviewee—a former womanizer became the better man for her. Her insights were fascinating."

Jazmine brought up the podcast on her laptop and clicked on the arrow to play it. Her voice came through the speakers, inviting and warm.

"Good evening and welcome to my new podcast, *Better Than Never*. I'm your host, Jazmine Johnston, and with me is the University of Washington's Professor of Romanian History..."

Jazmine took her seat back on the recliner, eager to see her friends' reactions. Ava sat on the edge of the love seat, wide-eyed as she listened. Carolyn's face was harder to read—her jaw set to stoic. Jazmine's recorded voice sounded strange to her own ears, yet she couldn't help feeling proud of the confident cadence she seemed to carry. She actually sounded like a professional interviewer. She listened with the other women as she set the stage for her topic and explained how her guest fit into the scheme of things, having landed a former adulterer who'd become faithful for and to her.

Her guest laughed and responded in her melodic accent. "We have both made our share of mistakes and learned from them. I am a different woman than I was twenty and thirty years ago. And he, a different man. When younger, I believed I must prove my worth through academics. The more degrees I earned, the worthier I became."

Ava groaned. "Is she saying I'm going to have to wait twenty years for the men my age to figure themselves out?"

Jazmine waited for Carolyn to quip something like, *You wouldn't be the only one who's had to wait that long*, but the woman continued sitting quietly on the sofa, her face draining of color.

"Listen more closely," Jazmine said. "She's talking about how we find our worth in ourselves—and how that can become a fix."

Ava nodded, her distant eyes appearing deep in thought. She turned to Carolyn. "You've built two publishing companies now. That must have been a major fix. I bet every book you put out was a high for you."

Carolyn said nothing, her mouth set in a grim line.

"When my husband was younger," Professor Mirea said, "he found his worth from being wanted by women. The more women who wanted him, the worthier he felt he was. And we all know it takes two to dance a tango, no? The fact is that I cannot speak for his first wife. What I can say is that my heart is in this marriage, and he is well aware of that fact."

"What the hell is that supposed to mean?" Carolyn asked.

Jazmine paused the show. "I think she meant he knows how much she loves him."

"And what does it say about where the husband's heart is? Isn't that question at the core of your podcast, Jazmine?" Ava asked. "Maybe he's still a philanderer and this professor just hasn't caught on yet."

"No, what she means is that *her* heart is in the marriage," Carolyn said through gritted teeth, "which implies that *mine* wasn't."

Jazmine's face grew hot. "Yours?" She felt the air in the room turn heavy. Her muscles clenched as she noticed Carolyn grinding her jaw, her face now flushing with color.

"I thought we agreed not to interview each other's exes," Carolyn said in a hushed, hoarse voice.

"Hoo-*hoo!*" Henry's volume rose steadily as the tension in the room did the same.

Jazmine glanced between her son and Carolyn, wondering whom to address first before either boiled over. She began edging towards Henry's corner. "Carolyn, I didn't know—"

"That's a little hard to believe," Carolyn said. "But what I really want to know is why *you* would dig up dirt on me?"

"I know you've been betrayed," Jazmine started in the warmest, smoothest voice she could manage, "professionally, in your marriage, and maybe even in previous friendships. But you made an accusation toward Ava when you first met her, and now me, and you know we love you—"

"I don't think you realize what a big deal this is," Carolyn said evenly.

"It *isn't* a big deal," Jazmine insisted. "Quentin's receptionist asked me about my topic. I didn't even have a topic yet, so I started telling her about what we've been talking about. She got all excited and referred me to her—"

"Stepmother," Carolyn finished. "Quentin's receptionist is Sophie. My *daughter.*"

Jazmine sat in shock, feeling as though her face might slide right off.

"And now," Carolyn continued, "thanks to this public broadcast, she's going to get the idea that I was in love with someone else the whole time. And if she thinks I was in love, she might figure out—"

"The professor never said you were in love," Jazmine argued.

"Figure out what?" Ava asked.

"And I had no idea that Sophie was your daughter," Jazmine insisted.

"Apparently we don't look as much alike as I thought," Carolyn clipped.

"What were you afraid Sophie might figure out?" Ava asked again.

Carolyn clasped her hands together so tightly that Jazmine could see her knuckles go white.

"I would appreciate your taking the podcast off the air," Carolyn said, "or the internet, or whatever."

"I can't," Jazmine said. "It's my final project for my Investigative Reporting Seminar. I don't have time to find someone else to interview, much less—"

"Interview *me*," Carolyn said, then pointed to Ava. "Interview *her*."

"Carolyn, maybe this isn't such a bad thing," Ava said. "This could be some of the real-life research you suggested we do at our last meeting. Just think about it for a second. How many of us get to hear from the new woman—get to hear the actual *why* he gets better?"

"Consider me enlightened," Carolyn said, stone-faced. "Tell you what, why don't you look up your ex's new girlfriend—"

"He doesn't have one," Ava said.

"How do you know?" Jazmine asked. "You haven't been cyberstalking him, have you?"

"No," Ava said defensively. "I mean, I check in sometimes, you know, just to see what he's up to."

"Well, when you see him in a selfie with a new girlfriend, you be sure to learn all you can from her," Carolyn said. "As for me, I'm waiting for Jazmine to delete the interview so I can get going."

Jazmine felt dizzy and nauseous, overwhelmed by the stress of getting this project done for her Investigative Reporting Seminar, and now she was being asked to delete it all—by the same person who'd pushed her to do it in the first place!

"Carolyn, I can't," Jazmine said. "I don't have time to start this over, and besides, nobody will listen to it, anyway. I can take it off as soon as my professor scores it."

Carolyn grabbed her watered-down Midori sour from the coffee table, the half-melted ice cubes clinking weakly against the glass. She held the glass up.

"Are you threatening me with a cocktail?" Jazmine asked.

"All it would take is for Isadore to tell Sophie about it and then Sophie will listen and then—"

"Carolyn, let's sit down and talk this over," Ava said, reaching for her arm to take the drink from her hand.

Jazmine watched as Carolyn wrenched her arm free with such force that the drink and the glass went flying. Jazmine ducked them both. She rose, her eyes trained on Carolyn, whose wide eyes looked past her, to where a boiling kettle shriek pierced the air.

Jazmine turned to find Henry, his hair and face soaked with the cocktail. She knew better than to reach to pick him up, squatting instead to wipe the alcohol from his face with a tissue.

"Is there anything I can do?" Ava offered.

"Clear the area," Jazmine said, her voice husky. "Get everything out of the way."

"Jazmine, I'm sorry," Carolyn said. "I never meant for that to happen. I was just trying to get Ava to let go of me and…"

Jazmine ignored Carolyn's ramblings as she grabbed for a train car with one hand and a piece of the track with the other—anything that might be thrown or used to hit himself in the head—when a light flickered from the corner of her eye, then went dark.

She froze, mid-crouch, and looked at her laptop. The glass Carolyn had inadvertently thrown now rested there, draining the rest of its contents into the keyboard.

A numbness settled over her. It couldn't be. Surely her laptop had only run out of battery. All she had to do was charge it and all of her research and term papers would reappear. And if they didn't, she'd take it into the IT desk at the U. They'd look at it, charge her a hundred dollars or two, and restore everything, no problem.

While Henry's high-pitched squeal continued to reverberate against the walls, she felt herself removed somehow, as though watching through a window as Ava held her head from the noise, and Carolyn reached for Henry to calm him.

"No!" Jazmine shouted, all at once coming back into herself. Her voice was low and breathless. "Don't you touch him. Just leave."

"Jazmine, please," Carolyn pleaded. "I'm just overwhelmed. It's all too much. Let me at least help with the laptop."

"All too much," Jazmine snapped, her memory instantly flashing to the moment Ben had walked out on her and their son. "If it's all too much, then *go*," she shouted and pointed towards the door.

Jazmine watched as Carolyn's bottom lip trembled. In fact, her shoulders and knees seemed to be shaking, as well. She seemed to open her mouth to speak, then closed it, opting instead to charge to the front door and out into the cool spring night.

Temptations

Ava

The coffee shop was busier than Ava would have liked, though it made sense that at this time of morning people would fuel up before heading to the office. It was a reminder to be thankful for a job that didn't get her out of bed two hours before dawn.

Ava glanced around the cafe and, seeing no Max in sight, took her place in line. At least this way, there wouldn't be that awkward moment of waiting to see if he would offer to pay, then faux arguing that she was happy to pay for herself before finally giving in to the chivalrous gesture. When she finally reached the cashier, she proudly ordered a Grande non-fat Chai and whisked out her credit card to pay.

Beep! Beep!

It was a low, humiliating mechanized tone that made the cashier's next words both inevitable and unnecessary.

"I'm sorry, it didn't go through." The barista didn't seem to think anything of it—probably happened all the time. "The reader can be sensitive. Give it another swipe."

But Ava knew better than that. She knew her card had been declined because the money was finally gone. And the last conversation she'd had with the attorney Carolyn's mother had referred her to had culminated only in a lowball offer from the school district that would barely cover her hospital stay, let alone her outpatient appointments—let *alone* her accruing legal fees.

Thankfully, she had a ten-dollar bill in her pocket. By the time she pulled it out, unfolded it, and told the barista to keep the change, her drink was ready at the other end of the counter. There would be no green tea for this girl—no more changing colors for anyone else. Last night's meeting may have been a disaster, but she'd at least learned to stay true to herself and her own interests from here on out. She just hoped their Red Flag Society hadn't been disbanded forever.

She couldn't help feeling guilty as she edged through the crowd of business suits and laptop cases—as though she were betraying her friends by meeting Max, the man they deemed untrustworthy. Instead, she felt the need to call and check on Jazmine—poor Jazmine who'd had to calm down her emotional hurricane of a son. She hoped everything had settled over the last couple of days so that Jazmine was able to head back to her classes this morning and begin the unfathomable job of redoing her project. And Carolyn—well, she still wondered what Carolyn had been so afraid of Sophie "figuring out."

When she reached the back of the café, a thirty-something guy said, "Hey, it's me."

"Hi," Ava replied, squinting to make him out. She was sure she'd never seen him before. She glanced around herself to see if he was speaking to someone behind her. Was this some kind of coffee bar pickup line?

But then, when he rose from the table and turned to pick up his cross-body satchel, she saw him speaking into a Bluetooth. And as he made his way out of his table space, Ava spotted Max seated directly behind where the man had been.

Max hadn't been late. In fact, he'd beaten her there. What was the opposite of a red flag? White? No, that was surrender. Transparent. Maybe that was Max's true color. At any rate, Ava made a mental note to text Carolyn and Jazmine about his punctuality. She would leave out the part, however, about how Max was so focused on tapping into his phone that he didn't notice her approach the table.

"Hello there," she said casually, as she slid into the chair across from him, admiring his black crew neck sweater under a black blazer.

Max looked up. "Oh, hey, there you are." Instead of his normal bedhead look, he'd combed his dark hair back with some kind of gel to keep it in place.

Ava slid out of her jacket as she waited for him to finish with his phone.

"Congratulations on getting Wes McBride," he said, adjusting his glasses.

"Thanks," Ava said, taking a sip from her Chai. "I'm super-excited. It's just that big names can bring big pressure, too. And it's not like he's signed yet, so…"

A notification dinged on Max's phone. He glanced at the glowing screen, then clicked it dark and flipped it over. Ava's stomach turned as she saw him do it. Damn.

"So how did the conference go for you?" she asked. "Anything promising?"

"The writers always have great ideas." Max lifted his cup of tea and took a sip.

Ava nodded. "I can't believe how many manuscripts I requested."

"We all do," Max said. "Half of them won't follow through on sending them, and the interns will sift through the other half and let us know if they've turned up any gold. But I don't need to tell you this."

"What do you mean?"

"It's not like you're a newbie at the agenting game."

"It was my first conference," she reminded him. "And I've still got a lot to learn. Howard's been very patient."

"He has?" Max asked.

Ava regarded Max curiously. "Why wouldn't he be?"

"Did you see how he acted on that panel?"

"Oh yeah," Ava said. "That was pretty out of character for him, wasn't it?" She considered confiding in Max about the underlying tensions between Howard and Carolyn. For all she knew, she'd never see Carolyn again, anyway. Why not dish a little gossip? But even if their friendship was over, Ava would always feel an affinity for the woman, and she knew she could never betray her. She took another drink of her Chai and decided against sharing anything.

Max shook his head and raised his eyebrows over the dark frames of his glasses. "I just don't get their generation."

Ava cocked her head. "What do you mean?"

"They act like they're here to guide us into a world of publishing that's already obsolete," he said. "We're the ones who should guide *them* through all the changing technology, but they keep us in our place, starting us with a single-digit percentage and making us work our way up like, I don't know, like fuckin' share-croppers."

Ava gulped, surprised at his sudden coarseness. There was no avoiding that flag. "I heard you signed three authors last quarter," she said, working to get Max back on a positive track.

"Sure did," Max said. "And Howard graciously took *his* percent out of *my* commission for completing and filing 'paperwork.' I sifted through the queries, read the manuscripts, edited them, pitched them to the publishers, and Howard gets a cut for the sole act of stamping his name on the contract."

"I'm sure it takes a lot of time to do those things," Ava gave a sympathetic shrug. She'd at least been in the business long enough to know that much. "It's all part of the process."

Max leaned in, his voice and eyes resonating a new intensity. "But it doesn't have to be. We're hunched over, panning through slush piles for flecks of gold when hundreds of authors are making six figures every *month* in self-publishing. Technology is turning the industry on its head. Our ship is sinking and our agency's idea of saving us is to fit us with life jackets."

Ava leaned in, too, trying to keep up with the changing metaphors. "What are you suggesting? We mutiny?"

Max raised his eyebrow again, his dark eyes glistening through his glasses. "We *revolutionize*."

Ava sat back into her chair, watching the steam from his tea slowly dissipate in the coffee shop air while she tried to process the meaning in his message. This business meeting and his revolution seemed directed at Howard Mercer Literary and it was hardly a 'for the good of the order' camaraderie-building session. Yet, Max must have seen something in Ava to impart his ideas to her—perhaps even include her in whatever he was hinting at.

Still, she was happy at Mercer Literary. She was happy to climb the traditional ladder—but to what, at this point? It would take months to see her McBride commission. At least Howard believed in her enough to provide a modest draw on commissions, in addition to her salary, so that she could fend off a few creditors. But Max had a point. How relevant would literary agents even be ten years from now in an ever-changing industry? She already knew a dozen or so agents who had switched to freelance editing in hopes of pay that was both better and more consistent.

"Figuring out how to revolutionize our agenting is definitely something to consider," Ava finally said.

"I'm done considering."

"What do you mean?" Ava asked. "You're leaving Howard?"

"Getting the ducks in order," he said. "Letting the authors know."

"You're giving up your authors?"

Max laughed. "I'm letting them know the advantages of going with me, versus staying with someone who can't even manage his money."

Ava's stomach began to roil. She couldn't imagine slinking behind Howard's back like that. At the very least, Max wasn't asking her to.

"And I need other agents," Max added. "A cohort of the best and brightest up-and-comers."

Her stomach plummeted, leaving a dark void at her core. Now she *was* being asked to leave Howard. "Sounds like a younger version of just another agency."

"No, a *cooperative* with various divisions for everything from editorial services to book cover design to agenting. You remember how Howard wouldn't let you pitch your father's book? You could do that with us. And whenever you sign a book, you get a fair percentage."

"*I* would get full commission?" Ava asked, although her mind kept stuttering over the part about her father's book—now a self-published e-book, ready to hit the online stores any day now. And here, she could have taken him the traditional route—something he'd always dreamed of.

"If you join us, absolutely."

"And who exactly does 'us' comprise?"

Max ran a hand over his hair, as though to be sure it was still slicked-back and hadn't gone wonky once it dried. "Roxi Fischer and I are heading this up. She's got some agents from her end, but you're the only one I know who could hook a multimillion-dollar author on her first shot. Having Wes McBride join our team would give us a major boost when we make the official launch."

Ava nodded, but instead of seeing Max's earnest face in front of her, she saw a vision of Carolyn and Jazmine behind him, waving red flags up and down, side to side. Roxi Fischer? Ava felt herself hating Max, if only for the reason that he'd proven Carolyn right. That's what they'd been chatting about before the panel and every other time Carolyn had seen them together. But there was so much more to loathe about him than the fact that Carolyn's intuition had been spot-on.

"With Howard flying out to New York next weekend," Max said, "we can talk up authors at the Seattle Literary Society Awards Ceremony. Forget those no-name writers at conferences. We're talking published, award-winning *authors*."

Ava continued to nod blankly, wishing she could rewind thirty minutes and un-know everything Max had just outlined. But she was stuck in play, trying to choose between the man who had saved her life and the man who had provided her livelihood. Max had saved her. Didn't she owe him? But, as Jazmine had mentioned, it was possible that he hadn't so much "saved her" as he'd come to her aid. And for that, he would forever have her gratitude—but she didn't owe him any more than that. Did she? For a people-pleaser like Ava, this was more than she could handle.

"Take some time to think it over," Max said, draining the last of his tea. "It's going to be quite the coup de état, and we'll go down in history as the young rebels that gave literary agents a new, even more legitimate place in the industry. But, like any coup, I can't give away the names of those involved, just like I will never tell anyone about this conversation. And I know you'll afford me the same courtesy."

Ava nodded, feeling more alone than she had after her breakup with Gavin or lying in that hospital room. She needed help with this. She needed Carolyn.

"It went without saying, I know," Max said as he nodded back. "It's like fate that I was first on that scene to help you on the ground. And as soon as you started working with us—I knew there was something about you. I knew I could trust you and connect with you in a way I don't connect with many people." Max's phone binged in another text. He glanced at the lit screen. "I've gotta jet."

"Of course," Ava said. "I should get going, too."

"Thanks for meeting up with me," he said, extending a hand.

Ava shook it and felt him give her hand a soft squeeze. She watched him as he headed out, knowing that Max may have found a pseudo-mentor in Roxi Fischer, but Ava had the real deal. If they were still on speaking terms, she wouldn't make any decisions until she had the chance to get some guidance from the best in the biz—Ms. Carolyn Ford, herself.

Carolyn

Carolyn read over the email to her editorial team, deliberating over whether her tone was too stern, too condescending, or occasionally, too humorous. She took a sip of chamomile tea and relaxed back into her leather desk chair, luxuriating in the sweet knowledge that she had the house to herself now that her mother was away on a five-day Alaskan cruise. In fact, she'd invited Sophie over for dinner tonight because they could share their first *real* conversation since she'd moved back to Seattle.

Carolyn could hear the distant huff of the city bus coming to a stop outside. When the doorbell rang, she dashed off a closing statement and trotted down the hall, Trixie yipping at her heels. Sophie stood on the front porch, covered in a red, hooded poncho, holding a plastic bag in each hand. Her eyes reflected the pale blue patches of sky and her cheeks and nose were ruddy from the evening chill. It was an image reminiscent of a spring sunset fifteen years prior, when Carolyn shook a cherry tree branch so that Sophie could twirl, the blossoms covering her strawberry blonde hair like pink snowflakes.

"Can't wait to dish these up," Carolyn said, reaching to help with the food. The aromas of green curry and peanut sauce steamed through and wafted into the air. She took the bags to the dining room table and reached inside for the takeout boxes. The three-star spices from the curries cleared her sinuses and caused her stomach to grumble.

Trixie's yips subsided as she sniffed the takeout aroma in the air. When Sophie took a seat at the dining room table, Carolyn noticed she looked somehow different tonight. Her hair was still cut in that severe, side-shaved style, but tonight she'd pinned the bangs back and had gone without makeup. Her complexion and her eyes both shone bright and clear. It was as though the mask had come off and Carolyn was sitting down with her natural, authentic daughter for the first time in years.

"How's the new job going?" Sophie asked.

"You mean my career running my own publishing firm?" Carolyn countered as she took the chair across from Sophie. She took daughter's plate and spooned up the Pad See Ew. "It's nice to oversee every aspect, being the control freak that I am."

"Mom, take it easy on the noodles."

When Carolyn regarded the plate for what seemed like the first time, piled high with broccoli balanced precariously atop the tofu and wide noodles, she laughed. "Sorry about that. Guess I'm a control freak with both my food ladling and my job."

"I thought it was a career," Sophie said, taking the plate from Carolyn to scrape half of its contents back into the takeout box. "But I'll chalk it up as maternal empathy, not control freaking."

Empathy? Carolyn pondered the trait. She'd certainly shown her share of empathy—with Marcus, with Morgan St. John, with Jazmine— and had paid the price every damn time.

She stopped herself. She wouldn't play victim today. And Jazmine was innocent. It had been a completely honest mistake that could cost what little relationship Carolyn had with her daughter. Now it was a race against time—or simply a matter of time—before everything blew up, and while Jazmine may have lit the match—however inadvertently—there would be no impending explosion if Carolyn hadn't created that particular fuse in the first place.

"Did you hear Isadore did a podcast?" Sophie asked.

While the sound of a burning fuse sizzled in her mind, Carolyn forced her facial muscles to go slack. She loosened her jaw and willed away every memory of that horrid evening in Ava's living room last week, listening to Marcus's bride relinquish any semblance of personal privacy or nobility, and for what? "Believe it or not, I don't keep track of your stepmother's goings-on. She has a podcast now?"

"No, she was a guest. But I guess it's safe to assume you didn't hear it."

"I did not," Carolyn said. "You?"

The pause told her everything she needed to know, which was the opposite of Sophie's eventual answer of 'no' before she, not too deftly, changed the subject. "So did that guy ever write you back?"

Carolyn froze. She thought that subject had been put to rest and somehow thought that feigning ignorance might be the best way to do that now. "What guy?"

"Mom, did he write you back? My study's due in a couple of weeks."

"Oh, of course. I can't stop fixating on your study," Carolyn said, setting down the serving spoon and taking her place at the table. She'd done her best to close the door on the memory of Howard under the streetlight, but those blue eyes of his pierced right through. "Yes. I'm afraid it's a no-go."

"Why?" Sophie asked, sitting across from Carolyn. "Is he married? Or was he one of the guys you turned gay?"

"Excuse me?"

"Grandma said—"

"Never mind that. He's engaged."

"To a man or a woman?"

"Does it matter?"

"Well, yeah. If it's a woman, you can change his mind. It's not like they're married, yet."

"What do you want me to do?" Carolyn asked. "Crash the wedding?"

"No," Sophie said glumly. She slurped down the rest of her bubble tea until the straw struggled with the remains at the bottom of the clear plastic cup. "Guess my study's a bust. I'll need a copy of the email, though, as a source."

"All I have is the email I wrote him."

"Then how do you know he's engaged?"

"Long story." Carolyn watched her daughter swirl the noodles aimlessly around her plate. "Honey, I've spent so much of my life looking back. Can't we look forward now?"

"So then, what if…" Sophie started, then shook her head.

"What if what?" Carolyn asked.

"Well, my study is about Gen-Xers and technology. Instead of re-claiming relationships, I could do a study on the use of technology to just, well, claim a relationship in the first place."

"I'm not following what you're—no. You don't mean I—"

"Join a dating site!" Sophie's eyes were wide again, and they sparkled under the low light of the vintage chandelier.

"I just started building Ford Publishing. I barely have time for you, let alone—"

"This is perfect!" Sophie squealed. "Let me grab my tablet."

"Oh, ho, ho, no," Carolyn said. "Anything we do will be done on my laptop. I don't want my passwords getting saved to anyone else's device."

"Where's your laptop?" Sophie asked, already out of her seat and crossing the living room.

"It's in my bedroom," Carolyn called weakly. She hadn't seen Sophie this delighted with her since she'd surprised her with a puppy on her tenth birthday.

Alone at the dining room table, Carolyn finally speared a piece of broccoli and brought it to her mouth, savoring the warm curry. She rolled her eyes at herself, wondering what she was allowing Sophie to get her into now—and for what? It's not like she hadn't tried her hand at online dating before, the endless merry-go-round of interviews. "So, what's your favorite food/music/movie/book/etc.?" It felt like McDating and there was only so much she could McTake.

Her daughter seemed so set on finding her a relationship, when the only relationship Carolyn was interested in rekindling with this silly venture was the one with Sophie herself. Perhaps this online dating experiment could finally allow her to connect with her daughter on a more adult level, single gal to single gal. She could be there for her in a way that she hadn't been able to be there over the last few years. And it could give her a way to put the past in her rearview mirror, where it belonged.

Carolyn set her fork back down when she heard Sophie's exuberant footsteps coming back down the hall until she appeared, laptop in hand.

"All right, what are you looking for in a guy?" Sophie asked as she set the laptop on the table and sat back in her chair.

Carolyn opened her mouth to respond, but no answer came. Single gals or not, the young woman sitting across from her was her daughter, for crying out loud. Still feeling the sting of Jazmine's betrayal with that podcast, the weight of opening up to anyone else with such personal longings, even—no, *especially*—her daughter, was enough to close the door of connection they'd just opened.

No, she could do this. Just keep it straightforward, that was all. The only problem was, she knew all too well what she didn't want in a man, but what exactly *did* she want? "It's important that he's educated."

Sophie smiled wryly. "Of course, you'd start with that."

"What's wrong with that?" Carolyn's voice came out more defensive than she would have liked. "Would you rather I date an eighth-grade dropout?"

Sophie slid the laptop over for Carolyn to enter her password. "Bill Gates was a dropout."

"He dropped out of college," Carolyn reminded her daughter.

"And now he's a gazillion-aire, so…" Sophie raised an eyebrow at her mother until they both broke out laughing—something Carolyn couldn't remember doing with Sophie since—since when?

"You don't want to come off sounding stuffy and, well," Sophie paused for the word, "overbearing."

"What would you propose, then?"

"Just loosen up a little, Mom. Why don't you pour us some wine?"

"Nice try," Carolyn said, reaching for the almost-empty bottle at the center of the table. "Ask me again in a couple of years."

Carolyn turned the bottle over in her hands. She hadn't had a drink since last week—the night before her meeting with Ava and Jazmine. Her muscles tensed at the memory—the glass flying across the room, the plutonium drink dripping down that ridiculous divot in Henry's hair. All for the sake of Sophie not hearing about Carolyn's emotional absence from her marriage because she'd been longing after the man she should have chosen. But Sophie hadn't heard it, so she said. Not yet, anyway. And if Jazmine had erased the podcast by now, perhaps Carolyn was free and clear. She pushed the guilt down, but she really needed to call Jazmine tomorrow and apologize. Definitely, tomorrow.

"So what website are we going to use?" Carolyn asked. "I keep hearing about some site where you swipe left or right—Kindling, or—"

Sophie laughed. "It's Tinder, Mom, and that's a hook-up site."

"Isn't that the point?"

Sophie's face pruned into a look of disgust. "Not when it comes to mothers—especially mine. Most free sites are hook-up sites. The more you pay, the more serious people seem to be—about having a relationship, I mean. And there are other groups you can get involved with that are in person—meet ups and events."

"How do you know all this?" Carolyn asked, eyeing her daughter warily.

"I'm on a couple." Sophie shrugged. "Most of my friends are, too."

"You're nineteen," Carolyn said. "You have your pick of thousands of young men at the university. That's not enough?"

"It's not about quantity," Sophie said. "It's about narrowing it down. If there's an algorithm that can align me with someone with similar interests, then why waste time on the ones who don't?"

"Apparently, you're the pro. Let me see how you do it on your profile," Carolyn said, her stomach suddenly queasy as she considered what kind of pictures her daughter may have posted.

Sophie shrugged again and typed into the address bar. A site came up with different pictures and group names. Carolyn tried to keep up with the titles as Sophie scrolled down the screen.

"Pythonistas?" Carolyn shuddered. "I never knew you were into snakes."

Sophie shook her head and rolled her eyes. "Relax, Mom. It's a coding meet up."

"Computers?"

"Yeah," she said in a tone that may as well have been, *Duh*. "But I am into snakes, too. Grandma even let me have a couple in high school."

"Surely she didn't allow you to have pythons?" Carolyn asked.

"No such luck," Sophie said as she clicked on a picture labeled *Seattle Cosplay*.

Carolyn skimmed the picture, filled with people dressed in costume. "Which one are you?"

"I'm not in that one." She scrolled down and pointed to a costume of a character Carolyn vaguely recollected from a graphic novel that Advance Imprint had put out a few years back.

"So, you…" Carolyn paused for the right terminology. "You 'hook up' with guys in costumes?"

"Oh my God, Mom, this isn't some kind of fetish," Sophie exclaimed. "Cosplay is a thing—like a hobby. And this is a way to meet other people who are into it. You know, similar interests. Don't you have any hobbies?"

Carolyn had to think about it for two solid minutes, which was telling when she couldn't come up with one. "Reading," she said, weakly.

"All work and no play…" Sophie shook her head and tsk, tsk, tsked. "Some things never change. Maybe you should try cosplay, Mom."

Carolyn laughed.

"What?" Sophie asked. "Is something wrong with *my* hobby?"

"Of course not," Carolyn said. "Cosplay sounds like lots of fun, but I can't imagine you'd want your mother trailing behind you dressed as what? Virginia Woolf?"

"Well, there you have it, Mom," Sophie said, the spark returning to her eye. "But enough of how your lovely daughter meets prospects full of panache and intrigue. Let's look at some dating sites for older, professional people."

"Could we find a different word for 'old' please?" Carolyn asked tiredly.

"Middle-aged?"

"Why don't we say 'mature' and leave it at that?"

Carolyn watched as her daughter typed in, "Dating sites for professionals over 40." The search results displayed several options.

"Let's try that one," Carolyn said, pointing at the screen.

Sophie clicked and pictures of model-handsome men popped up immediately.

"Oh, yes," Carolyn said. "Definitely the right choice."

"These are stock photos, Mom. Wait till you see the real ones."

Sophie slid the laptop over to Carolyn so she could type in her basic information. "What am I supposed to do for a username?"

Sophie bit her lower lip in thought. "You just came back to your childhood home from New York. You could call yourself the Homecoming Queen?"

Carolyn cringed. "That's not me at all."

"Oh yeah, remember those pictures Grandma pulled out? You were goth girl, all the way."

"Well, I won't be 'Goth Girl' here. How about, 'I'm-Only-Doing-This-For-My-Daughter'?"

"Too long," Sophie said dryly. "No personality."

"My Daughter's Dupe?"

Sophie rolled her eyes.

"Tired of Being Betrayed?"

"Mom, be serious. Guys don't want someone who's bitter. How about More Than Meets the Eye?"

"What's that supposed to mean? I have plenty that meets the eye."

"All I mean is that you're full of surprises. Ooh, 'Full of Surprises'?"

"No way."

"Fine. Let's just use your initials and a couple of numbers for now." Sophie clicked on the box for a free week's trial. A page came up for

Carolyn to type in her basic information and interests. At least this time, she had lists to choose from. Yes to indie movies and the symphony; no to all things sports and hunting. Within two minutes she had her checklist done.

"Let's skip the profile Q & A for now and jump right to the pictures," Sophie said, pulling the laptop back her way until it rested in a spot between them. She clicked on the button that said *See Your Matches* and smiled at Carolyn while the page loaded. Carolyn gave her a warm grin in return. Perhaps this would become more than just a college study for Sophie. And who knew? What if, with Sophie's cross-generational prompts, she just so happened to find a great guy to take her unraveled life and tie it back up in a lovely little bow?

Then, the pictures appeared.

Carolyn's face fell.

Sophie broke out laughing.

"This is what's out there?" Carolyn asked.

"What's with this one?" Sophie asked. They both tilted their heads to the left to see the picture that had been posted sideways.

"Not very tech-savvy," Carolyn murmured. "Why do so many of them take selfies from the driver's seats of their cars?"

"No idea—the guys on my sites do that too."

"Don't they have friends who can take pictures of them?" Carolyn asked. "And why are the ones over here wearing sunglasses and hats?"

"Guys wear hats and sunglasses all the time," Sophie said.

"I can't see them behind all of that," Carolyn said. "They may as well be wearing masks."

"'Down4Fun' doesn't look so bad." Sophie pointed to the top right corner of the screen.

"He's shirtless," Carolyn complained. "I think we can both presume what 'Down4Fun' is code for. And I don't want anyone who can't spell out the word 'for'."

"Damn, you're picky," Sophie said. "Guess you'll never ROFLOL, then."

"What's that?"

"Never mind. Let's just try a couple more pages and then we'll decide whether to try a different site."

"Sounds good," Carolyn said, reaching for her empty wine glass. "Would you like some more tea? I don't have the Thai kind, but I've got lots of choices and we could load it up with sugar and cream."

"Naw, I'm good," Sophie said, her gaze steady on the laptop screen. "You got any good pictures to add to your own profile?"

"Maybe I should put on a hat and some sunglasses and go sit in my car and take a selfie," she said on her way to the kitchen to open a new bottle of wine. As the Merlot sloshed into her glass, she couldn't help but pour a couple sips more than she probably should have. She was smiling—probably beaming, if she were to see her reflection. She felt almost giddy, like a college girl herself, talking about boys with her daughter. This never would have happened in New York. Perhaps she had Morgan St. John to thank for writing a hoax that would force Carolyn back to Washington State to revive her relationship with her daughter. Finally, all the planets and stars had seemed to align themselves in her favor. She held up her glass to the universe and drank the toast and a little swig more.

Heading back into the dining room, she found herself in an empty room.

"Sophie?" she called and listened for footsteps upstairs. Perhaps she'd needed to use the bathroom.

Carolyn caught sight of the face glowing from the laptop screen.

Her mind stuttered. How had Sophie found that picture? She must have gotten into her photo file to look for profile pictures and there it was.

But then, on the other side of the desktop, Carolyn noticed her work account—the one she'd been emailing from when Sophie had come to the door with their dinner. Had Sophie had gone into her "sent" mail? Carolyn clicked "History."

Dear God.

Most recent on the list gave the subject title: *Blast from 20 Years Ago.*

Carolyn's breath grew shallow, her head faint.

She searched the hallway, the bathroom. Empty.

She'd found him—his name, his picture.

Carolyn dashed back out in the hallway and looked toward the front door, which had been left wide open.

Jazmine

Jazmine trudged through the cherry blossoms on her way across the university's quad. Everywhere her dull gaze landed was the bright sign of spring—in the dew glistening on the lawns; in the trees' explosions of blossoms, seemingly overnight; in the thin veil of fog that gave it all sort of a romantic feel.

Or at least it would, were Jazmine not shrouded by the gloom brought on by Carolyn's fit of rage that had killed her laptop and took her files along with it, resulting in the imminent demise of her college career. Jazmine's phone had been inundated with Carolyn's apologetic voicemails ever since the other night, when she'd mistakenly tossed her cocktail at Henry. After a sleepless night trying to calm Henry, she wasn't ready to forgive just yet—not until she could find out whether her professor might give her an extension on the now nonexistent podcast.

The four months her dad had set were almost over, and she had nothing to show for all the work she'd done—all the time she'd spent away from her son as an investment in a brighter future. And now, all this brightness—the glaring sun, the winking dew, the snowing blossoms—wasn't the promise of a new beginning, but the reminder that, for Jazmine, this was the end.

Even her mind was taunting her, playing Quentin's rich, resonant voice in her memory, saying her name over and over.

"Jaaaaazmiiiine," came his voice again, followed this time by a warm, heavy hand on her shoulder.

Her head whirled, the fastest she'd moved in days. When her eyes lighted on Quentin, she relaxed—for a moment, anyway. Then she remembered how she must look, her face washed out and drawn, her whole demeanor slumped, resigned.

"You don't happen to have the next few hours free, do you?" he asked, breathing heavily as though he'd had to run to catch up to her. A breeze whipped the blossoms into a kaleidoscope of pink and white. It also blew the clean scent of soap and aftershave, and Jazmine noticed Quentin's hair was still damp from his morning shower. He took a step forward, apparently joining on her walk to the News Lab.

Jazmine thought for a moment. Her only purpose in coming to the campus today was to beg her professor for more time, which was pathetic and probably futile.

"My receptionist didn't show today and I was wondering..." Quentin trailed off to veer Jazmine around what appeared to be a small balloon animal. "Hey, is this something Henry might like?" he asked, crouching to pick it up.

Jazmine's mouth dropped as she regarded his earnest face, his large hands holding it out for her. The smile on her face felt like cracking plaster. What started as a snicker gave way to a full-on laugh.

"What?" he asked, his tone uncertain.

"It's a..." She bellowed into the morning fog. "It's a..."

"Looks like a little doggie, to me," he said, turning it at different angles in his hands. "Didn't you mention Henry says the word 'dog' now?"

Tears rimmed her eyes and she leaned over, feeling her abs rolling with the laughter. Breathless, she finally managed to say, "It's a condom."

She watched Quentin's smile freeze, his eyes grow wide. His hands opened and let the object fall to the bricks.

"The Sexual Awareness Center was passing them out today," Jazmine managed before laughing all over again. "I'm sure they weren't used, if that makes you feel any better."

If Quentin's dark cheeks could blush, they were surely doing so now. He reached into his shoulder satchel and pulled out a small bottle of hand sanitizer. "Let's keep this between us, shall we?"

"Of course," Jazmine said. "It wouldn't look good for you, offering a condom to a student."

Quentin's eyes widened even more. "It's not like you're *my* student," Quentin stammered. "But yeah. Pretty embarrassing." He wiped his hands on his slacks and shivered.

Jazmine wondered what he'd meant. If he hadn't thought of her as a student, had he only thought of her as Henry's mother? Then her mind tipped into a different reason altogether. Was there the slightest chance that he thought of her as a peer, or God willing, was he interested in her? No. She wouldn't let herself go there, no matter how endeared she was to this dignified professor's ability to laugh at his own awkwardness with the ridiculous rubber doggie.

"I'm sorry to hear that Sophie didn't make it to work," she said, ready to change the subject for his sake. "I hope she's okay, although," she laughed ruefully, "I wouldn't be surprised if her mother killed her."

"What's that now?" Quentin asked, wrinkling his nose at the off-hand comment.

Jazmine bit her lower lip, feeling a residual sense of loyalty to Carolyn.

"She—Carolyn, I mean—wasn't happy with me for the podcast interview," Jazmine explained. "I guess Sophie's recommendation for my guest was her stepmom."

"Carolyn's stepmom?"

"No, Sophie's stepmom."

Quentin spoke slowly and Jazmine could practically see his mind puzzling the pieces together. "Carolyn's...ex-husband's...current wife?"

"Exactly."

"And she's mad at Sophie over it—enough that she'd cause her to miss work?"

Jazmine shrugged. "I can only speak for myself when it comes to being the object of Carolyn's anger."

"Well, I've called for two days but she's not answering. I need someone to manage the office—especially this week, with this quarter's finals happening and next quarter's registration. I thought, if you had the time and wouldn't mind, that you could fill in for her. You'll be paid for your time, of course."

There wasn't much for Jazmine to consider. The proximity to Quentin alone cinched it. More than that, if this was a foot in the door for a job, she couldn't possibly turn that down. It probably wouldn't pay as much as the bus driving gig, but it might have more flexible hours and would be closed for holidays, and she'd have access to Seattle's best autism specialists.

"What would you need me to do exactly?" she asked. "Answer the phone?"

"And greet people as they come in. Call us in our offices when appointments arrive, that kind of thing. It's going to be crazy today, with some students turning in last-minute finals and others wanting to register for classes, switch classes, meet with professors to argue grades."

Jazmine opened her mouth to explain that she would be too busy throwing herself at the mercy of her professor to be able to help when Quentin added, "I'd sure owe you one."

"Oh, please." Jazmine waved his words away. "I owe you, and you know it."

"With all due respect, Ms. Johnston," Quentin paused and smiled slyly when Jazmine winced at the memory of their last exchange in his office. "I did that as a favor to Carolyn, so you can owe her as much as you want."

Jazmine considered Quentin's request and how lucky this really was. Serendipity, or kismet, or whatever they called it. Now that her degree was in jeopardy, she needed a job. She wondered how much it paid. And she *did* owe Quentin. But her thoughts were interrupted by Carolyn's voice, something she'd said weeks ago at the Cider House, and Jazmine decided she'd take her own shot.

"Be my guest," she blurted.

"What's that now?" Quentin asked for the second time in their conversation. "Are you inviting me out somewhere?"

"No." Jazmine laughed and leaned into his arm before she realized what she was doing and pulled herself back. "I'm wondering if you would be kind enough to be my next podcast guest. That's how you can pay me back."

She watched Quentin's face as he processed the invite. For the first time since her laptop had died, she felt a spark of hope. Sure, she'd have to rewrite questions and re-research and re-everything in just a few days' time if she was going to salvage her grade, but if Quentin just said "yes," it would at least be *possible*.

"Why do you think I'd be a good candidate for your podcast?" Quentin asked. "What did you call it? *Better Than Ever*?"

"*Better Than <u>Never</u>*," Jazmine corrected. "And Carolyn told me you'd be perfect."

"How's that?"

"Because she says you're the quintessential perfect man."

Quentin gave a low whistle into the morning mist. "I'm far from perfect. I've made lots of mistakes in my life."

"But you've learned from them?" Jazmine asked.

"Definitely."

"And you're a better man because of it?"

"I'd like to think so," Quentin said, "but better men can still make mistakes. Maybe we just work harder at learning from them."

"Then that makes you all the more perfect."

"You're the one with the halo," he said, his lips turning up at one corner. It was Jazmine's turn to wrinkle her nose, but he explained by turning to her, picking something from her hair, and holding it out to her.

A cherry blossom.

Jazmine smiled just as wryly and took the miniature flower. Then she reached up, stood on her tiptoes to pull a blossom from the crown of Quentin's head.

"It's no better in the fall, with all the leaves," Jazmine murmured. "But I'll take a blossom over a condom. You sure it's okay to offer a flower to a student?"

"Probably not," he said.

Jazmine brought her eyes up to meet his, and she knew this time that he didn't think of her as the mother of one of his subjects. It was more than that—maybe as much for him as it was for her.

"But I wonder whether it's appropriate for me to offer a flower to my temporary receptionist," he said.

"You help me with my final project so I can actually graduate, and I'll work on graduating and getting Sophie back," Jazmine said. "Then you can give me all the flowers you want."

No Going Back

Ava

Ava stood on the porch, knocking on the door of the same house she'd thrown up in what seemed like forever ago. She listened for the barrage of yipping from the feisty Chihuahua that Henry had called a "dod," but heard nothing. She knocked again, a series of panicked raps against the solid wood door. Maybe Carolyn hadn't returned her calls because she was too busy, or perhaps it was because she was still upset about what had happened last week at her late father's bungalow.

No matter—not after the text that had come in from Max that morning. It was the worst text she'd gotten since the day of her interview.

Get everything in order with McBride—we're moving ahead tomorrow!

Ava felt woozy and clung to the same porch railing. If this was happening tomorrow, she needed Carolyn's insight *now*! As she lifted her hand to pound the door again, it opened to reveal a young woman in a ratty UW Huskies sweatshirt, squinting into the sun over Alki Beach.

"Is Carolyn here?" Ava asked, breathless.

"Who wants to know?" The young woman's tone sounded more teen apathetic than guardedly suspicious.

Ava stood there dumbly. "Are you..." she paused, trying to remember the right name. She'd been so good with names at the conference, but now it seemed her brain had reached its limit. What had Carolyn said her daughter's name was? Shawna? Stella? Then, finally, "Sophia?"

"Sophie." The college student narrowed her makeup-less eyes as though trying to place Ava. With the dark circles underneath them, Ava wondered if she'd been cramming for finals—much like Jazmine would be doing if Carolyn hadn't soaked her final project in Midori sour. But then, Jazmine had said that Sophie was the one to suggest Jazmine interview Carolyn's ex-husband's current wife in the first place.

Ava closed her eyes, determined to stay focused. This was her last chance to get Carolyn's advice before do-or-coup time. The last thing she needed now was to be given the run-around by Carolyn's daughter.

The young woman in the doorway took a half-step back. "Sorry, she's not here," she said and started to close the door.

"I'm your mom's friend," Ava rushed to explain. "I work in publishing, too." She fished in her purse for her business card and handed it to Sophie. "If she isn't here, then maybe she could call me?"

Sophie looked at the card, turned it over in her hand, then studied the front of it again. "Howard Mercer Literary," she murmured.

"Yep," Ava said, rocking on her heels as she waited for Sophie to look up from the card. "I actually need to head over there now for work, so if you wouldn't mind letting your mom know that I really, *really* need to talk with her—"

"Lake Union?" Sophie asked, indicating the address on the card with her thumb.

"Yeah," Ava said, then added. "We work out of his house. It's super-nice, overlooking the lake and everything—"

"I'm actually heading that way," Sophie cut in again, "for an appointment. I wouldn't have to bother my grandma if I could I hitch a ride with you."

Ava opened her mouth to object. There was no way she could deal with chauffeuring Carolyn's daughter when she needed what little time she had left to decide whether to tell Howard what Max was doing behind his back. But before she could get a word out, Sophie was winding a black scarf around her neck and had already grabbed her coat off the entryway hook before closing the door behind her.

Ava followed her down the porch stairs, wondering what had just happened. Instead of leaving Carolyn's house with informed advice, she was leaving with her daughter in tow. She forced the warming spring air into her lungs. She would have to figure this out on her own.

As she sifted through her keys and clicked the car fob to unlock both doors, Ava noticed Sophie smile for the first time. Her expression was nice and all at once familiar.

"Nice ride," Sophie said.

Ava got into her used Toyota Corolla, wondering whether Sophie was just shining it on. But as her passenger got in, she hardly seemed to regard the car itself, staring out the windshield to something in another realm entirely. Ava clicked her seatbelt on and waited for Sophie to do the same. "Are you planning to strap yourself in?"

Sophie glanced away from the window as though just waking from a dream and not knowing where she was. "Oh yeah," she mumbled and pulled the seatbelt across her chest.

Ava started the car and pulled out, listening mindlessly to the radio until Sophie asked how long she'd been working for Howard Mercer Literary.

"Since Valentine's Day," she said as she reached over to turn the radio down a couple notches. Normally, this was where she would cringe at the events that had followed the interview, but she had more important things to process.

"What's it like?" Sophie asked. "Are the people nice?"

Ava gripped the steering wheel as she merged onto the West Seattle Bridge. She couldn't understand why the same young woman who would hardly say a word at her front door was suddenly curious about her job. "They've been great. I got hit by a bus after the interview—"

"Are you serious?"

"Yeah, the driver who hit me introduced me to your mom, actually." Ava tapped the brake as traffic crawled past the Seahawks' and Mariners' respective fields. "Anyhow, the senior agent was the first person on the scene, and he visited me in the hospital to make sure I was okay."

"Holy hell," Sophie breathed. "What did the boss say? I mean, he obviously hired you. That seems cool of him."

"Considering the concussion and how slowly I had to take things, Howard was incredibly patient with me."

"Seems like a standup guy," Sophie said. "I'll bet *he's* honest."

Ava wanted to ask, "As opposed to whom?" but as the 99-tunnel opened up next to the Space Needle and she slammed on the brakes for another traffic snarl, she found her thoughts interrupted by Gavin's voice through the car's speakers.

"Call Douglass and Burns to get a free consultation and don't settle for less than your pain and suffering are worth."

Ava's hand shot out to slam off the radio. That was the last thing she needed now.

"Damn," Sophie said. "Got something against ambulance chasers?"

"Only that one," Ava answered absently. "He's my ex."

Sophie picked off flecks of polish from her nails. "It's been ten years since my parents got divorced, and Mom still hates my dad. It galls her that he's getting an award for his writing—as if it means she lost to him, somehow—like they're in a competition, or something. She's not even a writer."

Ava nodded. While she knew she needed to return her concentration on what she should say to her boss, she found herself absorbed in this new take on Carolyn's history with Marcus, wondering if Sophie's comment had to do with either of them. At the same time, she held her breath for more prying questions from Sophie, but she stayed silent—silent enough that Ava could truly notice the shift happen inside of herself.

That damn commercial had been following her around for three months now, taunting her at every turn—bringing up the resentment, the yearning to have him back, the conversations she'd never have the chance to have, and the infinite questions that would never be answered. But this time, she felt…nothing. It was a mere annoyance, like the distracting buzz of a fly.

As she turned left onto Dexter Ave, she felt herself turning another, more figurative corner because she no longer saw herself in the victim's chair. It was Howard—Howard being victimized now—Howard who would never get to have a conversation or ask the important questions before Max stuck the knife deep into his back. It was Howard who would never get the chance to understand Max's dissatisfaction or to right it. Ava had deserved to know how Gavin had been feeling—to know how she could have adjusted to his problem, if that was even possible. Howard deserved that chance, too.

Ultimately, as Sophie had recognized without even knowing the man, Howard was a stand-up guy. As much as Ava appreciated Max's help on the accident scene and his subsequent hospital visits, he was the one in the wrong here. And while Ava was desperate for the money, and as flattered as she had been by Max's accolades, she knew the risks Howard had taken in hiring her as a newbie—with a concussion, no less. Sure, she would have thrived in this cool, young, revolutionary movement in the industry, but they never would have considered her without her having signed Wesley McBride. And it was *Howard* who had provided her that opportunity. Besides, he'd always treated her fairly.

"We're almost there," Ava said. "Would you like me to drop you at your appointment?"

Sophie shook her head. "I can walk." She was obviously worlds away as she looked back out the passenger window. Ava had lost her again.

They drove along in silence for the rest of the trip, the sun bright above them. Ava sat up taller in her seat, knowing without a doubt that as long as Howard did right by her, she would do right by him. She felt a surge of pride and resolve within herself.

When Ava pulled over alongside Howard's house, she scanned the side of the road for Max's car, relieved when she didn't see it. Only Dahlia's little Jetta and a pickup that probably belonged to one of Howard's neighbors. She set the emergency break and said, "Okay,

Sophie. Thanks for keeping me company. Hope your appointment goes—"

"I have to pee."

"Excuse me?"

"I *really* have to go," Sophie said, pressing her legs together. "I'll wet my pants if I have to walk six blocks. Do you think your boss would let me use his bathroom?"

"It would probably be fine," Ava said, amazed at how brazen Sophie was compared to her ever-sophisticated mother. "But you'll need to make it fast. We have some important things to go over…" She trailed off, realizing Sophie had already left the car and was headed up Howard's front walk. Ava bolted out of her door to join her.

It was Dahlia who inevitably greeted them at the front door.

"This is my friend Sophie," Ava told her. "She just needs to use the bathroom and then she'll be heading back out."

"Sure," Dahlia said. "I'll show you the way."

Ava shrugged off her jacket and hung it on the hallway hook. As nervous as she was for her impending conversation with Howard, she felt the smile lighting her face. It was as though a toxin had been surgically removed from her body. The toxicity of Gavin's addiction and Max's underhanded takeover. She stepped lightly down the hallway toward the meeting room until she heard a deep voice that didn't belong to Howard and stopped cold. The voice had a slow drawl that could only belong to Wesley McBride.

"…and then, she had the audacity to tell me *I* was the perverse one," he said.

The two erupted into laughter as though they were old college chums. They stopped only when they saw Ava in the doorway of the meeting room. Dahlia floated past her and back down to the mail pile on the hallway desk.

"Why, Ms. Perkins, so nice to see you again," Mr. McBride said and rose to shake her hand. He towered over her, a head taller than even Howard, who wasn't exactly short. He seemed bigger than ever in the meeting room, quite stocky in his flannel shirt and jeans.

"What a surprise," Ava said, giving his hand a quick shake.

"It came up spur of the moment," Mr. McBride said. "Howard wasn't expecting me, either. Sounds like my email didn't come through."

Ava nodded, her mind whirling through her past emails, knowing she hadn't seen one from Wesley for at least a week. As much as she wanted to believe that it hadn't come through, it was just as likely that Max had moved it from their shared email account into whatever new, separate account he was sharing with Roxi Fischer—especially if Wesley had been arranging a time to sign the contract. Howard needed to know immediately.

"Wes was just telling me about how he stumbled onto his great ending for the book," Howard said.

Ava winced. Her determination had been so solely based on signing Wes, she hadn't yet read the manuscript he'd emailed. And there on the meeting table was Howard's printed version, riddled with editorial markings. Weeks ago, Ava had learned that Howard went the old school hard copy way with the big authors.

"Go ahead," Howard encouraged her. "See if my edits match yours."

"Thanks," Ava said with as much sincerity as she could force through her desperation to warn her boss about Max. "I was just hoping I could steal Howard away for a quick minute?"

Wes looked taken aback and Howard's face registered pure confusion.

"I wouldn't ask if it wasn't crucial," Ava urged him. She fidgeted with the manuscript, flipping the pages when a certain line brought her shuffling back.

For my Annabelle—may you ever be your own.

Ava stopped, breathless. *Okay,* she told herself. *This was Dad's inscription. But they were friends. They shared all kinds of writing techniques. Even inscriptions, apparently.*

"Everything okay?" Howard asked, leaning in.

Ava flipped a page and read the first few sentences, and then the next few sentences of the manuscript she'd been working to format for self-publishing. Her father's manuscript.

"Something's wrong," she said and continued turning pages. The only thing different was that his trademark quirkiness had been deleted—and without the quirkiness, the narrative actually read like a Western.

But then, as she waited in the silence for a response to her sudden bout of dread, she noticed that Howard's perplexed gaze was looking just past her to the hallway, where Sophie stood, wringing her hands. Ava wondered where Dahlia had disappeared to and why she hadn't shown Sophie out after she'd finished with the bathroom.

"I just wanted to thank you for letting me use the facilities," Sophie said softly to Ava. She mostly stared at the floor when she wasn't stealing glances at Howard. But when she shined a shy smile, Ava noticed it—that subtle crinkle beneath her eye. She turned her gaze to Howard, who smiled warmly back at Sophie, his blue eyes every bit as bright as hers, and his own dimple underneath the same right eye.

Without turning her head, Ava glanced back and forth between the two until she felt woozy all over again. "No problem," she said, more loudly than she'd intended. "Why don't I show you to the door?"

"Actually, I'm a student at the University of Washington and I need to fact-check a study I'm working on."

"You said you had an appointment," she said through gritted teeth.

"This obviously isn't a good time," Wesley said, suddenly standing before them, his backpack slung over his shoulder. "We can talk later, via phone."

Howard held up a hand. "Please, Wes. This will only be a minute." He turned back to Sophie. "Who did you say you were?"

"Sophie," she said, extending a hand. "Sophie Wheeler."

"Wheeler," Howard said under his breath.

Ava watched Wes shift his backpack and sneak glances in her direction. Did he know that she knew?

"I'm doing a study on Generation X and the Tech Boom—"

"We're in the middle of a meeting," Howard said.

"Yes, maybe another time," Ava said, placing a hand to Sophie's elbow.

"Howard, I don't need to interfere in your personal business," Wes said. "Perhaps we can meet at a more convenient time for both of us." He squeezed past the three of them at the edge of the hallway entrance.

Carolyn's daughter yanked her arm away. "—more specifically how Gen-X'ers have used technology to look up old flames."

"Excuse me?" Howard asked.

"One of my subjects, Carolyn Ford, emailed you recently. I believe the subject line read, a 'Blast from 20 years ago'."

"What the hell is this?" Howard asked, as the gentle gleam in his eyes turned steely.

Ava gave Howard an apologetic shrug. "I just met her myself. She needed a ride."

"'Blast from 20 years ago?'" He glowered at Ava. "Are you also part of this kid's dating app study, along with your good friend, Ms. Ford?"

Ava wasn't sure what Carolyn's daughter was doing, but the girl had everyone on their heels. Had Carolyn actually sent some "Blast from 20 years ago" email? That would have been ancient history for Sophie. Why had Carolyn shared it with this pot-stirring kid of hers?

Howard tried to step around Sophie and called down the hallway. "Just give me a minute, Wes."

Ava felt the tension release from her neck and shoulders. Wesley wouldn't be signing any contracts tonight and Ava would be able to talk with Howard—once they got Sophie out the door.

As soon as the door closed behind him, Howard turned to Ava. "Is this kid here why you needed to talk with me so desperately?" Before Ava could answer, he whirled on Sophie. "Who *are* you? Is this a joke? A set-up?"

"Honestly, Howard, I just met her this morning," she said.

"But you're friends with Carolyn," he said. "Is she trying to poach Wes McBride? Are you working for her?"

"*I'm* not trying to 'poach' anyone. And we're just friends—nothing professional involved. It was a total fluke I even met her—through the bus accident after our interview."

Sophie raised her eyebrows. "She said you had a grand time at my grandma's house for drinks. Until all the upheaval, that is."

Ava's stomach roiled, and she feared she might heave again now, on yet another hardwood floor. She almost wished she would—anything to get out of from under Howard's interminable glare.

Ava was so tempted to turn to this conniving little chaos agent and stab her with a pithy warning shot, but she turned to Howard instead. "Look, I really need to tell you something—actually, two things now—important things. In private. You *need* to hear this—"

"At your interview, you said you knew Carolyn Ford," he said with an evenness that sounded forced.

"I was…" Ava stammered. "I was trying to impress you."

Howard snickered. Ava had never heard him snicker. He'd always been too cool and professional to *snicker*. "And you thought using Carolyn Ford's name was the way to do that?" he asked. "I hired you in *spite* of her."

Ava could hear Dahlia's footsteps finally click-clacking back down the hall. Thank God.

"What's that supposed to mean?" Sophie asked. "Do you hate my mom, or something?"

Howard ran his hands over his salt-and-pepper hair. "Look, *now* is not a good time."

Dahlia stepped in. "Why don't you and I set up an appointment with Mr. Mercer and we'll revisit your college project then."

"No need," Sophie said, re-wrapping her scarf around her neck. "I just wanted to let Mr. Mercer know my birthday is October 17, 2003. He can do the millennial math."

Sophie turned on her heels and walked back up the hallway. They listened to her footsteps clunk against the hardwood and then the deep boom of the heavy front door slamming shut.

"Why the hell would I care when her birthday is?" Howard asked, then blanched as he seemed to answer the question on his own. He staggered a couple of feet back until his hand found the back of a chair. "You need to go," he hissed at Ava.

"Are you firing me?" she asked, her voice shaky.

"Give me one reason why I shouldn't."

Ava pursed her lips and returned his glare. It would be so satisfying to blurt it out—to see the look on his face when he learned what Max was about to do.

"Go!" Howard's voice rose in strength. "Now!"

"Howie?"

They turned to find a thin woman in the still-open front door. Ava guessed she was in her early forties. The diamond on her left hand was four times the size of the one Gavin had given Ava.

Howard breathed, "You're early. I told you I couldn't do dinner until..." He trailed off, leaving behind an exhausted silence.

The woman's small voice dwarfed Howard's previous shouting. "You have a daughter?"

Carolyn

Seagulls swarmed the park bench as Carolyn tore off bits of her sandwich and tossed them in the air to feed the most aggressive birds willing to edge closest to her. She was too distraught to eat her lunch, and dinner was doubtful. The birds in front of her stabbed silently at the bread with their beaks, while seagulls circling overhead cried and cried and cried.

The sea lapped at the beach with a numbing rhythm. Any minute now, her mother would pass by on her afternoon walk. In the meantime, Carolyn inhaled the sea air and imagined herself rising and walking into the water until the Puget Sound swallowed her whole. Her new employees hardly knew her well enough to miss her, and it would probably come as a relief to those she'd deceived all these years.

Of course, she was being ridiculous. It was on her to untangle the web she'd so expertly spun over the years, and if anyone could do it, she could. But how?

She checked her phone for the zillionth time to be sure Sophie was still ignoring her texts. She didn't dare call Marcus to ask where their daughter was. She wouldn't doubt that Sophie had gone to him first.

While there was still a chance that a paternity test could come out positive for Marcus's DNA, the fact that Sophie was Howard's spitting image did little for Carolyn's optimism.

"They say seagulls are just rats with feathers."

Carolyn looked up to see her mother standing over her, clad in a mauve velvet jogging suit for her afternoon beach walk. At her feet, Trixie yipped and lunged at the seagulls until Vivian pulled back on the leash.

Carolyn shrugged and went back to shredding her sandwich for the birds. "Flying rats need to eat, too."

"Why don't you make some room for your mother and tell me why you're sitting in blue jeans and sunglasses on a workday afternoon?"

Carolyn slid over on the bench, her bottom lip trembling too much to be able to speak. Instead, as soon as Vivian sat down, she dropped her head to her mother's shoulder and wept.

For what seemed like the first time in Carolyn's life, Vivian remained silent, as though allowing her daughter's tears to tell her all she needed to know. Carolyn heaved sobs, breathing in the scent of her mother's face powder and Selsun Blue shampoo, while the Chihuahua sniffed around her ankles for any bits of sandwich the seagulls may have left behind.

"Rock bottom" had nothing on the new low Carolyn was feeling. Her surprise pregnancy, Marcus's constant cheating, the Morgan St. John hoax—all of them hovered miles above her now as she grieved the possible loss of her recently renewed relationship with her daughter. What did any other facet of her life—any success she might ever find—matter without Sophie?

Vivian finally broke the silence with a sigh. "I always wondered if there was something more behind that forensics project Sophie did last year at the high school."

Carolyn's shoulders slumped in both relief and resignation. She tossed a piece of bread and looked out into the distance where a man in a Seahawks hat was walking a dog. Finally, she breathed, "You know?"

"Oh please," Vivian said, waving the words away like so many flies. "I've known for years."

Carolyn straightened up and ran a finger under her sunglasses to dry her eyes. "When?" she asked. "How did you—"

"Give me some credit, sweetheart," Vivian said. "And isn't that beside the point?"

Carolyn shrugged again in surrender. "Are you upset with me for lying?"

"I'm livid with you for making me put up with Marcus all these years." Vivian reached for a corner of Carolyn's sandwich to toss to the flying rats. One of the screeching birds swooped and scavenged the morsel before the seagulls on the ground could snatch it. "And I'm sad you chose to lie to the people who needed truth the most."

Carolyn frowned, then threw her arms up limply. "What was I supposed to do? I'd been married to Marcus for three months by the time I found out I was pregnant. Should I have told him the baby might not be his? Or was Howard supposed to welcome me back to raise a child after I'd left him for someone else?"

"Howard!" Vivian snapped her fingers. "That's right!" The woman beside Carolyn beamed as though she'd won a senior speed-walking championship.

"It's not like I knew for sure, myself, you know?" Carolyn continued. "And once I'd convinced myself that Marcus was the father, I couldn't well decide to come clean with a *possibility* after Sophie had been born, much less as the years unfolded. What would have been gained at that point for my semi-functional family in revealing Sophie to be Howard Mercer's younger, female 'mini-me.'"

"Mercer!" Vivian lifted a victorious fist once again. "Howard Mercer, I remember now."

Trixie stood on her hind legs, her forelegs on Vivian's knees until she picked her up and set her in her lap. The dog licked eagerly at her Vivian's chin before turning three circles and lying down.

"When should I have come clean, Mom? When Sophie moved away to live with you? When Marcus married this…this new woman and invited Sophie to become a part of his life—their lives—again?"

"That gutted you, I know," Vivian said, her voice as smooth as her velvet jumpsuit. She put a hand on Carolyn's knee. "And it probably would have seemed like you were saying it out of revenge, at that point."

"That's exactly why I didn't. And there didn't seem to be any point in telling the truth about something that was still a matter of speculation."

"I suppose you could have run a DNA test without their knowing," Vivian said. "There are whole talk shows I've watched with Maury and Jerry that feature those revealing paternity tests."

Carolyn grimaced and shook her head. Leave it to her mother to utter a completely sound suggestion in one sentence, and then speak of Maury Povich and Jerry Springer as reasonable examples in the next, as though they were neighbors she knew personally from down the street.

Something niggled at the back of Carolyn's mind. "Tell me again what Sophie's high school science project was again—the one she won the award for?"

Vivian slowly turned to meet Carolyn's eyes, as though she could read exactly what she was thinking. "DNA lab work," Vivian said. "She must have spent at least three months testing and comparing various samples."

"Including Marcus's," Carolyn said dismally.

"That must be how she found out," Vivian agreed.

"You mean, she didn't tell you when she found out they weren't a match?"

Vivian shook her head. "I'm afraid I'm as surprised that she knows as you are. Poor girl's been keeping this inside for months now."

Carolyn's heart ached that her daughter could no longer trust her and would probably never trust her again. It crushed her to think of how fun it had been eating Thai and making up singles profiles. And then it hit her that making up for lost time had been her own agenda—not Sophie's. "She made up that college assignment to get me to tell her my old boyfriends—"

"—so that she could figure out who her biological father might be," Vivian finished.

The two women sat in silence, absorbing all that had happened right in front of them all this time.

"What now?" Carolyn asked numbly. "Obviously, I need to talk with Sophie."

"I don't think so," Vivian said. "Not yet, anyway. She's just found out that everything she thought was true was a mirage."

"But if she would give me a chance to tell her the whole story, maybe she'd understand."

"She will, eventually," Vivian said. "But she needs time to rebuild her world. And besides, you know Sophie. She's always been like a feral cat. Come towards her and she'll disappear. Let her come to you on her own terms and she'll trust you in her time."

"Then I should go to Howard. He must be reeling—"

"If, indeed, Sophie has told him."

"They're probably taking a DNA test as we speak."

Vivian nodded slowly. "In that case, there's one other person in this equation whom you don't seem to give much consideration."

"Who?" Carolyn asked. "Marcus?"

Vivian nodded again.

"Since when have you given that cheat any consideration?"

"Never," Vivian said. "But it seems to me you've lost the moral high ground when it comes to infidelity."

The words themselves sucked the air from Carolyn's lungs.

"I'm not judging you," Vivian said.

"You sure about that?" Carolyn asked. "Because I'm pretty sure you—"

"Honey, it isn't your fault he cheated," Vivian said, her voice kind, yet firm. "But your long-ago choice to marry the wrong man *is* on you."

Carolyn snorted and tossed the last corner of her sandwich to the seagulls surrounding them. "Like you would have wanted me to marry Howard."

"Who cares what *I* would have wanted?"

"I cared, Mom!" Carolyn shouted. "What kind of life would I have had with a garage band drummer?"

As a few more seagulls joined the afternoon feeding, Trixie squatted on her haunches and growled, the hair on her spine rising into a stiff little mohawk before she leaped from Vivian's lap and sent the birds flapping into the air, crying anew.

"Trixie, you stop that," Vivian scolded and pulled back on the leash. The dog strained and barked until, satisfied she'd done her job, she sat as tall as her tiny body would allow. Vivian took a hand off the leash and placed it gently on Carolyn's hand. "From the looks of Howard now, you would have had a very nice life."

"How was I supposed to know he'd turn himself around?"

"You weren't supposed to know anything, dear," Vivian said, taking a fly-away piece of Carolyn's hair and tucking it behind her ear. "But marrying a man because he seemed like the more responsible choice wasn't exactly responsible, was it? Would you want someone marrying you for any other reason but love?"

"Of course not, but there's so much more than that—"

"Save it." Vivian held up her hand and rose from the bench. "Marcus needs to hear it from you."

"Too little, too late," Carolyn said, shaking her head sadly.

"Would you rather he hears it from Sophie?" Vivian asked.

"Yes," Carolyn said without missing a beat.

Vivian crouched and lifted Carolyn's chin until their eyes met. "It's never too late to do the right thing."

Jazmine

Jazmine sat across from Quentin at his office table, watching as he leaned over to turn off the essential oil diffuser. Tension gripped her shoulders like a reflex when she heard Henry cooing from down the hall.

"He's fine." Quentin's voice was gentle. "Office hours are over and Sophie just locked the doors, so the little man's got her all to himself."

"It's just that he doesn't know Sophie, and it's hard to believe she's reliable enough…" Jazmine trailed off when she saw Quentin's soft expression.

"Sophie said it was an emergency," he said. "She was a little distant the first couple of days, but she's gone above and beyond the rest of the week, and she's determined to make up for you pitching in for her on Monday by helping with Henry while we record. But if you're uncomfortable, we can always reschedule."

Jazmine listened once again and heard Henry's giggles echo down the hall. "Doesn't sound like he'll be melting down anytime soon," she said.

"And if he does, we hit pause and finish up another time," Quentin said. "It's not like we're doing a live radio broadcast."

Jazmine clasped her hands nervously, ready to begin. Before this, she'd never felt nervous around Quentin and cringed to think of the ridiculous amount of time she'd spent that afternoon at home, trying on outfits and smoothing her hair back into a ponytail until it sprang into a perfect array of curls. But now that Sophie was back in her receptionist's seat, watching Henry for her in the Psych Department's front office, Jazmine was no longer Quentin's pseudo-employee, nor was she the desperate mother of an autistic boy. She was a fellow podcast interviewer, a soon-to-be Communications Grad with an impending successful career, and she was determined to prove herself as his equal—or as equal as she could be to a university professor. Quentin pressed the record button and gave a warm smile that allayed any sense of intimidation, most of which were her own projections.

"Good evening, and welcome back to *Better Than Never*. I'm Jazmine Johnston and my guest tonight is Child Behavior and Special Needs Diagnostician, Professor Quentin Sims from the University of Washington School of Psychology. Thank you, Dr. Sims, for joining me tonight."

"Happy to be here," Quentin said. His eyes gleamed; his full soft lips smiled encouragement. Jazmine glanced away, determined to keep her focus.

"You can hear more from Dr. Sims in his own podcast, *Insights and Information*. Lord knows I've learned a ton about my own special needs son, who's grown exponentially since Quentin evaluated him and referred us to a specialist in child autism."

"I appreciate the shout-out," Quentin said. "I'm glad *Insights and Info* has been helpful for you, and I'm guessing it won't be long until you're hearing from your listeners about how much your show has helped them—in whatever way that might be."

Jazmine felt her cheeks warm. "Your show offers answers. Mine only seems to offer more questions."

"That's where the experts come in," Quentin said. "You ask the questions; they'll give the answers. Here's a question for you: What answers are *you* looking for?"

"Let me think." Jazmine's eyes went wide when she saw Quentin's large hand reaching out toward her face. She felt herself moving to allow her cheek to settle into his palm, but then caught herself when his hand grazed past her jaw in order to pluck something from her shoulder. He held it up, beaming—another cherry blossom had caught in her hair on her way in. It was all Jazmine could do to breathe deeply and re-center herself so she could continue. "On *Better Than Never*, we look at past broken relationships and consider why so many exes go on to become the people they could've—even should've—been in the first place."

As she spoke, Jazmine took a paperclip from the desk and fidgeted, pulling it open, then twisting it back and around. She felt herself relax and thought about all the objects necessary to distract Henry and bring his nerves down. She'd never noticed that similarity between them before and felt a sudden closeness to him.

"For example," she continued, "a cheater who becomes faithful to the next partner. Or an addict who becomes sober. Perhaps a person who abandons one family becomes a glowing husband and father to the next." Jazmine paused when she realized she'd gotten a little too specific—too close to home. But Quentin seemed just as absorbed in watching her paperclip as she'd been in shifting it into its various shapes. Just in case, she added, "Or a devoted wife and mother, for that matter."

Quentin put his index finger over his lush lips. Had he seen through to her own, semi-sordid history? "Intriguing concept," he said. "So, how has your hypothesis held up empirically?"

Jazmine shrugged, wondering if he was testing her intellect with the professional lingo or if he truly saw her as an equal. "First of all, we consider why this happens."

"Why a person chooses to better himself?"

"Yes, but why at that time, in particular?" Jazmine replied. "Why doesn't he—or she—choose to get better within the initial relationship? Was the initial partner not worth it, or the second partner more so?"

"Or was he so broken up by the dissolution of the relationship that he realized change was in order before he—or she—could move forward?"

Jazmine froze, breathless. She couldn't imagine that the obsessively controlling Ben would have had such insight before finding his new wife. Not to mention her father, who seemed to feel no remorse for the way he'd ignored her after he moved across the world during her teen years. Without acknowledging his neglect, could he really evolve into the good guy he pretended to be now? She stared at Quentin, at a loss for words. His eyes shone like dabs of melted chocolate, earnest and sincere. Candid.

And then she realized. He'd been talking about *himself*.

"Ultimately, I believe it's important to consider the danger in overly generalizing these reasons when breakups vary from relationship to relationship," Quentin continued.

"Somewhat true, but commonalities emerge as distinct patterns when enough broken relationships are examined," Jazmine said, matching her professional jargon to his. "And, actually, the more intriguing question to me is how any jilted partner, or those fresh to romantic engagements for that matter, would go about landing a person who's earnestly strived to be his—or her—best self in the first place?"

"Maybe it's not a matter of 'landing' someone," Quentin said. "I would argue it's a matter of mutuality in this important life choice."

Jazmine felt her face fall. She was tempted to pull out the hackneyed term "chemistry," but thought better of it. "Are you saying a woman makes a choice to be emotionally abused and controlled?" She stopped, realizing Quentin had run the discussion completely off the rails, into territory for which she hadn't prepared herself—territory she knew more about than she ever would have wished for. It was all she could do from snatching her red jacket from the back of her chair and waving it around like the red flag Quentin had just sent up.

"If she's being held against her will, then no," Quentin said. "But if she has the ability to leave and find a healthy person to share her life with, yet she stays with the abuser, then yes, she is making that choice."

Jazmine put on her thinking face to cover for the way Quentin had thrown her off her game. She couldn't very well correct him, that Ben had been the one to leave *her*.

And then, Quentin took the paperclip that she was contorting within an inch of its life and poked the cherry blossom through the end. He twirled it in front of her as he went on to explain. "Let's just say a man wants to invest time in his career, thinking once it got going, he'd have more down time. But once that down time finally rolls around, he doesn't have anyone to enjoy that leisure time with, because his wife leaves him, citing neglect."

While Quentin's voice remained steady, Jazmine met his gaze, noticing the slightest change in his eyes, gleaming as always, but with no laugh behind them. And then she knew. This wasn't just some clinical example—this was about him. She couldn't imagine him neglecting anyone any more than she could imagine a woman who would choose to leave him. Neglect didn't seem so bad. Surely it was better than having someone watch your every move, controlling every mile driven, every penny spent.

"Wow," Jazmine murmured, thinking back to her autism sessions with Henry. "Bringing change starts with changing our own behavior."

"If you're looking for answers," Quentin said, "I'd start there."

A soft knock at the door reminded Jazmine that Sophie was on a tight schedule and would need to take off soon.

"Thank you so much for tuning in to *Better Than Never*," she said, rushing to sign-off before opening the door to her potentially noisy little boy. "And Dr. Sims, thank you so much for joining me. It was enlightening, to say the least."

Quentin gave a half-smile and a nod. "The pleasure was all mine."

He switched off the recording and, before he could rise to open the office door for Sophie and Henry, Jazmine reached for his hand and took the flower clip, plugging one end of the paperclip through the shirt button at his wrist and pulling it back out the other side like a cuff link.

Then Jazmine's heart gasped and held its breath. What had she just done? The silence pounded in her ears and she longed for the sound of that silly oil diffuser. They'd flirted before, in the courtyard, hadn't they? Surely it hadn't been her imagination. She realized her hand was still on his and felt the blood drain from her face until finally, Quentin reached towards her, then past her to open the office door.

"Sorry to interrupt," Sophie said as she poked her head through the doorway. "I really need to be going."

"Sophie's father has been nominated for an award at the Pacific Northwest Literary Society tonight," Quentin said.

"As have you," Sophie said to Quentin. Jazmine noticed that her smile and voice both seemed tight.

Quentin went to the coat hook in the corner of his office. "Now that I think about it," he said, shrugging on a gray wool trench coat, "it's the perfect place for a Communications major."

Normally, Jazmine would be wide-eyed in confusion over his feelings for her. Here he was, thinking he was being subtle in removing her flower cufflink at the same time that he was asking her out. Was it a guise to have a date with her or was he really just trying to give a student a leg up in her profession? She smiled broadly at the makeshift blossom pin.

Her smile faded when she noticed her son. "What happened to his hair?" she asked.

"I know I should have asked," Sophie said. "It looked pretty wonky with that piece shaven down the middle, so I fixed it."

"But how?" Jazmine breathed. "I didn't hear him screaming during our interview."

"Screaming?" Sophie repeated. "I'm sorry, did he want it that way? Was it a style choice?"

"God, no!" Jazmine laughed. "He throws tantrums."

"Oh." Sophie nodded and shrugged. "Well, I didn't do anything special."

"I beg to differ," Jazmine said. "You have a gift, truly."

Henry toddled towards Quentin, pointed at his hand, and said, "Wose."

"Oh, this?" Quentin asked, holding up the blossom. He casually handed the flower to Henry.

"What do you say about tonight?" Quentin asked Jazmine. "Would you be willing and able to attend the literary awards banquet?"

This time, Jazmine's wide eyes looked up from her son and met Quentin's. "You were serious about that?"

"You could hobnob with the Who's Who in the writing world. Find the next interviewee for *Better Than Never*."

Jazmine luxuriated for a moment in the way he'd used her podcast's name—as though it were a legitimate show. She hoped Lucinda would be available to watch Henry, followed by the familiar twinge of guilt that she was spending less and less time with her son and depending more and more on her stepmother. But then, tonight held the potential to find relationship writers for her podcast that could launch her platform into the stratosphere, not to mention the networking she could do with other nonfiction writers and journalists.

And, deep down in the recesses of her soul, there was still a possibility, no matter how minute, that this could turn into a real date.

"Willing, yes," she finally said. "I'll need to find childcare. Then I need to get him home. I don't know if I have enough time. Light rail doesn't leave for another—"

"I drove my car to work today," Quentin said. "If you feel comfortable, I could drive you to your stepmom's house and you could ask her when we get there."

Quentin was making it impossible to say no. And so, Jazmine pulled out her cell phone, scrolled to Lucinda in her contacts and said, "Yes."

Accolades

Ava

Ava hugged her father's manuscript to her chest as she counted down until the crossing sign finally flashed WALK. She stepped out onto the street amidst a throng of people, walking toward the Seattle Convention Center. A modest crowd milled about the sidewalk in designer trench coats and jackets, which surely hid designer suits and gowns beneath them. Ava couldn't help feeling that her consignment label—the same kimono wrap she'd worn at the conference—would give her away as the fraud she was. Unemployed and *still* no word from the attorney about the impending settlement, she could only hope that Carolyn might welcome her to join her table—that she might be able to bend Carolyn's ear about Sophie's bombshells at Howard's agency, the fallout of which having been Ava's abrupt dismissal from his firm. If anyone could guide her through this, it was Carolyn—and considering it was Carolyn's secret that had put her in this position, it seemed she owed her at least that much.

As the Convention Center loomed above, Ava gazed breathlessly at the way the building's modern industrial light fixtures glowed through the glass façade, radiating glitz and glamor. She followed the rest of the VIP crowd into the entrance hall where she exchanged her stylish invitation to Howard Mercer and Associates for a gilded program, hoping Howard himself wasn't lurking nearby to call her out on what she could only assume was now a canceled invite.

Bestselling authors of every genre gathered throughout the foyer. Some shrugged off coats and laid them over their arms. Her own arms were growing weary from the weight of her father's words. But then, in the middle of it all, she spotted Carolyn. She probably appeared serene to those who didn't know her, but Ava detected the glimmer of her jaw clench and noticed the white knuckled grip on her program. No matter. Desperate times. Ava sidled through the crowds for a moment with her friend.

"Hello, Ava," Carolyn said, all business—a far cry from the familiar warmth she'd shown at the conference. But Carolyn knew Ava had nothing to do with Jazmine's podcast interview, and so long as she was being polite, Ava surely had a chance.

"Carolyn," Ava said with a stoic nod, doing her best to mirror Carolyn's affectation for the evening. "Do you have an extra seat at your table? It's important that I talk with you—"

"About what happened with Henry," Carolyn said. "I know. Last I heard, we were full."

"It's not about Henry and it's *urgent*," Ava insisted. "You're going to want to hear this."

"I don't have time to talk now," Carolyn said, "but come find me in the banquet hall and I'm sure I can find a couple of minutes for you." She turned to leave but ran smack into Dahlia instead.

"Excuse me," Carolyn told her Ava's startled coworker—*former* coworker—who backed away and made to walk around her, when Ava registered the man holding Dahlia's hand. Wearing the same gray suit and striped tie from his commercials, he smelled of the same spicy cologne he'd worn on their first date.

"Gavin?" Ava asked.

Carolyn raised her eyebrows at Ava with an implied, *The Gavin?* Dahlia looked to Gavin, as though for answers. If the bastard hadn't bothered to tell Dahlia about Ava, then he certainly hadn't told Dahlia how he'd pushed his most recent ex to the brink of bankruptcy.

"Gutless. Coward," she hissed at Gavin. "Dating someone you know I work with?"

Gavin's face was plastered with the smile he always wore when she'd busted him for anything. "I didn't know whether you got the job."

"It's a good thing she did," Carolyn said. "Apparently she racked up quite a credit card bill putting a certain someone through law school."

Ava looked at Carolyn, who'd apparently shrugged off the professionalism in the name of red flag solidarity. "Yeah, well," Ava added, "you could have asked your new girlfriend here, apparently."

"Wait, did you two date?" Dahlia asked him.

Ava could tell that Gavin was distracted by his new girlfriend and this woman with Ava who seemed to know all about her finances. Yet all the while, he kept his eyes trained on Ava. "You can't choose who you fall in love with."

Sure, you can! Ava wanted to scream. *You could have chosen to stay with me!*

She took a deep breath, working to achieve some semblance of dignity and grace.

"You've got yourself a great guy," she told Dahlia, "especially now that he's..."

She was going to say *changed*—but then she noticed it.

The drink in his hand.

"Now that he's..." she stammered, looking back up at Gavin—the same old Gavin he'd always been. "He's..."

He hadn't become a better man after all.

Ava realized they were all waiting—Carolyn included—for Ava to finish her sentence. But then, a voice came on the other side of her. "Looks like you made a choice with that drink in your hand."

It was Jazmine, her hair done up in a spray of curls. Where had she come from? Had she made up with Carolyn already?

"Do I know you?" Gavin asked Jazmine, then looked at Carolyn. "Or you?"

"We're the Red Flag Society," Carolyn announced, "and we're here to save this poor dear time and money."

"What are they talking about?" Dahlia asked.

"Red flags," Jazmine repeated. "I'm sure you've seen 'em. Just don't ignore them."

Dahlia appeared just as puzzled, then glanced away as though wheels were turning, working to recall past suspicions.

Ava wanted to offer a few red flag examples, but once Gavin had narrowed his eyes at Jazmine, then at Carolyn, his glare finally landed back on Ava herself. For the first time, she felt perfectly at ease under his steady, laser beam scowl. He didn't even look away as he placed a hand on Dahlia's arm. "Let's go. I can explain inside."

Ava broke the staring contest with her ex to offer Dahlia her most pleasant smile. "He's all yours."

As Gavin whisked his new girlfriend away, the members of the Red Flag Society didn't bother stifling their laughter. It seemed a cease-fire had been declared between Carolyn and Jazmine in order to enjoy a moment at Ava's ex-boyfriend's expense.

"That man's still drinking," Jazmine said, shaking her head.

"Just like your Ben is probably still controlling," Carolyn offered.

"He's not *my* Ben anymore," Jazmine said. "But his new wife can have him. Like Ava said, he's all her problem now."

"So, if Gavin's still drinking," Ava started, "and Ben has the potential to still be controlling, then what's to say Marcus isn't still cheating?"

Carolyn's smile turned steely. Ava kicked herself for bringing up the subject, yet she needed to talk to Carolyn about her next steps now that Sophie had led to her sudden unemployment.

"I'll see you inside," Carolyn said.

"But I still need to talk—"

"Ava, we've been looking all over!"

Ava turned to see Max and Roxi approaching, a clipboard in hand. By the time she whirled back to Carolyn, her friend had disappeared into the banquet hall, and Jazmine was already strolling that way alongside a tall, broad-shouldered black man. Was that the Quentin Sims she'd heard so much about? She wished she were strolling along with them. She wasn't ready to face Max, let alone his viper partner.

Max leaned in, his usual cologne turned up to eleven. Above his black-framed glasses, she could see his eyebrows knit in concern. "Ava, I heard what happened at Howard's place. It made me sick."

"I could hardly believe it when Max told me," Roxi said, leaning in as well to complete the huddle. Her makeup-spackled face had been turned up to a level eleven, as well, making her appear clownish. Ava felt suddenly stifled and yearned for fresh air, but Roxi continued. "Who could treat anyone that way?"

Ava nodded along, at a loss for how to respond. This shark who prided herself on making writers cry was suddenly concerned about Howard's treatment of Ava?

But then, Roxi wasn't the only one acting out of character these days. Howard, who'd prided himself on being kind and open had shut Ava down.

"Think about it," Max urged her. "He came down on you for his own personal complication, totally unrelated to the business."

"Sounded to me like he got caught with his pants down," Roxi mused.

Ava grimaced at the inadvertently accurate analogy.

"Ava, join us," Max said, the two of them pulling their conversational triangle ever tighter, till Ava felt like they were circling her.

"First, I need to talk to—"

"Howard?" Roxi scoffed. "He's off at some conference, isn't he?"

Ava couldn't bring herself to argue that it was Carolyn she needed to talk to. And Wesley. Would Max and Roxi even want her anymore if they found out that Wesley had plagiarized his prize new work of fiction from a nobody like her father? Her heart sank at the answer she already knew.

"Look around you, Ava." Max made a quick sweeping gesture. "This is the perfect opportunity to plant seeds with the authors in there. I'll tell Howard about our transition as soon as he gets back."

"There's no reason to feel guilty," Roxi added. "The man fired you. You're literally a free agent."

"More like double-agent," Ava said. She bit her lip, still waiting to feel that surge of self-righteousness that should have come with the idea of joining forces with Max. After all, Roxi was right—she'd been fired while trying to warn Howard about the very coup in which she was about to be an integral part. Of course, Max knew nothing about her motives for driving to Howard's home office the day prior—only that Howard had lost it when—surprise—she'd unwittingly introduced, at a key meeting, his biological daughter.

But then, Ava reminded herself that this was the way it was in publishing. Agents changed agencies all the time. Quid pro quo was all about, "You stab my back, I'll stab yours." The thing was, after landing what she thought was her dream job with Mercer Literary, she wouldn't be joining Max and Roxi as pay-back—she'd be joining them out of sheer desperation to keep the money coming in, and if at all possible, to stay in the publishing industry. And Howard didn't need her—didn't even want her. Max and Roxi did—desperately so, it seemed.

"Well, if it isn't Ava Perkins."

She glanced towards the voice to see Wesley McBride fanning himself with his program.

"Long time, no see," he joked in his laid-back, slight southern drawl. "So glad to see you. Do you have a moment, if you don't mind discussing business at a swanky event like this one?"

"For you, I'll make the time," Ava said, feeling a whole new wave of confidence. Max and Roxi shared an encouraging nod with her to bring Wesley on board before they slipped back into the crowd.

The seasoned author walked her over to a corner of the lobby. "Ava, I'm not sure how to say this," he said.

"I know things at Howard's house were a little strained—"

"To say the least," Wesley said. "The way that man spoke to you was reprehensible."

Ava ran her hand over the glossy parchment of her program. "That's exactly why I left."

Wes raised his eyebrows and gave an impressed nod. "That's my girl. Not about to let yourself be bullied."

Ava wanted so much for Wesley McBride to believe that about her—and it was partially true, that she had left Howard Mercer and Associates. But she'd had enough of the partial truths, especially since they had yet to do her any favors. She squared her shoulders and looked Wesley in the eye. "I was invited to leave, actually."

Wesley regarded her thoughtfully. "That's why I decided I can't go with Howard Mercer. I had enough trouble with my last agent mixing the business and personal. I'm sorry it couldn't work out that you could be my agent."

"It still could, though," Ava said before he could walk into the ceremony. "I'm joining a new venture. We're going to take our authors into the future with all the technological advances happening on a daily basis—"

"Ava, I'm not sure about going with a start-up," Wesley said. "One of Mercer's selling points was his veteran status."

"Well, I'm sure glad to hear that," a familiar voice came from behind her, followed by a solid hand on her shoulder. "How are my favorite junior agent and pending powerhouse author?"

"Howard," Ava breathed. "You're here. I thought you were going to New York for the big conf—"

"I canceled," he said. "Too much going on. Decided to hunker down at headquarters."

Ava managed a shallow, unsmiling breath. She'd have thought Howard would feel stifled in a stiff suit—compared to the polo shirts and khakis he usually wore—but he seemed as relaxed as ever, a silver fox with his hair combed slick to the side—the George Clooney of literary agents.

"Ceremony's about to start," a woman said, her hands clasped around Howard's arm. Ava recognized her from his house yesterday— his fiancée, who'd stood in his doorway asking Howard, in shock, if it was true that he had a daughter. The dignified woman appeared every bit as delicate and sophisticated as a thirty-five-year-old Audrey Hepburn in her black, fur-trimmed, and belted overcoat. A silver chain had been woven into the twists of her chignon.

Howard took his arm from her wispy grasp and put it around her shoulders. "Do you mind finding our table while I talk with these two for a minute?"

"Nice to meet you, Mr. McBride, and so nice to see you again, Ava," she said. "I'm glad it could be under happier circumstances this time." She shared another smile with Wes and stepped gracefully towards the entrance to the ceremony.

It surprised Ava that Howard's fiancée—a woman she'd never formally even met—knew her name and treated her so warmly.

"Ava," Howard started, "I've been wanting to tell you how sorry I am for—"

"Howard, I—"

"No, you were right. It was my own personal bullshit," he said, drawing out the last word and glancing quickly at Wesley McBride for effect. "Excuse my language, but it's true. I let my private world overshadow my professionalism. I haven't heard from that girl since, so I'm guessing it was all a batshit crazy misunderstanding. Oops, there I go again." He threw his head back and laughed good-naturedly.

Ava nodded, stunned to learn that, by some strange mind-twist of verbiage from his mouth and into her ears, she hadn't been fired. She felt dizzy as her stomach sank deep into the dark recesses of her bowels.

"Why don't we go inside?" Howard asked, gesturing towards the banquet hall.

"Well, actually," Ava started. She glanced back across the lobby to see Max and Roxi chatting it up with a nominee.

"I owe you an apology, too, Mr. McBride," Howard continued. "How about we kick off this literary gala by making an appointment to sign that contract?"

"I'm afraid I've decided to go with Ava, here." Wesley's tone was matter-of-fact. He patted Ava on the shoulder, then folded his hands across his wide chest.

"Welcome to the team," Howard held out a hand to shake. "You're a member of Howard Mercer and Associates—a package deal, so to speak..." He trailed off and turned to Ava.

The blood drained from Ava's face. She knew she should say something, but her throat constricted and her mind drew a blank.

Wesley regarded Howard, his voice even-keeled. "Maybe you didn't understand, Howard. I'm going with Ava's new agenting co-op, or whatever it's called."

Howard mouthed the words *agenting co-op*.

Ava locked her eyes on Howard's and forced a steady tone. "You fired me."

"I never fired you," Howard said, then looked at Wes. "Honestly, what would make you think you were fired?"

"You told me to give you one good reason you shouldn't fire me, so I just assumed..."

She watched as Howard's face fell with the realization. "So, you're signing *my* author under a *different* agency?"

"I never was your author, Howard," Wesley said. "And it sure sounded like you fired Ms. Perkins—all because you couldn't separate church from state, home from work."

"You may not have a contract with me," Howard said sternly, "but Ava does."

Ava heard the line at the door go silent and felt the stares. She lowered her voice but kept the tone even. "I didn't know, Howard. It wasn't clear."

"You signed a contract when you took your job as a Mercer Literary associate," Howard said. "So what other agency are you working for? I don't know of any local agency that would poach a wet-behind-the-ears agent out from under—" He stopped and took a step back, his index finger pointing at someone approaching them.

Ava wanted to feel relieved when she saw Max heading their way across the lobby, but the growing crater in her gut told her things were about to take a turn for the much, much worse.

"Howard, I'm surprised to see you here," Max said nonchalantly. "What's going on?"

"Apparently," Howard's voice was halting and hoarse, "I've been betrayed."

While Howard leveled his glare at Max, Ava tried shaking her head at her new agenting partner, a signal to keep his mouth shut for now.

Instead, Max trained his own accusations of betrayal on Ava when he screeched, "You told him?"

Ava held her hands up to stave him off. "Max, listen—"

"We were supposed to wait until Monday," he hissed. "That was the plan."

"Let me be perfectly clear," Howard said evenly. "Both of you ingrates are fired. And you'd better hope your little 'co-op' works, because if I have anything to do with it, neither of you will ever work for another agency again."

Ava couldn't breathe as she watched Howard stomp off to the banquet hall. Surely he couldn't sue her for a contract that had yet to be signed with an agency that had yet to be launched.

"I'm sorry, Ava," Wesley said, placing his heavy paw on her shoulder, "but this is just too much drama for me. I know you'll do your father proud."

"Actually," Ava said, feeling her feet planting themselves into the ground, "we need to talk about my father."

"Why don't you send me a text and we'll get together over coffee?" Wes asked, clearly making way to depart.

"No, I'm afraid this can't wait," Ava insisted. "Your book. I was wondering about the inspiration."

Wesley regarded her for a long moment, his eyelids narrow as thought calculating his answer. "Well, your father certainly was an inspiration," he started, then chuckled and gave a little chin rub that showed he was looking back on a fond memory. "In fact, I was inspired by a trip your dad and I took back in '82."

Ava wasn't sure whether he was talking about a drug trip or an actual trip. Knowing her father as she did, it could just as easily be one as the other.

"Sir," Max insisted, "our agency will treat you better than any—"

Ava slammed her father's manuscript down on an empty chair beside them. She waited for Wes's look of recognition. "I believe *this* was your inspiration."

Max and Roxi leaned over to see the manuscript that Ava had brought from the enormous stack in her father's bungalow. Thankfully, he'd dated it when he typed it.

Wesley gave a slow nod, as though realization were gradually dawning. "I remember your father's work. I'm sure there were parts of it that inspired me. Some imagery may even have found its way into my book. Like an homage."

"Would you be willing to bet your career on it?"

The two stood staring at each other, almost daring the other to blink.

"Ava, let's arrange for that coffee to go over this."

"No, we're going to talk about this now."

"Can we at least take a step outside?"

Ava shook her head.

"Like I said, Ava, it was an homage to your daddy."

Ava cringed. It was bad enough that he was referring to plagiarism as an *homage*, but now he was calling her father *daddy*?

"I was going through a dry spell and I figured, what better tribute than to get his work published once and for all?"

"I'm already giving him that 'tribute'," Ava said.

"You're already having this manuscript published?" Wes asked. "How? Did Howard sign it?"

"I'm having it self-published," she mumbled, still feeling her father's shame over independent publishing. "With *his* name on the cover."

Wesley shrugged. "That's all fine and dandy if you don't want to make a penny on it." Then he leaned in and spoke with an intensity Ava had never heard from her father's best friend. "Don't you see, Ava? It was nothing short of serendipity to have you ask me to sign with you because *you* would make money on it too—the rightful heir to your dad's legacy."

"Right," Ava said. "20/80."

"First of all," Wes hissed, "that twenty percent commission could be hundreds of thousands with my name attached to this project. You try to self-publish and you'll be paying more than you ever bring in."

Ava looked at Max and Roxi for some kind of feedback on what this man was saying. Apparently, they couldn't comment on plagiarism, but shrugged and gave wide eyes full of dollar signs that said, *Just take the damn money!*

"And second?" she asked.

"Second…" Wes stammered. "We could make it 30/70."

Max and Roxi gave audible gasps and she heard them whisper to one another about how that never happens.

"And third…?" she pressed.

Wes tilted his head and pursed his lips. Finally and very reluctantly, "40/60. Final offer."

Roxi actually squealed at the prospect. Normally, Ava would have joined in for a happy dance around Wesley because these deals never happened between authors and agents. And Wesley wasn't wrong—her father's work could be seen by millions with the name Wesley McBride on the cover. And ultimately, her father was gone. It's not like he would know one way or the other. Or, if he was beaming down on her right now, maybe he was squealing right along with Roxi to take the percentage and get the hell out of debt. Maybe he wouldn't mind his old friend making a buck off of his work.

But something stayed her. Deep in her core, she knew she couldn't publish her father's work without his name. More than that, it was time for Ava to choose her own color—to make her own decision.

"I'm going to self-publish," Ava said. "I'm sure your dry spell will end sooner than later."

Max and Roxi stood speechless as Wesley turned his back on them both and swaggered back to the awards ceremony.

"I can't believe you screwed us over," Max snarled at Ava through clenched teeth. He took out his phone and started scrolling. "I've gotta do some damage control. Wesley was right. You're too much drama."

Max headed to the opposite end of the convention center while Ava stood in a daze. She waited for the inevitable tears to form, yet she found herself unexpectedly relieved. From Gavin to Howard, and now Wesley to Max, never had she been so thankful to be a free agent.

Carolyn

Carolyn sat at the big, center table in the Convention Center's banquet hall, sipping champagne and comparing titles with the editors from her imprint's parent publishing house. To her right, Carolyn's brainy, 30-year-old acquisitions assistant and editor, Isaac, gushed over their latest pitch. "It's a fiction title about the sole surviving World War II soldier who misguided his captain—and thus his entire platoon—into deadly combat."

"The remainder of the story is his struggle to redeem himself," Carolyn added, thinking it may as well be called The Carolyn Ford Story, although she was still waiting for the redemption part. After the Morgan St. John hoax, it seemed she'd come full circle in that regard, or at least she could now hobble her way for two-thirds of a lap around the track.

But she knew she was using her conversations with the key players from her publishing house to distract her from the key players in her life, surrounding her throughout the banquet hall—such as Dr. Sims, over by the stage. One of tonight's nominees for the non-fiction category, Quentin was her only award-winning author in this room—although he also happened to no longer be *her* award-winning author. Next to him stood Jazmine Johnston, highlighted by her high-volume laugh. Despite their recent bonding in the lobby as they joined forces against Ava's ex, Carolyn winced at the memory of the flying glass of plutonium that had possibly waylaid Jazmine's college career and probably ended their friendship. An in-person apology was in order. Just not here. Not now.

Looking closer, Carolyn couldn't help but observe Jazmine's smile—as broad and genuine as Carolyn had ever seen it. Her face glowed and her curls bounced this way and that as she stood schmoozing, head back and emitting the same tinkling gaiety that had filled her reprehensible interview with Isadore. Jazmine's giggling provided the perfect harmony to Quentin's baritone chuckles, as though they'd prepared a duet of laughter and mirth.

Thankfully, Jazmine and Quentin were too intertwined to pay much attention to Carolyn. In fact, Quentin appeared to be introducing Jazmine to several major literary agents, all potential career door-openers. Roxi Fischer was practically fawning over Jazmine. The whole damn room—in all its elegance and all her family and friends—only amplified her fast-unraveling life.

Sipping her champagne, she managed a surreptitious glance towards her ex-husband's table, but Marcus wasn't there—probably too busy hobnobbing with Seattle's literary elite. His wife—the great Isadore—leaned in on her elbows to say something private to Sophie. In a pewter, strapless dress, Sophie's buxom figure made her look older than her nineteen years. Sophie's pulled back hair allowed her habitually hidden purity to shine. Carolyn had to shake off the illusion that Sophie was that naive little girl, her sweet-faced baby, kindergartner, tween. But there was no mistaking her daughter's coming of age. How much had she missed of Sophie coming of age since she'd been too busy proving herself on the big Manhattan stage? And for what? Or, more importantly, once her daughter left her for the stability of Vivian's Seattle home, for *whom*?

Carolyn watched the teen nodding so adult-like to her stepmother. Carolyn didn't know what to think of her suave style, so smooth and totally unlike the chaos she'd been stirring up with her and Vivian lately. She took a gulp of wine, knowing an impossible conversation with her was inevitable. But not now, and certainly not here.

How had she repressed, rationalized, totally censored for so many years of this girl's life that Howard really was the father? Was this all so she could delude herself into taking the path of peace? She knew she had to tell them, to save some face by coming clean on her own—and here they all were.

Her mind replayed Vivian's urge to tell Marcus the truth. She pinched the back of her hand, chastising herself to stay composed. Now was not the time to crumble. She just had to get through the speeches, then make for a quiet exit out the back door. So much for the prodigal daughter returning to the literary scene of her younger days. Carolyn drained the last of the champagne from her glass.

Two tables away from Carolyn, Howard Mercer took his seat beside a waif-thin woman, who said something into his ear. Carolyn's stomach lurched at the sight of his flushed cheeks and steely eyes. Surely Sophie had gotten to him. But then, there was Sophie now, chatting away with Isadore as though she hadn't just upended the man's entire world, so maybe there was hope yet.

Carolyn was just wishing she could pull Ava aside to compare notes, in a sense, when she noticed that the junior agent wasn't sitting at Howard's table. In fact, there were two empty seats.

"Testing, one, two, three," a man in a tuxedo stood on stage, speaking into the mic and nodding to the sound person in the back of the room. The microphone shrieked the obligatory screech of all hot mics.

Carolyn winced until it faded, then rose to make her way to the powder room before the ceremony started. She hadn't walked past two whole tables before she saw Isadore floating across the room towards her, those million-and-one scarves fluttering like waves in her wake. She nodded coolly at Carolyn before descending on Jazmine. Carolyn grimaced at the overpowering waft of expensive perfume. Isadore kissed Jazmine on one cheek and then the other, as though they were long-lost friends which, Carolyn knew, was both logically and chronologically impossible.

She tried to walk past them when Isadore gestured her way and asked Jazmine, "Do you know Carolyn Ford?"

Carolyn stopped and said, with all the serenity she could muster, "She does, as a matter of fact."

Isadore nodded coolly at Carolyn. "Then perhaps you know that Ms. Johnston has a podcast."

"She just interviewed me for her next episode," Quentin said with all the warmth he'd shared when she'd last seen him in his office. It was almost as though he hadn't dumped her as his publisher and there really were no hard feelings.

"I'm afraid I've only been able to hear the first episode," Carolyn said, focusing her attention on Isadore. "You certainly seem to think you know a great deal about where my heart was during my marriage."

"Have you received any feedback about the interview?" Jazmine asked Isadore, blatant in her attempt to move the conversation back into neutral territory.

Jazmine's face fell as Isadore shot back at Carolyn. "Can you honestly say your heart had been in the marriage?"

Carolyn held herself back from smacking the smugness from Isadore's smile. "There you go again, Isadore. Such an authority. The rebound wife telling the world all about his flawed first wife, and never one honest statement about Marcus as a serial cheater. Are you so sure he isn't cheating on you these days?"

Carolyn drew back, realizing that her volume far exceeded ceremonial decorum. She heard a woman gasp from a nearby table. "Did you hear that? Serial cheater." All the surrounding tables seemed to come alive with whispers.

Isadore raised an eyebrow and the palms of her hands to Jazmine to signal the raw audacity of such a bold question. Blood rushed to Carolyn's face.

"Perhaps you should take this exceedingly personal conversation to a more appropriate venue," Quentin said, his voice quiet, yet as stern as a headmaster.

Or at a more sensible time, Carolyn realized just as a heavy hand landed on her shoulder and whirled her around.

"You really had us all fooled, didn't you?"

"Excuse me?" Carolyn asked, taking in Howard, who stood before her as formal as she'd ever seen him. His red face and steely eyes remained. Somehow, the bedraggled grunge band drummer came through the mussed hair and the intensity of his gaze.

"You come back to town, sniveling about how a hoax brought you down, when all the time it was you." Howard pointed an accusatory finger in Carolyn's face. "*You* were the hoax."

The surrounding spectators shushed at Howard's pronouncement. Guests at neighboring tables leaned in to hear more.

"No, Howard, I didn't know," Carolyn said.

"Didn't know what, exactly?" Howard asked, his finger still trained on her. "About Ava poaching my next big client for some agent 'collective'? That was all you, wasn't it? You're probably part of the collective, too, you two being 'besties' and all."

Carolyn tilted her head. Bestie sounded like Sophie's kind of slang. She wanted to argue that she would never poach a client—least of all from Howard—when the lights began to blink and dim. A voice over the microphone said, "We're going to ask that people please get seated, as the ceremony will commence in five minutes."

Howard whirled back on Carolyn. "Did you know that your friend, Ava, brought Sophie to my place?" Howard asked, ignoring the emcee. "Did you know your daughter created a scene in front of a client—lost me that client—almost lost me my fiancée, because she insists she's the child I never knew I had?"

Quentin wedged himself between Carolyn and Howard and that awful, ever-pointing finger. Howard took a half-step around Quentin's shoulder to go again at Carolyn, his finger still accusing her. "Look, we really need to take a breath here, Mr. ..." He looked at the name tag hanging from Howard's event lanyard. "Mercer."

Blocked by a chair, Quentin held out his arm, but Howard, fully lit with anger, slid further away from the larger man's blockade.

Carolyn glanced over her shoulder to see if Sophie had heard Howard's completely inappropriate exclamation, but instead, she saw Isadore and the blood draining from her face.

"Excuse me?" the woman asked softly.

A tap sounded against the microphone. "Two more minutes, everyone. We ask that you please take your seats." The emcee used his mic to emphasize his directive by pointing it at Carolyn.

Carolyn's tongue went numb, along with her will to continue this fight with everyone around her. For an instant, she thought she might pass out then and there—a welcome change from this public flogging, except that Isadore flung a stray end of scarf behind her and leaned into Carolyn's face to whisper in her ear.

"Please, please tell me that Marcus is her father," Isadore implored. "You would not have lied to our daughter—"

'Our' daughter? Carolyn could hear her neck crack when she whipped around. Staring at Isadore, she only managed to squeeze three words through a suddenly dry throat. "How. Dare. You."

"How dare you 'how dare' her," Howard said, pointing first at Carolyn, then at Isadore.

Suddenly, they were joined by Howard's fiancée, who put a hand on his shoulder. "Howard, please," the slight woman pleaded. Sure enough, Carolyn saw the engagement ring, with a diamond as big as a meteor. "Let's sit down—or we can leave, even. Just don't do this—not here."

"Not yet," Howard told her. "You can wait for me in the lobby."

His fiancée took her hand from his shoulder and adjusted the ring, as though trying to decide whether to take it off.

From behind, Carolyn heard Isadore excuse herself. Carolyn knew exactly where she was headed.

"I need to go," Carolyn blurted.

"I'll go with you," Jazmine said.

"No," Carolyn said, trying to move around her.

"Are you serious?" Howard bellowed.

Carolyn ignored him, finally pushing her way past Jazmine so she could follow the same beeline Isadore was making to Marcus's table.

"Carrie, get back here!" Howard shouted. "I have a right to know!"

Carolyn slipped quickly between chairs and attendees working to seat themselves at this inopportune moment. Her only saving grace was that Marcus still wasn't at his table. She caught up to Isadore and touched her elbow, all but pleading, "Don't do this."

Isadore ignored her the same way Carolyn herself ignored Howard shouting from behind.

Carolyn lunged for her scarf, trying to pull her back by the neck. Onlookers gave a collective gasp. Isadore snatched a champagne glass that Sophie had somehow acquired, and flung the bubbly at Carolyn, who ducked just in time for it to miss her and splash Howard directly in the face.

Champagne dripping down his reddening cheeks, Howard stepped forward, reached out, and grabbed Isadore's shoulders to hold her immobile. Her limp hand dropped the champagne flute where it landed on the rug.

Carolyn lurched around Howard and got in Sophie's face. The mother's tone wasn't so conciliatory. "Where's your father?" she demanded. As Carolyn's timing would have it, Marcus suddenly came strolling up behind Sophie's chair at their table.

"Which father?" Sophie asked, her voice full of snark.

Carolyn watched Marcus' face darken, his bright eyes suddenly confused. The commotion at their table had captured the attention of everyone in the banquet hall. Only Quentin's larger-than-life calm kept the security detail from approaching their table. Sophie must have noticed the change in Carolyn's face—and perhaps the change in the demeanor of Howard and Isadore. She gulped and her eyes grew wide with consternation as she turned around in her seat to see Marcus standing there.

"Why would you ask that, Sophie?" Marcus asked her. "What on earth do you mean, 'Which father'?"

Carolyn had never seen her daughter's face redden so suddenly.

"I didn't know you were… you were… standing there," Sophie stammered.

Carolyn twisted the end of Isadore's scarf in her hands and watched Howard look at the face of the man whom Sophie addressed.

Marcus took in the frozen ruckus around him until his gaze lit on Howard. "Get your hands off my wife!"

Howard immediately let go of Isadore's shoulders, the unexpected release sending her reeling forward and tripping over the champagne flute. She would have fallen into the next table if Carolyn hadn't been clutching the end of her ridiculously long scarf. Howard held up his hands, as though in surrender. His face, however, told a different story—one of having lost to that man one too many times.

"I didn't mean to hurt anyone," Sophie insisted. "All I wanted was to ace my senior forensics lab last spring. I thought I'd done it wrong—when our DNA didn't match up."

This wasn't a surprise. Carolyn had already pieced this together with Vivian at the beach, yet her mind skipped to long before Jazmine's podcast, all the way back to her morning coffee with Sophie in Vivian's kitchen.

"I need you to tell me who you dated before Dad," she remembered Sophie saying then, all under the guise of what Carolyn now understood was a bullshit Gen-X study. Carolyn had known that something was off—all that grilling in the name of how technology could rekindle relationships. Except, this had nothing to do with Jazmine's podcast or Sophie's having conned Ava into driving her to Howard's place. They'd all been pawns in Sophie's ploy to find out the truth about her own heritage.

"If I'm not her father, who is?" Marcus asked.

Carolyn opened her mouth to come clean at last, but then watched her ex-husband's face go ashen and gaunt as he fell into shadow. She turned to go back to her own table, but inches away now, lit only by the spotlight on the stage, Howard stood rooted to the floor, blocking her path. Far behind him, at the back of the room, Carolyn saw his fiancée putting on her coat as she walked out the door.

The Master of Ceremonies started welcoming the audience. Carolyn remained toe-to-toe with Howard, forced to resurrect their long-ago dance in the dark. But tonight, nearly two decades later in the dim of this hall, she was no longer afraid of the truth that the two of them were never meant to be a lasting couple, but also not callous to how he must be reeling. Carolyn realized that all the cards had long since been played, not as a hoax, but as young adults figuring their way through this rabbit hole of a life. She beheld his glistening eyes from what little stage light reflected their way, powerless to make any more denials or to fix the past. It wasn't that she didn't love Howard. Rather, she no longer saw those remnants in him of the garage band drummer she'd once adored down to the very seed of her being. And now, in Howard's pained glare fused with anger, she could see that he had maybe never seen her truth. She'd been a young woman who didn't reject him, but who had left him broken-hearted in order to do the right thing, the responsible thing.

Howard's eyes told a different story. He viewed her as the biggest fraud of them all.

Jazmine

As the lights dimmed, Jazmine took her seat, dying to tell Quentin about the contact she'd made before all this drama had consumed them. The top relationship radio personality in all of Seattle, Dr. Tamara Thompson, who had just made a deal with her to cross-promote each other. Dr. Tamara would be Jazmine's next podcast guest and Jazmine would do the same for Dr. Tamara on her radio show—her radio show!—as a relationship expert. Jazmine's breath caught in her throat. She may have come a long way since she started back to school, but she was no relationship expert. What she was, she realized with a sinking feeling, was screwed.

Of course, she couldn't confide any of this to Quentin now, nor could she ask him what the hell had gone down across the room, because the room had gone dark and the Master of Ceremonies was already cracking lame literary jokes. He'd probably prepared the one-liners ahead of time, but after the debacle a few tables over, it seemed like a desperate attempt to lighten the mood. While they'd shared a fun moment taunting Ava's ex in the lobby earlier, Jazmine had had enough of Carolyn's drama after the podcast fiasco. She could still see that drink running down Henry's face as he screamed.

She returned her attention to the emcee, who was now reading out the nominees for the year's top mystery novel. He tore open an envelope and called out a name Jazmine didn't recognize. Across the room, a woman with short, dark hair rose and made her way up to the stage.

As the author spoke, Jazmine glanced back at the still empty chair at Isadore's table. Recalling the miracles Sophie had worked with Henry earlier, Jazmine longed to get up and search for her. The least she could do was to be there for Sophie. She wondered what Carolyn would think about that. If nothing else, they'd be Even Steven. She could finally return the favor Carolyn had given her when she'd quelled Henry's tantrum at the cellular store—not to mention hooking her up with Quentin and the autism specialist he'd referred her to. She would no longer owe Carolyn a thing—not that Carolyn had ever asked. But with Jazmine's luck, talking to Sophie would be perceived as nothing but another—albeit, inadvertent, as always—betrayal. So, she sat and clapped along mechanically with the people around her for the mystery author's acceptance speech. Quentin looked at her with raised eyebrows, as though to ask how things were going and she stopped clapping long enough to give him a thumbs-up.

The emcee took the microphone again to announce the nominees for contemporary mainstream literature, none of whom Jazmine recognized until she heard Marcus's name at the end. She stole another glance at his table, where he sat looking haggard and dazed. Isadore sat stone-faced, her hand clasping his on the table. The empty chair sat ominously on the other side of her.

When the emcee called, "This year's award for contemporary mainstream goes to…Marcus Wheeler," Jazmine gazed across the room, watching as Isadore helped him rise from his chair and guided him around the table to make his way to the stage. The applause felt restrained, as though everyone were wondering, along with Jazmine, what this man—the center of the scene that had just happened in front of the stage—might reveal to them all.

As Marcus took his place behind the podium, Jazmine could see what Carolyn had seen in him however many years ago. He had a dark, brooding quality about him—one that had, according to Carolyn, served him well in attracting mistresses and carrying on extra-marital affairs. Even now, his hair grayed only at the temples, which gave him an even more sophisticated and intellectual allure. During their podcast interview, Isadore had seemed so confident that he was faithful to her; for her sake, Jazmine hoped she was right.

Marcus reached into his suit pocket, pulled out some index cards, and placed them on the podium. His other hand pulled reading glasses from his breast pocket and he put them on. The audience watched in silence as he squinted at the cards, fumbling with them. Finally, he tossed them over his shoulder, which drew nervous chuckles from the audience. Jazmine rolled her eyes at the obviously rehearsed gesture.

Marcus frowned as he took his reading glasses back off, fidgeting with them as he spoke. "From the time I wrote my first short story at the age of eight, my life has been spent writing fiction."

Jazmine listened, breathless. He had an authoritative voice—the kind that could coach a college football team or command the attention of all the attendants at a board room meeting.

"And tonight," Marcus continued, "I found out that most of my life has been a work of fiction." His voice broke at the end of his sentence.

A collective murmur passed through the crowd like the "wave" in a football stadium. Jazmine knew the man on stage wasn't exactly a stand-up guy. But as she sorted through her memories of her interview with Isadore and Carolyn's reaction, something sank in, and she found her heart soften for him.

Marcus held up the award. "I think the real winner tonight is Howard Mercer."

Heads turned in unison to the table for the Howard Mercer Literary Agency. Jazmine scanned the guests there, who all looked at one another, shocked—although none of them seemed to want to look at the middle-aged man who had been shouting at Carolyn before the ceremony began. But there he sat, the chairs on either side of him empty, as though even his own table were shunning him. She was dying to see Ava among them—to share a secret look that they'd be dishing about this later. Ava had been talking about sitting front and center at Howard Mercer's table at this awards ceremony for about as long as Jazmine had known her. So where was she now?

"Let's all give Howard a hand, shall we?" Marcus asked, as the crowd gave a scattered, confused applause. "This one's for you."

The audience emitted a louder collective gasp as he Frisbee'd the framed award at Howard, who ducked as it whirled over his head and clattered across the floor.

Quentin's brows furrowed at Jazmine in the dark, clearly confused. She shrugged helplessly, glancing around again for Carolyn or Sophie.

"Thank you, Mr. Wheeler," the emcee stammered, back at the podium. "I'm sure Mr. Mercer appreciates your accolades."

Even in the dim room, Jazmine could see Howard gritting his teeth. On the other side of the room, Marcus helped Isadore from her chair and they made their way down the hall, presumably to the coat check before making their way out into the night.

"Our next award for the night is for non-fiction." This time, Jazmine recognized the first name he read, Quentin Sims. As the tuxedo-ed man on stage read through the remaining finalists, Jazmine felt her hand covered in warmth. She looked over at Quentin, who gazed at the emcee so intently, she wasn't sure if he even realized he had reached over and placed his hand over hers, or if it was some instinct to reach out and grab the nearest rail as the train screeched to a stop, and she was that safety rail.

Sure enough, the emcee opened the envelope and announced Quentin Sims the winner of the Seattle Literary Society Non-Fiction Award for *On the Spectrum*. Jazmine wasn't sure whether to stand or remain seated, so she followed Quentin's lead as he rose, only as far as she realized he was heading toward the stage and not about to embrace her in his triumphant bliss. As he took his place behind the podium, Jazmine lowered herself back into her seat, acting as though she'd been adjusting the angle of her chair all along.

When Quentin spoke into the microphone, Jazmine felt her skin ripple with gooseflesh. It was exhilarating to see him up there, accepting an award for his work. And he was so gracious, thanking his publisher. Too bad Carolyn had run from the room just as the event was starting.

The table felt empty now, with both Quentin and Carolyn gone, but Jazmine didn't see herself at the table, either. She saw herself on that stage, just a few short years from now, accepting an award for her journalistic research. At least she could dream. Quentin had spoken on the ride over about his journey to this point, and he'd had every bit as normal a childhood as Jazmine. There was nothing extraordinary about Quentin—aside from the essence that made him *him*—that would preclude Jazmine from achieving similar success. He didn't come from a wealthy family and Jazmine had never had to endure racism the way he had.

She felt a vibration and lifted her hands to clap whole-heartedly for Quentin's big, well-deserved moment, but stopped short when she realized he was still speaking. The vibration was coming from her purse. She reached into the bag to turn off her phone so the soft buzz wouldn't disrupt Quentin's speech, but she couldn't find the switch, fumbling blindly as she was. Thankfully, it stopped, and she moved to put her purse back down—until it vibrated again, an insistent buzzing that told her something was amiss. She pulled out the phone, shielding the screen with her hand so the glow wouldn't disturb anyone around her, and peered at the screen, at Lucinda's misspelled and Filipina-accented text.

Henry at *hospatle*. Come *imediate*!

Jazmine gazed wide-eyed at the screen. What did it mean he was in the hospital? Had he choked or come down with a 103 temperature? Was he even alive at this point? Jazmine hated her stepmother more than ever for not including more, but she wasn't about to waste time texting or considering all the possible nightmare scenarios. She glanced at the stage, where Quentin was still speaking. She couldn't very well interrupt him, and anyone she could have asked to get the message to him—Carolyn, Isadore, Sophie—were long gone. She took up her purse and crouched as she ran to the nearest exit, leaving her coat and Quentin and everything else behind.

Commencement

Ava

Ava led Jazmine and Carolyn to the children's wing as they stepped in double-time through the corridor, the sound of their clicking heels reverberating off the walls. It was the one saving grace of the evening's upheaval that had landed Ava on the bench outside the Convention Center, so she happened to be there when first Carolyn had come barreling through the exit doors, followed by Jazmine, carrying her phone with that god-awful text. Ava knew a thing or two about god-awful texts, and somehow both hers from Gavin, and now Jazmine's, had landed them in a hospital that had become all-too familiar to Ava.

At the end of the hall, Ava spotted Jazmine's dad and stepmother talking to a doctor. As possible prognoses ticked through her mind, a sense of foreboding blanketed her like a fog. Had Henry fallen down a flight of stairs and broken bones? Had he and Jazmine's parents been in a car accident?

Finally, when they were within hearing distance, Jazmine huffed, "What happened?"

"I'm Dr. Takahashi." She held out a small, unmanicured hand. "Are you Henry's mother?"

Jazmine turned to her parents and repeated, "What happened?"

"Henry been having a fit," Lucinda started, when Jazmine's father put a hand on her arm.

"He hit his head against the wall," he said, his voice low and steady.

Ava and Carolyn both nodded to the doctor, who was still waiting for an answer about Henry's parentage. Ava shot Carolyn a side-glance and saw her adjusting her purse uncomfortably.

Dr. Takahashi glanced at her clipboard. "Mrs. Johnston, we need to discuss your son's prognosis."

"He hit his head during the fit?" Jazmine asked her parents.

Ava gave the doctor an apologetic shrug.

"You picked him up, right?" Jazmine looked back and forth from her father to her stepmother. "Dad? You didn't just let him go on pounding his head against the wall?"

"I wasn't there," her dad said.

"Lucinda," Jazmine pleaded. "You know you need to pick Henry up when he throws a fit—to put him in his padded playpen. Tell me you picked him up!"

Ava watched as Jazmine's wide, tear-glassed eyes looked around for answers—at her father, the doctor, Lucinda, the doctor, Carolyn, the doctor, and finally, Ava, who could only offer another powerless, apologetic shrug.

"Mrs. Johnston, Henry has suffered severe contusions and lacerations on his forehead, as well as some swelling and bleeding in the brain."

The three women gave a collective gasp.

"Swelling and bleeding?" Jazmine asked. Her eyes shot daggers at Lucinda as her voice raised in pitch. "In his *brain*?"

Ava felt Carolyn brushing up against her side. "Let's go," she murmured out the side of her mouth.

"She needs us," Ava whispered back.

"Lucinda was only trying to help you," Jazmine's father said.

"I try stopping him from hitting wall," Lucinda insisted, "but he keeping going and going. I thinking once he feel pain, he stop. But then he wobbling back and forth."

"Oh my God." Jazmine put a hand to her mouth, as if she might be sick.

Lucinda turned to her husband. "See how ungrateful is you daughter?"

"*Ungrateful*?"

"Just like when you were teenage girl, never writing back your father."

There was silence. Ava watched as Lucinda's face froze into a wide-eyed expression—as though she'd just bought herself some trouble.

"But you never wrote me," Jazmine said hoarsely.

"I wrote you a letter every week for three years," Jazmine's father said. "I didn't blame you for being too upset with me to write back. But we don't need to get into this now."

"I wrote you all the time!"

While Carolyn looked back and forth between Jazmine and her father, Ava watched Lucinda, realizing that someone had played interference with the mail back in the Philippines. Then, she saw the doctor jotting notes and had no doubt that CPS would be arriving shortly. She leaned over to Carolyn and whispered, "To the cafeteria? It's just down the hall, so we'll be able to stay close by."

"Perfect," Carolyn whispered and turned on her heel. Ava followed, knowing the cafeteria was the opposite way of the corner Carolyn was taking them, but the last thing Ava could think about now was eating.

"Jazmine didn't deserve the way I treated her," Carolyn said, her voice tight. Though she charged forward, her sunken, bloodshot eyes gazed absently at the over-waxed, gray-flecked tile under her feet. Somehow, despite whatever debacle had happened inside the ceremony, her hair was glossy as ever and meticulously combed into place, and she wore a designer trench coat and Jimmy Choo pumps.

"What do you mean?" Ava started, then remembered the podcast fiasco. "Carolyn, this has nothing to do with you. And besides, you can't blame yourself for that. You didn't know she'd interviewed your ex's wife—"

"And I didn't know that Sophie had figured out long before then that Marcus wasn't her father," Carolyn said.

Ava's chin dropped.

Carolyn veered toward the gift shop—no mention of the change in cafeteria plans. Ava followed along, letting the implications of this revelation unfold. Howard actually *was* Sophie's father. And he must have found this out tonight—*after* he'd found out that Ava had supposedly stolen his bestselling author. It was like a one-two punch with point-blank cannonball fists.

"All I know at this point is that I feel like *I'm* the one who's been run over by a bus," Carolyn said, absently running her hands over a sage pashmina scarf. "Only mine was a double-decker and it ran back and forth over me about fifty times."

Ava scanned a group of plaques with uplifting religious healing sentiments. "I know how much you love Jazmine and Henry, but why are you here with us when you should—I mean, you *could*—be working things out with Sophie?"

"What's there to work out?" Carolyn asked dully. "I've lost them both."

"Them?" Ava asked. "I thought you lost Marcus a long time ago."

"I'm talking about Howard," Carolyn said, "And from the looks of the empty seats at his table tonight, I would assume I'm not the only one."

"I thought I'd lost my job, okay?" Ava said, a little too defensively. Ava picked up a stuffed chick and smoothed its fluff. It had been a mistake—an awful, uncorrectable mistake. She kept going back and back and back to re-do it in her mind. Back to the moment at Howard's house, where he told her to give him one good reason he shouldn't fire her before telling her to leave the premises—only as she re-lived the scene with him tonight, she left with the understanding that she actually *hadn't been fired.*

"I tried to warn you about Max Volkov." Carolyn shook her head ruefully as she picked up a novelty mug. "So, you'll have to excuse me if I'm at a loss as to how you could trade in a job with most reputable agent on the West Coast for a slime ball like that guy."

"Max happens to be an up-and-coming agent," Ava said, her words as lifeless as the stuffed chick in her hands, "with innovative ideas to shift the industry into the technological—"

"Oh please," Carolyn said, waving the mug around as she spoke. "He's already smearing Howard's name all over town. Don't you see? He cheated *you* just as much as he cheated Howard because *you're* the one who's going to take the fall. Howard will see to it that you never work in publishing again."

"I know I'm screwed, okay?" Ava slammed the chick back on the shelf. Unfortunately, she slammed it into a frame, which tumbled to the floor, the glass cracking into three pieces. She lowered her voice when the gift shop clerk looked her way. "I lost my job, I caught Wesley McBride plagiarizing my dad's book—"

"He *what*?"

"I'm tens of thousands of dollars in debt, and it's only a matter of days before they come and repossess all of my—you know, possessions."

"Is everything okay?" the cashier asked, making her way to their corner of the store.

"It's fine," Carolyn said with a sudden breeziness in her tone. "Something slipped." She reached into her purse, pulled out a bill, and handed it to the cashier. "This should cover it."

"Accidents happen," the woman said, her voice uncertain. She cast back glances at them both as she shuffled back to her station. "I'll be back with your change."

"Keep it!" Carolyn called back, then whispered, "Ava, I had no idea. Why didn't you come to me?"

"I *did* come to you!" Ava insisted. "You weren't there. Unfortunately for me, Sophie was."

"What is that supposed to mean?"

Ava gave Carolyn the lowdown on Sophie's manipulation of getting a ride from Ava to Howard's house, only to tell him how he might be her father.

"Oh God," Carolyn said, steepling her hands over her face. "That's when she got Howard's DNA."

"Excuse me?" Ava asked. "All she did was use his bathroom."

"So, what do you think she took? Hairbrush? Toothbrush?"

Ava's jaw dropped. So that was why Sophie had used her.

Carolyn reached for a stuffed puppy. "A dod," she murmured.

Ava grinned sadly at her, remembering the night Henry had said his first word at Vivian Ford's house. She gave an almost imperceptible shake of her head as she thought about how they'd sat there, commiserating over their troubles with men and hoaxes and job interviewers who hadn't called back. All of them thought they'd hit bottom when they'd all been standing on the precipice of new opportunities and better lives—better *selves*—oblivious to the massive landslides that were about to take them so much further down.

"We should start heading back," Carolyn said, taking her olive branch puppy for Jazmine and Henry to the checkout counter.

When they made their way silently back to Henry's room, the corridor was empty. Ava wondered if Jazmine's parents were on their way back home, or if Lucinda was in an interrogation room somewhere, rationalizing her neglect to an agent from Child Protective Services.

As they stepped into the room, Ava stepped into an alternate universe, a world in which she was the visitor and Jazmine, bent from her chair so that her head lay on Henry's bed, sat on the patient's side of the room. Henry, who usually loomed larger than life with his autistic quirks and the ever-present threat of a meltdown, now lay sleeping under a web of wires—too still, too tiny for Ava's comfort. Under normal circumstances, the humming and beeping of the surrounding machinery would have undoubtedly sent the child into a frenzy.

Ava guessed that his head was probably clean-shaven underneath the tightly wrapped layers of gauze. She remembered the reverse mohawk he'd had the last time she'd seen him, after having pitched a fit when Lucinda tried shaving his hair. She knew he must have been completely unconscious when the medical staff had shaven his hair clean off, not to mention when they'd stitched up the slight zig-zagged line of stitches going up through the swollen bruise in the middle of his forehead.

She wanted to cry—for both Henry and his mother, who appeared just as shrunken as her son—the beaten-down way she'd looked to Ava when they first met in this same hospital, in a room almost exactly like this one. Since then, Ava had experienced an unexpected friendship with a woman she had watched morph from being hunched over, swollen-eyed, and devoid of hope into a straight-backed, returning college student—so stylish, sensuous, intelligent, and strong. The very accident that had rendered Jazmine out of work had spun the silver lining she needed to thrive. And now, it seemed life had beaten her back into her former self.

Jazmine didn't seem to register the rest of the room as she gazed groggily at the stuffed puppy by Henry's shoulder.

"I wanted him to have his own 'dod'," Carolyn said.

Ava smiled grimly at the little stuffed puppy Carolyn now tucked inside the blanket at Henry's shoulder. "What happens now?" she asked Jazmine.

Jazmine looked off in a daze and said in a flat voice, "I kill Lucinda."

"Do you want to talk about it?" Ava ventured.

Jazmine shook her head sadly. "It's my fault."

"What do you mean it's your fault?" Ava asked. "You weren't even there."

Jazmine met her eyes for the first time since she'd woken. "Exactly."

"That's bullshit, and you know it," Carolyn hissed.

"I should have been there," Jazmine hissed back. "Not out on some pseudo-date, talking up publishers. I put my son aside for a pipe dream. What kind of nightmare has he been living day in and out as I skipped out to my classes?"

"You'll be a better mother and Henry will sense it, if you allow yourself to have your own identity and life," Carolyn persisted.

"Lucinda's always been on me about showing Henry tough love," Jazmine continued, "letting him cry himself out, tantrum himself out, bang his head against the wall until…" Jazmine hid her face in her hands. It was the first Ava had ever seen her cry. She'd seen her worn down, exhausted, hopeless—yet through it all, she'd never shed a tear. Jazmine sniffled and wiped her nose with the back of her hand. "Until he felt enough pain to stop on his own." She smoothed the blankets over Henry's chest. "She was probably more worried about the blood stains on her wall than my son."

"Good God," Ava whispered.

Jazmine took a deep, shaky breath, her eyes glassy with tears. "I can't leave Henry with her anymore. I need to be with my son."

Ava nodded and bit her lip.

"But you're set to graduate," Carolyn said.

Ava's head swiveled back and forth on her neck, as though she were watching a tennis match. Since it was Carolyn who'd ruined Jazmine's final project, she could only imagine Jazmine retorting with something like, "Yeah, I'll be graduating, no thanks to *you*."

Instead, Jazmine threw up her hands and rose from her seat. "Don't you get it? I'm done—back to square one."

"Absolutely not," Carolyn spat.

Ava could understand Carolyn's reaction—Jazmine had come too far to give up now.

"Then what do you suggest, Carolyn?" Jazmine asked, her voice rising like it had with her parents. "It's not like I can afford to pay Sophie to take care of him all day long."

"I'll watch Henry." Ava's voice felt raw from having sat silent for so long. She cleared her throat. "It's not like I have a job to go to. I can send out resumes in between playing with blocks and trains."

"I'm tired of being everyone's charity case—"

Ava crossed over to Jazmine and put a hand on her arm. "You helped *me*, remember? I never could have afforded my dad's mortgage without your help."

Jazmine blinked a tear from her eye, leaving a shiny trail down her cheek.

"I'm stuck and you're stuck and I'm thinking we can get unstuck together."

Jazmine stood silent, her eyes on Henry as tears continued down her face.

Carolyn seemed to study them. Perhaps she thought Ava was enabling Jazmine to regress back into the person they'd first met—and maybe she was. It wouldn't be the first time she'd been accused of enabling. But Ava sensed that this would turn into so much more, the way good friendships can hold unexpected treasures.

"Sophie might be able to help with Henry, as well," Carolyn said. "Although you'll need to work that out with her directly since she won't be talking to me for…well, probably forever."

"It'll work out," Jazmine said, dragging her sleeve across her eyes. "We'll get you unstuck, too."

Carolyn rose and crossed towards them. "Can I join this group hug?"

Ava kept her right arm around Jazmine and reached her left around Carolyn. Without a doubt, she knew nothing was impossible once she felt the power of the three of them spark to life once again.

Carolyn

Carolyn sat at her office computer, working on an internet search for Ford Publishing's almost newly signed author, John S. Morgan. The middle initial did little to narrow down the million John Morgan's in the world, and what little platform he'd built for his name brand was seemingly only months old. Only half an hour until the meeting, the first step towards acquisition approval, not to mention a big first step towards showing some mettle around here. How could she beef up this veggie burger of his? A slew of her pressure-cooker deals in the Big Apple were far, far tougher than birthing this project. None of that meant a thing out here. 'What have you done lately' was now, 'Show us what you can do in the Emerald City, Ms. Ford Publishing big-shot?' This was her moment to shine, yet this particular author's dismal readership numbers left her looking dull and void.

Carolyn peered through the glass walls to the meeting room across the hall. She watched as interns scuttled about, setting up coffee, tea, and ice water. In the middle of the bustle was her own acquisitions editor, Isaac. Normally, he dressed for work in plaid button-up shirts and dark denim jeans. Today, presumably in honor of his first big pitch, he'd paired navy slacks with a long-sleeved, button-up shirt and a tie, all a far cry from the suits her editors wore for such meetings back in Manhattan. They were high end consignment suits, of course, but still.

She remembered her first big acquisition. There were two big firsts when she'd found herself firmly in the publisher's chair. One was championing the big name that made millions, and the other was discovering a gem that affected the publisher so deeply to the core that they couldn't wait to share it with the world. The money may follow eventually, and when the publishing cosmos aligned, the message was also at the core of the book's success. Isaac hadn't yet landed the million-dollar name, but Carolyn enjoyed watching his excitement over this project. It would allow him a great deal of latitude with this particular author, even if Carolyn was the one behind the scenes lending the sharp teeth this book would need to see the marketplace.

She rolled her chair a couple of steps towards the open doorway. "Isaac, can I see you for a moment, please?"

Isaac held up a finger to let her know he'd be there in just a minute. She raised her eyebrows and rolled back to her computer. No one at Ford Publishing would have stayed her with an index finger like that—but then, in Manhattan she never would have deigned, like now, to do a junior editor's job. She wanted to let him have his fun, but without a formalized author platform, she worried they were screwed before getting into the starting blocks. Scrolling through her emails, she skimmed for any that might help predicate sales volume numbers when her eyes landed with a big thud on the subject line that read—

"Blast from 20 years ago."

Carolyn's eyes grew wide. The voice that had come from behind her did not belong to Isaac. In fact, she knew the voice all too well.

"What the hell?" Carolyn asked.

"Don't be crass," her mother said. "I'm here with the lunch you so graciously penciled me in for a week ago." Vivian set down her paper bag on the worktable and pulled out the takeout boxes. Her hair looked and smelled as though she'd just come from underneath a salon hair dryer hood. "Did I see Harvey Mercer's name on that email you were reading? Sophie told me his fiancée left him after that awards event."

"His name is Howard," Carolyn corrected, stunned to hear that Howard's engagement was off, and wracking her brain to remember planning a lunch with her mother. "Look, Mom, I'm really sorry, but I double-booked myself. I have a make-or-break meeting in a half-hour I have to prepare for. I need to—"

"You need to eat, honey," Vivian said, opening two containers of chicken Caesar salad. The sunlight flooding through the window lit up her freshly dyed hair an unnatural burgundy hue—but then, was burgundy ever a natural shade for any woman's hair? It matched the frames of her glasses, though, which complimented an–olive-toned cardigan. "Oh, by the way, Sophie told me about the awards event—"

"Mom, seriously, I can't get into Sophie, or the awards ceremony, or any of that right now," Carolyn said. "You realize that I have an actual job to do, don't you?"

"Oh please," Vivian said. "Your work never stops."

"I need a break from family drama," Carolyn said, and before her mother could remind her that she had caused all the drama in the first place, she added, "Work *is* my vacation."

"I know, dear," Vivian said, setting out the plates and plastic forks. "That's your problem."

Carolyn rolled her eyes. "Aaand, here comes the psycho-analysis."

"You're using wit as a defense mechanism again, dear." Vivian took a chair at the table and made herself at home.

"And *you're* watching too much Dr. Phil," Carolyn mumbled back, just as the phone rang. When Carolyn saw it was the front desk, she picked up.

"The author is here," the secretary said.

"We're all set for the meeting," Carolyn said. "Send him up."

"Well, actually the author is—" the secretary started, but Carolyn hung up.

"Can't you see what you're doing here?" Vivian continued, stabbing at the salad with her fork. "Just like you did in New York, you're building a work fortress around yourself in order to close yourself off from the possibility of finding real love."

"'Work fortress,' Mom? Seriously?" Carolyn glanced at the phone, willing it to ring again—sending telepathic S.O.S. signals to the surrounding offices in desperate hopes that someone might come barging through the door the way they did every other moment of every other day, like a Manhattan subway turnstile every few minutes in this place. But not now. Of course, not *now*.

"And you've spent all these years blaming Marcus and that Harvey Metzger—"

"*Howard. Mercer.*"

"—using the same reflex to whine about *all* your exes improving once *you* were out of the picture."

"I've never once whined!" Carolyn insisted. "Honestly, when have I ever said anything remotely close to that?"

"But, honey, maybe now *you're* the better person for the next man who is better for *you*."

"I can't believe you eavesdropped," Carolyn said, though it hardly surprised her. Apparently, when Jazmine had brought Ava to the house to return the tablet, Vivian hadn't gone back down to watch her game shows. She'd entertained herself by listening from the stairwell to what wasn't any of her damn business.

"But honey, look at yourself—"

"I get it, Mom! I'm flawed! Everything is *my* fault!"

"Sweetheart, would you please shut *up*?" Vivian pounded her fists on the table. "I'm trying to tell you that *you* have gotten better. You're so much more confident now, making decisions based on what's right for *you*. You built yourself up from the ground in New York, you handled that hoax, and now you're building yourself up all over again here."

Vivian's words finally made it through Carolyn's ear canals and into her consciousness. She chewed on the words the way her mother chewed her salad, slowly and deliberately.

"Ms. Ford?" Isaac asked, his tall, skinny frame taking up a fraction of the space in the doorway.

"Please, Isaac, it's Carolyn," Carolyn reminded him gently. Although she preferred the more formal title, Seattle was all about the laid-back environment. "Mom, I need you to go now."

Vivian wiped her mouth with a napkin before setting it beside her salad bowl. A shadow of disappointment passed over her face.

"Let's meet for dinner this Friday," Carolyn said, desperate to move her mother out so she could usher in her new author. "My treat."

Vivian's face brightened, her eyes suddenly a-twinkle. "I know you're busy. Why don't I make the reservations?"

"Perfect," Carolyn said.

"It most certainly is," her mother sang as she gave a little "too-da-loo" finger wave.

Isaac nodded politely to Vivian as they squeezed past one another in the threshold of Carolyn's office.

Carolyn turned to face Isaac. "I thought you told me this guy had an amazing platform, but I can't find anything online."

"That's because it's a pen name," Isaac reminded her.

"Oh yeah," Carolyn said, heading back to her computer. "What's his real name again?"

"It's not *his* name, it's *her* name," he specified. "Oh, here she is now!"

Carolyn's jaw dropped when she saw the woman's figure fill the rest of the doorway.

"Carolyn," Isaac continued, "I'd like to introduce you to—"

"Morgan St. John," Carolyn finished for him. She felt her stomach roll over and die.

Isaac looked back and forth between them as Morgan's flushed cheeks drained of color. "You two know each other?"

"You obviously didn't do your research, Isaac," Carolyn said, working to keep her voice even. "I will not work with this fraud."

"Carolyn," Morgan stammered, hugging her arms around her long black trench coat. "I thought you were still in New York."

"It's Ms. Ford," Carolyn shot back, "and I see you didn't do your research either."

"But it's actually poetic justice, or full circle or whatever," Morgan bumbled, "because this book was my way to atone for what I did to you and everyone else affected by my—"

"Lies," Carolyn finished for her. "All lies. You run to a Seattle publisher to atone for ruining your last one in New York. You have some nerve—"

"Well, now she's writing fiction, so…" Isaac trailed off.

"No doubt," Carolyn said, stung by her own stupidity at having been stumped by such obvious, unimaginative name play. "John S. Morgan," she sneered. "She didn't even give us her real name!"

"Authors use pen names all the time," Isaac argued.

"Carol—Ms. Ford," Morgan said, "my story moved you enough to want to sign it. I have a platform with numbers in the hundreds of thousands, notoriety—"

Carolyn scoffed. "Oh, you're notorious, all right!"

"Ms. Ford," Isaac started, "I mean, Carolyn—I mean, Ms. Ford, you signed off on this project, and the meeting starts in ten minutes."

Carolyn leveled an even stare on her editor. "Then you and I have ten minutes to find another author to pitch."

"If Morgan goes, I go," Isaac said, his pointing index finger punctuating the statement.

"Then I wish you both the best of luck," Carolyn said, turning to her computer.

"This is bullshit!" Isaac exploded. "You know what? We can do better than this, Morgan. I've already had another agency approach me—one that puts the message over *money*."

Carolyn kept her eyes on the screen as she began clicking on files for other sub-par, sub-platform authors she might be able to talk up at the meeting.

"Really?" Morgan asked as Isaac led her out the door.

Carolyn could hear the two making their way back down the hall.

"Who?" Morgan's voice echoed.

"Max Volkov," Isaac replied.

Carolyn's laugh came out her nose, so hard that it hurt. But it didn't matter—didn't matter that they could surely hear her roaring with laughter from her office. She felt for Isaac, so arrogant in his youthful naïveté. He would learn his lessons the way Ava had.

Carolyn's fingers hovered over the keyboard as the idea of poetic justice settled into her mind until an idea began to take root. She looked through the glass wall to the meeting room across the hall where the editors were taking their seats and expecting her to give a polished report on the current trends in self-help and personal growth. She was supposed to pitch the latest prospective author, "John S. Morgan," whose name had already been printed on the agenda.

But Carolyn was done following trends, playing it safe. She was ready to dismantle the fortress and open herself up again.

Her mother was right. And Carolyn had known it for some time now.

She just hadn't been ready to take the risk.

Jazmine

On her way out to wheel the garbage bin to the curb, Jazmine noticed the mail truck pulling up along the sidewalk. She hesitated with the bin until it moved to the next house down the block, then made her way to the box labeled "Perkins" and found a stack of mail so thick, she wondered when Ava had last checked her mail. Catalogs for *H&M* and *Old Navy,* ads for insurance agencies, propaganda for the last voting season, coupons for pizza places and fast-food restaurants, and envelope after envelope of bills.

"Mail call!" she exclaimed as she walked through the door. She tossed the mail onto the table beside the door. The precarious stack of mail leaned, then tipped, sending the catalogues slithering to the floor. What was left was a manilla envelope, packed thick and addressed to her.

Jazmine tilted her head and studied it. She'd been having her mail forwarded to her father's house—no one knew she lived here. Except her father. And Lucinda.

All at once, the scrawl across the envelope became familiar, as well as the misspelling—addressed to "Jasmeen" Johnston. She could feel Ava's eyes on her as she picked up the parcel with a shaky hand, broke the seal and reached inside, knowing all the while that these were the letters—all of them addressed two decades back in her father's block-style handwriting.

Ava leaned forward. "Are those…"

"The letters," Jazmine finished. "From my dad."

"Wow," Ava breathed. "There must be at least thirty of them."

"At least," Jazmine repeated, running her thumb along the edge of the stack. Her father *had* written her all those years ago. He *was* a good man. Except that he was choosing to stay with her evil stepmother. Or was he? "Lucinda must be in some trouble to be sending these along now."

"Little late to make amends," Ava agreed.

Jazmine turned to take the letters to her room. It would take at least an hour to get through them all—two, if they brought up emotions. With Henry still in the hospital, she'd have the peace she needed to really delve into them and get some idea of how to proceed with her father—something she couldn't see ever doing, so long as Lucinda was around.

But then, she slid on one of the fallen magazines.

"Shoot!" Ava reached out to help steady her. "I should've picked these right up." She crouched down to do just that. "I'd much rather look at your mail than mine."

Jazmine wondered if she should pretend like she hadn't seen Ava wince at the sight of the bills she was collecting from the floor, or if she should avoid the subject of Ava's debt the way Ava had been avoiding her mail for who knew how long?

"Ava, I know it's none of my business," Jazmine started, "except that it kind of is, now that you've invited us into your life. Some of those bills appear to be..."

"Threatening?" Ava finished for her as she twisted open the cap on a water bottle. "Believe me, I know."

Jazmine sat down on the sofa. "Henry and I will be out of your hair as soon as I get back on my feet again."

"Take all the time you need." Ava took a swig of water before reaching for another bottle on the coffee table to hand to Jazmine, who reluctantly set down the stack of letters to take it.

"I'm hoping we'll be secure here for the foreseeable future," Jazmine said, taking the water. "If you don't mind my asking, just how much trouble are you in?"

"I'm declaring bankruptcy," Ava said bluntly. "And I'm looking all over the place for another job."

"I thought you signed that southern guy—"

"He writes Westerns," Ava corrected. "And I never signed him."

"And you still haven't reached a settlement with the school district?"

Ava gave a solemn shake of her head.

Jazmine bit her lip. She was hardly in any position to help Ava, but she did have one option open to her that had been closed the moment she'd seen Ava on the crosswalk that dark, fateful morning. It was the only way to move them forward, but it was such a huge step back.

Jazmine forced a quiet breath deep into her lungs. "Ava, I heard back from the district. I can start driving the bus again on Monday."

Ava shook her head. "No, Jazmine. You have your degree in communications now—or you're about to, right?"

Jazmine's mind flashed back to her interview with Quentin and the kudos her professor had given her on the final project. Then she calculated the days since the awards ceremony until she realized the date. She chuckled and gave a weak shrug. "Graduation is today."

"*Your* graduation?" Ava set her water bottle down. "Shouldn't you be there?"

"Doesn't matter." Jazmine shrugged. But of course, it mattered. She had fantasized about taking her diploma a thousand times, shaking the hand of the college president, and giving Quentin a sly side-smile as she left the stage. She tried to take another deep breath, but her chest felt as heavy as the box beneath her. "Thanks to Quentin helping me finish my final project, I've earned my degree."

"We need to celebrate," Ava said. "To toast my roommate's graduation!"

Jazmine gazed at her hands while a reflective smile played on her lips. "Only if Carolyn can make it."

"Guess that counts me out," came a voice from the open doorway.

The two women turned to find Sophie standing there, gazing down at the scattered mail on the ground.

"Not that I could have joined you in a real toast, anyway," Sophie continued. "God knows that after the train wreck I made of my dad's—Marcus's—award night, I'm done with champagne forever and ever, Amen."

"Nice to see you, Sophie," Jazmine said.

"Thanks," Sophie said, "although I doubt Ava shares the sentiment."

Jazmine turned to see Ava's mouth agape, her face draining of color.

Sophie buried her hands into her shredded jeans. "I owe you an apology, Ava. I went to lunch with Howard yesterday and told him about everything that had happened when I'd hitched that ride from you. He's a good guy. I guess if I had to find out my life was a lie, the truth isn't all bad."

"How were you able to find out for sure?" Ava asked.

Sophie shrugged. "Remember when I used his bathroom?"

Ava nodded slowly.

"I took a hairbrush."

"Wow," Jazmine and Ava breathed in unison.

Jazmine turned to Ava. "She's quite the detective."

"She's diabolical," Ava said. "I'm still wondering how she found out where I live."

Jazmine thought about it and then murmured, "Quentin must have told her."

"Sort of," Sophie said, her eyes darting around the room. "It was in the file on the temporary application they had you complete so you could fill in for me."

"Too bad you didn't bring him with you," Ava said, aiming a sly grin at Jazmine.

Jazmine sighed wistfully, then shook her head. "Carolyn's been bad enough. Don't you start in on me, too." She stole a look at Sophie and immediately regretted bringing up Carolyn's name. Thankfully, Sophie didn't seem fazed, or if she was, she hid it well.

"I couldn't have brought Dr. Sims, anyway," Sophie said, "since he's speaking at the graduation ceremony—wait, why aren't *you* at the graduation?"

Jazmine opened her mouth to explain but found her throat suddenly dry. It was still too fresh—too raw. She met Ava's eyes with a pleading look.

"Henry had an accident," Ava said softly. "He's in the hospital."

"Oh my God!" Sophie's apathetic exterior crumbled to reveal an expression of pure concern. "Is he going to be okay? Can I see him? Who's with him now?"

"Your mother." Jazmine watched for anger, but instead saw Sophie's expression soften. "He's pretty out of it, but at least my sweet boy is conscious."

"Do you hear something?" Ava asked.

"No, but I smell plenty of pot," Sophie said. "Got any around?"

"No, that noise," Jazmine said. "It sounds like it's coming from outside."

Jazmine turned towards the front door, still open from her trip to the mailbox. She wished she'd closed it behind her and twisted the deadbolt when she'd had the chance. She strained her ears for sound, wondering if it was a homeless wanderer or a rabid raccoon. But when she was finally able to make out a sound, it sounded more like a kazoo.

And then, just as she recognized the tune—"Pomp and Circumstance"—Quentin ducked his head in the doorway. He wore a black robe and a funny hat—like a puffy beret—and a silly smile, which lit up twice as bright when he saw Jazmine standing there. She barely noticed Sophie share a secret smile with Ava.

Jazmine's smile was invitation enough for Quentin to come through the door, still buzzing the graduation song through his lips like a mini-trumpet. One of his hands held a rolled-up piece of paper, as though it were a scroll. The other held a square graduation cap, which he held up as he approached and finished his song.

"May I?" he asked.

Jazmine bowed her head for her own personal coronation. "You may."

He placed the hat atop her head, adjusting the elastic until it fit. Lifting her chin to face him, he took the tassel and moved it to the other side. "It is my honor and privilege to bestow this degree on one Jazmine Johnston." Quintin presented her with the paper. "It's a pretend degree—you'll get your real one in the mail."

"I figured as much," Jazmine whispered back, feeling the glow on her cheeks. She bit her bottom lip and swallowed as Quentin cleared his throat to continue.

"Carl Jung once said, 'Your vision will become clear only when you can look into your own heart. Who looks outside, dreams; who looks inside, awakes'."

Jazmine nodded, unsure what was happening. Was Quentin giving her a private graduation speech? She could hear Ava and Sophie whispering to each other on the sofa and she held up a hand to stop him. "Ava could I have a word?" she called.

"Of course," Ava said.

Jazmine turned back to Quentin. "Would you mind giving us a minute?"

As Quentin stepped back onto the front porch, Ava made her way to Jazmine.

"He's *gorgeous!*" Ava gushed in a whisper that could surely be heard 'round the room.

Jazmine whisked Ava into the kitchen.

"Isn't your shift supposed to start soon?" Jazmine asked her. "At the hospital?"

"Crap!" Ava dug into her jeans pocket for her phone and checked the time. "Well, actually, I have about twenty minutes before I need to go."

"Or you could go now...?" Jazmine said, waiting for Ava to catch on. "And take Sophie with you."

"After what she pulled the last time I gave her a ride?"

"Please, Ava," Jazmine pleaded. "Henry adores her. She'll make your visit easier."

Ava shrugged. "Henry's never really warmed up to me, so I guess I could use the help." She reached for her purse on the coat rack.

"I can't wait to see the little guy," Sophie said.

Jazmine stepped aside with an appreciative smile as Ava scooted Sophie out the door.

"All right, then," Quentin's voice boomed as he came back inside, "where did I leave off?"

Jazmine listened to Quentin as he repeated the first part of his speech, which he'd obviously rehearsed for this occasion. She thought about his take-charge way and the red flags it should raise from her past experience with Ben. But Quentin's take-charge had a whole different face to it. Her ex's controlling had come from a place of low self-image—putting Jazmine down as a way to make up for what he had clearly been lacking—to make him feel above her and better. But Quentin—who was clearly so accomplished in so many ways—had always treated her as an equal. His take-charge came from a place of confidence, but he was comfortable enough in himself and his place in life to just...be.

"Last winter," he continued as though he were reading from a podium for the world to hear, "when you came into my office for guidance with your son, you never asked for a quick fix. In fact, you never saw his autism as a disability. You understood that he simply perceived the world in a different way—and rather than try to change his perceptions, you wanted to know how you could change your own lens, so you could view the world *his* way."

"Since I've known you, I've witnessed a dreamer who'd had so many doors slammed on her, somehow awaken into a cognizant, astute person who rouses those around her to do the same. You've found the gifts of writing and reporting within yourself and have used them to encourage others to look into their own hearts. God knows, you've gotten me to look into mine."

Jazmine took in a quick breath and held it as Quentin handed her the scroll with one hand and extended his other to shake. But it wasn't a brisk handshake, like the one she would have given the university president, had she crossed the stage at this afternoon's graduation ceremony. Quentin kept her hand in his as he continued.

"You're a college graduate, now. Officially. And as an alumna of the University of Washington, you are free to fraternize with school personnel."

Jazmine tilted her head and the tassel swayed against her cheek. Quentin's thumb rubbed her palm as though he were stroking a rabbit's foot, sending a jolt through her she hadn't felt in years. It was all she could do to keep her balance.

"You could, I don't know, have coffee with a custodian," he said. "Or hang out with one of the librarians."

Jazmine wrinkled her nose.

"Or, say, spend time with a certain professor."

Jazmine's breath caught in her throat. It was happening. He felt the same way. She hadn't imagined it. He'd been waiting, that was all.

In fact, even now, face-to-face, as she anticipated their first kiss, she realized he was waiting. He wouldn't risk making a move that might or might not be welcome. Jazmine stepped forward, put her hands on both sides of his face, and planted one on him, so long and so luscious that she felt her body melt into his. She was afraid she might melt right into the ground when Quentin put his arms around her and held her upright.

His lips were every bit as soft and strong as she'd daydreamed in her Public Relations and Mass Communications and Situational Management classes. And so it was that she spent the next few hours in the arms of a man who would never talk down to her, never control her, and never think of Henry as "less than normal." She found only answers in his kisses and she knew, most of all, that she was in the arms of her better man.

Enlightenment

Ava

Ava listened to the rhythmic slapping of Sophie's flip-flops against the glossy hospital tile as they walked along the same corridor she'd practically sprinted down with Carolyn just a week before.

"It's sweet to see Jazmine and Quentin getting on, don't you think?" Ava asked.

"Getting *on*?" Sophie replied. "Why do you think Jazmine was in such a hurry to get us out of there? Bet my ass that those two are getting *it* on."

"True," Ava conceded.

Sophie snorted. "They're probably hitting the sheets right now—christening your little cottage as we speak."

Ava grimaced. "I'd prefer to live in denial, if you don't mind."

"Pshh," Sophie spat. "No wonder Mom loves you so much. Queens of Denial, the both of you."

Thankfully, Sophie's attention appeared to be diverted by a handsome orderly so she couldn't see Ava's eyes go wide. What had Jazmine been thinking, pushing Ava to maneuver Sophie into the same tinderbox as Carolyn? The slightest spark could set the whole hospital ablaze. Worse yet, Henry would be set off in the crossfire. Ava needed an excuse to turn around pronto, or her friendship with Carolyn would be dead and buried.

Her mind spun with excuses. She could say that a work text had come in and she had to jet. Too bad Sophie knew full well that she was jobless.

Ava rifled in her handbag for her phone when Sophie asked, "Isn't this the room?"

Before Ava could respond, Sophie passed the propped-open door and poked her head in. "Hey, little guy!" she said before disappearing inside.

Ava stood in the hallway, her gut churning.

"Nice train pajamas you've got there," she heard Sophie say.

"Hoo! Hoo!" came Henry's little excited voice.

Ava could breathe again. Her shoulders slumped. The tension released. She peeked around the corner, gingerly.

"What's your problem?" Sophie asked. "Scared of the little man here?"

Ava watched as Henry grabbed Sophie's necklace pendant and turned it over in his little hands. Sophie's face positively beamed. Too bad Carolyn wasn't there to see it, Ava thought, and then remembered how lucky she was that Mama Ford had already left. Ava sent a quiet prayer of gratitude out to the universe for whatever had created that small blessing.

"Are you going to keep lurking or get your ass in here?" Sophie asked.

Ava straightened her posture and strode into the dim hospital room. The only lighting came from the sun glowing around the edges of the blinds.

The little boy blinked at her from his bed. The gauze wrapping was gone from his shaved head. The jagged cut on his forehead was scabbed and healing, and the bruises had gone from purple to green.

"Wow, look at this train puzzle!" Sophie exclaimed, rifling through the get-well gifts on the bedside table. Ava guessed half of them were probably from Quentin, with a few consolation gifts thrown in from Jazmine's guilt-ridden father and stepmother, and the rest from various friends. Sophie pulled the puzzle box from the pile and set it on the bed. The way she smiled at Henry, her face lit the room.

Ava marveled at how much Sophie resembled Howard, down to that dimple just above her cheekbone. And if Ava could see the resemblance, how had Carolyn failed to recognize it all those years? Seemed like more than denial to Ava. More like willful ignorance. But why would Carolyn choose a cheater over Howard Mercer, one of the most stand-up men Ava had ever met? Then she considered the possible closet full of Howard's skeletons. Hadn't he been in a grunge band or something? Not exactly the lifestyle for a family man. Still, nothing was reason enough to lie to two men about their paternity, or lack thereof.

Ava took a seat in the visitor's chair by the bedside table, listening to children's voices echo through the hallway. Outside the door, she watched a gowned child being wheeled down the hall, waving cheerfully at a doctor who passed the open doorway in a clown outfit complete with rosy cheeks and a bright red nose.

"Why is Henry in here by himself?" Sophie asked as she dumped the oversized puzzle pieces onto the bed and immediately locked two corner pieces into place. "I thought for sure my mom would be here watching him."

Ava gave a stilted laugh and asked, her voice a touch too shrill, "How awful would that have been?"

"You have no idea," Sophie murmured. "But I wouldn't put it past you."

"Put it past *me*?" Ava asked, wondering what all Howard had told his newly discovered daughter about her screwup—or, from his perspective, the betrayal of her leaving his agency with what would have been his biggest author.

"I get it, okay?" Sophie blurted. "I tricked you into taking me to Howard's—my… 'biological father's'—house. And now you get back at me by tricking me into facing my mom."

"Now that's just crazy-talk," Ava said, waving Sophie's words away. Sure, there was the prosaic payback of losing Ava her dream job, but neither Jazmine nor Ava would ever make a plan that put Henry in the middle of their battle. Plus, Jazmine was too wrapped up in Quentin to do that kind of plotting. "I would never do that to you," Ava said.

"Of course not." Sophie sorted through the train puzzle, connecting two more edge pieces together. Henry reached for them and took them back apart, lining them up on the bed cover. "But getting me to forgive my mom—which won't happen in this lifetime, by the way—would have gotten you back into her good graces."

Ava maintained her smile through gritted teeth. Best to ignore the girl and her half-baked and only theoretically correct assumptions. The air in the room had turned balmy, stifling. Sophie had her number, in a way, but the plausible denial belonged to Ava. Where was Carolyn, anyway? Ava reminded herself that the woman's absence was a grenade dodged.

And then, Ava saw an opportunity to get Sophie to open up and give them the information they needed to puzzle back together this massively broken family. "Look, I know this isn't my place..." Ava trailed off because this was the most truthful statement she'd made in months. "...but you did kind of drag me into this, so I'm going to ask it, anyway."

"Let me guess," Sophie cut in, her voice almost bored, as though she were reciting state capitals. "You're wondering if I could at least listen to Mom's side of the story?"

"Seriously, how do you do that?" Ava marveled.

"Do what?" Sophie kept her gaze on Henry as she helped him lay out the puzzle pieces from largest to smallest.

"You're incredibly intuitive," Ava said. It was probably what made her so good with Henry. The only other person Ava knew with that kind of intuition—and who had the same magic touch where Henry was concerned—was Carolyn.

"Yeah, well, look what intuition got me—a whole new father."

"Because of that school project?" Ava asked.

"How did you know about that?" Sophie asked. The suspicion in her eyes showed she'd been knocked off-kilter.

"Well, you *did* use me to get into Howard's house," Ava said wryly, "so you could get your hands on his hairbrush or toothbrush for the DNA."

"Oops," Sophie said.

"Oops?" Ava repeated. "I lost my job and all you can say is 'Oops'?"

"Oop," Henry repeated and pointed towards a spot on the floor.

"Ava, I said, 'Oops' because I dropped a puzzle piece. It fell under the table there. Can you get it for us?"

Ava leaned forward in her seat and reached under the bedside table, her fingers grazing some kind of leather strap. She froze. She hadn't brought a purse and all Sophie had carried here was her phone. Was it possible that Jazmine had left her purse here? Sure, it was. And now that they were roomies, Ava could easily bring it back to her.

"Anyhow, do you really think it was *intuition* that kicked in for that lame-ass school DNA project?" Sophie asked.

Ava lifted the puzzle piece and Sophie wrenched it away.

"If I was going to figure out who the hell I am, I needed to become my own private investigator. I couldn't exactly count on my mother."

Of course, this all came down to Sophie's mother. In fact, Ava knew she was deluding herself all over again with that purse. She pulled the purse gingerly, just an inch or two toward her, until she could make out the Louis Vuitton label.

Jazmine couldn't afford a Louis Vuitton any more than Ava could afford a Chai latte these days, which meant only one thing: Carolyn was in the building somewhere. Sophie's mother would surely come back through that propped-open door any minute. Any *second,* more likely! As nonchalantly as she could manage, Ava shoved the luxurious purse back even further than where she'd first found it. Her pulse quickened and she felt herself breaking into a sweat in the stuffy room. It wasn't her fight, her relationship, but deep down, Ava dreaded that thought of being caught in the crosshairs. And it wasn't only the inevitable battle between the mother and daughter that shook her—it was the thought of Henry, the most vulnerable, anxious little boy in the world, melting down in the midst of it all.

"Henry seems a little tired," Ava said, watching as Sophie shrugged off her hoodie. "Maybe we should take off—" She stopped short, wishing she'd thought to glance at the open door before she'd spoken, because there, just outside the jamb, stood Carolyn herself.

"Feel free to go, then," Sophie said, her intuitive sleuthing incapable of sensing her own mother's presence. "I could spend all afternoon with Henry."

"Dod," Henry chirped.

"God?" Sophie asked. "What do you think he wants? To pray?"

"Dog," Ava corrected and nodded toward Henry, who was now reaching for the stuffed animal by his pillow. She remembered when Carolyn had bought it for him last week in the hospital gift shop.

Sophie squealed and petted the toy's head as though it were a real dog. Jazmine had mentioned how good Sophie was with Henry, but Ava was especially impressed by the wise way she let Henry hold the 'dod' while petting it along with him, somehow knowing that possession was nine-tenths of the law in keeping the peace with this kid.

"It's adorable!" Sophie said. "Where did you get this little cutie?"

Ava watched Sophie's gaze follow Henry's pointing finger.

"Sophie?" Carolyn asked faintly, shifting a small plastic bag from one hand to the other. "What are you—"

"Doing here?" Sophie finished. "Oh please, like you don't already know."

Carolyn's wide-eyed look of consternation landed on Ava.

"It wasn't my idea," Ava stammered, rising from her seat. "It just happened." With any luck, she could make a quick exit before the first grenade was thrown.

Carolyn was clearly working to keep her voice measured as she asked, "What do you mean, 'idea'?"

"You can drop the act, Mother," Sophie said matter-of-factly as she rose from Henry's bed and took her phone from the bedside table. "Your stooge did you proud, just now, asking me all those questions, trying to get me to spill all my feelings—"

"I knew nothing about this." Carolyn's eyebrows knit together, her expression completely bewildered. "Wait, Ava, why *did* you bring her here?"

"I, I mean 'we'," Ava gestured toward Sophie, "we're giving Jazmine some privacy." It all sounded so trite when she said it.

"What a crock," Sophie countered. "Both of your dear friends thought you and I could hug and make up." Sophie stood and collected her phone from the table. "Just like all those cheesy novels you sell, where all the threads tie up in a pretty little bow at the end."

"Ava, I don't know in what world you thought this was appropriate," Carolyn began in a measured tone, then seemed to soften when she added, "but thank you."

Braced to defend herself against another Carolyn Conniption, Ava came up speechless. *Thank you?* Instead of writing Ava off for meddling, Carolyn was grateful?

"Oh, that's classic," Sophie said, her voice sounding suddenly choked. "In what world did you think it was appropriate to keep the truth from me? In what *world* did you think it was appropriate to keep me from my *real* father?"

"Hoo-hoo!" Henry chimed, but his tone this time was different, more strained, more the way he had sounded at Jazmine's father's house at the beginning of that unforgettable meltdown.

Ava moved in front of Sophie. "Maybe you and your mom could take this out to the hall while I keep watch over Henry."

Sophie scoffed. "Maybe you should mind your own business. Besides, I thought *you* were leaving, what with Henry being so tired, and all."

"Sophie, please," Ava pleaded, "just go outside and listen to your mom—"

"Ava, *stop*." Carolyn all but shouted, the desperation in her voice and body palpable as she put up a hand to her, then turned back to her daughter. "You need to understand, this woman here has troubles. She's a...you know, she's an...enabler!"

"Excuse me?" Ava asked, her mouth completely agape at the audacity that Carolyn would dredge up her highly personal history with Gavin and apply it here. It felt as though Carolyn had just thrust an arrow through the one soft spot in Ava's armor—that spot of delicate trust.

"She thinks she can fix other people's issues," Carolyn continued, then shot Ava a glare every bit as pointed as the arrow she'd just shot. "She doesn't understand boundaries."

Sophie turned from the door and said, "You can act like the victim all you want, Mom. 'I had no idea you were here,'" she mimicked her mother in a high-pitched voice and continued. "'I had no idea you might have a different *father*.' All that time you complained that Dad—*Marcus*, that is—cheated on you, and there you were, fucking around on him from the very beginning."

"I never cheated on your—on Marcus," Carolyn said, sounding more defeated than aghast. "He'd left for New York. I thought it was over when Howard and I—"

"You see that?" Sophie turned to Ava, throwing up a hand in exasperation. "She never owns up—not once. It's always someone else's fault with her. You, of all people, should know that."

"*Hoo! Hoooo!*" Henry's voice rose as he wrung his little hands.

"Sophie, maybe you should leave," Carolyn said, her voice soft and measured. "I am very sorry this happened."

"Oh, *now* you're sorry." Sophie threw up both hands this time, on her way out the door. The only sound left in the room was the air vent and Henry's persistent hoo, hoo, hooing.

Ava stood rooted to the floor, afraid that if she tried to move, her shaking knees would take her down. As Carolyn took Sophie's place on Henry's bed and presented the stuffed animal from the gift shop bag she'd been holding since she'd shown up in the doorway, Ava wondered what she'd been sorry for, exactly—how far back her *I'm very sorry this happened* went. Her chest tightened. What if Ava's actions had been the final nail in her friendship with Carolyn? What if she'd made Carolyn sorry she'd ever met her?

"So, whose idea was it?" Carolyn asked, her voice low as she redirected Henry towards the "dod" and away from his imminent hysterics.

"Sophie came by the house," Ava said softly. "She wanted to apologize and tell me that Howard won't be suing me. He'll never want to work with—let alone see me—again. But at least he won't be suing me."

"That's good news," Carolyn said, "but it still doesn't explain why you would bring Sophie here, to force a reunion between us."

"Because Quentin came by next, and Jazmine wanted to be alone with him, and I figured you'd be gone by the time we got here."

Carolyn nodded thoughtfully. "Then it was never a set-up," she said, helping Henry stay focused on his newest toy.

"Think about it, Carolyn. If Sophie thought this was a devious plot and was dead set on never ever seeing you again, then why didn't she bolt before we got to the hospital?"

Carolyn chuckled. "Maybe my girl hasn't completely slammed the door on me, after all."

"We've got to believe it's open a crack," Ava said. She listened to the hospital HVAC system whoosh through the ceiling, considering what to say next.

Carolyn rose. "Have you seen my purse?"

Ava crouched near the floor and felt around under the bed for the thousand-dollar designer bag, sending a silent prayer for the mother-daughter relationship to work itself out. Carolyn had become so much more than a publishing mentor. She'd become a mentor on how to embrace adulthood, on becoming a better woman. She deserved every happiness.

"Meet me at the Cider House tomorrow, at seven o'clock," said Carolyn, her voice back to its authoritative self. "And bring Jazmine."

Ava's lungs filled with air—and hope—once again.

Carolyn

Carolyn sat at the same Cider House table, tapping her freshly manicured nails to the same Latin-jazz fusion guitar coming from the corner stage. As the guitarist's fingers moved deftly across the strings, she couldn't help noticing once again that one of them was free of a wedding ring. And again, she couldn't help noticing his Harry Connick Jr. type of vibe.

Not that it mattered, of course. She knew how these things went—the ole *he's probably taken, he's not into women, or he'd just as soon ask out someone Ava's age.* And what did she want with a guitarist, anyway? His full-time job was probably working as a curbside busker at Pike Place Market. But then, that's the same reasoning she'd used with Howard in his band days and look where that had gotten her.

Across the restaurant, she noticed the same sad woman at the same half-hidden table against the brick wall—the woman the waiter had told them about before, who wouldn't know a red flag if she had to salute one on a daily basis. If she could join the woman at her sequestered table, Carolyn would tell her to give up now and enjoy a life of solitude. She eyed her own reflection in the wine glass—sleek red bob, green eyes, and red lipstick, and reminded herself that it wasn't so bad, being married to a career. It wasn't so lonely at the top.

Except that it was.

She watched the entrance, willing Sophie to walk through it. She conjured a far more significant conversation in her mind, of how she would take accountability for what she had done—of how she would try to apologize for something that a simple *sorry* could not begin to address.

But when the door finally breezed open, it wasn't Sophie. Jazmine came strolling through, a purse slung over one shoulder and an envelope in her hand. She looked smart in her plum-colored, faux leather jacket. The light glinted off her dark-framed glasses as her heels clacked along rustic floorboards to Carolyn's table.

"How's Henry?" Carolyn asked as Jazmine took her seat.

Jazmine's eyes lit up, beyond the new-lover glow that Carolyn almost immediately recognized. "They're going to release him tomorrow."

"He's progressed in such an incredibly short amount of time," Carolyn said. "I need to tell you how out of line I was in the way I reacted to your interview with Isadore. Were you able to salvage any of your final project?"

"Doesn't matter." Jazmine shrugged. "I wound up interviewing Quentin, instead."

Carolyn gave an impressed nod, her eyes shining with a hint of amusement. "He mentioned that at the ceremony—but let's not go there, other than to say that you two make a dashing couple."

Jazmine's cheeks glowed pink. "He's been wonderful to me," she said. "As have you."

Carolyn gave her a warm grin and placed her hand on top of Jazmine's, happy to have added matchmaker to her repertoire, as inadvertent as it had been.

"What are we having tonight, ladies?" the familiar waiter said from above the two women. His work uniform consisted once again of a black T-shirt tucked into belted black skinny jeans.

"I'll take a glass of Pinot grigio," Carolyn said.

"Hey guys," said Ava, breathless, as she moved around the waiter and took her seat between the two women. She shrugged off her jacket to reveal a light, pastel sweater that was perfect for spring. "Looks like I'm just in time to order."

The server narrowed his eyes and studied the faces of each woman at the table. "You gals have been here before, right?" He tapped the order into his tablet and murmured, "I think I remember our Midori girl. And you are…" The server paused, studying Jazmine. "You're cider."

"He's good!" Ava said, clearly impressed.

"Damn good," Jazmine agreed.

"Well, it is a Cider House," Carolyn said. "Odds are people are going to order it."

"Wait a minute, aren't you The Red Flag Girls?" he asked glancing back and forth between them.

Carolyn nodded, feeling a sense of elation.

"All right, I'll be right back with a Pinot, cider, and a Midori sour," he said, turning to go just as Ava held up her index finger.

"Forget the Midori. I'll take a Pinot, too."

"This is pretty dry." Carolyn regarded her near-empty glass.

Ava shrugged. "I figured I'd graduate from drinking 'liquid candy' and try on a martini or wine."

"You could order the specialty here," said Jazmine. "Can't go wrong with hard cider."

"Or if you insist on drinking wine," Carolyn said, "start with something sweet, like Riesling."

Ava crinkled her nose. "Reese-ling?"

Carolyn watched the slim waiter glide back across the wooden plank floor back to the bar. She couldn't help stealing another glance at the guitarist. This time, he caught her eye and shined her one of those sexy, lopsided Harrison Ford-type grins. He finished his song, to light, sporadic applause, and took a long, sensual pull from a cider bottle.

"Sorry I got here late," Ava said. "I stopped home to check the mail, but I guess the mail truck hasn't come through yet."

"I just got here myself," Jazmine said. "And I brought you the mail."

Carolyn watched Jazmine reach into her purse for a small stack of envelopes and hand them to Ava.

"What about your mail?" Ava asked. "Did you get anymore old letters from your father?"

Carolyn tilted her head, intrigued.

"No, but I read the ones I got," Jazmine said, then turned to Carolyn. "Lucinda finally got my dad's old letters to me—the ones she admitted to at the hospital."

"That was gracious of her," Carolyn said with a hint of sarcasm. Then, her shoulders went slack. "I don't suppose I can judge her. It's not like I'm innocent in the keeping-my-daughter's-father-from-her department."

"Willful ignorance is different from willful deceit," Ava said, fidgeting with the envelopes in her hand.

"Arsenic is different from cyanide," Carolyn argued. "But that doesn't make one better than the other."

"At any rate," Jazmine said in apparent effort to steer Carolyn away from self-flagellation, "Dad says she's in the Philippines now, visiting family, supposedly." Jazmine shrugged. "Probably more like a separation."

"Do you think they'll divorce?" Ava asked.

"Not likely," Jazmine said. "But things will be different now, for sure. If nothing else, it's been great spending more time with my dad. I thought he was such a deadbeat. Turns out, he was a decent guy all these years."

"Wow," Ava said in awe. "You've got the better man *and* the better dad!"

Jazmine gave a tentative nod. "He's not perfect. I mean, he still left me to deal with my mom alone."

"But he's trying," Carolyn said, knowing all too well the feeling. "And both you and Henry will be better for it."

"All right, enough about me," Jazmine said. "Ava was about to open her mail."

Carolyn grinned. It always amused her to see Jazmine take the role of the interviewer, leaving the spotlight to others. Yet, at the same time as Jazmine showed her innate talent as a media host, Carolyn noticed Ava's breaths grow shallow and her cheeks drain of color.

"Is this it?" Ava asked. "Is this where I find out whether they'll pay the medical bills?"

"None of us will know that until you open it," Jazmine said.

Ava sat, staring at the top envelope in her hand.

"Well?" Carolyn asked. "Why all the suspense?"

"I'm just thinking about all the things I could do if I had money," Ava said, tucking a beachy wave of hair behind her ear. "I would help Jazmine with childcare so she could get on her feet—"

"Hey now, I'm doing just fine," Jazmine said. "Quentin hooked me up with a retired couple, the Hendricksons, who are helping with childcare." Then, she sat up a little straighter and added, "And, I'll have you know that I've had enough people listen to my podcast that a couple of small advertisers are actually taking interest."

Carolyn wanted to take advantage of the moment, to tell Jazmine what she had in store for her. But they would come to that soon enough. For now, there was an envelope still sitting unopened in Ava's shaking hands. "If they settle for millions, you could always buy stock in a fledgling publishing house," she half-joked.

"But what if it's nothing?" Ava asked.

"It's not like anything could get worse," Jazmine said. "It would just stay the same."

"The status quo being that I'm unemployed and tens of thousands of dollars in debt," Ava reminded her. "I'm sure it sounds silly, but so long as I don't open this letter, there's still a chance that things could change, you know?"

Carolyn watched as Ava gazed into Jazmine's eyes and saw that Jazmine, indeed, knew. Carolyn had been there herself. In fact, she was there now. Here she'd prepared herself for a business-type meeting, but her mother's words still rang in her ears. *Work fortress.* These two young women had been open to her all this time, entirely vulnerable, while she'd donned her polished, professional mask more times than not. She'd been viewed as a fraud in New York and now with Sophie and Howard. If there were two people in the world she felt safe to come clean with, it was the two women sitting on either side of her.

"Ava, I know you see me as a sort of…" Carolyn paused for the right word, "icon. But I need you to know that I'm struggling. Going from New York's publishing industry to being locked into the middle rungs of a large corporate publisher in Seattle—I'm going stir-crazy."

Carolyn paused as the server arrived with a tray full of drinks, setting one in front of each of them. She took a grateful sip of her Pinot.

"I know there were lawsuits," Jazmine broached gently. "Has any of that resolved?"

"Thankfully, no one was able to prove my negligence, since the recording of Morgan St. John's shenanigans wasn't released until long after the book had gone to print."

"Hallelujah," Ava murmured.

"The financial status of Ford Publishing, while lean, is affording me one shot to resuscitate my career. I've already begun to invest in establishing a modest, yet professional presence in Seattle—to be closer to Sophie, just in case—yet still able to draw from my many Manhattan publishing related connections. My Ford Publishing entity may be on life support, but I'm determined to see this little company revive and thrive."

"How lean are Ford Publishing's finances?" Ava asked.

Carolyn took a deep breath. She'd never been this vulnerable, but then, New York's Advance Publishing had never been in such dire straits. "To be honest, I really need to hit the ground running. This first year will be a make it or break it proposition for me."

"Carolyn, I had no idea," Jazmine said. "You may be an icon to Ava, but you are a lifesaver to me and my son. If there's anything I can do, I hope you won't hesitate to ask."

"I'm here, too," Ava said. "Whatever you need."

Carolyn chuckled, feeling freed and—for the first time since she'd been in love with Howard—like herself. "What I need first is an acquisitions editor."

"Really?" Ava asked. "I know this is a much smaller scale, but I was an acquisitions editor for—"

"*Klipsun*, I know," Carolyn said. "That's why I'm offering you the position. I plan to take you under my wing as my own personal protégé. At the very least, no matter what is in that envelope, you won't be going back to being unemployed."

"Which means you can finally open your mail," Jazmine added.

Carolyn watched as Ava gingerly opened the envelope and withdrew the letter. She unfolded it and skimmed the page until her eyes turned glassy. The young woman gaped and what little color was left in her face paled entirely—so much so, that Carolyn nearly leaned over to catch her in case she passed out. Ava brought her hand to her mouth.

"Oh, sweetie, I'm so sorry," Jazmine said, reaching over to caress her shoulder.

"It's fine," Ava said. "They're paying the hospital bills in full."

"That's great news," Carolyn said.

Ava nodded but didn't look so sure. Carolyn felt for her—knew she had inherited her father's mortgage and had accrued all kinds of debt over the past few years. She opened her mouth to make the proposal she'd brought them here for when Ava tore open another envelope from the stack Jazmine had brought.

Ava shook her head and used a cocktail napkin to wipe her eyes. "Don't be sorry." More tears slid down Ava's cheeks as her face broke into a smile like Carolyn had never seen. "My father's book," Ava said. "The one I self-published. He got his first royalties check."

"That's good, right?" Jazmine ventured.

Ava nodded with a little hiccupy cry. "Thirty-five dollars."

Jazmine's wide eyes moved back and forth over the page. "Hell, girl, a thousand more checks like that and you can pay off your father's house!"

Ava bit her lip and nodded, folding her hands on the table the way Carolyn had always done to start her business meetings. "My father left that book for me—his dedication told me to 'ever be my own'. I want to be my own in the publishing world. I want to make my mark."

The server approached the table with a tray of drinks. He served Ava first, then Jazmine.

"You are looking at Ford Publishing's new Editor-In-Chief," Carolyn announced, looking Ava in the eye. With a broad smile, she extended a hand to shake on it.

"I thought I was your acquisitions editor?" Ava asked.

Carolyn shined a warm, wry smile. "Your determination earned you an instant promotion."

The waiter set down Carolyn's glass, already frosty from the cold wine. "You gals are publishers?" he asked, clearly impressed. He then lowered his voice to a conspiratorial whisper. "Please tell me you'll be publishing a book about those red flags you all talked about last time. That woman over there sure could use that wisdom in volumes— especially if you've found any solutions." He pointed to the darkened table across the floor. "She's still batting zeroes."

Carolyn glanced across the pub to the woman but found her own eyes drifting back over to the guitarist. He sat on his stool, immersed in closing out a slow and soulful instrumental number. She began to look away before Jazmine and Ava could catch onto her moth-and-flame diversion but noticed him flagging over their server, who skipped off to the corner stage.

"Drink up, ladies," Carolyn said. "We'll need to get going soon."

"Already?" Ava asked. "I'm afraid we've focused so much on me tonight. I'd love to hear more about how you and Jazmine are doing— Henry, too."

Carolyn savored her wine and fell into a brief euphoric daze. The music from the stage sounded vaguely familiar. A pop song. The Beatles? She grinned. "Paperback Writer." She shook herself back into the present moment. "Our next stop will focus on all of us—especially Jazmine."

Carolyn watched Jazmine and Ava exchange a puzzled glance as the guitarist swept into the chorus of the song. The server was back yet again, as coy as ever, to set down a folded paper before her.

"What's this?" she asked. "I said the night was young, but it seems a little soon for the check."

The server shook his head, grinning so mischievously that his eyes actually sparkled. "Our musician wanted to reciprocate. He's wondering if *you* take requests."

"The guitar player?" Ava squealed.

"What are you waiting for?" Jazmine asked. "Read it!"

"I never made any request," Carolyn said before the waiter's Cheshire Cat smile gave him away.

"I couldn't help myself in requesting such an appropriate song on your behalf," he confessed. "Since I work here, I had to say it came from you. Besides, I'm a huge Beatles fan. As for your note, trust me, I had nothing to do with his handiwork there."

"Trust you?" Carolyn said and winked at her friends. "After a stunt like that." Be that as it may, Carolyn's cheeks burned as she unfolded the note and scanned it.

"Well?" the waiter asked. "What do you think?"

As Carolyn glanced back at the stage, Ava inspected the note by peeking over her new boss's shoulder. Then, in her best male voice for Jazmine and the waiter to hear, Ava read the note aloud. "I'm taking requests. Name the restaurant, and I'll make reservations for next weekend."

Carolyn blushed and folded the note back up. Then, to deflect the sudden prospect of a love interest, she turned to the waiter and wagged a finger. "Which is it? Are we your Red Flag Girls or your Paperback Writers?"

He gave a sly smile and clasped both palms over her raised hand. "Why don't we just…let it be?"

Jazmine

Jazmine stood alongside Ava as Carolyn slid a card through a slot and let them into the dark, empty building. The only light was leaking through an open office door at the end of the hall where Jazmine could hear a vacuum cleaner running. "This place is spooky as hell," she whispered.

"Almost feels like we're breaking the rules, doesn't it," said Carolyn. "But we're engaged in our first order of business, so you can use your regular 'inside' voice."

Jazmine and Ava followed her down the corridor and veered left down another hallway. Carolyn stopped, held out her hand like a game show host, and announced, "This is our wing."

"Wow," Ava gushed.

"Nice," Jazmine agreed, wondering if she could negotiate having an office here, a quiet getaway beyond the chaos of her home life.

"And this," Carolyn slid the same card through another slot, "is Ava's office."

When she swung the door wide, Jazmine followed Ava through.

"Are you serious?" Ava asked, clearly in awe. Jazmine didn't blame her. The office was spacious with a view of the Puget Sound.

"Not exactly," Carolyn said. "Your office is in that cubicle at the back of the room."

Jazmine burst out laughing before she could stop herself. But when she saw Ava's face fall, she put an arm around her shoulders. "Hey, at least you *have* an office."

Jazmine watched as the corner of Ava's mouth curled up into a grin. It felt good to be back in the fold of these friendships. It felt…right.

"Now let me show you one more room," Carolyn said, turning and leading Jazmine by her hand.

"Can I stay and check out my new digs?" Ava asked.

"Later," Carolyn said. "This involves you, too—as well as your first acquisition."

Jazmine shrugged. "I didn't realize this was going to turn into a business meeting," she said. "Maybe I should take off. I'm sure Dr. and Mr. Hendrickson are ready for a break from my sweet child."

Jazmine and Ava followed the publishing icon back into the hall and passed offices encased in glass, the blinds drawn for the night.

"We're looking for women's empowerment," Carolyn continued. "A new take on the old standbys. Someone with a platform—a blog readership or a…" Carolyn scanned her card to open the door. She turned on the lights.

"Whoa," Jazmine said, gazing around the room in wonder. There was all kinds of recording equipment and microphones—all shiny and new, and all enclosed within sound-proofed walls.

"Or a podcast," Ava whispered, filling in the blank of Carolyn's hanging sentence.

"Is this where you guys record?" Jazmine asked.

"Bingo," Carolyn said. "Audiobooks, advertisements, you name it. You can record here and, if you're willing to sign some paperwork, we'll put it on the company website. We can use it to promote the upcoming book."

"What's that now?" Jazmine asked, as if it were just dawning on her that she herself was exactly who Carolyn and her new sidekick were looking to acquire.

Carolyn pulled another paper from her folio, this one lined with numbers. She reached for her reading glasses, placed her index finger on the line she wanted, and read, "'*Better Than Never*: Four-thousand listeners in only two podcasts.' That's almost viral. We'll build a nice platform for potential readers with your impressive social media launch. I'd say that 50,000 in a year is achievable. In fact, I've already pitched it."

"But do they even want it?" Jazmine asked.

"Would I be saying any of this if they didn't?" Carolyn asked. "I told them that one of my interviewees already had an acquisition for us and to fully expect it to be on next year's list of their bestsellers."

Jazmine felt years of tension release, while a whole new pressure took its place. She had finally reached the point of knowing she was truly going to be better than she had ever been. Yet her life had been stuck in limbo for so long, she wasn't prepared for it to happen so fast. And a book? Really? "You realize I'm not a novelist, right? I'm a journalist—and a novice, at that."

"This would be a nonfiction title," Carolyn corrected. "Journalists often publish collections of their columns."

"Oh my God!" Ava squealed. "We can compile your podcasts into a book! What do you think, Jazmine?"

Jazmine took a breath so deep that her chest swelled before she exhaled the stream of air. "I think I've never felt so lucky."

"Luck has nothing to do with your talent," Carolyn said. "Shall we take a seat and test this out?"

"It's getting late." Jazmine thought about the retired couple she'd met in Quentin's office who'd volunteered to watch Henry for the evening. "I don't want you to feel you have to sit around while I figure out all this technology. I can come back another time."

"Since you started talking about podcasting," Carolyn said, "I've actually put in some time to learn the basics, and I think we should do a show."

"Now?" Ava asked, then leaned in and whispered, "but we're not exactly, you know, sober?"

"You can speak up, Ava," Jazmine said. "The microphones aren't on yet."

Carolyn began logging into various devices and hooking up machinery. "Make yourselves comfortable."

"I don't have any questions prepared," Jazmine insisted as she took a seat at a circular table.

"It's not like the three of us have ever lacked anything to talk about," Ava said with a shrug as she took the next available chair.

Jazmine chuckled, but a wave of self-consciousness had her and Ava sitting in silence the rest of the time it took for a fully absorbed Carolyn to get the recording equipment ready to roll. Finally, she placed microphones in front of them. Jazmine wondered how much her trepidation and uncertainty showed.

"Great chance for a test run." Carolyn's fresh, late-night enthusiasm was not to be denied. "And who knows? Maybe our relaxed inhibitions will reveal a brilliant revelation. It's not like we have to put it online."

Jazmine and Ava shrugged to each other.

"Perfect," Carolyn said. "In three, two…" She held up one finger and then pointed at Jazmine to start.

"Welcome back to *Better Than Never*," Jazmine started, "the podcast that begs—and I mean *begs*—the question: *Why do our exes improve their behaviors after our relationships with them?*" Jazmine smiled when she saw Ava beaming at her. "For this episode, I'm honored to be joined by two women who helped me articulate this question. We will be working together on an upcoming book. I'd like to welcome Ford Publishing's own Editor-in-Chief, Ava Perkins."

"Thank you," Ava said, her cheeks growing rosy.

"And my publisher, Carolyn Ford."

"Glad to be here," Carolyn said.

"Since I began this podcast, I've received dozens of emails from both men and women who say they've been through the similar experiences." Jazmine paused again when Carolyn smirked at the word *dozens,* now that the number was sure to rise considerably. "Ava, why don't you begin by telling us about your experience with your ex-fiancé?"

Ava's eyes grew wide. The question must have caught her as flat of foot as Carolyn's impromptu podcast had.

Carolyn gave the charades gesture that film was rolling, begging with her eyes for Ava to speak.

"My ex left me because he was an alcoholic," she started. "He'd shown no interest in recovery when we were together, and when he finally joined Alcoholics Anonymous, he dumped me."

"Did he give any specific reason for cutting ties with you?" Jazmine asked.

"He called me an *enabler*," Ava said.

"And were you?" Carolyn asked.

"Hey, why am I being grilled here?" Ava asked. "Why don't we talk about you?"

"We will," Carolyn said. "My point is that he became a better person, sure, but what did you learn from the experience?"

Ava held up her hands in an exasperated shrug. "That I'm an enabler, apparently."

Jazmine caught Carolyn's eye and they both chuckled. Ava looked perplexed at first but grinned despite herself.

"What does that really mean," Jazmine asked, "to be an enabler?"

Ava glanced back and forth between the two of them as though she might cry. Jazmine held her gaze, hoping the warmth in her eyes might help.

"It means I aided and abetted him drinking by not standing up to his daily drinking habit," Ava finally said. "I endured his behavior, his excesses in silence and at any cost. Mostly injuring myself."

"You like to feel needed," Carolyn said.

When Ava nodded, Jazmine gestured her to the microphone.

"I think I *needed* to feel needed," she said. "He was an up-and-coming lawyer, and who was I?"

"You thought being needed made you worthy of him," Jazmine murmured in thought. "My ex let me know in no uncertain terms that I wasn't worthy. Ever. Nothing I did was right. I couldn't clean the house right, couldn't handle money. All the years I spent trying to prove myself to him, I ultimately lost myself."

"Why did you stay with him?" Ava asked.

This time, it was Jazmine who shot Ava a wide-eyed exasperated expression. She was the host of this show. She'd never intended to share her life, much less get this personal. "We had a child."

Carolyn leaned forward. "Since then, you've raised that child on your own and you finished your bachelor's degree. Have you proven your worth to yourself?"

Jazmine nodded, then spoke into the microphone. "Definitely."

"So then, you're a better person for the next person in *your* life," Ava chimed.

Jazmine felt a smile spread across her face and said, with more emphasis this time, "Definitely. As are you."

"As are we all," Ava said, looking at Carolyn to take her turn.

"When my ex cheated, I thought I wasn't good enough," Carolyn started. "I proved myself by building a publishing firm from the ground up. Turned out I was burying my head in my work to protect my heart from any more torment. I lost so many chances at love—mainly the time I lost with my daughter. I regret, more than anything in my life, never being able to retrieve those little moments with her."

Jazmine studied Carolyn's face, wondering if Sophie might be listening—wondering, in fact, if Carolyn was counting on Sophie hearing this explanation. "What have you learned from your experience?" Jazmine asked.

"I took what I thought was the responsible path. I ditched a garage band drummer because I assumed he had no career potential and got together with a man with a clearer path for professional success."

"So, you left a man you truly loved for a man who cheated on you?" Jazmine asked.

"That was my first mistake, yes," Carolyn said. "And it devastated all parties involved."

"You're human, remember?" Ava reminded her. "I'm guessing the drummer had his share of issues, too."

"He was into the music scene," Carolyn said, "in its entirety."

"Sex, drugs, and rock 'n' roll?" Jazmine asked.

"Addiction?" Ava murmured.

Jazmine watched as Ava's wheels turned, as though her friend were connecting the dots of her former boss's life ordeal to her ex-fiancé's addiction. More than that, Jazmine was beginning to realize the real reason for this podcast: A public confession. Atonement.

"When I found out I was pregnant, three months into my marriage, I knew there was a possibility that the baby didn't belong to my husband. DNA testing was much harder to come by then—impossibly expensive—and if she turned out to belong to…the drummer…I would be ending my marriage to go back to tell him about his daughter and risk winding up alone to raise her."

"But without a DNA test, you could feign ignorance," Jazmine said. "Why not assume he was the man you ran off with to Manhattan and no one would be the wiser?"

"Exactly," Carolyn said. "But as she grew into her teen years, the resemblance to the musician made it obvious that we were all living my lie. And now, because of that lie, at least five people are paying the price."

Jazmine folded her hands on the table. "What if you could do it over again as the person you are now?"

Carolyn chuckled. "I'm a completely different person now. Publishing taught me to take risks and fend for myself."

"Which means you're a better person, too," Ava offered.

"Once the people whose lives I gambled with believe it, I'll believe it too. I've proven to myself that I can carry my own water bucket, but that doesn't mean I've gone through life without getting some other people wet."

"Hopefully they'll make the time to let you explain this to them so they can come to their own conclusions," Jazmine said. It dawned on her that Carolyn had long needed to make a confession to those in her world that she might never be able to say these things to directly. It explained the decision to do this late-night podcast, and it hardly mattered if her decision tonight was spontaneous or planned. She needed this, like Ava needed not to be so needy. Hell, maybe the booze fueled the lack of inhibitions tonight. Jazmine smiled and spoke. "And speaking of conclusions, I think we've reached the end of today's edition of *Better Than Never*. Thank you so much for sharing your time with us."

The Better Women

Ava

Sitting in a newly opened coffee shop, Ava took an unapologetic sip of her frothy Chai latte. Through the steam, she stared at her laptop screen. Her bank account showed a plus-sign for the first time in months, now that she'd deposited her settlement, her first paycheck from Ford Publishing, and her father's most recent book sales. Surely he would have overcome his mortification at having a self-published book if he could have seen his name on the bestseller's lists. Granted, his named hovered around number fifty on each list, but it was *his name*, and it sent her heart soaring and all but fluttering around the ceiling beams. Finally, she straightened up and clicked on the button to make a payment. She was actually *making a payment!*

"Oh, hey," a voice said above her.

Ava turned her head left to see what looked like a model ready to strut a runway.

"Dahlia!" Ava gushed, her smile suddenly feeling forced. "So nice to see you!"

It had taken Ava every ounce of will to force herself out of bed at five-thirty that morning, and there was Dahlia, every hair in place, her makeup so impeccably applied that it didn't look like she even wore any. Puh-*lease*! She probably woke up at four o'clock each morning to beautify herself so that Gavin could think he was waking up to her natural beauty.

"Yeah," Dahlia said, folding her arms. "Well, hope you're doing okay, after that whole mix-up with Howard."

"I am." Ava nodded, holding herself back from thrusting her laptop screen in Dahlia's face to show her just how well she was doing now. "Did he get the flowers I sent?"

"He did," Dahlia said. "It meant a lot to him—the gesture, I mean. He wants to reach out—tell you how terrible he feels about the whole thing. But he's been pretty swamped with work, not to mention his new, bouncing college-aged daughter."

"I totally get it. Can you let him know not to feel guilty about the…" Ava paused for the right word. "About the debacle at his house?"

"Of course," Dahlia said, already losing interest in the conversation enough to check her phone.

"Well, I hope you're doing all right," Ava said, assuming the conversation had come to a close.

"Doing great," Dahlia said, looking up from the phone to glance around the coffee shop. "I was actually supposed to meet someone a few minutes ago."

"Ah," Ava said, blowing the steam from her Chai. She wondered if it was Gavin, but then she didn't care. "An author?"

"Naw," Dahlia said. "Meeting up with a guy before work." She looked to the door, as though waiting to match a person with a picture from a singles profile. "At least this one says he's not a heavy drinker."

"Gavin didn't work out?" Ava asked.

Dahlia shrugged. "If that's what you want to call it. Ever since the Seattle Literary Society event. I don't know how you put up with it for as long as you did."

Ava nodded again, staring into the steaming Chai while two sides of her competed to sort through Dahlia's words. There was the old her that latched onto the fact that Gavin and Dahlia were over, and that he was single once again. But then the new and improved her knew it didn't matter. Even if he still had feelings for her, he'd gone back to drinking.

"Well, this guy's ten minutes late, so..." Dahlia trailed off, then held up her coffee. "Enjoy your morning."

Ava watched Dahlia exit through the side door into the parking lot. The words about how she'd put up with Gavin for as long as she did still buzzed in her ears. There was a time when Ava would have taken this as a compliment. Now, she knew the point wasn't *how* but *why*. Why had she put up with it for so long? The woman at the Cider House had been waiting forty-five minutes for her date; Dahlia wouldn't put up with being held up for more than ten minutes.

As the steam dissipated from her Chai, Ava felt a bigger fog lifting. Gavin hadn't become a better person for someone else because he hadn't become better, period. At the same time, Dahlia hadn't changed her colors to become his drinking buddy, and she certainly hadn't depleted her savings to save him. The very trait that Ava had considered ideal—her undying loyalty—had been nothing but a liability, not to mention desperation in its purest and most pathetic form. Like Carolyn, she had been willfully blind to what had been right there in front of her.

That was the bad news.

The good news: Ava now knew she would never again allow herself to enable someone else's toxicity. Just being friends with Jazmine and Carolyn had a maturing influence. The next man she chose to spend her time with would be worthy of her trust.

"You have a nice smile," a man said from the next table.

Ava looked around to see whom he was addressing. When she saw the surrounding tables were empty, she looked at each of his earlobes for a Bluetooth. Nothing.

"Thanks," she said, and felt her cheeks grow warm. "It's been a good morning."

He took a sip of his coffee and went back to his paper. Ava was surprised she hadn't seen him come in. Perhaps this was Dahlia's date, a whopping ten minutes late. The morning rush could easily have held him up. But then she thought about the woman sitting at the table

against the brick wall at the Cider House, waiting endlessly on men—
and making endless excuses for each one's weird and bad behavior.

Of course, this could be some other man entirely, having nothing
to do with Dahlia at all. She found herself flashing forward, imagining
mornings with this guy, trading sections of the paper as they read
through it together. She had a sudden itch to reach into her purse and
give this man one of her new, glossy business cards.

Then it hit her. Ava had seldom read a print newspaper, and here
she was, morphing herself into someone else for a man who'd said all
of five words to her. At age twenty-seven, she was $50,000 in debt and
changing colors faster than a disco ball.

Ava slipped her laptop into her satchel and strapped it over her
shoulder. She picked up her Chai and passed the man on her way to the
door, shining her brightest smile as she said, "Enjoy your morning."

Carolyn

Carolyn inhaled the breeze coming up from Elliott Bay. She'd expected her mother to be home when she got back from work so they could walk down to the restaurant together. But the house had been devoid of either her mother or daughter. She'd noticed Vivian had been making more trips to the university to visit Sophie.

As she reached the main drag and rounded the sidewalk corner, the restaurant came into view and the salty air caught in her throat. She'd been so desperate to get her mother out of her office last week that she'd blurted the first restaurant she could think of—Christo's—the one Howard used to take her to after a long shift of endless data entry. There, they'd share a pizza and drinks before he dropped her at home. She hadn't been back since she'd left for New York, and while it had undergone its share of updates in the past twenty years, the memories swelled and surged.

Walking through the door was like walking into the past. It almost didn't surprise her to see the same woman behind the hostess podium, and she knew the woman's husband was probably still cooking away in the kitchen. The owners wouldn't recognize her, of course, after all this time.

A server passed in front of her, carrying a silver water pitcher. She took her place in line at the hostess podium, scanning the restaurant for her mother.

"May I have the name on your reservation?"

Carolyn returned her gaze to the hostess station, where the woman stood poised to look up her reservation, which no one had needed back in the day. The place had undergone a bit of upscaling.

"Ford," Carolyn said.

"Ford," the woman murmured, typing the name into a tablet. "Right this way."

Carolyn followed the woman to the same corner table she used to share with Howard. What Carolyn hadn't expected, however, was to see Howard sitting there now, looking tired but calm, sipping a mug of coffee. Was this a joke?

And there, across from Howard, sat their daughter. Her hair was chin length now and also dyed lavender.

"I…I…" Carolyn stammered, "Sophie, you have to believe that this is nothing more than a weird coincidence." She turned to the restaurant owner to clarify. "I'm here for dinner with my mother—Ford, party of two."

The hostess furrowed her brow. "The only Ford reservation I saw was for a party of three."

"Three?" Carolyn asked, feeling increasingly awkward standing in front of Sophie and Howard's table. She made the mistake of looking out the window to the white-capped waves of the Puget Sound, which caused her stomach to churn even more. "But there's no reason you two would be under a reservation for Ford, right?" She held herself back from pointing out that Sophie's last name was Wheeler and Howard was a Mercer. No use fanning the ever-burning embers that Sophie should have been a Mercer in the first place.

"Grandma apparently worked her magic to get us all together," Sophie said dryly, tucking a piece of hair behind her ear. The slant of the waning sun lit up her eyes.

"But if that's the case, wouldn't we all be a party of four?" Carolyn asked. "Where is your grandmother, anyway?"

"Come on, Carrie," Howard said. "You should be able to smell a con job by now."

Carolyn shifted her weight from foot to foot, not knowing whether to make up a lame excuse to leave or forcing herself to sit with this incredibly awkward family triangle.

"Have a seat, Mom," Sophie said. For a moment, Carolyn wilted gratefully at the invitation. Her daughter *wanted* her here. But then Sophie added, "The people across from us are trying to leave. You're in the way."

Carolyn grimaced when Howard broke into a chuckle.

Sophie turned to her newly discovered father. "What?"

He dabbed his mouth with his napkin, as though to hide his smile. "Oh, nothing."

"Your server tonight will be Marcella," the hostess said. "She'll be here to take your drink order shortly." She turned on her heels and headed back to the front podium.

"Please know that I had nothing to do with this ambush," Carolyn said.

"That's obvious," Sophie said.

Carolyn unbuttoned her coat. "I know you thought I'd asked Ava to bring you to the hospital, and now this—"

"Mom, I know more than anyone what a scammer Grandma is," Sophie said.

"Howard," Carolyn started.

"You're sorry and you didn't know," Howard said. "I get it."

Carolyn pursed her lips. He obviously didn't get it at all. But then she saw the softening of his eyes that showed an understanding that only came from having a shared history. This was awkward for him, too, sitting at the same table they'd sat in just around the time that Sophie was conceived.

"I would like to know what Vivian was thinking, though," he continued.

Sophie reached for a spanakopita from the appetizer plate. "She's thinking that this is the part where we all make up and become one big happy family."

"Surely your mother isn't *that* deluded," Howard said.

Carolyn felt her lungs deflate. For that flicker of a moment, she'd even deluded herself.

Sophie snickered. "Grandma Vivian? Deluded?"

Carolyn giggled, relieved by Sophie's ever-present, tension-breaking humor. "Now there's an understatement to end all understatements."

Sophie's snicker gave way to a full-on laugh. Howard looked back and forth between the two. Carolyn wondered if Howard thought he was sitting with a family of lunatics.

Carolyn wiped a tear from the corner of her eye and forced a deep breath to get back to whatever this was that she needed to at least pretend she understood. "I believe I know my mother more than anyone, and I think this is her way of saying, 'It is what it is. Time to deal with it and move forward.'"

"As one big happy family," Sophie repeated.

"As whatever shape it takes," Carolyn said.

Howard still sat in shock, probably astonished at the genetic creature that he and she had launched into this world. Carolyn realized how strange it was that this biological truce of theirs could take any shape at all. But for years she'd been on the outside looking in on the family that was—and would hopefully continue to be—Marcus, Isadore, and Sophie. Here, amongst the remnants of a disaster of her own making, she had the potential to be on the inside, at least—if these two would leave that door open to her.

"Don't think that you're forgiven." Sophie looked sternly at her mom.

"I second that," Howard said, reaching for his glass of ice water.

"But I heard your interview," Sophie continued, "where you explained how everything happened. And why you did what you…well, did."

"I listened to it, too," Howard added. "When Sophie shared it with me."

"And I've thought about it," Sophie said. "I've talked with Grandma about it a lot, and I want you in my life."

Carolyn felt her throat constrict, her eyes burning with tears.

"It won't be the same," Sophie warned her.

Carolyn nodded and shared a look with Howard. "Everything is different now."

Howard nodded back, leaned in, and with a quiet drumroll of his fingers on the edge of the table, he finished with a flourish. "So, where do we start?"

Jazmine

Henry struggled in Jazmine's firm grasp, but she couldn't imagine ever loosening her hold on him again. "It's okay, baby," she murmured in his ear as she fumbled through her keychain for the right key to Ava's bungalow.

The little boy whined to be put down until Jazmine pushed the door open to reveal a living room she almost didn't recognize. Amid a colorful, balloon-filled room was a giant banner that read, "WELCOME HOME!" And there, in front of it, were Carolyn and Ava whispering, "Surprise!"

Jazmine looked from them to her son, who would have melted down immediately at a typical, overstimulating party.

She herself felt rooted to her place just inside the front door, holding her hand to her mouth in surprise as she marveled at the streamers, the tray on the coffee table filled with snacks separated into their own categories of apple slices, cheese slices, and celery sticks—and all of them lined up in order from smallest to biggest.

And her friends—who had custom-made this celebration just for her son—filled the room with the warmth of their beaming smiles.

Carolyn held out a tall, icy glass.

"Hard cider?" Jazmine asked her.

"I picked up a growler for us from the Cider House," Ava announced.

Jazmine set Henry down gently so she could take the frosty glass. Henry raced into the middle of the living room to run circles around the train track her friends must have set up on the floor before she came home. She lifted her cold glass high and thanked her friends before savoring her first sip. Jazmine intended to savor the moment itself as one of those memories not to be forgotten. The cider held the flavor of an elixir. "Hear, hear," said her two friends.

"Dod," Henry said. "Dod, dod, dod."

Jazmine watched him peeking into a gift bag.

"You got him presents, too?" she asked her friends.

"That one is from Quentin," Carolyn said. "And the other beside it is from Sophie."

Jazmine looked to Ava, shrugged, and mouthed, *Sophie?*

Ava held out her hands, palms up, as clueless as Jazmine about this new development.

"Hoo! Hooooo!" Henry sang.

As Jazmine watched her son place the new engine on the track, she held herself back from asking the question she'd wanted to ask the moment she'd opened the door: What did I do to deserve all of this?

But she knew the answer. It was the same answer as it was when she'd lost her marriage, her job, her home, and almost her son. What had she done to deserve it?

Nothing.

Jazmine knew now that she'd done nothing to deserve life's downs, just as she'd done nothing to deserve to meet Carolyn or Ava or Quentin. Yet, being at the wrong place on that icy hill on the wrong snowy morning had turned out to be some kind of kismet, which had opened doors that had previously been bolted shut. She'd taken advantage of each opportunity presented and had achieved dreams that had been unachievable less than a year prior.

"Are you lost in space?" Ava asked Jazmine as Carolyn poured two more glasses of cider.

Jazmine shook her head. "Just spacing out."

Henry toddled over to Sophie's gift bag and pulled out a new conductor's cap. Carolyn and Ava chuckled as he set it sideways on his head and went back to the track.

Jazmine grinned and held out a hand for Ava to take. "I was just thinking about how far we've come since meeting each other."

"What started as a support group, launched a podcast," Carolyn mused.

"Which means it's not just us anymore," Ava added. "*Better Than Never* will open us up to God knows how many women."

"And men," Carolyn added.

Jazmine felt her breath shudder in her chest. She hadn't thought of it that way. It had always been about exploring the question of why Ben, Marcus, and Gavin had somehow managed to better themselves for Isadore and Dahlia, and the whatsername that Ben had married. Of course, Ava had mentioned that Gavin was still drinking, so he hadn't changed at all. And Jazmine had received a few fan emails from a listener asking her to give her advice about living with a controlling husband. Some of the details seemed so familiar to her—so Ben-like—that she couldn't help wondering if the woman asking her these questions actually *was* whatsername.

But ultimately, Jazmine knew their original hypothesis had been flawed from the start. The journeys of their exes wasn't the point. It was Jazmine's journey of taking control of her life again. Ava and Carolyn, too. It was Carolyn's journey of coming clean from her own fraudulent past. It was Ava's journey of finding her own colors, rather than changing them for other people.

It wasn't in their power to figure out what had made their exes change, or why. It was in their power to better themselves. When Jazmine joined her friends in sitting in a circle on the floor around Henry's new train track, she knew she could handle whatever their friendship had in store for them. And while the magnitude of their shared endeavor overwhelmed her, they were all the best they'd never been.

Acknowledgments

An infinity of gratitude goes to Laurel Leigh for teaching me how to write and to Andrea Hurst for teaching me how to plot. Their friendships made me a better writer and a stronger woman.

Thank you to the people who read this book for feedback and critique: Laurel Leigh, Andrea Hurst, Paul Hanson, Brandon Bryson, Debbie Byrum, Rozemary Van Dyke, Ella Blackwood, and Nate Christensen. And many thanks to my eagle-eyed editors, Lydia Caudill and Mark Scott. This book would be nowhere what it is today without expert insights and guidance from Scott MacFarlane. Thank you from the bottom of my heart.

Thank you to my encouraging family—Mom, Carey, Tim, and Jordan—for reading countless scenes and giving honest feedback, and to my late, great father and my stepmother for their excitement over my publishing contract. I typed my first attempt at a novel on my father's PC when I was fourteen; our last conversation included telling him that my book had been accepted for publication. It was a full circle that meant everything to me.

A special thank you to my daughter for her patience while I wrote, revised, and workshopped this project. You're my real-life character.

Thank you to Karen Brees, who encouraged my editing and introduced me to Black Rose; to Reagan Rothe, creator of Black Rose Writing, for his persistent guidance and for taking chances on new authors like myself; and to David King for the beautiful layout and cover design. What a thrill to find an audience for this book!

Lastly, my appreciation for the men who inspired this book by going on to become someone else's Mr. Right—and a full, frosty wine glass of Pinot gris raised to *all* the folks out there who won't settle for less. More power to us all!

About the Author

Cate Perry has a B.A. in English Literature and a Masters in Secondary Education. She has taught English for over twenty-five years and works as a developmental editor. An alumna of the Squaw Valley Writers Workshop, she has multiple publications and was recognized as a top ten and a Judge's Favorite in Ink and Insights Writing Contests.

Cate likes to sing and play guitar at open mics. According to her daughter, she tells bad mom jokes; according to Cate, they're hilarious. Always a picky eater, if Cate could be a Spice Girl, she'd be "No Spice." She lives in beautiful Skagit Valley with her daughter, two cats (Dora and Jasper) and two dogs (Nikki and Minnie).

Note from Cate Perry

Word-of-mouth is crucial for any author to succeed. If you enjoyed *Before the Next Mistake*, please leave a review online—anywhere you are able. Even if it's just a sentence or two. It would make all the difference and would be very much appreciated.

Thanks!
Cate Perry

We hope you enjoyed reading this title from:

BLACK ROSE writing™

www.blackrosewriting.com

Subscribe to our mailing list – *The Rosevine* – and receive **FREE** books, daily
deals, and stay current with news about upcoming
releases and our hottest authors.
Scan the QR code below to sign up.

Already a subscriber? Please accept a sincere thank you for being a fan of
Black Rose Writing authors.

View other Black Rose Writing titles at
www.blackrosewriting.com/books and use promo code
PRINT to receive a **20% discount** when purchasing.